NIGHT FISHING

About the Author

Glenn R. Parsons is the author of over 100 scientific papers and numerous popular articles on fish and fishing. He also wrote two widely used textbooks, Sharks, Skates, and Rays of the Gulf of Mexico and Introductory Fish Biology: An Ecophysiological Approach. A Professor Emeritus at the University of Mississippi, he previously served as Director of the Center for Biodiversity and Conservation Research at the University of Mississippi. He is internationally recognized for his work in shark biology, having secured millions of dollars in research funding. He also testified before Congress on environmental issues and delivered a TED talk on shark conservation, both of which can be found online. He lives in Oxford, Mississippi, where he spends time writing, fishing, composing music, playing guitar, and enjoying his grandchildren. He is currently working on a historical novel entitled The Road Through Ruin: Remembrances of a Boy Soldier. More about Dr. Parsons and his books can be found at www.booksbyglenn.com.

NIGHT FISHING

Glenn R. Parsons

This is a work of fiction. It is not based on real people and any resemblance to persons, living or dead, is entirely coincidental.

FIRST EDITION

Glenn can be reached at glennp1776@gmail.com and your comments/questions are welcome.

DEDICATION

This novel is dedicated to my wife, Cheryl.

Night Fishing Reviews:

"I can see it becoming a movie with Ryan Gosling as the lead."

"Exciting storyline…lots of twists and turns."

"Truly a fun read. A feel-good thriller."

"Great book. It has everything you need in a thriller."

"Characters are well drawn and pacing is steady."

"Good summer beach read."

"Fun read that includes unique characters and plot twists."

"The author keeps you guessing as he weaves this tale through the lives of a cast of colorful southerners."

Cherokee Summer Reviews:

"Fast-paced and fun!"

"A thoroughly enjoyable read!"

"Characters vividly created!"

"Wonderfully, insightful and funny!"

"A feel-good read that's ending will leave you spellbound!"

"A cross between 'A Christmas Story' and 'Stand by Me"

The Road Through Ruin: Coming soon.

NIGHT FISHING

SYNOPSIS

Jesse Gates, a marine biology PhD student, notices alarming changes in the sharks he studies off Dauphin Island—anomalies that threaten both his research and his future. On a research trip with his dog, he finds an abandoned shrimp boat run aground on the island. The Coast Guard investigates and makes a surprising discovery. When island residents begin dying in gruesome, inexplicable ways, CDC agent Dr. Cherie Belon arrives to investigate. As Dauphin Island is sealed under quarantine, Jesse, Cherie, and Sheriff Robert East race to uncover the source of the outbreak before it reaches the mainland. Exploding victims, bionic sharks, a psychopathic terrorist, pirate treasure, and a category-5 hurricane collide in *Night Fishing*, a relentless, edge-of-your-seat, brain-teasing thriller.

CHAPTER 1

June 23, 1989. Northern Gulf of Mexico, F/V Crimson Tide, 40 miles south of Mobile Bay, Alabama, 4 AM

The tiger shark had followed the boat for several hours, first drawn by the low-frequency sounds that a working shrimp boat creates and further reinforced by the smell of dead and dying fish trailing behind. A twelve-foot female, too many days had passed without food, and she was ravenous. The thirty-eight pups she carried in her swollen belly were even hungrier. The crew working on the deck of the Crimson Tide knew that, on most nights, the dark waters around the fishing vessel were filled with large, hungry sharks as the boat moved slowly at no more than a few knots.

Captain Tom Armstrong turned the bow of the vessel upwind into the 4-foot seas that had been building since midnight, attempting to provide some relief for his crew working on the back deck. An 18-knot southeast wind was a little worrisome. He punched the button on the VHF radio to check the weather forecast and took a sip from a cup of cold, bitter coffee. Standing in the darkened wheelhouse, the only lights being the green glow of the navigational electronics, he steered the vessel between the brightly lit gas rigs that now dotted the waters of the Gulf of Mexico.

Like most commercial fishermen, Captain Tom was an independent spirit, gladly accepting the tough, dangerous working conditions for the freedom of the open seas. Tom was built like a steam locomotive—short, muscular, with a drill-sergeant jawline and silver hair. He wore a University of Alabama ball cap, a red T-shirt, yellow farmer-john foul-weather gear, and dirty white shrimper boots, the standard footwear for all fishermen along the Gulf Coast. Tom was straight as an arrow and no-nonsense. Tom glanced at the dimly lit photo of his wife and kids on the console and smiled; a reminder that he had a family to support, and nothing was more important than that. He was arguably the best shrimper in the northern Gulf of Mexico.

The strain on the rigging and winches demonstrated Captain Tom's remarkable skill in locating shrimp. This was yet another large haul, and after the four trawl nets were emptied onto the rolling deck, the crew would spend at least the next hour sorting shrimp. After a series of maneuvers, the trawl bags were hanging suspended above the rear deck. A few tugs on the bag tie-offs caused the trawl's contents to spill out across the bright white deck.

Retrieving the nets or "haul-back" could be dangerous business, and all hands had to be aware of what was happening around them. The risks on deck were only exceeded by the hazards of falling overboard. Like Pavlov's dogs, the sounds and smells of decades of shrimp trawling in these waters had conditioned sharks to follow the vessels, their reward being a free meal as hundreds of pounds of unwanted "trash" fish were shoveled overboard.

"Hold what you got!" yelled Chris, as the four huge trawl bags, swinging slowly in time with the rolling boat, dripped slimy water across the deck. The rear deck where the men worked was awash in the glaring lights set high in the boat's rigging. The light sparkled jewel-like from the sides of the thousands of fish trapped in the trawl netting, their deciduous scales falling like snowflakes onto the deck.

Chris Franklin was Tom's best deck hand and had worked on the Crimson Tide for 8 years. A native of Pascagoula, Mississippi, Chris had worked in and around shrimp boats since he was a small boy and knew no other occupation. Tall, wiry, and heavily tattooed, years of chain-smoking, hard-drinking, and two failed marriages had left Chris with two estranged kids, a chronic cough, and one testicle. Lately, the 10 or so days at sea were the only time when he took a sober breath. Captain Tom had come to accept the fact that the first few days on board would be tough for Chris, but a bit of "drying out" would see him morph into a different person and an excellent deckhand.

The cook and second mate, Carlos Flores, set the brake on the huge winch, sending a shudder through the entire vessel. Easygoing and an extremely hard worker, Carlos was dark-complexioned, about five feet tall, and almost the same width. Close-cropped, dark hair, and hands the size of catcher's mitts, Carlos wore a plain white t-shirt and khaki work pants cut off at the knee. An emigrant to the U.S. from Cuba, his father had worked the fishing fleets in the Caribbean, and it seemed natural that Carlos would do the same. The three men formed a veritable "shrimping machine."

"Gordo!" barked Chris over the thrum of the diesel engines, using the second mate's nickname, "Dump the port trawls first!"

Carlos grabbed the tie-offs and quickly jerked the bags open, whereupon a myriad of sea creatures flooded the deck: stingrays, fish, small sharks, crabs, starfish, and, of course, shrimp. Carlos had learned years ago that you had to be careful when handling many of the animals that fell from the trawl. Mantis shrimp, odd-looking creatures that shrimpers called thumb-splitters, could inflict a serious wound; blue crabs could almost pinch a finger off, and if you were stuck by a stingray or catfish spine, the wound could fester and, at best, you could be laid up for days, or at worst, you could lose a limb.

The two men grabbed several trawl baskets and squatted on deck to begin the tedious sorting process. The shrimp were tossed into the baskets according to their size, and the rest of the catch was directed out of the scuppers and into the sea. Sharks that circled the boat gorged themselves as they slashed through the cloud of dead and dying fish that drifted on the ocean surface.

Captain Tom stood in the wheelhouse and spoke over the ship's hailing system. "How does it look?"

"Damn good!" Over the noise, Chris had to yell toward the bi-directional speaker that allowed communication to and from the wheelhouse. "I'm guessing about five baskets, mostly white shrimp, sixteen to twenty count."

"We should be finished with this trawl in about thirty minutes," said Carlos as he tossed a particularly feisty crab overboard.

"If this wind continues to pick up, we might have to cut this night short and drop anchor," said Tom. "I don't want Gordo to fall overboard and give some shark a stomachache. Probably some kind of gov'ment regulation against that."

"I don't think sharks like Cuban food anyway," quipped Chris.

"I think they like Gringos better," retorted Carlos weakly. He noticed Chris's hands shaking as he sorted shrimp from "trash". "You OK amigo?"

"Yeah. I'm struggling some, but I'll be over it soon enough. I could use a shot, or five, of whiskey. But that ain't happening."

"When we finish, I will make you a drink that we use in Cuba that helps."

"You got some rum stashed somewhere?"

"No, no. It has tomato juice, pineapple juice, coconut water, tabasco, apple cider vinegar, salt, ginger, and cilantro."

"Oh yeah, that sounds wonderful. Look at the size of this bad boy!" said Chris, holding up a very large shrimp.

"What's the largest Tiburón you've ever seen?"

"English, buddy, English," scolded Chris.

"Sorry, what's the largest shark you've ever seen?"

"That would be old Hitler, an albino Great hammerhead that hangs out around the Sunshine Skyway Bridge in St. Petersburg, Florida. I was fishing that bridge when he came to the surface and scarfed my bait. That son-of-a-bitch was 25 feet long, if he was an inch and pure white. His hammer was this wide." Chris held his arms out as wide as he could reach.

"Hold tight!" shouted Tom through the hailing system as *The Tide* plowed through a large wave, sending a shower of water down on the men.

"Qué fuerte!" exclaimed Carlos. "That's cold. Captain, why don't you see if you can find a smoother road than this one!"

"I'll see what I can do. How much longer before that deck is cleared?"

"Almost finished with the port trawls," said Chris. "We'll dump the starboard trawls directly. I reckon we will be finished just before sunup."

"Let me know as soon as you have things squared away back there. I'm gonna slowly steam for calmer waters. We got more weather coming in, and it's gonna get worse."

Tom set a course for the Mississippi Sound and turned on the autopilot. A navigational device, the autopilot holds a particular course indefinitely but requires human intervention to navigate between islands, through channels, and around buoys.

"Works for me." Carlos grabbed a shovel and began heaving the last remains of the trawl into the sea. He stood for a moment gazing overboard as an unusually large tiger shark, its muscular flanks dappled with grey stripes, rose into the lit surface water and leisurely grabbed several floating fish. A cold chill crept through him as the dark shape disappeared back into the depths from where it came.

"*Dios Mio*!! You're a big one!" Carlos crossed himself and uttered a short prayer of contrition.

"Go ahead and dump the starboard trawls." Chris's command snapped Carlos out of his macabre thoughts.

Carlos walked to the starboard side of the vessel, pulled the tie-off on one of the two remaining trawls, and the contents spilled out. As the bag emptied, a barnacle-encrusted, metallic cylinder fell from the net and clattered across the steel deck. The impact triggered an internal mechanism that opened a valve, releasing its pressurized contents.

"What the hell!?" Carlos instinctively stepped away from the strange object. "That damn thing is making a hissing sound!"

Chris was paying no attention to the events on the back deck as he placed the freshly sorted shrimp in the salt-bath chiller that would instantly freeze the catch before they would be stored in the ice-filled hold. The Crimson Tide had an unusually large chiller, testimony to Captain Tom's shrimping ability.

Carlos bent over to get a better look at the object. "Do you smell that?" Despite the wind, an overpowering, unusual smell enveloped the rear deck.

Carlos shouted over the din of diesel engines and the gathering storm. "CHRIS! Take a look at this thing."

"What the hell?" An impatient Chris walked back to the rear deck to stand next to Carlos.

Carlos pointed at the mysterious object that lay among the dead fish on deck. "That thing was making a noise. I don't like this worth a damn! Did you smell that?"

Chris nudged the cylinder with the toe of his white, shrimpers' boot. "I don't hear nothing, and I smell fish....go figure? It's just trawl-trash. Probably fell off a tanker. Toss it overboard and let's finish up. I'm hungry, and my bunk is calling my name."

"I'm not getting near that thing!"

"Oh, good Lord." Chris hefted the cylinder overboard and then returned to his task. As it hit the water, another valve opened, and a stream of bubbles trailed from the object as it dropped into the silent depths.

Suddenly, loud music blared from the ship's hailing system, causing both men to start, as Captain Tom tuned to the country station broadcasting out of Biloxi.

Johnny Cash's *"Ring of Fire"* baritone boomed from the speakers.

"DIOS MIO!" exclaimed Carlos, whose nerves were now on edge. Carlos's heart raced and pulse quickened. Adrenaline flooded into his circulatory system, preparing his rotund body to fight or to flee. Just as suddenly, a sickening nausea swept through his gut, and his body temperature began to rise. Air rattled in and out of his lungs with each labored breath. Beads of glistening sweat appeared on his face and arms. A dazed look spread across Carlos's face, and his normally tanned complexion turned ghastly pale. Carlos's hands began to tremble uncontrollably, and waves of spasmodic muscle contractions wracked his entire body.

"Gordo, hand me those baskets."

Unable to speak, Carlos said nothing.

"Carlos! What's wrong?" said Chris, shocked by the sudden change in his appearance.

"I.........I.........AHHHHHHHHHHHH."   A gut-wrenching scream cut through the din of diesel engines and pounding waves. Carlos lost bladder and bowel control simultaneously. A quivering mass of flesh, he fell across the ship's railing and heaved dark, clotted blood into the blue Gulf waters. Blood seeped from every orifice, soaking through his clothing, splashing onto the stark white deck, and mingling with the fish slime and water.

Even without the two-way communication system, Captain Tom would have heard Carlos' tortured scream in the wheelhouse.

"What in God's name!?" Tom almost jumped from the captain's chair. A cold chill ran up his spine as he rushed out of the wheelhouse toward the rear deck.

Carlos stood on shaky legs, turned toward Chris, and mumbled something unintelligible. Chris ran toward him and tried to catch him as he fell toward the railing again. Carlos projectile vomited blood and bits of flesh that splashed across the pile of unsorted catch and covered Chris. He drew back in revulsion. As the boat rolled, the bloodied heap that was Carlos tumbled overboard just as Tom pushed through the rear door of the ship.

The sight that met Tom was horrific. Chris stood on the rear deck covered in carnage, his body now also wracked in convulsions. The reddening sky of dawn seemed to accentuate the hellish scene. Chris's arms outstretched and his contorted face framed by the blood-red sky, a primal scream pierced the early morning. Tom caught Chris just before he fell to the deck, lowering him slowly onto the pile of fish. As Tom knelt beside his dying friend, the boat rolled, and blood that had pooled on deck sloshed out the scuppers and streamed down the side of the ship as Johnny Cash continued to sing.

The bloody red cloud mixed with the white wake of the ship as the autopilot steered the vessel toward the glaring lights of the casino coast.

*****

Carlos's body slowly descended into the silent depths as the cloud of blood carried down-current. The tiger shark trailing the vessel hungrily picked up the dead and dying fish that rained down from the surface, but it was not sated. Now sensing something altogether different, the shark first bumped the object to test its palatability and then slammed into it, rending a bloody piece of flesh from the torso.

CHAPTER 2

Mopan Archeological Research Station, Belize, C.A., May 25, 1987

The Belize Defense Force helicopter sped across the tops of the jungle canopy, leaving frightened toucans and howler monkeys in its wake. In a swirling cloud of dust and jungle detritus, it landed in a clearing near a series of hastily constructed, open-walled shelters, military surplus tents, and partially uncovered Mayan ruins. The shelters protected groups of individuals from the blistering tropical sun and sudden, torrential rains that marked the beginning of the rainy season in Belize. Workers bent over recently discovered Mayan artifacts arranged on tables, meticulously cleaned and cataloged each item.

The chopper stayed just long enough to deliver two passengers who, with heads bowed beneath the spinning rotors, ran towards the nearest shelter. One individual held a black AR-15 assault rifle and wore the jungle-camouflaged uniform of a Belizean Defense Force soldier. The two individuals gestured as the soldier continued across the compound to a small shelter that commanded a view of most of the area. Dr. Hector Fernandez, the Belize Minister of Archaeology, headed to a large military surplus tent, tossed his briefcase onto a make-shift desk, and sat down with a heavy sigh. Hector wore the standard archaeological dig attire, a light grey, double-pocketed field shirt and khaki pants. Short and musculature, his wire-framed glasses and "Margaret Mead" style field hat that covered his dark hair gave him the stereotypical archaeologist appearance. Hector had dedicated his professional life to the study of Mayan culture.

Dr. Eliana Fernandez approached her husband and kissed him lightly. "I hope you have some good news to give us?"

Hector and Eliana were about as unlike in appearance as possible. Eliana was truly a beauty. Tall, slim, dark-eyed, and raven-haired, she could have graced the cover of any beauty magazine. She wore jeans, a loose-fitting blue top, and a ball cap, her ponytail pulled through the hat at the rear. However, Eliana's interests went far beyond the merely superficial, which was fortunate for Hector. She was an internationally recognized expert in pre-Columbian linguistics. Hector and Eliana had met at the Center for Mesoamerican Archaeology at the University of Colombia, where they both studied pre-Columbian archaeology.

"I wish I could say it was good. I met with practically the entire National Assembly and got no commitments at all. I wasn't optimistic about continued funding, but I had to try."

"Did you show them the photos of our most recent finds?"

"Of course. But it was a complete waste of time," said Hector dejectedly. "Most of them had no interest. It was just so much lip service. We've got enough money to last perhaps two more months if we tighten our belts. It's so disappointing."

"Don't worry, Cariño, I know something will come through. Perhaps a private donor could help us?"

"Maybe. Senator Garcia showed the most interest. He said he would see what he could do. He has connections with various charitable groups and wealthy people who have an interest in antiquities."

A look of concern, Eliana asked, "Are you talking about Senator Darien Garcia from Belize City?"

"Yes." Hector rose and paced worriedly across the dirt floor. "I know what you are going to say. He is poco limpio and would probably sell his own mother for a few pesos, but what are we to do?" pleaded Hector. "We are making discoveries here that will rewrite Mayan history in this area. If we have to abandon this dig and leave it unprotected, the jungle will quickly reclaim all we have done. Even worse, when we leave, it's certain that looters will destroy this entire site. Word is slowly leaking out about this location, and those photos I handed out will make it even harder to protect. The Guatemalan border is only a few kilometers away, and terrorists frequently cross over into this area. These artifacts sold on the black market could purchase an arsenal of weapons."

Somewhat perturbed, Eliana replied, "I know these things."

Hector sighed deeply and turned to gaze out into the Belize rainforest. "I'm sorry. I was venting."

At that moment, a soiled and sombrero-wearing worker emerged from a rainforest path and ran into the shelter. He removed his hat as he entered the shelter. "Doctor Fernandez! Ven rapido, muchas cosas! Many things!"

"What is it, Miguel?"

"Come… quickly!" he said, out of breath. "The new site!"

Hector rose, and he and Eliana hurried down the path toward the easternmost portion of the site. Excavation of this recently discovered area revealed a central courtyard between two large temples surrounded by numerous smaller structures scattered across a large area. Stone walkways and retaining walls crisscrossed the site. Two years of excavation had uncovered many structures, but the immensity of this temple complex was just beginning to be realized.

As they arrived, laborers were busy clearing debris away from a low doorway and passage that angled downward into the darkness. To protect any delicate artifacts that might be present, Hector had given specific orders that only Eliana and he were to enter newly discovered areas. The light from the noonday sun shone down a passageway littered with Mayan artifacts: pottery, jaguar and human effigies, and stone slates covered with Mayan hieroglyphs.

Hector and Eliana stood in the entrance. The stale air was heavy with an ancient odor, the sharp, mineral scent of limestone, and the smell of time compressed into the dust that lay on the chamber floor.

"Puchica!" said Hector excitedly, as he tried to take in the scene in front of him. "This is unbelievable!"

"Oh, my goodness!" Eliana knelt in the passageway and closely examined the glyphs carved into the stone walls. "These are some of the most beautiful inscriptions I have ever seen."

Equipped with carbide headlamps, they proceeded slowly down the hall, being careful not to disturb the precious items. A menagerie of nocturnal insects secreted from the sun scurried across the walls and floor, away from the harsh lights.

Hector did not hear a word Eliana spoke as fifty feet from the door, the passage opened into a large chamber. The walls here were adorned with intricate Mayan paintings, their colors almost as vibrant as the day they were rendered. The images portrayed Mayan Priests who appeared to be conducting ceremonies unfamiliar to Hector. Around the walls stood an array of large, covered, ceramic vessels.

"Eliana! Look at this!" called Hector as he slowly moved around the perimeter of the room, illuminating ever more beautiful images. "What is going on here?" said Hector to himself as his attention was drawn to one particularly disturbing image. In a scene of conflict, a Mayan Priest was juxtaposed against an image of *Buluk Chabtan,* the Mayan god of violent death.

He then turned his attention to the many ceramic vessels. Each jar was inscribed with repeating images of *Zotz,* the bat. Eliana entered the chamber behind him.

"I have never seen vessels of this type," said Hector.

"The bat is the symbol of protection," added Iliana. "The Maya believed this symbol would provide protection or ward off enemies."

"Perhaps the symbols on these vessels protect their contents."

"Or perhaps to protect people *from* their contents?" queried Eliana.

"That had not occurred to me."

"That's why you pay me the big dinero," quipped Eliana.

"It's a good thing I married you because I could not afford you otherwise," joked Hector. "This is very peculiar. All the vessel lids are sealed, and the effigy on the lid is not one I recognize. It must be undocumented."

Hector knelt beside the row of vessels that lined the wall and carefully lifted one. "This one is unsealed."

Hector carefully lifted the lid. "Oh my god!" he gasped, placing a hand to his head, "this is a codex!"

A book made by the Maya, the codices were fabricated from long sheets of paper called *huun,* produced from fig tree bark. The paper, folded like an accordion, was used by Mayan scribes to record important religious, historical, agricultural, and astronomical events. Only four codices had ever been found, and those few documents were critically important in deciphering the meaning of the Mayan written language. However, a complete understanding of the Mayan language was as yet unavailable.

Hector's hands trembled as he gingerly extracted the document, revealing horizontal columns of Mayan glyphs in colors so brilliant they could have been written last week. "The quality of these is extraordinary. The vessels must have preserved them from the elements." He carefully handed the codex to Eliana, who was equally awestruck.

"This is incredible! All of these jars may contain codices?" said Eliana.

"This could be one of the most important finds in all Mesoamerican archaeology!"

"And we've only got two months to document this discovery," observed Eliana.

"Then we better get to work".

CHAPTER 3

Four weeks later.

After another grueling day under almost unbearable conditions, Eliana and Hector had retired to their tent as the day darkened around them. A white-noise, drizzling rain fell against the tent fabric. Nightfall and the beginning of the rainy season brought a cacophony of sounds: the constant mechanical buzz of cicadas and the staccato calls of a myriad species of frogs, punctuated by the melancholy sound of nightbirds searching for their mates. A kerosene lamp that hung from the center pole illuminated a tent strewn with artifacts in various stages of documentation. After having worked late into the night, Hector lay on his mosquito netting-enshrouded cot, while Eliana sat at her desk, poring over notes and transcriptions of the Mayan glyphs.

Despite a herculean effort, the rainy season was upon them, when all activities would have to cease. A portion of the artifacts had been cataloged, but with little time and even less money remaining, they grudgingly realized that they would have to abandon the site.

"We could spend the rest of our careers describing the material we have already found, and we have no way of knowing how much more remains on this site," commented Hector. "We'll have to begin packing up all of the artifacts tomorrow…ahhhhhh," Hector yawned mid-sentence, "…excuse me, for shipping back to the Department of Antiquities."

Caught up in the examination of a codex, Eliana did not reply.

"Mi amor, please take a break. I fear your health is suffering."

"Just a little longer, Cariño." She spoke without looking up.

Eliana's work further documented the violence and warmongering that characterized the rise and fall of Maya society. Structured into various city-states, the mighty cities of Tikal, Calakmul, and Caracol waged war for territory, resources, and prisoners used in sacrifice. The cause of the collapse of Mayan civilization was one of the great mysteries of archaeology.

Hector got out of his bunk to look over Eliana's shoulder. He bent lower to more closely examine the colorful glyphs Eliana had painstakingly copied onto the loose page in front of her. Hector picked up the leather-bound notebook that contained the finished material and leafed through the pages. "This is incredible work! You have an amazing eye."

"Thank you cariño." Eliana leaned back in her chair and rubbed her tired eyes. "I am close to decoding this series of glyphs. The first two codices were relatively straightforward. Several accounts of warfare between Mayan city-states, bloody battles, and the military exploits of the warrior-king *Shield Jaguar*. However, several glyphs are unknown to me, and some of the interpretation eludes me."

"Perhaps I can help," offered Hector.

"Well, for example, this is clearly a "bat" glyph that appears in unexpected places along with several unknown glyphs."

"Is it one of the known bat glyphs?" asked Hector, yawning again.

"No, it differs in several features. It is the same glyph found on the outside of many of the vessels. But I am struggling with Codex Three. It is completely different. It seems to be a grocery list of unrelated items, along with depictions of priests engaged in rituals that I have never seen before. I don't think they have ever been reported. For instance, here is a depiction of *Lady Xooc* performing a blood-letting ritual."

Lady Xooc was the wife and aunt of *Shield Jaguar* and is believed to have been the most powerful Queen in all of Mayan history. Bloodletting, an important aspect of Mayan culture, was believed to provide the Maya a means of obtaining advice from their ancestors. The gruesome ritual was accomplished using an obsidian blade, sharks' teeth, or a stingray spine, and the toxin present on the spines may have enhanced the experience. The loss of blood and the toxin may have further induced the trance-like state that carried the individual to the boundary between the living and the dead.

Eliana continued. "The symbols for blood, bats, various plants, and several glyphs I don't recognize figure prominently in Codex Three."

"We don't have to finish this now," said Hector as he gave Eliana a quick kiss. "We'll have plenty of time when we return to Belize City."

"You are right," admitted Eliana. "Just five more minutes and I will stop."

CHAPTER 4

Hector drifted off, and five more minutes became two hours before Eliana fell asleep, her head on her desk. She slept fitfully; her dreams filled with Mayan glyphs and strange rituals. In one particularly vivid dream, she looked down from above at *Shield Jaguar,* who sat at a torch-lit altar high atop a massive step pyramid, a freshly extracted human heart pulsating in his right hand. Adorned with jade, gold, and an elaborate headdress, the Mayan King peered into a blood-filled ceramic vessel, while his assistants cast powdered material into the mix. The mixture roiled with increased agitation as each powder was added to the vessel. A dark mist rose from the vessel and shrouded the altar. Suddenly, Eliana found herself gazing through the eyes of an assistant as she added the final ingredient. Thousands of bats, their eyes shining with a blood-red inner light, burst from the vessel and encircled her! Eliana gasped and called out in the night.

Startled by her outcry, Hector jumped from his cot and stood over her, looking very concerned.

"Eliana, are you OK?" Hector held her in his arms as she panted uncontrollably. "You frightened me! You're soaked with sweat."

"I'm so sorry," said Eliana, sitting upright and trying to catch her breath. "I just…had the most terrible dream."

"I'm aware of that. I awoke when I heard you talking in your sleep."

"I was talking in my sleep? I never do that…do I?"

"I've never heard you before. That is why it was so strange."

"What was I saying?"

"It was mostly nonsense about blood and bats."

"I was dreaming about *Lady Xooc.* I was a participant in one of her blood-letting rituals atop a pyramid. It was very disturbing."

"I imagine it was, mi amor."

"Perhaps I have become too immersed in this work."

"Right as you awoke, you said something about a recipe?"

Eliana paused as a distant look crossed her face. Hector could tell she was deep in thought. "That was it!" Eliana's excitement was palpable. "That was it!!" She stood up and kissed him fully on the lips. "Do you know how much I love you?"

"I am not sure what I did, but I will take it nevertheless."

"Codex Three! I said it was a laundry list of unrelated items. It's a recipe!" Eliana pumped her fist. "In my dream, we were mixing ingredients into one of the Zotz vessels. It must be the recipe for something important. A medicinal or perhaps a hallucinogen. With the notes I've made, I think we could reconstruct the mixture exactly."

"But do you think you could identify the materials from the glyphs?"

"I am almost certain that I can."

"Probably would not be a good idea to spend time concocting hallucinogens. There are already too many mind-altering drugs in this part of the world."

"Agreed," said Eliana with a laugh. "But we could provide my notes to a medicinal chemist along with the material needed to recreate the compound. Perhaps a valuable medicine or therapeutic of some kind. I have to write this down immediately." Eliana returned to her desk and quickly made notes about the incredible possibilities that might be found in the codex. It took only a few minutes to describe the procedure for reproducing the mysterious compound. "That's it! If this is some useful medicinal, it could fund our studies for years."

"I think that is a great idea, but let's not get ahead of ourselves. It requires years of research to take a natural product from crude extract to an approved medicine. We can investigate this further when…" Hector stopped mid-sentence. "What the hell was that?"

A burst of automatic weapons fire shattered the early morning stillness. To prevent revealing himself, Hector crouched behind the tent flap and peered across the compound. Their BDF-assigned guard lay in a pool of blood near the copter pad. A group of shabbily dressed individuals brandishing automatic weapons moved menacingly toward the tents. One individual waved a pistol as he barked orders. The men had already removed workers from their shelters and placed them on their knees on the copter pad.

"Oh my God!" whispered Hector as he pulled his knife from his pocket.

"Eliana, take this knife, cut the rear panel of the tent, and go into the jungle NOW! There are armed men in the compound, and Juan-Carlos has been shot. Remember our contingency plan. I'll be right behind you, and we will meet at our pre-arranged spot."

"But…"

"Go NOW!"

From the look on Hector's face, it was clear that arguing was pointless. Eliana quickly made a vertical slit in the tent fabric and quietly slipped through and into the jungle. Provisioned with a small supply of food and water, a boat moored on the Mopan River was to be used in the event of an emergency.

Hector could only imagine what was taking place outside as the compound filled with sporadic gunfire, angry shouting, and frightened screams. He immediately went to his shortwave radio and spoke as quietly as possible into the microphone.

"Mopan Archaeological Station, Mopan Archaeological Station, to anyone receiving this message. We are being overrun by armed men! Need help immediately! I repeat, we are being taken over by armed men! Please send help immediately!"

As he continued to transmit, Hector reached under the mattress of his cot and removed a holstered 9 mm, *Smith and Wesson*. Pausing briefly, he checked to see that it was loaded and inserted the gun into his waistband.

Arturo "the Bear" crossed the compound and, pointing his pistol, directed his men toward the row of tents that sat at the jungle's edge.

"Search those *rapidamente*!" barked Arturo. A man burst from a tent and ran toward the jungle. Arturo aimed and squeezed off several shots in quick succession as the luckless worker fell mortally wounded.

This group of men, originally driven by a misguided socialist/Marxist ideology, had quickly devolved into a terrorist group. Wanted in several Central American countries and the U.S., their leader, known only as Arturo "The Bear", parlayed drugs, hostages, and stolen property into supplies and weapons to ostensibly fund his twisted goals. Short and muscular, with a pockmarked face and greasy black ponytail, he wore tattered jungle fatigues and a Fidel Castro-style field hat in honor of his hero. A frightening visage, the few teeth that remained behind his thin lips were stained from years of pot smoking, and a deep scar ran across his nose and cheek. His well-used machete hung from his belt; a favorite possession that he found useful on numerous occasions for disciplining his men, "persuading" his captives, and occasionally just for enjoyment. Devoid of conscience and extraordinarily cruel, he used torture or murder without hesitation to advance his ideology. Originally from Colombia, Arturo had been educated in the social sciences and simultaneously radicalized at the University of Chicago.

Hearing voices coming from one of the larger tents, a bandoliered guerrilla approached cautiously, his battered AK-47 resting on his hip and aimed at the tent flap.

"You come out now, comrade, or it is going to be very bad for you." The guerrilla pointed his weapon toward the tent door.

Unintelligible words came from the tent as the guerrilla sprayed the flimsy shelter with a burst of gunfire. He cautiously stepped through the shredded tent fabric, weapon held at the ready.

"Mopan Archaeological Station, come in Mopan Archaeological Station..."

The nervous guerrilla started and quickly turned his weapon toward the short-wave radio from which Hector had broadcast before escaping.

Using the butt of his gun, he smashed the radio, pieces falling across the tent floor. As he ransacked the tent, a smile crept across his face as he held the jade and gold artifacts that were found among the many other items. The guerrilla stood over the desk where Eliana had worked and turned pages of the notebook that lay open. Although not an educated man, he suspected that the detailed images and descriptions on those pages might also be valuable. Slipping the gold and jade pieces into his pocket, he left the tent to report his findings to Arturo.

Hector slipped away moments before gunfire erupted behind him. As he ran down the trail, AK-47 slugs ripped through the jungle around him. The only thought in Hector's mind was to find Eliana. He looked down to see that, in his panic, he had left wearing no shoes. The Acacia thorns scattered along the path were almost unbearable, and his feet bled from the wounds. After putting some distance between himself and the guerrillas, he ducked away from the trail and crouched silently by a large Ceiba tree, listening for the sound of pursuers. Convinced no one was near, he quickly removed his shirt, intending to use it to wrap his bleeding feet before continuing.

Hector paused as he heard a rustle that was quite nearby. He reached for his pistol to discover that it was missing. Turning his head slowly in the direction of the sound revealed that he sat dangerously close to a *Fer-de-lance* viper that lay coiled near his thigh. Hector knew that a bite from the snake was a death sentence, even from a small one, and this one was massive.

His mind racing, he tried to assess the situation. Knowing his leg was easily within striking distance, he needed to remain perfectly still. Hector heard louder rustling again just to his left, and out of the corner of his eye, he saw a large tapir that was moving steadily in his direction. Growing to more than 450 lbs., these rhino relatives had been known to attack and kill humans. Accompanied by a small calf, mother tapirs were highly unpredictable. Although partially concealed by the Ceiba tree, the direction the mother and calf were moving would momentarily bring them close by.

Mauled to death by a hormone-enraged tapir or having one's insides liquified by hemotoxic venom were patently miserable ways to die. Suddenly, Eliana appeared in his mind's eye, and an intense calm came over him. He knew what he had to do, but he had to act quickly. Holding his shirt in his right hand, he extended his arm toward the viper, simultaneously bringing the shirt into full view of the tapir. The tapir instantaneously charged toward the menacing object. The viper struck and, as luck would have it, injected a dose of venom into the jowl of the tapir as it passed. Hector tossed the shirt toward the viper. The enraged tapir turned on the viper and mauled it unmercifully. Hector quickly scrambled up the Ceiba tree out of harm's way, at least for the moment. The tapir with calf in tow ran screaming into the bush as the venom permeated its facial tissues.

With no time to waste, he immediately came down the tree. Retrieving the now bloodied shirt, he tore it in half, wrapped each foot, and took off at a jog. The Mopan River was still about a quarter-mile away, but the fear that Eliana was in danger drove him on. Nearing the river, he cautiously approached, listening for any unusual sounds, and quietly called for Eliana. Receiving no reply, he cautiously moved along the riverbank to where the boat was hidden. Hector suddenly found himself confronted by terrorists with assault rifles leveled at him, and Eliana held captive with a pistol to her head.

"So happy that you could join us, señor!"

CHAPTER 5

Mississippi Sound near Dauphin Island, Alabama, 10:00 PM, June 25, 1989.

Jesse Gates lay on the bow of his center-console, open fishing boat, gazing at the star-filled night sky, feeling small against the vastness of the sea and the heavens. With the gentle sound of distant surf, a softly rocking boat, and a calm sea, he was in his happy place. Night fishing always reminded him of the many hours he spent as a child with his dad on the lakes of South Alabama. Bongo, his young golden retriever, lay beside him sleeping. Fishing rods in their holders, his lines disappeared into the dark waters. The bioluminescence tonight was strong, creating an eerie green trail as the slow-moving tidal current passed by his fishing line. A meteor streaked across the dark sky. Hopefully, a shark would rise to take his bait, and he would be one step closer to earning his PhD in Marine Science.

Jesse reached over and scratched Bongo on the head. "It's not looking so good, is it? We may get skunked tonight, big boy."

Bongo shifted position and put his head on Jesse's chest.

"Good dog." Jesse scratched his head a bit more vigorously.

An unseen pod of dolphins breached in the distance, and each exhaled audibly. Bongo tensed, turned his head in the direction of the sound, and let out a quiet "whoof".

"Calm down, boy. We're not chasing any dolphins tonight."

Jesse's thoughts were always on his dissertation research project. It seemed like only yesterday that he had been admitted into the doctoral program at the University of the Gulf Coast to investigate shark biology. Fortunate to have received a research fellowship from the University's Oceanography Lab, the award allowed him to use the facilities and provided a small stipend for his living expenses on Dauphin Island, where the lab was located.

Has it been four years already? thought Jesse. Although he had landed and released hundreds of sharks to study the stress of capture, the project had slowed lately, and it felt as though he would never finish his degree.

Not your typical academic, he cared little for the trappings of scholarly life and preferred to be on the water as often as possible. Enamored with the adventures of Thor Heyerdahl, Farley Mowat, and Jacques Cousteau from an early age, he was an "old school" field biologist and naturalist. Jesse always wore the same clothes: a T-shirt, shorts, and tennis shoes. Tall and thin with blonde hair and a full beard that he kept closely cropped, he looked like he just stepped out of central casting. But Jesse was nothing like those Hollywood wannabes. His southern drawl and easy-going manner revealed his backwoods upbringing. Tough, never afraid of hard work, and with a shallow threshold for BS, he had no patience for the arrogance bred in academia's ivory towers.

"Better check those baits." Jesse got up and reeled in one of the two lines he had cast out over an hour ago. "And the bait is untouched," said Jesse sarcastically. "Blast it!" For good luck, he spat on the half of a fish impaled on a large hook and cast the line out again. He then went to the bow, checked the anchor line to make sure it was holding, and sat down again with a sigh.

Jesse had anchored his 21-foot *Key West* off the western tip of Dauphin Island, a typical Gulf of Mexico barrier island that ran east to west along the coast of Alabama. Long and thin, barrier islands helped protect the mainland against the hurricanes that regularly assaulted the northern Gulf of Mexico during the summer and fall months. These islands also created a sheltered area of brackish water between the island and the mainland, the Mississippi Sound.

Completely uninhabited, the western end of Dauphin Island comprised approximately 20 miles of dunes, beaches, salt marshes, and dense cypress swamps. This remoteness provided a home for hogs, foxes, and alligators, and the waters teemed with sharks, dolphins, sea turtles, and the occasional manatee. In addition, people interested in escaping modern life, or those contemplating illegal activity, were irresistibly drawn to the west end. Under the cover of darkness off-shore of the west end, struggling shrimpers from the mainland sometimes rendezvoused with Colombian cartel, drug-running "fast boats". Overpowered and overloaded, a fast boat could deliver smuggled cargo from Central or South America and transfer it onto a locally registered shrimp boat to be brought to the mainland. On occasion, bales of marijuana, locally known as "square grouper," could be found washed ashore on the island after smugglers tossed their contraband into the sea ahead of being boarded by federal authorities.

Some of the healthiest shark populations in the Gulf of Mexico were found in the waters around the west end, and Jesse was hoping for an exceptional evening of shark collecting. However, after over two hours with no bites, hopeful optimism was beginning to slip away.

"Well, Bongo, looks like we've wasted most of this evening soaking bait."

Bongo momentarily raised his head and looked toward him.

The words were barely out of Jesse's mouth when a fish suddenly took his bait, causing his fishing reel to sing out.

"Fish on!" Jesse lunged for his rod and began to rapidly reel.

Bongo knew the routine and leaped to his feet, barking excitedly.

"Oh darn!! This is a small one," said Jesse, feeling relatively weak tugs against his line. He quickly brought the fish to the side of the boat. The spotlight attached to the center console of his boat revealed what he had captured.

"Crap, it's an electric ray. This does me no good."

In truth, the electric ray was one of Jesse's favorite marine fishes. In the Gulf, they were relatively colorful with dark brown splotches on a pale background. Their most amazing characteristic was their ability to deliver a strong electric shock, over 200 volts in some cases. The electric organs could be discerned as two large, kidney-bean-shaped structures on the upper surface just under the skin. The largest specimens were dangerous to handle since the voltage produced by these organs could stun a person or throw the heart into cardiac arrest. Previously shocked by smaller specimens, he was amazed by the feeling that was produced. Always the scientist, on a recent trip, he shakily recorded the effect in his field notebook with cold objectivity:

"June 15, 1986: Captured small Narcine specimen. Intense shock delivered to right arm while trying to release the ray. Arm completely numb for several minutes. Tingly feeling in arm as

effect wore off. Feeling is identical to when your foot goes to sleep and when feeling returns. Note to self- Don't do that again!"

His rod in one hand and a landing net in the other, Jesse scooped up the ray and brought it into the boat. The fish lay motionless on the deck while Bongo ran excitedly around it, barking.

"Bongo, stay back!" commanded Jesse as he attempted to hold the dog away from the fish. But it was all in vain as he leaped over his outstretched arm and planted his wet nose right on the ray's prominent electric organs.

"YEEEEEEEEP!"

The effect was immediate and catastrophic. The current passed through Bongo's small brain, causing him to bark at a pitch Jesse had never heard any canine produce. The dog fell to the deck unconscious, right on top of the ray. Mouth agape and tongue hanging, he could visibly see Bongo's muscles contract and relax as the fish repeatedly shocked the luckless canine.

"BONGO!" yelled Jesse. Grabbing the dog's leg, Jesse could feel the pulses of electricity pass through his hand. Fortunately, the current was now weak, allowing him to extricate Bongo. He carefully placed the dazed canine on the deck as Bongo slowly regained consciousness.

"You OK, boy?" asked Jesse while cradling his head in both hands. Bongo began to lick Jesse's hands as the connections in his brain began to re-establish themselves.

"I'll bet you won't do that again, huh?"

Jesse lifted the ray from the deck using the fishing rod, held it suspended over the live well, and cut the line with the knife that he always kept on his belt. The fish unceremoniously plopped into the boat's live well, no worse for wear.

"I'm gonna hold onto this fellow and put him in my aquarium. What do you think about that idea, boy?"

Bongo barely moved. The dog's first electroshock therapy had turned, at least for the moment, a previously Manic Mutt into Mr. Mellow.

Jesse rebaited and sent his line out again. A full moon had risen over the Gulf, and he was optimistic that it would have a positive effect on his catch. The increased illumination and tidal currents provided by a full moon were known to alter the behaviors of many marine organisms. He did not have to wait long. "ZEEEEEEEEEEEEEEEEEEEEEEEEEEEEEEEE"

The mechanical buzz of one of the large reels was music to his ears. As line rapidly spun off the reel, Jesse quickly removed the rod from its holder. Flipping a switch to engage the crank, he gently reeled up any extra slack and pulled quickly back on the rod to set the hook. This was the critical point in shark collecting. If the bait was held loosely in the mouth, the hook would simply pull out. If the line was not kept taut against the struggling fish, it could throw the hook during the ensuing fight. Jesse had witnessed leaping sharks throw their hooks in mid-leap, the hook flying free through the air, and the shark lost.

Most frustrating of all was when a small shark, having been captured, was attacked by a much larger shark. The series of events was always similar. A hooked shark would suddenly go berserk, leaping repeatedly from the water in an attempt to escape a much larger predator, the line would suddenly go limp, and, upon retrieval, nothing but a shark's head would remain. It always puzzled Jesse how unerringly a large shark would cleanly sever the head without itself becoming hooked. Almost like it knew it had a hook in it!

"Fish on!" declared Jesse as he cranked away at the struggling shark and started the timer on his Casio watch. "This feels like a good one."

Jesse's doctoral research project required that sharks be quickly landed, a blood sample be taken from a relatively unstressed shark, and the animal be released but kept on the line for the next blood sample. After repeatedly retrieving the same shark at predetermined time intervals and drawing blood samples, stress-induced changes in the shark's physiology over time could be monitored. It was a constant source of concern that the success of this project, and thus his professional future, hinged on his fishing ability. In retrospect, choosing this project might not have been the best career path. However, the necessary lab work was tolerable, the fieldwork enjoyable, and he hoped it would be completed within the year.

Bongo, now more like his old self, barked excitedly. Jesse cranked the reel like a man possessed, brought the fish to the boat, and quickly lifted the shark over the gunnel. A small bull shark was the perfect fish for his study. The shark thrashed violently for a few seconds before Jesse subdued it using a wet towel, drew a blood sample from its fin, released the still-hooked shark back into the ocean, and checked his watch.

"Ha!" exclaimed Jesse with a fist pump. "Captured, blood taken, and released in one minute and thirty-six seconds! What do you think about that, Bongo?" Upon hearing his name, he resumed barking and dashing about. At additional fifteen-minute intervals, Jesse reeled the shark in to obtain four more blood samples, a complete, one-hour stress series, and hopefully, another small step toward completing his degree.

CHAPTER 6

"Well, one shark is better than none, right, Bongo?"

Jesse had continued fishing late into the night with no other captures. A late rising, full moon provided light enough to clearly see the west end of the island from where Jesse was anchored.

In the distance, a brightly lit boat approached. Jesse recognized it as a friend and local crab fisherman, Gino Patronas. They first met after Jesse had run out of gas, and Gino towed him to shore. Gino lived on the island and often met Jesse at the Neptune Club, a bar and restaurant popular with locals. Gino's muscular arms and upper body were a testament to the many years spent pulling crab traps out of the Mississippi Sound. He wore dirty, yellow farmer-johns, a sun-bleached Red Man chewing tobacco ball cap, and no shirt. Black curly hair and dark-complexion, too many years in the intense, south Alabama sun had sun-damaged his face and arms. Jesse was puzzled that no matter the time of day, he always seemed to have a five o'clock shadow.

Gino cut his motor several yards away and allowed the momentum to close the distance. As the boat approached, Bongo suddenly got very excited.

"Hey, Jesse. How's it going?"

"Yap, yap, yap, yap." Bongo continued to vocalize.

"Pretty good. What brings you out here so late?"

"I thought you might have been the SOB who has been messing with my crab traps. I came out to see if I could catch him."

"Yap, yap, yap."

"Any luck?"

"Nah. But when I catch em, he is gonna have a conversation with my little friend." He pulled a 38 Special from his pocket. "Piece of crap taking food off of my family's table. You ain't out of gas ag'in are yah?"

"No, heck no! I guess you'll never let me forget that."

Gino's boat was just a few feet away, and Bongo was now extremely excited, barking, shaking, and jumping around.

"Yap, yap, yap, yap."

"Settle down, Bongo," commanded Jesse. "Crazy dog!"

"What in hell's gotten into that dog of yours?"

"He's just happy to see you, I guess."

When Gino was finally in range, Bongo immediately leaped onto his boat, squatted, and dropped a large pile of dung onto the bow. He then quickly jumped back into Jesse's boat. Jesse could not stop laughing.

"Damn it!" said Gino. "Did you teach that dog to do that?"

"You're kidding, right?" said Jesse between guffaws. "It would probably be easier to teach a mule to sing opera. He had to go, and I guess you were the next best thing. Actually, that's the smartest thing I've ever seen that dog do."

Gino filled a bucket with seawater and flushed the dog turds into the sea.

"What are you doing out here?"

"Still catching sharks for my research project. But I'm not having much luck at the moment. Only caught one shark this evening."

"You're fishing on the wrong tide. High tide is later tonight, and that's when you'll start picking some up."

"Yeah, well, I'll be out here all night camping on the island. Maybe I'll have better luck later. How's the crab fishing these days?"

Jesse posed the question and immediately regretted it.

"If the damn government would just leave us alone, it would be great. But the bastards are regulatin' me out of business. I guess they don't want no crab fishermen working in Alabama anymore. I'm about ready to pull up stakes and move to Louisiana. I hear they got no regulations over there. You can do as you please, and there are plenty of crabs."

Gino knew that Jesse had worked for the Alabama Department of Conservation before going back to graduate school, and he was baiting him for another argument about fishing regulations. Having no desire for verbal sparring, he didn't take the bait.

"Maybe that's the best thing to do, Gino. Although I would hate to see you go. I think you're a nice guy, no matter what people say. I know Bongo would miss his floating litter box," added Jesse with a snicker.

"Go to hell!" said Gino good-naturedly. "I guess I'll head for the hill. Be careful if you run around out here at night. I would hate to have to bail your ass out again."

"I'm not. I may fish from shore a bit. My running lights are out, so I won't be going anywhere. I'll be camping on the island. Tell your better half I said hello."

"I will. I'll monitor channel 16 on the VHF at home, so if you have any trouble, just give me a call."

"I appreciate it. Be safe, my friend!" added Jesse with a wave.

Gino pointed his crab boat in the direction of the launch and motored away. Jesse pulled anchor and, in the bright moonlight, headed the short distance to the island. With a dying wind, the reflected moonlight gave a quicksilver appearance to the glassy waters of the Mississippi Sound.

Jesse ran the boat onto the lee side of the island, and as soon as the boat touched the island, Bongo jumped, took a quick leak, and took off up the beach like his butt was on fire. Jesse walked the boat anchor far up the dunes and planted it securely in the sand.

After quickly pitching his small backpacking tent, Jesse got a driftwood fire going. He sat on an overturned pickle bucket and read a week-old *New Orleans Times-Picayune* newspaper that was left on the boat from a previous trip. The headline about the Tiananmen Square protests saddened him: "*Beijing Blood Bath, 57 Killed by Chinese Troops.*"

Bongo returned shortly to the campsite with a dried, mummified raccoon in his mouth, a prize he had found on his beach romp.

"Good grief Bongo! Get that thing out of here," demanded Jesse.

He tried to chase the stinky mutt out of the campsite, which Bongo interpreted as play and began running around, dragging the carcass with him. Jesse finally separated him from his evil plaything and, picking it up with a piece of driftwood, heaved it into the Mississippi Sound. Bongo took off, dove into the water, and retrieved it.

"Damn it dog!" yelled Jesse. He began chasing him again and finally got him to drop it. This time, he walked across the island and tossed it into the surf coming in from the open Gulf of Mexico. The waves sufficiently deterred him from retrieving it. Disappointed, Bongo whined and reluctantly followed him back to the campsite.

Jesse had not prepared well for this trip, expecting to catch enough fish for frying. However, he had several large mullet he planned to use as bait, and quickly prepared them for the pan. Although the freshness of these particular fish was in doubt, they were purchased from a local seafood market and were not specifically sold as bait fish. The fish turned out to be delicious, and Jesse ate his fill.

After dinner, Jesse sat at the water's edge and fished for a couple of hours. Bongo, completely exhausted, lay in the sand next to him. The night sky was cloudless. He could not remember seeing so many stars and was treated to a minor meteor shower. Remarkably, the meteors burned red and green as they streaked through space. Always the scientist, he wondered if perhaps the different colors were caused by their being composed of different materials. A particularly bright, green one blazed across the sky and made a hard right turn toward Mobile.

"Whoa, that was weird!" he said out loud. "I must be really tired, Bongo, because meteors can't do that." He dismissed it as two different meteors that crossed paths at right angles to each other. That would explain it, he thought. And then a meteor made three loops around the night sky before plunging into the waters of the Mississippi Sound.

"Son of a…!" He stood up to see if he could spot where the meteor had entered the water. Bongo stirred slightly, too tired to be interested in anything he had to say.

"My mind must be playing tricks on me, boy."

It was now past midnight and he decided he was too tired to think straight and definitely too tired to fish.

"Let's go Bongo. Time to call it quits."

They made their way back to the campsite and turned in. Bongo followed and flopped just outside the tent door. Originally, he had planned to allow Bongo to sleep inside the small tent, but the stench of coon carcass that hung heavily from him prevented that.

As soon as Jesse lay down, even though he was exhausted, his mind raced over the events of the day. The school of whale sharks that had almost capsized the boat, the Pelican that spoke perfect Spanish, who selfishly drank his last *Coke*, and the band of angels that played Hank Williams tunes on their harps while flying around a nearby shrimp boat.

Jesse jumped up and turned on the flashlight to check everything. Dismissing it as just a vivid dream, he lay back down. But as soon as he closed his eyes, his mind spiraled out of control. A mix of strange emotions swept over him, and then the hallucinations resumed. Scarlet monkeys, sharks swimming through fountains of orange light, and multi-colored lightning bolts flashed through the tent fabric. Jesse burst out of the tent, tripped over Bongo, and face-planted into a dune. Bongo started barking frantically, but then came over to be comforted. He gently licked his face. When Jesse opened his eyes, instead of Bongo, he saw the face of a red-eyed, horned demon. He screamed, shoved the creature aside, and sprinted back into the tent. The flashlight revealed nothing unusual, and no sign of the dog. For the rest of the night, as long as the light was on and he stayed awake, things were mostly fine. But whenever he turned off the lights or closed his eyes, he entered a surreal world full of color, strange creatures, and fear. At the peak of his hallucinations, he was about to use the radio to see if he could reach Gino for help, but the visions finally faded in the early morning hours, leaving him exhausted and worried.

CHAPTER 7

At sunrise, Jesse found Bongo asleep in the bow of the boat. As was his way, the dog had no memory of the events of the evening. He jumped out of the boat and raced around Jesse, eager to start the day.

"Sorry about last night, buddy. I don't know what was going on, but I thought I was losing my mind. This has been a tough trip for both of us. I think we'll call it quits."

Jesse opened a package of sliced, white bread and fed him almost the entire loaf. Bongo scarfed it down, barely chewing. He broke camp and loaded his meager camping equipment into the boat.

"I think we will head in around the south side of the island if the seas aren't running too high. Maybe we can find you some pelicans and seagulls to bark at."

On these fishing trips, Bongo liked to ride in the front of the boat, barking furiously whenever a seabird came in sight. That was Jesse's signal to swing the boat in the direction of the fleeing bird, and he would go completely crazy, barking and shaking. He never seemed to tire of this game. A particularly large pelican diving for bait fish appeared off the starboard bow, and the chase was on. Jesse hit the throttle on his 250-horsepower *Mercury* and followed the path of the fleeing bird. The chance of even getting close to the bird was slim, but that never dimmed Bongo's enthusiasm.

Bongo was in his customary position, right in the bow of the boat, when suddenly a full-grown dolphin appeared in the bow wake just below him on the starboard side. The crazy dog, overcome with excitement, pounced onto the back of the speeding mammal. For a fraction of a second, it appeared that he was standing on the back of the beast. It is said that dogs age seven years for every human year, so their lives are compressed into a much shorter period of time. Due to this altered perception of time, it's possible that Bongo felt like he had a good five-minute ride on the back of that dolphin. However, a single thrust of its powerful flukes caught Bongo in the chest and somersaulted him across the water. Jesse quickly throttled down, circled, and grabbed him by the scruff of the neck. Heaving him back into the boat, he feared the worst. However, after a couple of shakes, which thoroughly soaked Jesse, Bongo resumed his spot on the bow, ready for another ride.

Jesse's attention was suddenly drawn toward the island.

"Hmm, that looks peculiar." He slowly motored toward a boat that was out of place on this lonesome stretch of Dauphin Island.

Cautiously steering through the swells that had been building since sun-up, he pulled his binoculars from the dry box and focused on a shrimp boat that was run aground near the beach. Jesse had been gifted a pair of high-quality Zeiss binoculars that had come in handy on countless occasions. He could see waves breaking against the hull of the ship. A large number of seagulls sat in the rigging, and many flew around the back deck. After observing for several minutes and seeing no one on board, an ominous feeling came over him.

"That doesn't look good. I'd better report this."

Jesse removed the VHF microphone from its holder and turned the channel selector to 16, the emergency channel.

"Coast Guard Station Dauphin Island, Coast Guard Station Dauphin Island, Coast Guard Station Dauphin Island, this is Research Vessel Bongo, Bongo, Bongo. Over."

Having never officially named his twenty-one-foot *Key West*, Jesse used his dog's name for the vessel.

"This is the Dauphin Island Coast Guard station. Please go to channel 12, repeating, channel one two. Over."

"Research Vessel Bongo going to channel one-two and standing by. Over"

"What is your situation, Captain? Over," came the officious reply.

"I am just off the south side of Dauphin Island, about one and a half miles from the west end of the island. I'm looking at a shrimp boat ran hard aground. It is listing several degrees to port, and it appears to be abandoned. I can't reach it due to sea conditions, but I can read the name on the stern. It's the Crimson Tide. Over."

"We had a report of that vessel being out of communication two nights ago. Can you tell the condition of the vessel? Is anyone on board? Over."

"The boat looks OK, other than the list and the fact that it is hard aground. I've seen no sign of anyone around. Over."

"Thank you, Captain. We are dispatching a vessel now. Over."

"You will have no trouble finding it if you just run down the south side of the island. Do you want me to stand by until you get here? Over."

"If your situation allows it, we would appreciate that. Over."

"We got a steady 3-foot sea, but it's tolerable. R/V Bongo standing by. Over."

Jesse returned the VHF microphone to its hook and killed the engine.

"No use wasting gas waiting on the coasties."

The VHF radio suddenly came to life.

"Bongo, Bongo, Bongo. Golden Eagle, Golden Eagle, Golden Eagle. Over."

Jesse grabbed the microphone and replied. "Go ahead, Golden Eagle. Over."

"Captain, the Crimson Tide belongs to Tom Armstrong. He was south of Mobile two nights ago, and no one has heard from him since. There was some bad weather that came through, but it shouldn't have caused him any trouble. I hope he is OK. Over."

"Captain, I can't tell if anyone's on board, and I can't approach the boat due to this chop. The Coast Guard is on the way. I will let you know what they tell me. Over"

"I would appreciate that, Captain. I am friends with Tom and his family. I pray that he and his crew are alright. I will put in a ship-to-shore call to his wife. Golden Eagle standing by on channel twelve. Out."

"Well, Bongo, we'd better get everything in order and put our PFDs on. The coasties will probably do a vessel safety check and ticket us if we don't have things in order."

Jesse put on his personal flotation device and located his fire extinguisher, flares, and a Coast Guard-required sound-producing device, an air horn. A Coast Guard "response boat small" soon appeared on the horizon, headed in his direction.

"Here they come now, Bongo. That was fast! I want you to be on your best behavior, OK?" said Jesse while vigorously scratching him behind the ears.

The Coast Guard vessel with four individuals slowly idled up to the R/V Bongo and stood off about 30 feet. Bongo began barking.

"Good morning, Captain," said the individual who seemed to be in charge. "I'm Ensign Carlisle."

"Good morning, sir. Nice to meet you." Jesse steadied himself against the boat's railing. "I'm Jesse Gates. I'm working on a PhD research project and spent last night trying to catch sharks for my project. I was headed to the dock and spotted the boat that had run aground. I've never seen a shrimper do that. Plenty of pleasure boaters, but never a shrimper. Something doesn't look right."

"Thanks for reporting this," said the Ensign.

"No worries. I always try to be aware of what's going on. It can be dangerous out here, and I know many of the fishermen who work these waters. I had a terrible night last night, and we are anxious to get back to the dock."

"No luck fishing?" asked Ensign Carlisle.

"Very little. I camped on the island and didn't sleep a wink all night. Had the craziest dreams that were more like hallucinations than dreams. Some of them were like wide-awake nightmares. I thought I was losing my mind," added Jesse.

"Did you happen to have mullet in the last 24 hours?" asked the Ensign.

"Why yes. I had some last night. Why?"

"Have you ever heard of hallucinogenic mullet poisoning?"

"You're joking, right?"

"Not at all," said Carlisle. "It's very rare, but there have been a couple of reports of it on the island over the past few months."

"You don't know how glad I am to hear that," said a very relieved Jesse. "I genuinely thought I was having a psychotic episode. I almost radioed a friend of mine, Gino Patronas, to come get me."

"It's a good chance that Gino would have been hallucinating himself last night," said one of the Seamen.

"You know Gino?" asked Jesse.

"Oh yeah. I saw him at the *Neptune Club* last night. He was pretty plastered."

"Captain, we are required to conduct safety inspections of all vessels that contact us," said Ensign Carlisle. "Have you had an inspection before?"

"Yes sir, although it has been a while."

"If you will toss us a line, we will pull your boat to ours. We'll do this quickly and then hit the beach to investigate the stranded vessel. Hopefully, they just ran aground and are somewhere on the island now."

"I hope you are right, sir," said Jesse as he tossed a line to one of the seamen.

When the boats were close to each other, Bongo began barking excitedly, and Jesse suddenly realized what was about to happen.

"BONGO... NO!" yelled Jesse as the dog jumped on the Coast Guard vessel, deposited a respectable pile of feces on the deck, and leaped back again.

"Sir, I am so sorry! said Jesse, embarrassed. "That's the second time he has done that in as many days."

"I guess he doesn't like the Coast Guard, huh?" said one of the seamen.

"He just gets excited around new faces and that loosens up his bowels...I guess."

"Toss that line back," ordered the Ensign as the boats drifted apart again. "Get the wash-down hose and clear that deck. Captain, we will assume you have all the required equipment."

"I do, sir," said Jesse.

"Good enough."

"If you don't mind, I would like to hang around until you check out the boat," said Jesse. "I was just contacted by a shrimper who overheard our conversation on the VHF. He knows the Captain of that vessel and his family."

"No problem," replied Ensign Carlisle as they pulled away and turned toward the beach.

"Good job Bongo. No disrespect to the Coast Guard, but my fire extinguisher is out of date, and you may have just saved me a citation," said Jesse as he scratched Bongo on the head.

CHAPTER 8

"Seaman Rodgers, Seaman Jones, prepare to board the vessel when we approach," ordered Carlisle. "Stay in constant radio contact."

"Aye aye, sir," replied the men in unison.

"We have to do this quickly between waves or risk swamping," said Carlisle as he surveyed the stranded ship with his binoculars. "The trawls are still hanging over the rear deck, and two of the trawl bags were never emptied. That's curious!"

Carlisle continued to examine the Crimson Tide through his binoculars for a few minutes, noting the time between waves and the vessel's position relative to the shoreline. Although the vessel was aground in shallow water, the Coast Guard's rapid deployment vessel was designed for operation in just these conditions.

"Take her in, Seaman McClain."

The seaman piloted the vessel into the surf zone between two swells. In the momentary calmed water between breakers, McLain nosed the bow up to the stranded vessel, whereupon the two Seamen quickly scrambled over the railing. McLain expertly backed away, turned hard to port, and gunned the engines to climb over and away from the wave forming behind them. They stood off the beach awaiting a report from the shore party.

"Oh my God! What is that smell?" complained Rodgers as they cautiously entered the wheelhouse.

"Smells like a lot of spoiled seafood and something burning," replied Jones. "Not to mention all the seagull crap that's covering everything."

"No one in the wheelhouse," said Rodgers. This vessel was underway and on autopilot when it ran aground. It's still in gear, and all the electronics are still on. Let's check the rest of the ship. I'll go through the galley. You go to the stern and come through the rear hatchway. Check the bunk rooms and I'll go down into the engine room."

"OK," said Jones as he exited the wheelhouse and walked the narrow deck to the rear where the trawls were hanging. Seagulls perched in the ship's rigging took flight as he approached.

"Oh Lord! That explains the smell." Jones covered his mouth and nose with the crook of his arm. The deck was strewn with decaying sea creatures. Two trawl bags, packed full of spoiled shrimp and fish, still hung over the deck, cooking in the summer sun. He unclipped the hand-held VHF radio from his vest.

"Coast Guard Vessel 219, Seaman Jones, come back. Over."

"Go ahead, Seamen Jones. Over," replied the Ensign.

"Yes sir! We entered the wheelhouse and found no one. The back deck is covered with rotting trawl trash and seagull crap, and two trawl bags were never emptied. It stinks to high heaven back here. Rodgers is down in the engine room now, and I will take a look in the bunk rooms. We will continue to investigate. Over."

"Report back as soon as you have finished, and we will pick you up. Standing by."

"Aye, aye sir. Over and out."

Jones pushed open the rear door, entered the bunk rooms, and made a cursory inspection. He was just finishing as Rodgers came up the stairs from the engine room below.

"Nobody in the engine room," said Rodgers. "Very weird. A bowl of half-peeled potatoes was on the galley table, and there was a pot of something left on the hot stove. Whatever it was is burned to a crisp."

"I found three bunks that someone had slept in, and their clothes and personal items are still there," added Jones. "It looked like someone was poking around in the bunk room. Maybe looking for valuables. What we have here is a clear case of alien abduction."

"I dare you to report that to tight-ass Carlisle."

"Yeah, right."

"What we have here is a drug deal gone bad," added Rodgers. "Pretending to be shrimping and picking up drugs instead."

"If that's true, there should be no shrimp stored in the hold," said Jones. "I'll go down the hatch and check the hold. If full of ice and shrimp, then that shoots your drug theory."

"I'll look around the back deck if I can stand the smell!"

They both pulled the large hatch off the cold storage hold. "God, an inch of sea gull crap all over this hatch. Disgusting!" Rodgers wiped his hands on his pants as Jones lowered himself down. Rodgers remained upwind of the stench and poked around on deck.

"Nothing but a lot of bad sushi up here. I wonder if there is any shrimp in the brine chiller," said Rodgers to himself as he lifted the lid on the chiller. "Well, well, there's still frozen shrimp in here."

He grabbed a hand net that was hanging close by and poked around in the chiller looking for more shrimp.

"Oh my god!" Rodgers drew back in revulsion as a bluish-hued, pockmarked, frozen face emerged from the sub-zero water. The chiller cover slammed shut as he slipped on the slimy deck.

"JONES, GET UP HERE!"

Jones scrambled out of the ship's hold to find Rodgers pale and fear-stricken.

"Dude, we got a stiff in the chiller, and I mean stiff, he is frozen solid."

"Don't screw around man!"

"Look for yourself," demanded Rodgers.

Jones lifted the chiller cover and slammed it immediately.

"Oh my God! That is one ugly sight!" Jones went to the ship's railing and leaned over it, taking deep breaths. "I think I might puke."

"Radio Carlisle," said Rodgers. "Tell him we need to get off this ship right now!"

"Give me a second." Jones paused for a few moments to gather himself and then removed the radio from his belt. "Coast Guard Vessel 219, this is Seaman Jones, come in. Over."

"Go ahead, Seaman Jones," replied Carlisle.

"We are requesting immediate pick-up. Over."

"What is your situation? Over."

"Sir, I think it best that we not discuss this over an open communication line," replied Jones. Over."

"Very well. We are coming your way now. Over and out."

"What the hell do you think happened to that guy?" asked Jones. Both men stood at the railing watching the boat as it approached, anxious to be off the Crimson Tide.

"I have no idea. None of this makes sense. The holds are full of shrimp and ice. It looks like someone went through the cabins looking for something, but what of value would these poor bastards have? These guys were shrimping, not running drugs."

"How in hell did he end up looking like that and stuffed in the chiller, and where is the rest of the crew?"

"I don't know, man. I just want off this damn boat," replied Rodgers. "Here comes Carlisle. Let's go."

The vessel pulled up to the side of the Crimson Tide, and the two seamen climbed aboard. A perfect extraction, McClain powered through a wave and stopped just outside the surf zone.

"Report, Seaman Jones," ordered Carlisle.

"We found a body in the salt bath chiller!" said Jones, out of breath.

"A body?"

"Yes sir. Frozen stiff. It was horrible. His face looked like gumbo."

"Frozen, my God! A murder?"

"Sir, I can't say."

"It doesn't look like a drug deal gone bad to me, sir," added Rodgers. "The holds are full of ice and shrimp, and food was being prepared in the galley. The navigational electronics were left on, and the vessel was in gear and on autopilot when it ran aground.

Whatever happened was fast, and it happened while they were shrimping."

"You mean nobody ever shut the engines down?"

"Yes sir," said Rodgers. "I would guess the prop is chewed all to hell, digging into the sand. The engines likely over-heated and died since sand and sediment probably clogged the engine cooling system."

"That explains why the two trawl bags were never emptied," said Carlisle. "So you think something happened that incapacitated the crew and the autopilot ran it aground?"

"I think so, sir," said Jones. "Another curious thing. It looked like someone went through the bunk room looking for something. Drawers and cabinets were left open, and clothes and stuff were thrown around the room."

"Maybe they were just very sloppy shrimpers?" suggested Carlisle.

"Possibly, sir. But this was more than your average sloppiness. It appeared that three people were on board since three bunks were being used. But we only found one person, the fellow in the chiller.

"Any thoughts on what might have led to this?"

"Sir, I have no clue."

"Good work, men," said Carlisle. "We'll turn this investigation over to the local authorities. McClain, swing by that student's vessel. Let's keep our distance this time."

McClain motored over to where Jesse sat with his fishing line out.

"Mr. Gates. You can head to the dock. We appreciate you reporting this," said Carlisle.

"Was there anyone on board?" asked Jesse.

"Sir, it is best that we not comment on what we found."

"Uh oh! That does not sound good," said Jesse. "I had a shrimper contact me about this just a moment ago. Any suggestions on what I should tell him?"

"I recommend that you tell him that we couldn't give you any information. That's all you can do."

"That will work, I guess. Y'all have a great day," said Jesse as he fired up his outboard and headed for the dock.

CHAPTER 9

"You're not gonna believe what happened to me and Bongo on our last sharking trip!"

Jesse sat in the lab at the University, working to process his most recent samples. Donated to the University in the 1950s, the two-story, former Coast Guard building was built with hurricane-proof, steel-reinforced poured concrete and was simple and entirely utilitarian. About as attractive as an oversized cinder block, the building sat on the island's east end. Cold fluorescent lighting, industrial gray floor tiles, and black, slate countertops characterized the "low bid" look of a repurposed university research lab. Most of the workspace in Jesse's lab was filled with various pieces of equipment, some portable for use on a research vessel and others strictly for laboratory use: microscopes, a blood gas analysis machine, a spectrometer, etc. The only bright spots in an otherwise dreary space were the "Blues Brothers" poster on the wall and the classical music playing from the boom-box.

Jesse was behind in his lab work. Recent rough seas along the coast prevented him from shark collecting but provided the opportunity to catch up on blood analysis and data workup. Processing samples required him to transfer shark blood into small tubes that he placed in a centrifuge. Centrifuging the samples separated the blood cells from plasma, and the constituents of the plasma could be analyzed to provide a chemical profile reflecting the shark's stress level.

"Did y'all run out of gas again?" asked Christina Carrigan, a fellow graduate student.

Christina stood in front of an instrument that displayed the chemical profile of the plasma samples Jesse had collected. Constituents like lactic acid, pH, glucose, and antibodies were key stress indicators. Changes in these blood parameters could signal that the animal was under stress; the larger the change, the higher the stress level.

Christina spoke with a southern drawl, having arrived at the University from Mississippi at the same time as Jesse. Known as "CC", she was considered brilliant by most accounts. CC had finished high school in record time and was on track to complete her PhD well before Jesse. It was common for graduate students to help each other out, and CC assisted Jesse with his blood analysis. In return, Jesse helped her with her project. She was an Irish beauty — petite, red-haired, and fair-skinned. Her blue eyes were her most striking feature, and Jesse often found himself captivated by her look. Unfortunately, her fiery personality clashed so intensely with Jesse's easy-going nature that anything beyond friendship was out of the question.

"I guess I'll never hear the end of that."

"Not as long as I'm around," said CC sarcastically. "Could you answer a question for me?"

"I will try."

"Why is it that almost every time you go out, something weird happens?"

"I don't know. Just lucky."

"I would not call that lucky."

"How come?" asked Jesse sincerely. "It's the unexpected that makes life interesting. The same old thing over and over again is hardly a way to go through life. Boring. Boring."

"I'm not like you. I prefer things to be ordered. I don't respond well to chaos. Unexpected turns of events tend to frighten me."

"You just need to lighten up. Accept what the world serves up, examine it for insights, and make the best of it. The possibility of discovering something completely new and unexpected is what keeps me interested in science. And by the way, some of the most important scientific discoveries resulted from completely unexpected events, chance encounters, and even mistakes. Penicillin is a good example. Isaac Asimov said that the most exciting phrase in science is not "Eureka!", but rather, "That's funny…""

"Are you gonna tell me what happened or just lecture me?" asked CC impatiently as she loaded more plasma samples for analysis.

"Oh…yeah. Bongo and I camped on the west end, and I was tripping all night."

"What do you mean by tripping?"

"I mean flying monkeys, light trails, colors that you could taste, flaming sand dunes…you know, hallucinations."

"I didn't know you were into that kind of thing, but I am not surprised. LSD, mushrooms?"

"Oh no, nothing like that…mullet."

"Mullet?" A confused look, she turned from her analyses to face Jesse. "You mean the fish, or is that a new drug reference?"

"I apparently poisoned myself by eating mullet I bought from Castellanos Seafood. It's called hallucinogenic mullet poisoning, and it was not fun. I looked up the symptoms in the campus library, and they are exactly what I experienced."

"Get out!" exclaimed CC. "I've never known anyone who has had more crap happen to them."

"The Coast Guard told me about it when they came to investigate the boat that ran aground."

"What boat?"

"When we were coming in, we saw a shrimp boat that ran aground on the west end. I reported it to the Coast Guard. It was a boat called the, uh…Crimson Tide."

"The Crimson Tide?" asked CC, surprised. "You found the Crimson Tide?"

"Well, yeah. You heard about it?"

"Everybody on the island knows about it," added CC as she stopped analyzing samples altogether and approached Jesse. "You haven't heard?"

"Heard what? I've been out of touch for a while. I slept an entire day trying to recuperate from that shark trip."

"They found a corpse on board. The body was identified as the boat captain. I think his name was Joe or something like that."

"Oh no!" exclaimed Jesse in distress. "Was it Tom Armstrong?"

"That was it!"

"I spoke with another boat captain over the VHF while I waited for the Coast Guard. He knew him and his family, but I had no information at that time."

"They towed the boat in two days ago. It's down at the Marine Patrol station. The rumor is that it was some kind of drug deal gone bad, but the folks who knew Captain Tom say there's no way he was dealing drugs. I heard that the body is being kept in a walk-in freezer down at the docks. They're still investigating."

"Oh man," said Jesse, shaking his head. "I was told he had family."

"A wife and two young children."

"That just sucks!" said Jesse sadly as he finished up the last of the blood samples. "Do you have numbers for me?"

"They're printing out now." She tore a printout off the machine and handed it to Jesse. "Here you go. You owe me."

"I know. You're the best!" replied Jesse. "I think I still have mullet left if you'd like to come over and have some."

"I'll pass."

"I know, I'll buy you dinner this Thursday. We can go to the Neptune Club."

"You mean for the free buffet that they have every Thursday night?" asked CC sarcastically.

"You saw right through that, didn't you? OK, you can order off the menu as long as it is under $5."

"The last of the 'big spenders', huh?"

"Hey, I'm a poor graduate student," said Jesse, slightly offended. "I'm on a tight budget until I graduate and find a real job."

"Sorry. I was just poking fun at you," said CC, realizing she had crossed a line. "Is this a date?"

"You can call it that if you want, but with free food, there'll be a bunch of other graduate students. You know what they will think if we come in together."

"So, you think we should keep our forbidden love secret, like Romeo and Juliet?" She put both hands over her heart, stood too close, and used her thickest Southern drawl. "Or maybe like Scaw-lett O'Hara and Rhett Butlah."

"OK, now you're just getting weird!" Jesse backed away and turned to walk out of the lab. "I'll see you on Thursday at the Neptune around 6."

CHAPTER 10

"JESSE!" yelled the group of graduate students in unison as he pushed his way through the door of the Neptune Club.

An unpleasant mixture of cigarette smoke and frying fish filled the air of the most popular and unassuming bar and grill on Dauphin Island. Jesse immediately remembered why he didn't care much for *The Neptune*. He figured he could subtract a couple of months from his life expectancy for each evening he spent there, breathing secondhand smoke and eating deep-fried food. The jukebox blared Merle Haggard as two busy waitresses moved between tables spread across the room. From a nearby, smaller room with two pool tables came the clacking of billiard balls and drunken laughter. There were much better places to eat on the island, but the bait that kept the fish coming back to The Neptune on Thursdays was the free buffet. Pork and beans, sliced white bread, hushpuppies, runny grits, and fried mullet made up the menu. After recent events, Jesse's stomach clenched a bit as he passed the Spartan buffet and thought about eating mullet. Still, he figured he could make a meal out of the rest of the food. He wondered if he would ever be able to eat mullet again.

"Ayyy!" replied Jesse with a Fonzi-esque two thumbs up.

"CC!" shouted the students together as she came in just behind Jesse.

The group consisted of fellow graduate students who were residents of the university's research laboratory on the island. The Gulf Coast Oceanography Laboratory provided limited financial support, workspace, and ready access to the Gulf of Mexico and the Mississippi Sound. Some students worked as teaching assistants, while others, like Jesse, held fellowships that provided a stipend while pursuing their degrees.

The students had pulled a couple of tables together near the windows that looked east out onto the Mississippi Sound. An almost full moon rose over glassy water whose mirror surface was interrupted only by an occasional leaping fish. Jesse and CC pulled up chairs and sat across from each other at one end of the table.

"Jesse, what's this I hear about you and some kind of mind-altering drug?" said Ross Jenkins as he took another pull from a long-neck Budweiser.

Ross was Jesse's closest friend and, along with CC, often accompanied him on his shark trips. He was slight in build, sporting a dark beard and mustache, and was a good 6 inches shorter than Jesse. Ross tended to be a smart-aleck, which Jesse enjoyed. As the poster child for attention deficit disorder, Ross's intelligence, quick wit, and kindness outshone his personality quirks.

"Hallucinogenic mullet poisoning," said Jesse very matter-of-factly. "It was no fun."

"Do you roll mullet or smoke it in a pipe?" asked Ross, laughing hysterically. Ross's favorite comedian was himself, particularly after a few beers.

"I'll tell you this," replied Jesse, "I ain't eatin' any of that mullet on that buffet."

"See if you can get that waitress's attention," said CC. "Could you pass me one of those menus, Elaine?"

"Have y'all heard the latest about the Crimson Tide investigation?" asked Elaine, a fellow graduate student, as she handed CC a menu from across the table. "They found a shrimper's boot washed up on a beach over in Biloxi, and it had a human foot and part of a leg in it. It was one of the crew members."

"Oooo, wicked!" said CC.

"How did they know it was from that boat?" asked Ross. "Shrimper boots and gloves wash up all the time. Man, that's a big Marlin they got hangin' on the wall, ain't it?" added Ross, his ADD kicking in.

"Not with human parts in them, they don't. Plus, the boot had a name written on it," said Elaine. "I don't recall what it was, but he was a crew member on the Crimson Tide."

"I think it was a Mexican name," interjected Bryan, another graduate student.

"Whatever," said Elaine. "They are trying to keep it all hushed up, but you can't keep anything secret on Dauphin Island. My cousin works for the Marine Patrol, and he said there were three on the boat: the captain and two crew members. They think the boot guy went overboard or was thrown overboard, and sharks ate most of him. The whereabouts of the third person is unknown. He thinks the missing crew member had something to do with it. They say the guy had a drug problem."

"That's what I've thought all along," said Bryan.

"But this is where it gets really weird," added Elaine. "They found a frozen body in the brine chiller."

"Double-wicked!" said CC with a devilish grin.

"OK, you're freaking me out CC," said Jesse as he headed toward the buffet table. "I'm gonna grab some food."

"They were actively fishing when something happened real sudden-like because some of the trawls hadn't even been dumped when it ran aground on our fair island," continued Elaine. "It was the boat Captain frozen in the chiller."

"I'm telling you this has got drug smuggling written all over it," said Ross. "That missing crew member is on a beach in Mexico somewhere snorting cocaine."

"But they were shrimping when something happened unexpectedly," said Elaine.

"Maybe a wave hit the boat and washed everyone overboard," said CC.

"Maybe a rogue wave," added Jesse, returning with a plate from the buffet, *sans* mullet.

"What's a rogue wave?" asked CC.

"A rogue wave is an unusually large wave that is far larger than any other waves that precede or follow it," said Jesse. "The mysterious disappearance of several large ships has been attributed to them. The loss of the *Edmund Fitzgerald* is believed to have been caused by a rogue wave in Lake Superior."

"Who or what was the Edmund Fitzgerald?" asked CC.

"You know, from the Gordon Lightfoot song? The ship that sank in Lake Superior? Jesse sang a verse from the song.

"Not familiar with it," said CC. "And by the way, don't quit your day job."

"Everybody's a critic," retorted Jesse. "Some believe rogue waves can reach 100 feet or more."

"But don't you think a huge wave would have torn the superstructure off the boat and wrecked everything on board?" asked CC.

"True," admitted Jesse. "Although I was a distance away from the vessel, I saw no major damage."

"You can go down to the Marine Patrol dock and see the boat," said CC.

"I guess I need to do that," mumbled Jesse, his mouth full of food. "This is absolutely the worst hushpuppy I have ever tried to eat. It's grainy, dry, and fishy."

"Jesse," said Ross. "That's not a hushpuppy."

"Sure it is," said Jesse as he picked one up from his plate and scrutinized the bite he had just taken out of it.

"What color is the inside of it?" asked Ross.

"It's orange. Hmm, that's strange."

"That's battered, deep-fried, mullet roe. You're eating a mullet ovary."

"Gross!" said Jesse as he let the mass of fish eggs fall out of his mouth onto his plate.

"The testes are white on the inside. They're much better than the ovaries," said Ross.

"I'll keep that in mind," replied Jesse with a shiver.

From across the room, two drunken patrons approached the table. Brothers Frank and Charlie Peron were bullies when sober, but practically terrorists when drunk. Both overweight, Charlie, the elder brother and the more obnoxious of the two, was balding and wore clothes that looked like he had slept in. His fat face was cherry red. Both worked on the offshore oil rigs. Neither was married, and after weeks on the oil rig, they spent all their waking hours over-indulging in every vice they could lay their hands on. Frank was more clean-cut and was only slightly less drunk than his brother. They were both mean drunks, and from their demeanor, they were clearly looking for trouble, and nerdy college students were always an easy target.

"Do one of you rich kids wanna play pool?" asked whiskey-soaked Charlie, slurring his words. "I'll even spot you three balls."

"No thanks," said Ross, looking around the table at the other students. "We're good."

"What about you, blondie?" Charlie leaned against the table right in front of Jesse.

"I could spot YOU three balls and, even if you were sober, I could beat you like a bass drum," replied Jesse. "But I'm not gonna take advantage of a drunk."

"What you talking about?" asked Charlie, punctuating the sentence with a belch. "I ain't drunk. I think you just a chicken-shit little surfer boy. Don't I know you from somewhere?" A quizzical look on his face.

"Yeah, we met at the Country Club over martinis," replied Jesse. "Hey, I've got an idea, why don't you go find some cows to tip or bunnies to torture?"

"I ain't never been to the Country Club."

"That was a joke, dick-weed."

"Well, what do we have here?" said Charlie, now turning his attention to CC and leaning over her uncomfortably close. "You about the prettiest little thing I ever saw in here. You want a real man to teach you how to play pool? I'll let you use my special cue stick and balls," added Frank with a leer.

"When you find a real man, you let me know," said CC coldly, "and get out of my face!"

Jesse felt the anger building inside him, and anger management was a challenge he had faced for many years. He knew that if this anger turned to rage, he would struggle to control himself. Trying to recall some of the anger management techniques he had recently read about, but failing, he rose from his seat. Positioning himself between CC and Charlie, he pulled his 8-inch field knife from the scabbard on his belt and began cleaning his fingernails with it.

"Personal hygiene is a priority for me." Jesse gave Charlie a look that could only be described as evil as he held the knife point up at eye level and scrutinized the blade. A flash of light caught its tip. "I gutted two deer with this knife last season. They were about your size," added Jesse as he pointed the knife at Charlie's fat belly.

The look in Jesse's eyes sent a chill through Charlie, and he immediately backed away.

"Come on, Charlie," said brother Frank as he grabbed his arm. "They're just a bunch of pussies."

"Clearly, Frank is a lot smarter than you, Charlie," added Jesse.

"You better watch your back, surfer-boy!" growled Charlie, walking away.

"That's a physical impossibility," retorted Jesse calmly.

Jesse put his knife away and returned to his seat. His hand trembled slightly as he drank from a glass of water.

"Holy cow!" said CC, wide-eyed. "I don't know who I was more worried about, that scumbag or you."

"If looks could kill, those dudes would be pushing up daisies," added Ross. "Would you have used that knife?"

"I was just cleaning my nails," said Jesse with a smile. "They can get so dirty when fishing. I had a run-in with those two on the water a few months ago. They ran that sorry-looking old boat of theirs across one of my fishing nets. There was no doubt it was intentional. Let's just say we had words and leave it at that. I wasn't about to let that idiot start in on CC."

"Gadzooks!" said Ross in a terrible British accent. "It seems that Sir Jesse complaineth too loudly over the honor of the fair maiden CC."

"Is something going on between you two?" asked Elaine.

"NO!" answered both Jesse and CC simultaneously.

CHAPTER 11

"Bongo, settle down back there!" yelled Jesse out the window of his lime-green, 1968 Chevy El Camino as they cruised the only road that ran the length of the inhabited portion of Dauphin Island.

"He wants to ride up here with us." Ross had asked to come with Jesse to check out the Crimson Tide that was moored at the Marine Patrol Station.

"I'm not putting him up front. He's been chewing on everything, and he crapped on the deck of the Coast Guard boat the last time we were out."

"What? Are you kidding me?" Ross, unable to keep from laughing, put both feet up on the dash. "That ain't good. Surprised they didn't arrest him for marine pollution," added Ross, chuckling. "Hey, there's a Tennessee tag on that car."

"He just jumped on their boat, dropped a big deuce, and then jumped back on mine. He did the same thing to Gino Patronas's boat."

"No big deal. Gino probably deserved it."

Jesse pulled away from Ross' apartment and headed toward the Marine Patrol Station. Bongo ran from side to side in the back of the El Camino, barking at everything that passed.

"That dog is gonna drive me crazy. I don't know what has gotten into him lately."

"Probably got brain-damaged by that electric ray."

"But that requires you to have a brain in the first place," added Jesse.

"True."

Jesse and Ross pulled into the parking lot of the Marine Patrol Office under a dull grey sky. A single fat raindrop landed on the windshield of the El Camino as they got out and headed for the dock. To their surprise, the Crimson Tide was nowhere to be found.

"OK, where did the boat go?" Jesse stood on the dock looking at several vacant boat slips.

"Mullet!" exclaimed Ross, pointing across the Mississippi sound toward a large school of leaping fish.

"Ross, try to focus!" implored Jesse.

"Sorry."

"Let's check in the office. See if they can give us some information."

Jesse and Ross walked to the front of the Marine Patrol building and entered the reception area. A young woman sat in the lobby poring over a thick three-ring binder. She looked up as the two entered. Jesse briefly caught the gaze of the woman sitting in the lobby and was instantly captivated by her stunning hazel eyes. With an olive complexion and long, black hair pulled back, she wore jeans and a loose-fitting *Allman Brothers Band* T-shirt.

"Good morning, gentlemen," said the middle-aged receptionist from behind her glass-fronted cubicle. "Can I help you?"

"Jesse?" said Ross when he realized his attention was drawn away from the business at hand. "Jesse!" he repeated this time more imperatively.

"Oh, sorry," said Jesse, suddenly coming back from thoughts of romance. "Did you see that girl in the lobby?" Jesse motioned with his head in the direction of his interest.

"And I'm the one who is supposed to have ADD?" quipped Ross.

"Yes, Ma'am," said Jesse apologetically while turning to face the glass. "We were looking for the Crimson Tide. It was supposed to be docked out back."

"It was moved yesterday."

"Do you know where they took it?"

"I'm sorry, young man. I don't know. Why are you interested?"

"I was the person who found the boat and called the Coast Guard. I was also in contact with a shrimper who was a friend of the boat's captain. We heard he was found on the boat. Is that true?"

"Sorry, but I have no information on any of that. You could perhaps speak to Dr. Belon."

"OK", said Jesse, "Where can I find him?"

Jesse started when he heard a French-Cajun voice from behind say, "That would be her, not him."

Unbeknownst to Jesse, the young lady with whom he had been so smitten had overheard the conversation and crossed the lobby to stand directly behind him. She extended her hand to Jesse and, when they drew close, a spark of static electricity jumped between their fingertips.

"I'm Cherie…ouch," said the stranger with a wince.

"I'm so sorry," said Jesse, nervously. "The dry air in this lobby and this polyester carpet created a charge differential that…" Jesse stopped as he caught himself rambling, and then added… "static electricity."

"Or maybe animal magnetism," said Cherie with a smile. "I'm Cherie Belon. And you are…?"

"Jesse Gates. My pleasure."

"Nice to meet you, Dr. Belon," said Ross, extending his hand. He was disappointed when he was not treated to an electric spark.

"Please call me Cherie. I overheard you say that you found the Crimson Tide?"

Jesse, still taken by the vision of loveliness that stood before him, was having trouble collecting his thoughts.

"Uh, yes, we, I mean, I found it," stuttered Jesse. "Well, it was me and Bongo, or Bongo and I to be grammatically correct, so it was…"

"Yes," interrupted Ross. "Jesse found it on the west end of the island."

"Bongo?" queried Cherie, smiling.

"My dog. He's outside in the truck."

"You knew the captain of the boat?" asked Cherie.

"No, I was contacted by another boat captain when he overheard my conversation with the Coast Guard over the VHF," said Jesse, finally starting to gather his thoughts. "He told me that he knew the captain of the boat. I was collecting sharks when we found it."

"Are y'all commercial fishermen?"

"No, we're both graduate students at the Oceanographic lab here on the island. I'm studying biological oceanography and Ross, chemical oceanography."

"You're scientists?"

"Yes, we hope to be PhD scientists one day," said Ross.

A couple with two children entered the lobby and approached the receptionist.

"Fellows, would you mind stepping outside with me for a moment?"

Although puzzled, the trio left the office and walked to the shady area where Jesse's El Camino was parked. Bongo, tied in the back, began his frantic barking as they approached.

"Is that a '69 El Camino?" asked Cherie.

"A 68. Are you interested in classic cars?"

"I am a huge car buff. I don't have the funds to purchase anything nice, but my Dad and I have been restoring an old '55 Thunderbird back in Baton Rouge."

"Wow! That's a nice ride!" In his mind's eye, Jesse pictured Cherie smiling seductively, driving a bright red T-bird down a long, sunlit, country road, her hair flowing in the breeze.

"It will be someday."

"Wasn't there a 289 cubic inch engine in the T-bird?" asked Ross.

"No, it had a 292 engine. Ford came out with the 289 in the 1963 Fairlane."

"You certainly know your cars, lady!" said Ross. "Jesse's an autophile like yourself. Isn't that right, Jesse?... Jesse?"

Still caught in his fantasy, Ross' question brought him back to reality. "Huh? Oh, yes, I am."

"This must be Bongo?" asked Cherie as she leaned over the truck bed. The dog attacked her with his tongue, licking her face and hands. "That's a good boy!" Cherie scratched him behind his ears and spoke in the sing-song manner that people used with pets and babies. He flipped over on his back in the bed of the truck.

"Well, you've done it now," said Jesse. "He wants a belly rub. Let me warn you, though, if you rub his belly, he'll love you forever."

Jesse found himself falling hard for this young lady. Beautiful, a classic car enthusiast, loves dogs, and that Cajun accent!

"I think he likes you more than he does me," said Jesse. "You're from Baton Rouge?"

"Oh… yes. Sorry," said Cherie, turning away from the dog. "Originally, but I live in Atlanta now. I'm an agent for the Centers for Disease Control. I was sent to look into the Crimson Tide death.”

“Oh, crap!” said Jesse.

“Uh oh!” said Ross, concerned.

Cherie now had their full attention.

“There is no need for concern. The Crimson Tide was towed to an undisclosed location where access can be controlled. We felt that was the best thing to do under the circumstances.”

“And what are the circumstances?” asked Jesse.

There’s a possibility that the captain and crew were exposed to an infectious agent. By isolating the ship, we hope to ensure that no others become infected, if that’s actually what we’re dealing with. You’re both scientists, so you know that’s the prudent thing to do.”

“Of course,” said Ross.

“We’ve got lots of samples to evaluate before we can say anything definitive. This may sound unkind, but it was fortunate that the boat captain was found in the brine chiller. The body was quickly chilled and partially frozen, which resulted in tissue samples of extremely high quality. In many cases, the diseased tissues we have to work with are highly deteriorated and poorly preserved, which makes our job much harder.”

“So, you believe the captain was infected with something and fell into the chiller?” asked Jesse, puzzled.

“We believe he was exposed to something, but are not sure what it was. The condition of the body and the tissue necrosis we observed is not consistent with any other explanation. The samples are being taken to Atlanta for examination. If it’s an infectious agent, we will find out in time.”

“So, you’re a microbiologist?” asked Jesse.

“Yes. A Public Health Microbiologist. I specialize in infectious agent identification and disease transmission. You’re studying biology, Jesse?”

“The biology of sharks. I’m working on a project involving the physiology of sharks. How they respond to stress. It requires me to do a lot of shark collecting since I have to have living sharks for my study.”

“So, you have access to a boat?”

"I do. My research vessel. It's a *Key West*, center console, very sea-worthy."

"Would it be possible for you to take me to the spot where you found the Crimson Tide?"

"No problem," said Jesse, thinking that he would love to escort this young lady anywhere. "When would you like to go?

"Immediately, if that is possible. I understand that there has been no rain on the island since you found the boat, and I need to examine it before any moves in."

"Uh…OK." Jesse paused momentarily, a bit surprised by the urgency. "I'll go by and get my boat. You want to meet me at the public boat launch in, say, 30 minutes? Will that be enough time?"

"Yes. I just have to swing by the motel and get some things. I'm staying at the Palms Motel. I am so grateful for this!"

"No worries. Put on something that you don't mind getting wet if you need to go ashore. I think I can get you close to the beach, but you might have to get your feet wet."

"I grew up around water. I was on the swim team in college and a lifeguard when I was in high school, so I don't mind getting wet. See you in a bit." Cherie walked to her CDC vehicle, a white Crown Vic, and drove away.

Jesse and Ross climbed back into the El Camino and left the parking lot.

"Do you want to go along?" asked Jesse.

"No. You can drop me off. I have work to do, and besides, I don't want to cramp your style with the lovely Dr. Belon!" added Ross with a hint of sarcasm.

"Shut up!" retorted Jesse.

CHAPTER 12

Jesse hooked his boat trailer to the El Camino, and he and Bongo headed for the boat launch. Upon arrival, he found Cherie waiting at the ramp. He swung the trailer around and backed the boat down the ramp. Cherie got out and approached the truck window. She carried a waterproof bag and wore sunglasses and shorts over a bright blue, one-piece bathing suit.

"This is going to be a serious distraction. Dirty and thankless work, but somebody's gotta do it! "

"Is the drain plug in?" she asked.

"Yep. Obviously, you know about boats."

"A little. I used to fish with my dad in the bayous around Baton Rouge."

"If you would grab that bow line and hold the boat when it floats away from the trailer, that would be great. I'll remove the straps and back it down, and when it floats off the trailer, I'll pull out."

"Got it."

Jesse backed up, allowed the boat to slide off the trailer, parked, and got out.

"I'm going to unleash the *Kraken*, so gird your loins!" announced Jesse from across the lot as he untied Bongo from the rear of the truck.

"Uh…what?" asked Cherie from the dock.

Bongo, now unfettered, leaped from the truck, made a beeline toward Cherie, and body-slammed her. Cherie managed to maintain her balance and held the boat fast while he rained dog kisses down upon her.

"BONGO! Get in the boat," commanded Jesse. Bongo jumped from the dock and missed the boat entirely, belly-flopping into the green Gulf water. He swam out, shook himself off, ran back down the dock, and launched himself again. Fortunately, Cherie had drawn the boat closer, and he landed in the boat like a goose on a frozen lake. Gathering himself, he jumped onto the bow of the boat, ready for a ride.

"That's a unique dog!" said Cherie between laughs.

"Unique is one way to describe him," replied Jesse, shaking his head. "He loves people and boats, kind of like me, so he is in Nirvana right now."

"Gird your loins?" asked Cherie, puzzled. "Never heard that one before."

"It means prepare yourself. I can be esoteric at times. Some would call it nerdy."

"No worries. I'm something of a nerd myself."

With all passengers on board, Jesse idled out of the harbor.

"We have to go slow for a bit. It's a no-wake zone until we get beyond that bridge over there…" Jesse pointed toward the Dauphin Island Bridge in the distance, "…and then I can open it up. It looks like it will be fairly calm, so we should make good time once we get out in open water.

"No problem. This will give us time to talk some more. You mentioned shark collecting earlier. How is shark collecting different from fishing?"

"It really isn't other than the fact that we take data and samples, and then release all the animals alive. We are issued a collector's permit by the state in whose waters we are working. We can't keep any of the animals captured for personal use. Our collecting is very enjoyable, but it truly is a lot of work."

"So, what are you trying to accomplish with your research? You mentioned stress."

"I'm interested in how different species of sharks respond to stress and how that response changes with season, with environmental change, etc. From a conservation perspective, it could lead to methods to decrease the mortality of sharks captured by fishermen. Many sharks are released alive after they are caught, but unfortunately, many of them die after release. Sharks are not very stress-tolerant. I document their levels of stress by looking at various blood parameters after a stress event."

"I would guess you look at lactic acid levels?"

"Very good…and several other parameters."

"I would love to see your results sometimes."

"Absolutely. Typically, when I begin describing my project, folks' eyes roll back in their heads or they suddenly remember they need to be somewhere."

"I find it fascinating. I am, after all, a biologist. Jesse, there's something that I did not tell you earlier that you need to know."

"Oh?"

"I said that there may have been an infectious agent involved."

"Yes, I recall."

"Have you ever heard of Ebola?"

"Oh, my Lord!" exclaimed Jesse, now very concerned. "I took an advanced virology class in graduate school, so I know about the disease. I know that it's a very bad virus."

"We don't know what happened to the captain and crew, but we can't rule out Ebola. We have to consider worst-case scenarios, or we would not be doing our job, which is to protect the public. It will take a little time to process the samples, but we hope to identify the agent quickly, if there is an identifiable agent."

"Cherie, the lab on the island is pretty well equipped. We can perform all of the standard histology and microscopic techniques, and we also have a transmission and scanning electron microscope. You could perhaps do some of the analyses here. That would speed things up, would it not?"

"You have a transmission electron microscope?"

"We do, and coincidentally, I took a graduate course in electron microscopy. We can do all the sample preparation, and we can take a look at what you have using the scope after hours. But I have a concern."

"What's that?"

"Could there be a risk of infection from the tissue samples?"

"Absolutely not. The tissues have been chemically preserved, and nothing could survive that treatment."

"Sounds like a plan to me," said Jesse with a smile. "We're about to leave the no-wake zone. We need to get our minds right, so take a look at those cassette tapes in the overhead and choose one to play. I like to have music when we run out."

Cherie opened the overhead storage compartment, took out several tapes, and riffled through them.

"Oooo… what about Bob Marley? I love reggae."

"Good choice! Crank it up so we can hear it over the engine noise and hold on."

Cherie stood next to Jesse and braced herself against the center console. "My loins are girded!"

"Ha!" laughed Jesse. He throttled up the outboard, the bow of the Key West began to rise, and the boat planed off.

To the reggae strains of *Buffalo Soldier*, Jesse, Cherie, and Bongo cruised offshore of Dauphin Island with the dog in his customary place in the bow, barking at every bird, fish, and dolphin he spotted. A light chop on the Mississippi Sound sent vibrations through the vessel, Cherie's hair bouncing in time. Jesse located the exact spot where the Crimson Tide ran aground. He slowed the boat and angled in towards the shore.

"Look, look!" Cherie pointed excitedly at a disturbance on the surface of the water. "A huge school of stingrays right beside the boat."

"Those are called cow-nosed rays. I've seen schools as large as a thousand individuals."

"Awesome, they swim so gracefully!"

"This is the spot, and we are in luck. There's little surf this morning, so we can anchor in water shallow enough for us to wade to shore if we need to. I'll tie Bongo in the boat because he'll go crazy on the beach. He has plenty of shade, and maybe he will just go to sleep. Wishful thinking, however."

"Where was the boat located?"

"Do you see that sand spit?" Jesse pointed toward the beach as he dropped anchor. "It was out from that spit. You can still see where the hull plowed through the sand and where the propeller gouged a hole in the bottom."

"Let's go to the beach and have a look." Cherie removed her shoes and shorts. She grabbed her camera and, holding it over her head, carefully entered the water. Jesse threw off his tennis shoes and jumped overboard. The two waded toward the beach.

"What are we looking for?"

"I don't know. When the boat was towed, the question of an infectious agent was not a consideration. I wondered if there might be something overlooked."

Cherie walked westward along the water's edge, photographing the area. She paused and examined anything that was out of the ordinary. She then walked back along the upper beach toward town, again taking additional photographs.

"Do folks often use the beaches along this stretch of the island?"

"Rarely. The paved road ends miles away, and the only folks that might come out this far would be teens on dirt bikes or three-wheelers."

"What do these look like to you?" Cherie pointed to tracks high along the beach.

"Those are the tracks of a dirt bike."

"They came from the direction of town and stopped just here. The worrisome part is that they don't continue westward, and then they head back toward town again." Cherie and Jesse continued walking along the beach. "There are also footprints here. Looks like someone wearing tennis shoes got off their motorcycle right where the boat was located, and walked toward the water."

She bent down, placed a small ruler next to the footprints for scale, and took multiple photographs of the prints and tire tracks. She then measured the length and width of the footprints and recorded them in a small notebook.

"Maybe this will help identify who this was."

"Cherie. I don't like the look of those clouds!" Jesse pointed toward a line of thunderstorms forming off toward New Orleans. "We'd better head back, I'm afraid a storm is building."

"I hope you're wrong, for all our sakes," replied Cherie ominously.

CHAPTER 13

With amazing regularity, Jesse's biological clock woke him every morning at sunup. He lay in bed listening, wishing his biological clock would SHUT THE HELL UP!

"Crazy dog," muttered Jesse sleepily.

His thoughts immediately turned to Cherie and the events of the day before. They had agreed to meet for breakfast at the Blue Crab Cafe before heading to the oceanography lab. Since it was Saturday, there would be few people to question why they were in the lab, and Jesse hoped to impress her with his skill using the electron microscope. He also wanted to share the data he had collected so far regarding his PhD project.

Jesse made a quick cup of coffee, opened a can of dog food, and plopped it into Bongo's bowl. He pushed through the door onto the screened porch, where the dog awaited excitedly.

"Down, down!" commanded Jesse as he barked and leaped up at him. Jesse put the dish down, and Bongo inhaled the food in about three bites. At night, and when Jesse had to be elsewhere, he kept Bongo on the screened back porch of his secluded rental cottage. A sign nailed across the gable read *Castaway Cottage*. The house was owned by a university faculty member who rented it to graduate students working at the oceanographic lab. Raised high on stilts to avoid hurricane tidal surges, it was Spartan but comfortable. The screened porch was Jesse's favorite feature. He could keep Bongo out of mischief, and he enjoyed spending mornings sitting on the porch with a cup of coffee. Commanding a view of a small bayou just behind the cottage, Jesse loved to observe the goings-on in and around the swamp—the large gator that often sunned on the opposite shore, the myriads of bird species inhabiting the live oak trees, and the large tarpon that occasionally rolled across the water's surface. For Jesse, this was truly God's Country.

The cottage faced north, and for much of the year, both the rising and setting sun could be watched from opposite ends of the porch. On this occasion, the morning sky was fiery red across the entire horizon, reminding Jesse of the old maritime adage, *"Red sky at morning, sailor take warning."*

"Looks like it's gonna be a hot one today, boy!"

Jesse finished his coffee, took a shower, splashed on some Old Spice cologne, and stood before the bathroom mirror. He realized that he had just spent an unusual amount of time grooming his beard and mustache. Jesse had decided, a few years ago, to let his facial hair grow out, thus concealing his baby face. After putting on his cleanest dirty shirt, he threaded his belt through his jeans and knife scabbard and buckled it.

Jesse checked to see that Bongo had plenty of water before leaving. Sensing a ride in the truck, the dog shook excitedly as he approached.

"You can't go with me today, big boy, but I'll bring you a treat back this afternoon."

With Bongo barking his disapproval, Jesse started up the El Camino and pulled out onto Bienville Boulevard. Since he was going to arrive ahead of his 7 AM date with Cherie, he stopped at the *Quickie Mart* and grabbed a copy of the *Mobile Press-Register* newspaper. He entered the café and took his usual seat as an elderly waitress approached. Jesse often had breakfast at the Blue Crab, and he knew all the waitresses.

"Good morning honey."

"Hi, Marie. Y'all been busy this morning?"

"Oh, middlin," said Marie as she turned the cup over that sat before him and filled it with coffee. "You gonna have your usual honey?"

"I'm expecting someone, so let's hold off until she gets here."

"Oh, a lady friend! Does that mean it's over between us?" asked Marie jokingly.

"No, I think it will be OK for us to continue seeing each other." Jesse gave Marie his biggest smile.

"Did you see that article in the paper about the shrimp boat they found on the island?"

"No, I just got the paper."

Marie opened the paper, folded it over, and pointed to an article entitled *Mysterious Death on Dauphin Island*.

"This is not gonna help business. We got enough problems without this kind of crap!" Marie walked toward the kitchen. "I'll come back when your lady friend gets here honey."

"Thanks, Marie."

Jesse read through the news article and was just finishing when Cherie came through the door. He waved to her from across the room. Even though she wore shorts and a T-shirt, Cherie looked more fetching every time he saw her. But in truth, she could have been dressed in a potato sack, and Jesse would have felt the same.

"Good morning. I hope you had a restful evening."

"I'm afraid not." She slid into the booth across from Jesse and rubbed her eyes with the heels of her hands. "I haven't slept well since I've been on the island. I need coffee!"

"I'm sorry," said Jesse sincerely. "Our waitress will be back in just a moment. Here, take mine. I haven't touched it, and it's still hot." Jesse slid the cup and saucer over.

"God bless you!" Cherie added milk to her coffee and took a sip. "This is actually very good coffee. Probably the first good coffee I've had since I got here."

"The food here is pretty good, also. Are you not sleeping? Is the hotel room uncomfortable, or is it work, or both?"

"The room is fine. Something has been troubling me about this investigation, and I don't know what it is."

"Unfortunately, this will not make things better for you." Jesse handed her the newspaper and pointed to the article.

"This is BS!" Disgusted after reading the article, she handed the paper back to Jesse. "Nothing but rumor and speculation. Where do they get this stuff? The CDC has made no official statement about this."

"Like we said before, it's a small island and rumors spread fast. Imaginations will run wild if there are no facts to contain them."

Did you notice this article on the same page about the history of plague in the U.S.?" asked Cherie.

"I didn't notice that."

"Some dim-witted journalist is leading readers to make a connection between the plague and this death. There has never been a single case of plague in the Southeastern U.S. This kind of irresponsible reporting just chaps my buns!"

"All the more reason for us to take a look at those tissue samples as soon as possible," said Jesse.

"Absolutely."

"So, Cherie, could you tell me about your job and the CDC? I have, of course, heard of the Center for Disease Control, but I know very little about it. It sounds interesting."

"It's actually the Centers for Disease Control, plural, because at present, it consists of several different centers. My position is within the Center for Infectious Diseases. Which is pretty much self-explanatory. As a field agent, my job is to investigate public health threats. If there is a report of a possible infectious agent, they send me out to ascertain the risk."

"How do you determine risk?"

"A lot of footwork and a lot of lab work. We actually try to generate data and formulate a hypothesis about what happened and then go about falsifying that hypothesis, that is, I try to disprove my hypothesis."

"I know all about hypothesis testing," said Jesse. "Scientific research is the same whether it is marine biology or epidemiology."

"That's true. If we find there is an infection from a pathogen, we do contact tracing to determine how many people the infected individual has come in contact with. That's where the footwork comes in. We identify those people and inform them of the situation. Find out if they have been ill. We ask them to limit contact with others for a period of time, if possible. Obviously, we keep monitoring hospitals for people admitted with symptoms."

"So, if you find others that are ill and the pathogen seems to be spreading, what then?"

"We quarantine everyone who has been in contact with infected individuals. If we see continued spread, the Director of the CDC can order a lockdown. On an island like this, a lockdown could be used to try to prevent the spread to the mainland."

"That would make a lot of people very unhappy on Dauphin Island."

"Which is better, unhappy or dead?"

"Point taken."

"I don't know if I will continue as a field agent. We just opened a brand-new biosafety level-4 facility at the CDC. They may reassign me to work in that facility."

"What does biosafety level-4 mean?"

"The different levels refer to the degree of isolation and protection needed to safely investigate a particular pathogen. A level-1 would mean that the agent is not a risk to healthy humans. It is the minimum risk level. Level-4 is required for the highest-risk agents. Those would be agents like Ebola, smallpox, hemorrhagic fever, and plague that pose extreme risks to human health."

"How do you safely work with a dangerous virus, like Ebola?"

"Very carefully! The facility is air-tight, and only authorized personnel can enter. In a level-4 facility, there are multiple airlocks you must go through to enter and exit. Full-body protective suits must be worn to enter the facility. You are connected to a breathing hose, so you are never exposed to the air of the facility at all. Nothing goes in unprotected, and nothing goes out without it being decontaminated; that includes the air as well as wastes, which are completely incinerated."

"I don't know if I could work in an environment like that. It sounds dangerous."

"We have highly trained technicians who do the actual lab work. I'm guessing I will be more on the experimental design and data interpretation side of things. Changing the subject, could I ask you a personal question, Jesse?"

"Sure thing."

"What's with the knife?"

"Oh. Does it make you uncomfortable? I'll take it off."

"No, no, I was just curious."

"Well, I got in the habit of carrying it because I am on the water a lot. I use it for cutting line, mending nets, cleaning fish, etc., etc. I also use my "mullet gun" a lot, at least I did use it a lot when I was fond of eating mullet. I kind of lost my taste for mullet."

"Mullet gun?"

Chuckling, Jesse explained. "That's what I call my cast-net. Mullet are found in very large schools near the surface of the water. You can cast-net them and haul in 50 fish with one throw. A cast net is a circular net that spreads open across the water when you throw it on a school of fish. I always wear my knife when cast-netting ever since I read a story about a fellow who was cast-netting and, as luck would have it, dropped his net right on top of a very large hammerhead shark. The shark freaked out, and because mullet fishermen tie the rope of the cast net to their wrist, the shark pulled him overboard. He couldn't get the line off of his wrist. The shark dragged him through the water, and he drowned. The dead shark and the man were found washed up on a beach in Boca Raton, Florida, still tethered together. If he'd had a knife, he could have cut the line and saved himself."

"Oh, my goodness!" said a wide-eyed Cherie.

"A knife can be your best friend. I should also add that I used to compete in knife-throwing competitions."

"I did not know that knife-throwing was a thing."

"Oh yes. There were several teams at my college. I wasn't the best, but I was pretty good. We got first place in a competition."

"By the way, I appreciate you helping with this, Jesse."

"You're quite welcome. But I have a confession to make. My interests have not been completely charitable. I enjoy your company."

"Me too," replied Cherie with a smile.

"Where is that waitress?" asked Jesse as he looked away to hide his embarrassment.

CHAPTER 14

Finishing breakfast, Cherie followed Jesse to the Oceanographic Lab. Located on the island's east end, it commanded a view of the Gulf of Mexico to the south and the Mississippi Sound to the north. Entering the building, they went to the second-floor electron microscope facility. Cherie carried a small ice chest containing tissue samples taken during the autopsy of Captain Tom.

"Typically, only graduate students are around on Saturdays," said Jesse as he unlocked the door to the lab. "It will take a few hours to prepare the samples before we can put them on the electron microscope. Tissue preparation is so tedious."

"I know. I've done it many times. But proper tissue prep is critical."

To visualize the inner structure of the cell, a transmission electron microscope is required. However, it is not just a matter of placing a chunk of tissue under the scope and seeing what is there. The tissue samples must be preserved, dehydrated, stained, embedded in a block of resin, and then cut into extremely fine sections. Those sections can then be examined and the cell structure visualized using a beam of electrons that passes through the fine tissue slice.

"Here's how nerdy I am," admitted Cherie. "When I was 10 or 12 years old, I would spend hours looking through a small microscope I got for Christmas. Absolutely, amazed by the tiny things swimming around in a teaspoon of pond water."

"I know that feeling of amazement. I get it almost every time I am at sea. If we prepare this tissue carefully, I hope we will be amazed at what we see inside these cells."

"I hope we find nothing that looks like a virus."

"How many samples do you have?"

"I had to smuggle these out, so I don't have everything, but I've got samples from the skin, the large airways of the respiratory system, the lungs, and the liver. If this is an airborne infectious agent, it should be present in the respiratory system, but since we don't know what we are working with here, there is no telling what we will find."

"You smuggled them out?"

"Yeah, kind of. Some weird power struggles are going on at the CDC, which I don't understand. I'm doing this "under the radar," so to speak."

"I'm used to doing things off-the-record, and I can relate to political BS. You would think that the academic elite would be above that sort of thing, but believe me, they're not. Let's get those samples processed."

Jesse and Cherie gathered the necessary chemicals and glassware and laid them out on the lab bench. The tissue samples were placed in the appropriate chemicals to start the process.

"While we wait for the tissue to finish, let's go down to my office, and I can show you my research work. That is, if you would like to see it."

"Absolutely. I would love to better understand your project. Wait! You're not trying to lure me into your office to show me your "etchings," are you?"

"Uh, what?" asked Jesse, obviously not familiar with the cliche.

"Oh, just a dumb joke. Lead the way."

Jesse's office was conveniently located in the computer lab, where he had access to an IBM PC. The two sat in the green glow of the CRT monitor as Jesse inserted a 3.5-inch floppy disk into the drive.

"Here's all the data I have so far. These graphs describe the stress response in several shark species," said Jesse as he pointed to the glowing monitor. "This graph is for the bull shark. You can see that lactic acid levels quickly increased throughout the stress response. Blood acidity increased accordingly."

"What's significant about this?" asked Cherie.

"I'm trying to establish a baseline of information against which we can compare across species, seasons, or different environments. Changes in the stress response, say for example, an unusually exaggerated response, might indicate a problem in the population of bull sharks. This work can hopefully be applied to shark conservation in the future."

"Is there concern about shark populations? It seems that most of what you hear about sharks is negative. I'm guessing that a lot of people would be glad if there were fewer sharks."

"That's true, unfortunately. But I believe that the general public will one day have a better appreciation for the importance of all marine species, including sharks."

I hope so," replied Cherie.

"Actually, I still have some data from the last few shark trips that I have not included on this graph."

"You want to key-punch them in now?"

"We can." Jesse glanced at his wristwatch. "We've still got plenty of time. Let me get out my data sheets."

Jesse removed the sheets from a drawer and placed them on the desk in front of them.

"These are bull shark lactic acid values," He quickly punched the numbers into his database. "Now I will re-run the graph, and *voila*, those values will appear shortly on this graph. It is amazing how only a few years ago you would have to get out graph paper and plot your data by hand with a pencil."

"Computers have certainly changed things."

"You can see the new values here are similar to the ones taken previously," Jesse tapped on the computer monitor with his index finger. "Hmm, that's weird. Some of these values are much lower than they should be."

"Which ones?"

"These two sharks show little change in lactic acid over the entire stress experiment. I probably key-punched them wrong. Let me find all the data for those sharks."

Jesse reached again for his data sheets and perused the columns of values.

"Those are sharks #113 and 114. Those lactic acid values are not typos, but they're way off. Glucose, blood acidity, and lactic acid are all off. How could all of the measurements be wrong?"

"Why do you think they are wrong?"

"The blood parameters of those two sharks should not be different from other bull sharks I've examined over the past few years." Jesse scratched his head, puzzled. "Same species, captured on the same day or only a few days apart in many cases, and blood processed identically. I guess I messed up the measurements, but I don't know how."

"That happens sometimes," said Cherie sympathetically.

"I'll have to sort this out later. Your tissue samples are just about ready."

Jesse and Cherie left the office and walked back to the electron microscope lab. Jesse opened the door to the small room that contained the electron microscope and switched on the light.

"This is a nice scope," said Cherie as they sat down before the large instrument. The CRT screen dominated the instrument panel. "Not as good as the one we have at the CDC, but this will work very nicely."

"The resolution of this machine is about 1.5 nanometers." Jesse turned on the microscope and began to make adjustments.

"Technology today is simply amazing!" added Cherie. "It just blows me away that we can look inside something as small as a human cell and even visualize cell components; the nucleus, mitochondria, etc."

"Only in the past 100 years have we come to recognize the incredible complexity of the tiniest living things," said Jesse. "The most complex machine ever created by man, the Space Shuttle, is a crude toy compared to even the simplest cell."

Jesse got up and turned the lights down to better visualize the tissue. Sitting practically shoulder to shoulder with Cherie in the darkened room and smelling her perfume was very off-putting for Jesse, and his hand trembled a bit as he adjusted the controls on the microscope.

"You smell nice," said Jesse. "That perfume is very familiar to me."

"Why, thank you," said Cherie. That's not surprising; it's Prell shampoo. I never wear perfume. I always thought Prell smelled like gardenias."

"That's it. We had gardenias around our house when I was a kid. I love that scent.
Isn't it amazing how particular smells can take you back to a very specific place and time?" added Jesse. "Gardenias remind me of playing hide and seek with my friends when I was a kid. I often hid behind a large gardenia bush."

Jesse continued adjusting the microscope settings to obtain the clearest image. "How large is the Ebola virus?"

"Ebola is about 80 to 100 nanometers. The smallest viruses are about 20 nanometers. Human cells are 100 to 1000 times larger than Ebola. We should be able to find them easily with this microscope if they are there. Let's pray that we find no Ebola, but if we do, we should find them in the liver so we can look there first."

"OK." Jesse loaded a liver tissue slice into the instrument. The tissue sample slowly came into focus as Cherie and Jesse leaned toward the screen. "Voila! Liver cells at 1000x magnification. This is an excellent tissue section if I must say so myself."

"Can you zoom in on this area here?" asked Cherie as she pointed to a region of the cell.

"The magnification and focus controls are here, and you can move around the field of view using these controls."

"Oh, thanks." Cherie adjusted the controls and increased the magnification. "Most of the tissue looks normal, although there is some destruction in this area." Cherie pointed to the screen. "It's often hard to tell if the tissue destruction is a result of a virus or if it was a secondary infection."

Cherie increased the magnification to 5,000x and used the controls to scan across the field of view.

"Do you see anything that looks suspicious?"

"Not at this magnification. There are plenty of disrupted cells, but no sign of virus or bacteria. I wonder if this is just some kind of toxicological damage. Might be cirrhosis of the liver? He could have been an alcoholic."

"I don't think so. I didn't know him, but I was told he was a straight-up family man and a faithful Christian. Besides, heavy drinking and being a boat Captain don't go well together and almost always end in tragedy. Tom had been a Captain for many years."

"There doesn't appear to be any evidence of an infectious agent in the liver. I'll go up to 50,000x magnification."

"Crap! These sections aren't as good as I thought they were," admitted Jesse. "They should be very clear, but everything is all cloudy."

Cherie drew close to the screen, attempting to discern the cell structure through the haze. "Although it is hard to make out, I don't see anything that looks like virus particles."

"I am sorry, Cherie. It looks like I screwed up the tissue preparation."

"I don't know. It could be due to the extensive tissue destruction, not cell prep. Can we take some images of this along with some of the undamaged cells?" asked Cherie.

"Absolutely." Jesse shot several photographs, and the small 3 x 5-inch "instant" photos were available within a few minutes. The two continued examining the various tissue samples with the same result. Jesse took photos of everything.

"This looks more like physical damage that might result from some kind of toxic agent like nerve gas or mustard gas. All of this background clutter is irritating. I don't understand why it is here."

"Well, that sounds like good news to me. You don't think it's Ebola?" asked Jesse.

"It doesn't seem to be. Ebola is terrible, but the good thing about it—if there is anything good—is that it 'burns' itself out very quickly. That is, it tends to appear, kill quickly, and then disappear. If humans became carriers of Ebola, it could spread more effectively among populations, and the result could be devastating. You may have heard of Typhoid Mary. She was a real person who was a carrier of typhoid fever. Since she was a cook, she infected many people, and some died. Unfortunately, we are still no closer to understanding what happened on the Crimson Tide. If this were an infectious agent, let's hope that it has burned itself out."

"Do you mind if I hold onto some of the copies of these photos?" asked Jesse. "I took a lot of duplicates."

"Sure. That's the science nerd in you, isn't it?"

"Yeah. These are cool photos, and I might be able to use some of them for my graduate work. We are required to give presentations before the entire department on various aspects of biology. Maybe I'll do one on the liver and its role in metabolism."

"That would be interesting. Take whatever you would like. I don't think these will do the CDC any good."

Cherie gathered her samples and electron microscope images, and the two exited the building. She sat in her CDC vehicle as Jesse stood outside her car window in the parking lot. He knew she could be called back to Atlanta at any time, and he worried that this might be the last time he'd see her.

"Cherie, if you find the shark research interesting, and if you'll be around a while, would you like to go shark collecting with us?"

"I would love that!"

"I'll call you at the motel as soon as the weather looks promising. Hopefully in the next day or so."

"Looking forward to it and thanks again!" said Cherie as she smiled and drove away.

CHAPTER 15

"Palms Motel," said the front desk attendant.

"Yes, could you ring room 103, please?"

"One moment."

Phone in hand, Jesse stared out the window of his cottage, watching the waves as they rolled across the Mississippi Sound. There were no white caps, but it was clearly too "bumpy" for shark research this morning. However, these waves, fueled by the onshore winds of a warming summer day, would soon dissipate, and conditions would improve. Jesse had already checked his VHF weather feed to confirm that seas would be "two feet or less" after midday.

"One moment," replied the attendant.

The phone rang four times before Jesse heard Cherie's unmistakable Cajun accent.

"Hello."

"Hi Cherie, it's Jesse. How are you this morning?"

"Very well thank you. And yourself?"

"I'm good. I was calling to let you know that I'm planning a shark-collecting trip. The seas are a bit too rough this morning, but they're supposed to lay down later today around noon. Would you be interested in going along? We could use an extra set of hands."

"Actually, that would be perfect. I have a conference call this morning, but after lunch, I will be free."

"That's great!" said Jesse.

"I can either pick you up or we can meet at the same boat launch as before, say around 12:30?"

"Thank you so much for the invitation! You don't need to pick me up; I'll just meet you there. See you at 12:30."

"See you."

Jesse rang up Ross and CC to confirm their help. He then spent the morning in his office going over data before retrieving the R/V Bongo and heading to the boat launch. Ross, CC, and Cherie were already waiting when Jesse arrived.

"Howdy folks!" said Jesse as he got out of the El Camino. "Y'all have already met, I see?"

"Yes," said Cherie. "We've just arrived. We were just talking about sharks. I'm really excited about this! I've never seen a live shark before." Cherie's excitement was palpable.

"We appreciate you coming along," said Jesse. "We can always use the help. I've done this work alone, but it is much more difficult by myself."

"Plus, it's reckless to be on the water by yourself," added CC. "Particularly if you are handling sharks."

"I know, I know," said Jesse sheepishly. "I'm extremely careful when out there. But you know, sometimes I just need time alone, and why not kill two sharks with one stone? Hey, that rhymed! Maybe I'll write another song."

"Did Jesse tell you he plays guitar and is a songwriter?" asked Ross, speaking to Cherie. "He plays really well, but no one has ever heard any of the songs he has written."

"I didn't know that. Why Jesse, you are a man of many talents."

"Not really," replied Jesse.

"He is being modest," said CC. "He's really good on the guitar."

"I would love to hear you play," said Cherie.

"I'm not really an entertainer, but I would love to play for you sometime. Well, folks, we are burning daylight. Let's get this show on the road."

After flawlessly launching the boat and an easy ride out to his favorite shark spot, the crew anchored and had fishing lines in the water before 1:30. Two rods were set with standard fishing line, and a third, larger rod was set with heavy, 100-pound test line. The latter was baited with a large, whole frozen fish. To hedge their bet, Jesse put a block of frozen *chum*, ground fish parts, in a mesh bag and hung it overboard. As it slowly thawed, the mixture would release a scent that sharks found irresistible.

"Now we wait," declared Jesse. "Let's put some music on. I can tune to a station out of Mobile, or we can put in a cassette tape."

Ross lowered the anchor overboard and tended it to make sure it caught the bottom. "A cassette is fine, as long as it's not Bob Marley. You play that tape every shark trip, and I'm sick of it."

"There's no accounting for taste," said Jesse, and gave a wink to Cherie.

"I read a study that reported that sharks respond positively to reggae music," said Cherie and winked back at Jesse. "Didn't you know that?"

"Are you serious?" asked an incredulous Ross.

"No, I was just kidding," replied Cherie.

"How about the Allman Brothers?" asked Cherie. "I actually met Duane Allman a couple of years ago in Baton Rouge at a concert."

"Very cool," said Ross. "If I had to listen to a single album for the rest of my life, it would be *Eat a Peach*."

"You are in luck!" said Jesse. "I don't have *Eat a Peach,* but I've got *Fillmore East*," said Jesse as he pulled the cassette from the center console and pushed it into the player.

"Awesome!" said Ross. "Changing the subject, did you hear about the fellow who got shark bitten yesterday?"

"Really?" asked CC. "Was it serious?"

"No, it was some dude who was fishing. He caught a blacktip shark. Said it took him three hours to get the shark to the boat. When he got it on the boat, it went crazy. Biting everything. Grabbed his boot and sliced his leg. Said the shark would not let go of his boot. It only took a few stitches, but it could have been a lot worse."

"Three hours to land a blacktip shark?" questioned Jesse. "That ain't right. It might take twenty minutes at most for the largest blacktip."

"I don't know," said Ross. "That's what the news article said."

"Cherie, we should go over the routine for when we catch a shark, assuming we do catch one." The words were barely out of Jesse's mouth when one of the reels began to click ever so slowly. The reel then went silent.

"Probably just a crab pulling on the bait," said Jesse. "Cherie, I'll let you record data. Here's the field notebook, and here are the data sheets where…"

Jesse paused and turned away from Cherie as the reel clicked again and fell silent.

"CC, take that rod out of its holder," said Jesse.

"Aye, aye, Captain!" said CC good-naturedly.

"ZEEEEEEEEEEEEEEEEEEEEEEEEEEEEEEEEEEEEE EE…"

CC barely had the rod in her hands when the line began furiously spooling off the reel. She immediately set the hook and began to quickly reel.

"Good job, CC!" said Ross encouragingly. "Cherie, record the time of day to the second!" Jesse grabbed the landing net. "Then record the time the moment we obtain a blood sample."

"Got it," replied Cherie.

"Ross, reel in those other two rods so they are not in the way."

Despite fighting furiously, CC had the small shark at the side of the boat in less than a minute. Jesse expertly directed the shark into the landing net and brought it on board. As soon as the shark hit the boat deck, it went berserk, biting anything in range of the business end of the animal.

"Everybody, please be careful!" reminded Jesse as he grabbed a large, wet beach towel and threw it over the head of the shark. "This sometimes calms them, sometimes not."

The shark continued to thrash furiously.

"Well, that didn't work. Ross, grab a syringe and needle. I'm gonna let you draw the blood while I hold the shark."

"Whew, this is a lively one!" said Ross.

Jesse flipped the shark over and, kneeling over it, secured it between his knees. Ross crouched over and drew a blood sample. As he extracted the needle, the shark began thrashing wildly again. Ross's hand slipped, and the needle went deep into Jesse's thigh.

"Hey!" exclaimed Jesse as he drew away from the needle. "Dude, you injected me with shark blood!"

"I'm sorry," said Ross, clearly upset and embarrassed. "It… it… flinched."

"Do we have enough left for analysis?" asked Jesse.

"Yeah, there's plenty."

"Crap, man, that stings," said Jesse, rubbing his leg. "You gotta be more careful."

"I'm sorry, man."

Jesse removed the towel and quickly returned the shark to the Gulf.

"Cherie, did you get the time?" asked Jesse.

"Got it. It took two minutes and 49 seconds from the time it was hooked until blood was drawn."

"That was a bit slower than usual because the shark was so manic," said Jesse. "It will be considerably less active with each successive blood draw. The shark will be least active when we draw blood at 60 minutes, since it will be pretty stressed out. Now we keep the shark on the line but let it swim unencumbered for 15 minutes and repeat the procedure. Cherie, write down that it was a blacktip and male. We can get a length after the last blood draw."

"CC, how is it doing?" asked Ross.

"It's peeling line off like crazy," said CC as she held the rod and watched the spinning reel. "It's a good thing you have plenty of line on this reel."

"Crap!" exclaimed Jesse disgustedly, "I hope it's not being chased by a larger shark. Nothing we can do but wait."

Fortunately, no large predator was attempting to eat the shark, and the 15-minute period passed quickly. CC quickly reeled the shark in, and Jesse landed it and placed it on the deck for another blood draw. As if nothing had happened, the shark went berserk again.

"Holy smokes!" complained Jesse. "This shark is still going crazy. This is one feisty fellow!"

Blood drawn, time recorded, and the shark placed overboard, CC watched as the line peeled off. "Wow! He's going nuts again. I think we caught the bionic shark."

The procedure was repeated over an entire 60 minutes with the same results. The shark never seemed to tire at all.

"OK, I'm whooped," said Jesse, sighing heavily after cutting the line and releasing the shark at the end of the experiment. "And my leg hurts where Ross stuck me."

"I am very sorry about that," said Ross apologetically.

"It wasn't your fault," said Jesse. "I've been stuck with a syringe before, but never had any shark blood injected into me. I guess you could say that I am "blood brothers" with the blacktip shark now. That was definitely not a typical stress response. That sucker just never tired out."

"I guess he ate his *Wheaties* this morning," said Ross.
"Guess so," said CC, who was equally exhausted.

CHAPTER 16

"OK, slight change of plan," said Jesse. "We're gonna let Cherie catch the next shark since she has never caught one. CC, would you record data this time? Let's just put out two rods, the large one and one of the smaller ones."

"Ten-four," said Ross as he and Cherie ran the baits back out and placed the butt of the rods in their holders.

"We do a lot of waiting on this project," said Jesse to Cherie.

"No problem. I am enjoying this. It's refreshing to get out of the lab for a change and to work with an organism that you don't have to use a microscope to see. Thank you again for inviting me."

"It's our pleasure," said Jesse. "I'm just glad that we caught a shark. There are days when we just soak bait and never catch…."

"ZEEEEEEEEEEEEEEEEEEEEEEEEEEEEEEEEEEEEEE EEEEEEEEEEEE"

"But apparently not today!" exclaimed Ross. "FISH ON!"

As the reel sang out, Cherie attempted to take the rod from its holder. The force the pulling shark created on the bent rod prevented her from removing it. Jesse rushed over to help her and grabbed the rod.

"Whoa! This is not a small shark." Jesse extracted the rod from the holder with difficulty. "Ross, quick, grab the Bimini belt from the center console and put it on Cherie."

"With pleasure," said Ross, perhaps too enthusiastically. Ross fastened the Bimini around Cherie's waist.

"What's this for?" asked Cherie.

"It's used for large game fishing." Ross knelt before Cherie and adjusted the belt. "When Jesse hands you the rod, put the butt into this socket here on the front of the belt. It will give you better leverage so that one hand can be used to pump the rod and the other to reel in line."

"Cherie," said Jesse, "just so you are aware. This is a large shark, so you will need to keep a good hold on the rod at all times. I need you to move to the bow of the boat and get as comfortable as possible. You can prop the rod against the railing to take some of the tension off of your arms, but keep the rod tip up at all times."

"OK," said Cherie as she cautiously made her way to the front of the boat. Suddenly, the shark made a "run" and the line spooled out at an incredible rate."

"Oh, my goodness!" exclaimed Cherie as she sat heavily on the deck of the boat. The heavy rod bent at an acute angle as she propped the rod against the railing and held on for dear life.

"Do you need help?" asked Jesse.

"No, I'm good so far," said Cherie nervously. "But I'm losing line on this reel fast."

"I'm gonna tighten the drag down a bit to slow the loss of line from the reel," said Jesse as he turned the drag adjustment on the side of the reel. "That will slow it down, but it means more pressure on you when the shark attempts to take out more line."

"I understand," said Cherie, tension in her voice.

"Look at that!" exclaimed CC while pointing toward the horizon. "It just leaped out of the water."

"Holy cow, it's a mako shark!" said Jesse excitedly. "It looks like it cleared the water by 10 feet. I have never seen a mako this close to shore. This is really unusual. Ross, pull the anchor in as fast as you can. We can't sit on anchor while dealing with this shark. It will "spool" us if we do."

Ross quickly pulled the anchor, and the boat began moving, pulled along by the swimming shark.

"I definitely don't want to get spooled," said Cherie through clenched teeth as she attempted to regain some of the line lost during the jump. "By the way, what does that mean?"

"It means the shark stripped all of the line off the reel down to the bare spool," said CC. "If that happens, the line will break and we'll lose the fish."

"There it goes again!" shouted Ross. "Jump number two was just as high as the first one. Amazing! Hey, there's a sea turtle over there."

"Keep your rod tip up!" said Jesse. Do you want someone to take over for a while?"

"No darn way! I don't give up that easily. My loins are girded!"

"That's the spirit!" said Jesse, laughing. "When you get the opportunity, pull the rod toward you and then quickly reel line in as you let the rod move away from you again. By pumping the rod and reeling, you can regain some of the lost line."

Cherie began pumping and reeling in line as the boat was slowly pulled into offshore waters. Jesse went to the wheel, started the engine, and slowly moved along in the direction of the shark to take some of the tension off of Cherie.

"Cherie, when I move the boat forward, you can reel in additional line, but keep pressure on him the entire time. Make sure you keep the rod tip up, particularly when he jumps."

"OK."

"There he goes again!" said CC. "That's jump number three. And there's another one. Jump number four. He shows no sign of tiring out."

"Jesse, how long do these fights generally last?" asked Cherie, her voice clearly revealing the stress. "My arms are starting to feel like spent uranium!"

"It's hard to say. Mako's are excellent fighters, but he shouldn't last much longer if we keep tension on him. Just let us know when you want to take a rest. One of us will spell you."

"Holy smokes!" yelled Ross. "He just jumped three times in a row. How many does that make now?"

"That's seven total jumps so far," answered CC.

"Amazing!" exclaimed Jesse. "Another bionic shark, I guess."

"I'll give it a few more minutes and then let someone else take over," said Cherie.

"CC, do you want to give Cherie a breather?" asked Jesse.

Suddenly, the line went limp.

"Uh, oh, I think I lost it," said Cherie dejectedly as she quickly reeled the loose line in. She stood and walked to the stern of the boat.

"Oh, that's too bad," said CC.

"Crap!" said Ross.

"Did I do something wrong?" asked Cherie, still out of breath.

"No, no, you fought it perfectly," said Jesse. "The leader broke, or the hook may have straightened. My guess is that it probably *tail-whipped* the leader. If the shark's tail strikes the line repeatedly during a fight, the shark's rough skin will weaken the leader and make it more likely to break."

Jesse took the boat out of gear and turned off the motor.

"That happens sometimes. Truthfully, I am not sure what we would have done with a shark that size. It wasn't huge; shortfin makos can grow to about twelve feet, but it was larger than we could comfortably handle. Although I was hoping we might have tagged it and released it if we could have just brought it to the side of the boat."

"Wait!" said Cherie suddenly. "I feel something on the line. The line is going straight down."

Jesse leaned over the transom of the R/V Bongo and looked down into the clear Gulf water. "It's still on, and it's right under the boat!" said Jesse. "IT'S COMING STRAIGHT UP!"

Suddenly, like a submarine-launched nuclear missile, the mako erupted from the water at the stern of the boat, giving them an up-close and personal view of arguably the world's most beautiful and impressive shark. As all eyes looked skyward, the shark pirouetted in the air, revealing the brilliant blue dorsal surface, the starkly contrasting, pure white of its underbelly, and its coal black eyes. The sunlight glinted off the rock-hard muscle that packed every inch of its 8-foot body. To Jesse, there was a savage beauty in this act of desperation as it seemed to hang motionless in the air before landing in the boat with a resounding crash.

And then all hell broke loose! CC screamed. Ross dove for the front of the boat. Jesse tried to step back as the tail of the fish knocked his feet from under him, and he landed on top of the thrashing shark. Jesse could do nothing but hang onto its back as it went berserk. The force of its powerful tail tossed an ice chest from the boat, snapped a fishing rod like a twig, and sent a tackle box flying across the deck, spilling its contents. Jesse, attempting to limit the damage, held the shark tightly.

"It's destroying the boat!" screamed CC.

"Ross," yelled Jesse, the anger building in him, "throw me that towel NOW!"

Ross grabbed the towel and tossed it to Jesse. Jesse, growing angrier by the second, placed the towel over the shark's eyes and held it there. The shark calmed noticeably but continued to move its tail rhythmically, as if swimming through a tranquil lagoon.

"Somebody hand me some rope out of the front compartment," commanded Jesse breathlessly as he continued to hold the shark.

CC tossed him a length of rope, whereupon Jesse carefully wrapped the rope around the head of the shark to secure the blindfold. "Hopefully, this will hold until we can get him back in the water."

"Get him back in the water?" asked an incredulous Ross. "Dude, you got a forklift in your back pocket?"

"I'm not letting this beautiful animal die! We'll get it back in. Ross, hand me a needle and syringe. We may as well take a blood sample while we have the opportunity."

"Seriously!? exclaimed Ross, very concerned. "After what happened a while ago. His tail will break my arm if I try to take blood."

"We're not going to take it from the tail. Warm-bodied sharks like this mako have a large artery that travels along their flanks. If we can find it, it should be an easy blood draw. Famous last words, since I have never done this before. Ross, stand next to the center console when you draw the blood, so it will shield you if he starts thrashing again. Put the needle in about a quarter of an inch right about here," explained Jesse as he pointed to a spot on the side of the shark.

"Alright," said Ross nervously, his hand shaking. Ross inserted the needle into the mako, and it went off like a Roman candle. Jesse held tight and rode the shark until it calmed again.

"For Chrissake, man, I'm a chemist. I can't do this!"

"Then give the needle to CC!" said Jesse, frustrated and growing angrier by the minute.

"I've got this," said Cherie, taking the needle from Ross.

Cherie gently inserted the needle and drew a quantity of dark crimson blood into the syringe on the first attempt.

"Good job!" said Ross.

"Alright, we are going to get a firm purchase on this shark and heave it overboard. I pray that it will cooperate long enough to get it out of the boat. However, if it starts thrashing again, just let go and get away from it. CC, stand beside me and hold onto this rope. When he goes overboard, the rope will pull the blindfold off."

"I'm not caring for this plan," said CC as she wrapped the rope around her hand and wrist.

"Me neither," said Ross.

"I'll take the end with the teeth in it," said Jesse. "Cherie, Ross, you guys hold the tail firmly. I repeat, if it goes crazy, just drop it and get away from it. OK. Everybody ready? On three, we'll lift and toss the shark over the side."

"Ready, 1, 2, 3, lift!"

The shark stayed relatively calm, and they managed to get the animal onto the top of the transom. Teetering on the edge of the boat, it fell into the water with a splash. Unbeknownst to them, the shark had bitten down on the towel and the rope as it was released. The shark charged toward the depths with the rope and towel held firmly in its mouth and entangled around CC's hand. CC screamed as she was pulled overboard and disappeared.

"OH GOD!" screamed Cherie. "JESSE, DO SOMETHING!"

Like a scene from *Tarzan of the Apes*, Jesse pulled his knife from its sheath, put it in his mouth, and dove overboard. Ross and Cherie were left alone, staring at the calm ocean surface, unaware of the tragedy that was developing below them.

As soon as Jesse entered the water, he could see CC descending quickly, bubbles streaming from her mouth, as she struggled. The mako dashed about wildly as it pulled against the dead weight while continuing downward. Jesse swam as hard as he could, attempting to close the distance, but it was obvious that it was futile. As he descended, the pressure-induced pain inside Jesse's head was almost intolerable. He had to stop swimming momentarily to manually equalize pressure by pinching his nose to force air into his inner ear. The fear he felt for CC now turned to anger when he realized that she was no longer struggling, and the trail of bubbles had disappeared. Inexplicably, the mako made a turn toward the surface. The rope lost its tension as the shark passed close to Jesse on its ascent. Jesse recognized what was about to happen. The shark was going to attempt to make another leap! Jesse realized that when the shark leaped and the slack rope snapped tight, it would likely dislocate CC's shoulder or worse. A rage welled up inside him as he swam even harder, attempting to reach the line before the shark could reach the surface.

Not knowing what to do, Ross and Cherie were left speechless, their mouths agape as they stared over the railing at the spot where they last saw CC and Jesse. Ross began to pace nervously, and Cherie quickly pulled her tennis shoes off.

"I'm going in," announced Cherie.

"Me too," said Ross as he went to the railing, preparing to go overboard.

"Ross, someone has to stay with the boat. I was a lifeguard for years, so I know what I am doing."

"But...."

"Stay on the damn boat!" demanded Cherie as she dove in.

Jesse was just about out of breath when he reached the looping rope. He took the knife from his mouth and sawed through the line. The shark bolted away and disappeared into the blue. Pulling an unconscious CC to him, he grabbed her around the chest and began swimming to the surface. However, given the depth and the little oxygen that remained in his lungs, he knew he was not going to make it with the added weight. His lungs were about to explode. The urge to inhale was overpowering, but Jesse knew that if he inhaled water, it would be all over for both of them. He began to have tunnel vision, a sure sign of oxygen deprivation. And then a miracle. Cherie appeared out of nowhere and grabbed CC by the other arm. Together, they towed her to the surface. Without a moment to spare, Jesse broke the water's surface and gasped for air.

"Jesse, can you make it to the boat?"

"Yes," said Jesse between gasps.

"I've got this." Cherie turned CC on her back, grabbed her under the arm and around the neck, and began pulling her to the boat. Ross immediately motored toward them, and the three pulled CC on board. She lay lifeless on the deck as Cherie began mouth-to-mouth resuscitation.

"Oh my God!" said Ross.

"Jesse," said Cherie between breaths. "Check for a pulse."

Jesse placed two fingers on the inside of her wrist. "Her pulse is very weak, but she has one, thank God."

"Hang on, everyone!" Ross buried the throttle and had the R/V Bongo flying low. Cherie continued resuscitation while Jesse got on the VHF radio and turned to the Coast Guard emergency channel 16.

"Mayday, mayday, mayday!"

CHAPTER 17

"Dispatch to Chief. Dispatch to Chief. Come in." The radio in the early 1980s patrol car accidentally left on full volume crackled to life, startling its occupant and shattering the stillness of the bayou where Chief of Police Robert East had stopped to watch a large gator slide through the black, stained water.

The voters of Dauphin Island had returned Robert East to the position of Chief in four consecutive elections. He had just started his 14th year and was comfortable in the job. Crime on the island was almost non-existent other than petty theft, parking violations, and the occasional DUI, mostly by tourists, and Bobby liked it that way. A veteran, he was tall, slightly overweight, with a full head of grey hair that he combed back, Elvis style. A wound he had received in Vietnam left him with a limp. Famously politically incorrect, the people of Dauphin Island loved his no-nonsense, cut-to-the-chase approach to law enforcement.

Chief East jumped. "Damn it!" He tossed his binoculars on the seat next to him, grabbed the microphone with his left hand, and turned the volume down with his right. "Come back, Dorothy."

"Just got a report of an automobile accident out on Bienville Avenue about a quarter mile past the 4-way," said the dispatcher.

"Anyone hurt? Come back."

"I'm afraid so. I've already dispatched the ambulance. A Mr. Clarence Todd, who called this in, is waiting at the scene. Come back."

"I'm on my way. Over." Chief East hung the microphone on its hook, switched on the lights and siren, and gunned the big police interceptor engine.

"Standing by," replied Dorothy.

Chief East approached the address to find an ambulance with lights flashing pulled off of a long stretch of Bienville near a shallow bayou. He parked behind the ambulance and got out. Two EMTs administering CPR were crouched over an individual who lay at the water's edge, while a third individual stood on the roadside several feet away. Some distance off the road, in a couple of feet of water, sat a Chevy Impala against a large cypress tree, steam rising from the crushed front end of the car.

"How is he?" asked Chief East as he approached the crew trying to revive the victim.

"I'm afraid he didn't make it," replied one of the EMTs as he stood, blood covering his scrubs. "We are just going through the motions." The second EMT continued CPR, but it was clearly a lost cause.

"We got here within minutes of the accident and pulled him from the car. Started work on him but could never get a pulse."

"Must be a tourist, he's got North Carolina plates," said the Chief, pointing toward the damaged vehicle.

The individual who stood away from the accident approached and extended his hand to Chief East. "Officer, I'm Clarence Todd. I saw what happened."

"Thanks for calling this in, Mr. Todd. I'm Chief of Police East. Can you tell me what you saw?" said the Chief as he pulled a notepad and pen from his shirt pocket.

"I was behind the car when he swerved and skidded to avoid striking a dog that crossed in front of him. He almost went into the bayou. It must have frightened him because it scared the crap out of me. But he didn't lose control. He narrowly missed the dog and continued driving for a distance."

"What happened then?" asked the Chief as he wrote in his notepad.

"It was strange. He continued driving for a while, suddenly accelerated, and was going like a bat out of hell when he left the road and ended up in the swamp. He never even hit his brakes. I know because his brake lights never came on. His brake lights were working because they came on when he swerved to avoid the dog. I stopped and waded over to the car. He looked so bad that I was afraid to move him."

"Was he conscious when you got to the car?"

"He did not seem to be. It was horrible looking. He was slumped over the steering wheel, covered in blood, and was not moving at all. I don't have first-aid training, and so I drove immediately to the *Stop-and-Shop* to call for help. The ambulance was here in minutes. I was afraid to move him and just rushed to find a phone. Chief, did I do the wrong thing?" asked Clarence earnestly.

"Not at all. The sooner the emergency folks get here, the greater the chance of surviving an accident. Was he driving erratically before he encountered the dog?"

"No. I was behind him for several blocks, and there was nothing strange about his behavior."

"No one else in the car with him?"

"No, sir. None that I saw."

"Mr. Todd, can I get your phone number and home address in case I need to get some follow-up information?"

"Yes sir. You can also reach me on the island at the Sundowner Lodge. We are from Birmingham and vacationing here for the next two weeks."

"Sorry you had to witness this on your vacation!" said the Chief as he wrote down his contact information.

"No problem. I just wish I could have done more for the poor soul," said Clarence sadly as he walked back to his car. "I hope your day gets better, Chief."

"Your's too."

The emergency crew loaded the body into the ambulance as Chief East spoke with one of the EMTs.

"There are no skid marks anywhere," said the Chief as he looked along the highway where the car left the road. "He was going like a bat out of hell when he left the road."

"Chief," said the EMT. "He's covered in blood, but we can't find any major lacerations on him. He had massive blood loss. But there's no sign of a major injury. He has some cuts and contusions from when he hit the steering wheel and dash, but nothing that would explain that amount of blood loss. It is strange."

"Based on what I've seen, I would guess that he had a heart attack," said Chief East. "He inadvertently hit the accelerator when he lost consciousness and ended up leaving the road."

"I guess that's possible," replied the EMT as he closed the rear door of the ambulance. "I'll say this, he looked like a day-old corpse when we pulled him out."

"I guess I'd better take a look at the vehicle," said the Chief.

"Hope your day gets better, Chief," said the EMT as they drove away.

"I hope so too!"

Chief East removed his shoes and socks, rolled his pants legs as far up as he could, and waded into the bayou. He was not happy about taking a stroll through a south Alabama bayou, particularly with that bull alligator he was watching earlier, fresh on his mind. He reached the rear of the vehicle, wiped some mud from the license plate, and recorded the number. He glanced in the back window.

"No empty beer cans, no whisky bottles." He took out his pen and notepad and jotted down the observations.

The driver's door was open, and he leaned in to get a better look. "My God!" Blood and body fluids covered the dash, windshield, and front seat of the vehicle. "It looks like someone slaughtered a hog in here!"

Chief East returned to his car, took a paper towel from a roll he kept under the seat to dry his feet, and put his shoes back on. He picked up the microphone and radioed the dispatcher.

"Dorothy, come in," said the Chief.

Dorothy put away her fingernail file and picked up the microphone. "Come back."

"Could you run these plates for me? Come back."

"Hold on, let me get a pencil." A brief pause, and Dorothy replied. "Go ahead."

"It's North Carolina, BSW 1676. See if that person is staying on the island. Come back."

"I'll do that right away. How bad was the accident?" Come back."

"It was bad. The EMTs are taking him to the clinic, but he'll be pronounced DOA. Come back."

"Oh my!" replied Dorothy. "I'll call you as soon as I've got the information on those plates. Come back."

"Thank you! Over and out."

"Standing by," replied Dorothy.

CHAPTER 18

"It was my fault completely," said Jesse. He and Cherie sat on either side of CC, who lay in the bed at the small Dauphin Island clinic.

"No, it wasn't," said CC. "I have no idea why I wrapped that rope so tightly around my wrist."

"Jesse saved you," added Cherie. "He dove in after you and cut the line that was tangled around your arm. If it hadn't been for him… well, I don't want to think about it," added Cherie as her voice began to break. She leaned over CC and hugged her.

"Hey," implored CC. "I'm OK now. Just a few bruises. I'm frankly not sure why I'm in this bed."

"Cherie is the one who saved you," said Jesse. "I was winded when she showed up. She helped bring you to the boat and gave you CPR all the way back to the Coast Guard Station. She's the hero here."

"Sounds like it was a team effort to me," said CC.

"Ross brought the boat to us quickly. He had the R/V Bongo "flying low" back to shore," said Jesse. "So, you're right, it was a team effort."

"Where is Ross?" asked Cherie.

"He had something at the lab he had to take care of," said Jesse. "He knew you were gonna be OK after the EMTs took over. He said to tell you he would come by later to see you. Although I don't think you'll be here much longer."

"I am leaving today, whether he discharges me or not!" said CC.

"Just take it easy for a little while," implored Cherie. "They just want to make sure there are no complications."

"I don't understand the amount of fight that was left in that shark," said Jesse, still perplexed by the shark's behavior. "After fighting and jumping as long as he did, he should have been pretty much worn out. Sharks are typically good for one run, maybe two, but then they just pull without a lot of enthusiasm, and you can reel them in pretty easily. They tire pretty quickly. That mako and the small shark before it seemed to be as fresh when we released them as when they were first captured."

"Should you have the doctor look at that place on your leg?" asked CC. "It looks pretty angry."

"Nah, it's fine." Jesse rubbed the large, inflamed welt on his thigh where Ross had injected him. "It was sore for a while, and I felt kind of feverish, but it's OK now. As a matter of fact, I've had this strange craving for human flesh lately," added Jesse as, with teeth bared, he playfully pretended to bite CC on the forearm.

"Hey!" exclaimed CC. "Do I look like shark bait?"

The door opened, and a lab-coated individual entered the room. "How are you feeling, Ms. Carrigan?"

"Dr. Nolan, I feel like getting out of this bed and leaving, that's how I feel," replied CC, a little snarky.

"So far, everything looks good, and if you feel OK, then there is no reason for you to be here. However, just for my peace of mind, I want to do one last examination, and then we'll discharge you."

"Doc, we are very grateful for you taking such good care of CC," said Cherie earnestly.

"I haven't done much," replied the doctor. "Immediate CPR and getting CC quickly into the hands of the EMTs was far more important than what I've done. The fact that she is a very healthy young lady also contributed."

"Doc, I would prefer that my parents not find out about this if that's possible."

"You're covered by your student health insurance, and your medical records are confidential. That's your decision to make, but don't you think they should know?" asked Dr. Nolan.

"It would only worry them needlessly," replied CC.

"We'll wait outside," said Jesse as he and Cherie got up from the bed. "Let me know when you are ready to go, and I'll drive you home."

"Thanks, Jesse!"

"Don't go far," said Dr. Nolan. "This shouldn't take long."

"We'll be just outside," replied Jesse as they walked out. The two sat down in the small, dreary waiting room. Worn, green Naugahyde chairs and the requisite beach sunset print hung on the wall. His elbow on the armrest and his head propped against the palm of his hand, Jesse gazed darkly out the picture window.

"I feel terrible about this."

"Jesse, it was not your fault, and she's fine now."

"I keep running the events over in my mind. She almost drowned. Safety is a major issue for me, and I placed her in danger."

"It was an accident and you saved her life," said Cherie as she took Jesse's hand in both of hers, "and I am not going to let you beat yourself up over this."

Jesse turned and looked Cherie in the eye. "Thank God you were on the boat today!"

At that moment, a man, gingerly holding a crudely bandaged and bloody right hand, entered the waiting room and proceeded to the receptionist's window.

"Can I help you, sir?" asked the woman at the desk.

"I think I need some stitches," replied the injured patron.

"Let me guess," said the receptionist. "You were fishing, and a shark bit you?"

"How did you know that?"

"You're the fourth one this week," replied the receptionist as she handed him a clipboard. "Can you fill out this form for me, or do you require assistance?"

"Yes Ma'am, I can fill it out. I'm left-handed."

"If you'll have a seat, Dr. Nolan will be with you shortly."

"Thank you," replied the patron as he took a seat across from Jesse and Cherie.

"Did you hear that?" whispered a stunned Jesse to Cherie. "Four people bitten by sharks in a few days!"

"Is that unusual?"

"Very. It would be extraordinary to have four shark-related injuries on the island all year!"

The injured individual got up, gave the clipboard back to the receptionist, and returned to his seat.

"You recall that Ross mentioned someone else got bitten as well. And these are just the injuries that are being reported. I've known fishermen who used a piece of duct tape to bandage an injury and kept right on fishing. Never got medical attention."

"That's a very ill-advised thing to do," said Cherie. "A flesh-eating bacteria infection is dangerous stuff!"

"Excuse me, sir, I overheard you say you got bitten by a shark. What happened?" asked Jesse to the injured angler.

"I was fishing on the east end, between the jetties, and hooked a small blacktip shark. I was trying to unhook it when it grabbed my thumb and sliced the crap out of it. The little bastard! Excuse my French."

"Have you caught many sharks before?" asked Jesse.

"Hundreds of them. I've been vacationing on Dauphin Island for years, and we just arrived yesterday. That was the first shark I caught this year. The funny thing is that I have never seen a shark fight like that little prick did. Blacktips act crazy when you hook them, but this one was like it was possessed. Took me forever to land it."

"I'm very sorry!" replied Jesse. "By the way, I'm Jesse Gates, and this is Cherie Belon."

"Nice to meet you. Bob Travis," replied the patron as he extended his uninjured hand. "It's nothing a few stitches and a few drinks at the Neptune Club won't fix. Be careful if you do any shark fishing."

"We'll be careful," said Cherie.

"Mr. Travis, the doctor will see you now," announced the receptionist.

"Y'all have a good day."

"You too," replied Jesse.

"This is very peculiar," said Jesse quietly after they were alone. "Sharks around the island are displaying behaviors that are unheard of. I just don't know what to make of it."

"Would a behavioral change be that surprising?" asked Cherie.

"Absolutely!" replied Jesse. "I've been shark fishing for a lot of years, and I've never seen sharks act like this. I'm gonna speak to the receptionist," added Jesse as he stood.

"Excuse me, Ma'am," said Jesse as the receptionist looked up from her paperwork.

"Yes sir, what can I help you with?"

"I heard you say that there had been four shark bites in a few days?"

"That's right."

"Do you know where they got bitten?"

"You mean where on the body or where on the island?"

"Well, both, I guess."

"All the injuries were on the island, and if memory serves, there were two bites on the hand, I think one on the arm, and one on the leg. I recall that the young man who was bitten on the leg was surf fishing on East Beach. That's all I can tell you."

"Thank you, Ma'am." Jesse returned to his seat.

"Did you hear that?"

"I did," replied Cherie.

"Fishermen are being bitten all around the island. They are behaving the same as the sharks we caught today. Those strange blood values that we were looking at in the lab. I wonder if that reflects this change. If their physiology has changed, it would be unprecedented."

"What would cause a change like that?" asked Cherie.

"I am clueless. But I know one thing. I've got to go back and check all of my most recent data to see how many sharks show a depressed stress response and see if I can determine when the change occurred."

"Good idea. Jesse, I need to tell you something about the investigation."

"What's that?"

"We had a staff meeting yesterday morning to review our findings. The CDC is going to conclude that there is no public health threat. They will be sending me back to Atlanta in the next few days."

"Well, that's good, I guess." Jesse was clearly conflicted regarding the news. "How did they come to that conclusion?"

"They have no idea what happened to the Crimson Tide's Captain and have been unable to identify an infectious agent. They are leaning toward some kind of foul play. Maybe drug-related."

"What do you think?"

"It's BS in my opinion, but please don't repeat that, I could lose my job."

"I won't say anything."

"The CDC Director does not like to admit that we don't know. The scuttlebutt around the center is that he has aspirations for a higher government position and doesn't want to do anything that reflects poorly on him. He spends all his time in "cover his butt" mode."

"Then he should rise quickly in the ranks of government."

"Definitely. He'll probably be in the White House one day, which is a scary thought. You know, I have a gut feeling that we've overlooked something in this investigation. But for the life of me, I don't know what it is. It keeps me up at night."

"Will you let me know when you get called back to Atlanta? I would like it if we could stay in touch. You know, uh, about the investigation."

"Of course I will."

"I'll be on a research cruise for the next few days, and then I'll be in the lab for a day or so working up data. I'm the *Chief Scientist* on a cruise on the oceanographic labs research vessel, the *R/V Charles Regan*."

"Chief Scientist. I've never heard of that before."

"It just means that I'm in charge of the scientific party and the research that we'll be conducting."

"Is the boat named after someone in President Reagan's family?"

"No. It's spelled R-e-g-a-n. He was a noted British biologist who worked on fish. I'm not sure how his name got put on our large research vessel, but someone was apparently a fan."

"Are y'all going to be shark fishing?"

"Yes. But not with rod-and-reel. This is a long-line cruise where we will be catching sharks with a line that we set out that has about 200 hooks on it. We can catch a lot of sharks."

"Sounds like fun."

"Sometimes. But it's a lot of work and, if it's rough out there, it can be almost unbearable at times. The boat is nicknamed *"The Chuck Regan"* and all the graduate students call it the *"Up-Chuck"*, for obvious reasons."

"Gird your loins, huh?"

"Not sure I can gird my loins well enough for some of these trips," answered Jesse with a grimace as he began to recall some of his worst moments on previous trips. "I just have to work through the sea sickness when it sets in."

"I am sorry," said Cherie. "Why don't you just use your boat?"

"My boat is too small to go far offshore. In deeper water, we can catch bigger sharks and species that we don't typically see inshore. Like that mako. They're more common farther out. We might even catch a great white shark."

"Cool!"

"When we get in, I have to immediately process blood samples in the lab, which will take the better part of a day, assuming we catch a lot of sharks. I hope I get to see you before you have to leave."

"I hope so, too."

At that moment, the door at the rear of the waiting room opened, and a smiling CC entered the lobby.

"Do you need anything else from me?" asked CC as she approached the receptionist's desk.

"No, you are good to go," replied the receptionist. "Just be careful out there."

"Oh, believe me, I will!"

CHAPTER 19

Missionary Sisters of the Eucharist Abbey, San Cristobal, Guatemala. Nine months earlier.

In the early morning hours, before the fierce Guatemalan sun broke over the tops of the Sierra Madre Mountains, Sister Maria Lopez enjoyed walking through the cool abbey garden. She smiled to see the myriad tropical butterflies that graced her garden, along with an occasional hummingbird. Deep in prayer, she wore a head covering and the traditional, colorful clothing that identified her as an indigenous community member. The bright scarf she wore over her head framed her kind eyes and tranquil expression. Sister Maria strolled and prayed as her hand brushed the tops of the medicinal plants that grew there. The preparations the sisters made using these plants were the only medicines to which the impoverished inhabitants of this region of Guatemala would ever have access. Located along the eastern frontier, the sisters founded the congregation to bring *the word* to unchurched areas and to serve the poor. A rustling from the garden's far corner interrupted Sister Marie's blessings. Twice in the last few weeks, a neighbor's pig had broken out of its pen and damaged a large garden area. She paused and clapped her hands loudly, attempting to frighten away the apparent intruder.

"Shoo, SHOO!" shouted the sister.

"Ohhhh," came a low moan from across the garden.

Sister Marie, startled by the sound, cautiously threaded her way between the rows of plants toward its source.

"Blessed Mother Mary!" She gasped and crossed herself as she gazed upon a barely conscious, ragged, skeleton of a man lying amongst the plants. Marie rushed from the garden and into the Abbey. She burst through the door where Sisters Ana and Sophia were preparing their simple breakfast.

"Sisters, come quickly! There is a man in the garden."

The three returned to the garden and knelt beside the stranger.

"Who is he?" asked Sister Ana.

"I do not know." Sister Maria placed a hand upon his forehead. "He is burning up with fever! Sister Ana, get his feet.

Sister Sophia and I will take his arms. We will put him on the bed in the storeroom."

The Sisters carried him into the Abbey and gently laid him on the small bed used by visiting nuns.

"Sister Ana, bring soap and a wash basin of water."

"Yes, Mother Superior."

"Sister Sophia, what do we have for treating fever?"

"We have quinine and ginger extract. Do you think it is malaria?"

"It could very well be. He is covered with mosquito bites. Bring that and some drinking water. He is extremely dehydrated. Quickly now!"

*****

Hector was confused when he opened his eyes. A bitter taste in his mouth, his hands trembled uncontrollably as the room began to come into focus. He did not recognize his surroundings. A yellowed statue of Jesus, an image of Mother Mary on the wall, and the angel that knelt in prayer led him to believe that he was in Heaven. "Wh..where am I?" asked Hector weakly.

Sophia gasped and raised her head. "Sisters! He is awake!" She rose and came to his bedside. "You are at the Catholic Mission in San Cristobal. You are safe."

Hector groaned as he tried to sit up.

"No, no, you mustn't get up," insisted Sophia as she gently placed a hand on his shoulder. "You will pull the IV from your arm. You have been very sick." Sophia removed the wet cloth from his forehead, rinsed it in cold water, and gently placed it on his head again. Sister Maria and Ana entered the room and joined Sophia.

"Oh, thank you, Blessed Jesus!" said Ana upon seeing Hector with his eyes open.

"How, how… long have I been here?" asked Hector weakly.

"We found you in our garden four days ago," said Maria. "You were close to death. It is a miracle that you survived."

"Four days? How is that possible?"

"You were delirious the entire time. You had malaria but your fever broke yesterday and thanks to our Holy Father, you are much better now.

"The last thing I remember…was being in the forest," Hector paused and attempted to wet his lips. "My…mouth… is… so dry. Could I please…have some water? There is a terrible, bitter taste."

"Yes, yes, of course." Marie turned to a pitcher on a nightstand and poured water into an earthen mug. "That's the quinine you're tasting. We've been giving you quinine to treat the malaria." She held his head up while Hector drank deeply.

"Oh, thank you, Sister!"

"You kept repeating the name Eliana," said Sister Ana. "Is this someone you know?"

When Hector heard his beloved Eliana's name, the memories came flooding back. The starvation and cruelty, the loss of his beloved, the miserable trek through the jungle. The emotions rose in his chest and choked his words. "She…she… was my wife." Hector turned away and began to sob. "She… is… gone now," said Hector through the tears.

"Oh, I am so sorry." Sophia took Hector's hand and held it to her cheek, which seemed to ease his pain.

"Could you tell us your name?" asked Maria.

Hector took a moment to compose himself as best he could. "My name is Hector Fernandez. I am the Belize Minister of Archaeology. Or at least I was."

"Are you the Dr. Fernandez who has been missing for months?" asked Maria, surprised.

"Yes. We were taken by Bolivarian Revolutionaries and held captive. So much pain..." Hector paused in mid-sentence as he struggled to remember. "Caged… like an animal. My poor Eliana… As God is my witness, I will find… Arturo… and…" Hector's voice trailed off, and he fell asleep.

"He said Arturo!" said Sister Ana. "He must mean the Arturo who has terrorized people all over Guatemala."

"Sisters, I read about this last year," said Maria. "A group of researchers disappeared from the rain forest in Belize. I believe it was near the Concepcion River. It was assumed they were all dead. I don't think it was known that Arturo was involved."

"He must have suffered terribly!" said Sophia, still holding his hand. "I believe he is going to be OK."

"I think so. We must give special thanks to the Lord this evening for delivering him."

"Mother Superior," said Ana, "could I speak with you for just a moment?"

Maria rose, and the two retired to the hallway just outside the storeroom. "I had a vision last night while in prayer."

"A vision?"

"Yes Mother. In my vision, I saw a man in a battle against demons. He endured many hardships but was delivered from evil by our Heavenly Father. I believe the arrival of this man at our Abbey was providential. I cannot explain how or why I know this, but he possesses information that will save many lives. He must be returned to his home as quickly as possible."

"Sister Ana, you are sure of this?"

"Yes, Mother Superior. As sure as I am standing here!"

"Then I will leave for the Abbey in Mopan without delay. I must report this to Father Enrique. There is a phone there where we can reach the authorities."

"Godspeed, Mother Superior."

"God Bless you, Sister."

CHAPTER 20

A buzz of activity surrounded the 100-foot *R/V Charles Regan* as it sat tied to the dock at the Oceanographic Laboratory. Even a relatively short trip of a few days required a great deal of supplies, and all hands busied themselves loading long-line gear, fishing rods, food, ice, and bait. Although not designed for offshore work, the vessel had been outfitted for marine research, and Jesse had many fond memories of heaving his lunch over the rail in rough seas. To silver-line that dark cloud, he made a goal to "hurl" in every major ocean of the world. At present, he had "christened" the North Atlantic Ocean, the Caribbean Sea, and the Gulf of Mexico. With a little luck, the sea would be calm on this trip, and Mother Ocean would give up some of her bounty for Jesse's research project.

Jesse's head was a mix of excitement and anxiety as he stepped aboard the vessel. These trips could mean a windfall of data for his research project, but they were unquestionably the riskiest activity in which he participated. In fact, the same commercial fishing methods used on board the research vessel were the very reason that made commercial fishing the most dangerous occupation in the U.S. Thrashing sharks, sharp hooks, and knives in rough seas would make an OSHA inspector apoplectic. Even when not fishing, a rolling boat deck presented perils that most people never had to deal with. Jesse had once slipped when he was on deck at night while the boat was underway and almost gone overboard. He was not wearing a life jacket. If he had gone in, he often wondered how long it would have taken for the crew to notice he was no longer on board. He also wondered how long he could tread water because there was no swimming to shore out in the open Gulf of Mexico.

Jesse felt a slight wave of nausea as he caught a whiff of diesel exhaust, a smell that he had come to associate with sea sickness. Aside from the exhaust plume that emanated from the idling engine, the below-decks on the boat always smelled of mildew and diesel. Apparently, diesel fuel was a permanent ingredient of the concoction that could be heard sloshing around in the bilge, particularly in rough weather.

Jesse stowed his bag below deck in a top bunk, a strategic move since you did not want to be sleeping below a seasick researcher in rough seas. He had made that error only once on a previous cruise and was greeted, when he awoke, by a swollen barf bag tied to the bunk above him, swinging in time to the motion of the vessel. As quickly as possible, he climbed the ladder back into fresh air. He went into the wheelhouse where Captain Curtis Williams and the first mate were making preparations. The captain was of average height, thin and wiry, with a ruddy, sun-damaged complexion. His light brown, crew-cut hair was typically covered by a white cowboy hat that he thought made him look like Hank Williams, a distant cousin. To say Curt was unusual among shrimp boat Captains was an understatement. Although he had no education beyond High School, he was the most accomplished individual Jesse had ever met. Curt held a Captain's license, a pilot's license, a salvage diver's certification, and he was a Korean War veteran, a deep-water diver, and a voracious reader. Even among academics, Curt could hold his own in discussions of a variety of topics.

"Good morning," said Jesse as he stood in the wheelhouse door.

"Morning," replied Captain Curt, looking up from a navigational chart that was laid across a small table in the wheelhouse.

"Good morning," said the first mate.

"You ready for this trip?" asked Curt.

"As ready as I will ever be. What does the weather look like?"

"Well, it could be better. We got some storms predicted to move through our area, but they should not hit until late tomorrow. We should be able to get some long-line sets in before they arrive."

"Do you think we can do six sets ahead of this weather?"

"We'll give it our best try. We can do six if you don't mind doing some long-lining after dark?"

"I'm OK with that if you are," answered Jesse. "If we have calm seas, I think we should."

"Do you have coordinates for where we want to do our fishing?" asked the first mate.

"I have them here." Jesse pulled a sheet from his field notebook and gave it to the first mate. "The plan is to make sets from shallow to deep water. The first set will be at about 50 fathoms, the next one at 100, and then two sets out beyond the 500-fathom contour," explained Jesse as he pointed to the locations on the chart. "We can then repeat the 100 and 50 fathom sets on the way back in. I am really interested to see what we catch in those deep-water sets. We will have a two-hour soak time for each set, and most of the hooks will be equipped with hook-timers."

"As long as the weather holds, that should work," added the first mate. "Captain, we should be fishing the shallow water site at around 8:00 this morning, don't you think?"

"That's about right. By the way, what are hook-timers?" asked Curt.

"It's a little invention that I've been working on to use on these trips. When the shark takes the bait and pulls on the line, it pulls away a magnet that starts an electronic timer. When we land the shark, I will know just how long it has been on the line."

"Interesting," replied Curt.

"I'll be able to correlate changes in the blood chemistry of the sharks with the time spent on the line."

"Works for me," replied the first mate.

"I'll have everybody ready by the time we get to our longlining spot," said Jesse. "I guess I'd better go thaw out some bait."

"Turn that sea-water hose on back there and run water over the bait in that big-ass ice chest. That will thaw it quickly," suggested the Captain.

"I'll do that." Jesse started out the door as the captain spoke.

"Before you go, who do we have for the Scientific Crew this time?"

"I'm Chief Scientist, and we have Ross Jenkins, who you know, and two undergraduate student volunteers, Chris Stevens and Rick Lanier."

"That will work." Curt recorded the names in his logbook. "Where's CC?"

"She had a little mishap and was unable to go." Jesse decided to avoid the details.

"Uh oh!" said Curt. "Nothing serious, I hope."

"Well, it could have been, but she is Ok now," said Jesse, still feeling guilty about the near tragedy. "I'll tell you about it later."

"In that regard, I need emergency contact information for each person, and before we get underway, we will have our safety meeting on the fantail."

"OK. I'll let everyone know. How long before we're ready to shove off?"

"We're almost finished topping off with diesel, so it will be in about 20 minutes."

"Aye aye, Captain." Jesse left the wheelhouse and walked to the stern of the vessel.

Off toward Pensacola, a fiery orange ball was just peaking over the horizon as the *R/V Charles Regan* steamed out of the Intracoastal Waterway and into Mobile Bay. Black diesel exhaust poured from the stack and drifted toward Mobile in the light morning breeze. Having been conditioned by the multitude of shrimp boats working the area, raucous pelicans and gulls flew close behind the vessel, hoping to score an easy, early morning breakfast of discarded fish. Carried along by the bow wake, a pair of dolphins swam and leaped from the water just ahead of the ship. Always a good sign, many fishermen believed dolphins brought good fishing. The research vessel entered the ship channel as it headed due south and steamed past the deserted, lonesome Mobile Bay Lighthouse. Originally located on the east end of Sand Island, the hundred-year-old lighthouse now sat alone on a small rocky pedestal. The lighthouse was orphaned and left behind when the sandy island around it migrated west, carried along by the persistent longshore current.

Research cruises always involved a great deal of time spent riding between longlining locations. If there was a strong tailwind, following seas, and if the hull was recently cleaned of barnacles, the *Up Chuck* could manage a blistering 14 miles per hour. The slow pace meant many verbal battles were fought, card games won and lost, and off-color stories told around the small galley table. College football was always a popular, although sometimes heated, topic. After watching the Mobile Lighthouse grow ever smaller in the distance, Jesse had retired below deck and sat at the galley table, accompanied by Ross and the two undergraduates.

"Good lord, I will never get used to the smell in here!" complained Ross.

"Same here," said Jesse with a frown. "Just wait until the First Mate fires up that stove and starts cooking dinner tonight. That combination of mildew, diesel and frying steaks turns my stomach."

"Has there been any news about the hurricane?" asked Rick, one of the volunteers. "The last thing I heard was that it was still in the Caribbean."

"I don't know," said Ross. "Let's check the weather and see what's going on." He got up, turned on the VHF radio, and switched it to the NOAA Weather Radio channel. The four sat listening intently as the storm's strength, location, and direction were broadcast.

"Nothing we can do about this, folks," said Jesse. "May as well just carry on until we see where it's projected to strike.

"That's true," agreed Ross. "It's way down in the Caribbean, and even if it comes this way, it will take days to get here."

"I appreciate you guys helping out," said Jesse, speaking to the volunteers. "If y'all decide to do graduate work in oceanography, this kind of thing looks great on your resume."

"No problem," replied Rick and Chris together. "When we get to our first longlining station, what do we need to do?" asked Chris.

"I was about to go over that," said Jesse. "We'll first take some oceanographic data, such as depth, salinity, and water temperature, and then toss a radar buoy overboard with the longline attached. That buoy allows us to locate the longline using the ship's radar when we night-fish."

"You can see the buoy on radar?" asked a volunteer.

"Absolutely. It might be difficult to find a longline that has been left adrift after dark without a radar buoy."

"Cool."

"While the ship is moving forward slowly, the heavy mainline will unspool off the back of the boat. The baited leaders will be ready to be clipped onto the mainline. We'll use cut fish as bait that is thawing in an ice chest on the rear deck.

"What kind of fish are we using for bait?"

"We normally use menhaden. But on this trip, we have Spanish mackerel. A seafood company in Bayou La Batre donated about twenty cases of frozen mackerel to the Oceanographic Lab for us to use. I am curious to see if it works better than menhaden."

Rick, your job is to untangle and remove the leaders from the wash tub where they are stored. I need you to check the hook-timers and make sure they are working properly before baiting them." Holding a hook-timer in his hand, Jesse broke the magnetic connection that activated the timer and showed it to the volunteers. "When a shark takes the bait and breaks this connection, it will start the timer and we will know how much time has elapsed since he took the bait."

Wow, this is high technique stuff," said Rick. "These are battery powered I assume?"

"Yes. Check each one and if the hook-timer is not working, just toss the leader aside."

"OK."

"You then hand the leaders to Ross or Chris, who will bait the hooks. We will have two people baiting hooks because that is the slowest part of the process."

"Chris," said Ross, "run the hook right through the meaty part of the body so it doesn't come off easily."

"Aye, aye."

Jesse continued. "After the hook is baited, you will then hand the leader to me, clip first. When I have the clip firmly in hand, and before I clip it to the main line, you will toss the baited hook overboard. It's very important that the hook be overboard in the water when I clip it to the leader. When the leader gets clipped to the mainline, the hook must have no opportunity to snag one of us or to tangle around someone's foot. If that happens, you will go overboard with the line. So, make sure the baited hook is overboard before I clip it to the mainline."

"Yes sir! Do you think we will get to see some sharks?" asked Rick.

"Definitely," replied Ross.

"Awesome! I've never seen a live shark before."

"By the time the trip is over, you will probably be sick of seeing sharks," added Jesse.

"I doubt that," said Rick. "I think sharks are fascinating."

"Me too!" added Chris.

Suddenly, the ever-present drone of the diesel engine subsided as the ship slowed and then stopped. The hatch cover opened, and the first mate shouted down through the opening above.

"Jesse, y'all come topside quick!"

"What's going on?"

"There are thousands of sharks up here!"

Jesse led the way as all hands raced up the ladder and into the sunshine. Fully above the horizon now, the sun shone fiercely on the white deck and wheelhouse. Jesse held a hand to his forehead to shade his eyes while they adjusted to the brightness. The crew stood against the port railing, gazing in the direction of the rising sun. The fiery ball gave the tranquil ocean the appearance of molten glass. Across the distant horizon, silhouetted sharks could be seen rising vertically from the water, twirling like a Russian ballerina, and falling back with a splash.

"Wow!" exclaimed Rick as everyone stood in awe of an 8-foot shark rocketing from the water and spinning wildly near the boat.

"Those are spinner sharks. Anyone want to guess why they call them spinners?" said Jesse jokingly. "We see them out here all the time."

"Y'all look over there," said Captain Curt, pointing across the bow toward the west.

"Holy smokes!" uttered Jesse, mouth agape, as he and everyone on board were completely surprised by what appeared before them. The excitement, particularly among the volunteers, was palpable. Across a huge swath of ocean, almost as far as the eye could see, were sharks rising and spinning in the air. There appeared to be hundreds spinning simultaneously. The number of sharks above the water at any moment was truly astonishing, which meant there had to be many thousands more below the water in a school the size of which had never been recorded.

"Never in my life have I seen such a thing!" uttered Jesse in total shock.

"Holy cow," said Ross. "Those are all adult spinner sharks." He ran below and quickly returned, holding his Canon

AE1 camera. "No one is going to believe this if I don't get pictures of it."

"Captain, have you ever seen this before?" asked Jesse.

"I've seen plenty of spinner sharks in my 40 years on these waters. And I've seen huge schools of rays and other fish. But I've never seen anything like that," said Curt, just as amazed.

"Well, guys, I told you we would see sharks on this trip," said Jesse. "I just didn't think they would be flying through the air."

"Jesse, why do they do that?" asked Chris.

"No one knows. It may be a feeding strategy, but that's just an educated guess."

"Shouldn't we set out the longline?" asked Rick.

"That's an excellent idea," replied Jesse. "Captain, any reason why we can't set the longline in that school of spinners?"

"We're out of the shipping lane, so yes, we can do that."

"OK, everybody," announced Jesse to the scientific crew, "we'll make our first set in 10 minutes, so gird your loins."

CHAPTER 21

After only a few minutes of steaming, the *Up-Chuck* was in the thick of the school of spinner sharks. Looking overboard into the water, the sleek, grey bodies of large sharks could be seen cruising as far down as the eye could see. The sun, glinting off those closest to the water's surface, gave the sharks a coppery hue.

"Holy moly!" exclaimed Rick. "There are hundreds of them down there. Carbon copies of each other. You don't want to fall overboard, huh?"

"They wouldn't hurt you," explained Jesse. "These sharks are looking for a nice-sized, live fish to chow down on. Humans are just too big to be recognized as a prey item."

"Well, I don't think I want to take that chance."

"OK, Captain, we're ready to deploy the radar buoy," shouted Jesse toward the open door of the wheelhouse.

Captain Curt engaged the diesel engine, and the ship headed north-west, setting a course and speed to match the long, low swells coming across the Gulf. This "following sea" would minimize the pitch and roll of the boat and provide as much stability as possible while the crew worked on the rear deck. Jesse and Ross picked up the large radar buoy and tossed it into the churning boat wake.

The thick, black mainline was stored, wrapped around a large wooden spool, and mounted horizontally on an axle that was fixed to a heavy steel cradle. The spool turned slowly like a gargantuan fishing reel, as the line peeled off, crossed the fantail, and disappeared into the depths behind the boat. Jesse sat on an overturned five-gallon bucket and allowed the line to travel through his hand as he awaited the arrival of two knots tied in the line that indicated where each leader would be clipped.

"Number one, going out," announced Jesse as he clipped the baited leader between the double knots. "You guys help me keep count. I need to record how many hooks we send out."

"Here's number two," announced Ross as he handed the leader to Jesse.

The line continued to spool off the reel at a slow pace.

"Number two going out," said Jesse.

This continued for the next several minutes as leaders 3, 4, and 5 were clipped onto the line and sent overboard at a leisurely pace.

"Just like a well-oiled machine!" Jesse clipped leader 6 to the mainline and sent it overboard. "Hey guys, I can feel tugging on the line, so we've already picked up a shark. That's unusual but not surprising given the number of sharks in this area."

The spool turned more quickly now as the line began to spool out faster.

"Rick, go up to the wheelhouse and tell the captain to throttle back on it some. I don't want these knots coming faster than we can get the leaders ready," said Jesse as he clipped leader 7 followed quickly by leader 8.

A change in the sound of the diesel engine signaled that the Captain had throttled back on the engine. Leaders 9, 10, and 11 quickly appeared as the crew tried to keep up with the pace.

"Rick, tell him to throttle back some more!" ordered Jesse. "We're having trouble keeping up."

Rick ran forward and quickly returned.

"Captain says that's as slow as he can go."

"Crap!"

Jesse sent leader 12 and then 13 overboard. Number 13 dangled from the mainline that now spooled out away from the boat at a very shallow angle. The bait skipped across the water, and as soon as it went under, a large spinner shark took it like a big-mouth bass hitting a topwater lure. The shark sped away with its prize as the mainline began ripping off the spool.

"Damn it!" exclaimed an agitated Jesse, who rarely used expletives. The spool began turning wildly, and the line, pulled along by the shark, raced away at blinding speed.

Instinctively, Jesse tried to slow the line using his bare hand.

"Son of a…!" Jesse released the line from a rope-burned hand. "Captain!" yelled Jesse toward the wheelhouse. "Shut it down!"

The engine throttled back, and the forward movement of the vessel slowed and then stopped. However, the line continued to spool wildly out.

"Cut the line," yelled the first mate in a panic.

Jesse pulled his knife and grabbed the line with his good hand. The line continued to speed away, and Jesse received a second rope burn. The powerful shark began dragging the spool and steel cradle across the deck. The entire rig was about to go overboard, and this research cruise would come to an abrupt end!

"I can't stop it," yelled Jesse, his anger rising. "We're gonna lose the whole thing. Back down on it! Back down on it!"

A shudder travelled through the entire ship as Captain Curt put the diesel in reverse and throttled up. The vessel slid backwards into the shallow swells, causing seawater to slosh up and onto the deck. Ross and Don grabbed the spool to prevent it from sliding off the boat, but it was still turning too quickly for Jesse to handle.

"Faster, Captain!" yelled Jesse. "I still can't cut it!"

The engine rpm increased. Now the entire back deck was awash in seawater. Each time the vessel slammed into a swell, water was thrown upward and rained down on the crew, drenching everyone. Spilling over the threshold of the rear hatch, water poured into the laboratory. Either because the vessel's backward movement exceeded the forward movement of the shark, or the fish made a course correction, the line finally went limp and drifted under the boat. Jesse grabbed the heavy line and sawed on it with his knife. It was not easy, but the line finally parted, and the cut end vanished overboard.

"Shut it down, Captain," yelled Jesse as he plopped down on his five-gallon bucket, exhausted. "We got it."

"Holy smokes!" said Ross.

"That was awesome!" declared Chris as the two excited volunteers high-fived each other.

"No! Not awesome," said Jesse, shaking his head and wiping seawater from his face. "And now we got another problem."

"What?" asked Ross.

"The mainline is caught in the propeller."

"Crap! Seriously?" said Ross in disbelief.

"Look." Jesse pointed to the mainline visible below water, tethered to and traveling away from the underside of the boat. "We backed down on it, and the propeller picked it up."

Captain Curt hurried to the back deck to check on the crew.

"Wow!" said Ross with a sigh of relief when the engine noise faded. "You forget how nice it is to be without the constant drone of the engine."

"Sorry, Captain," said Jesse as Curt joined them. "Next time, I think I am gonna skip leader number 13."

"Well, it's not the first time we got something caught in the wheel, and it won't be the last," said the Captain sympathetically. "We've got scuba gear on board. I'll have to go down and cut the line out."

"Let me do it!" said Rick excitedly.

"I appreciate the enthusiasm, Rick, but are you scuba certified?" asked Jesse.

"No, but I used to borrow my brother's dive gear and dive in a quarry back home."

"That won't get it," said Curt. "There are only two certified divers on the boat, me and Jesse, and it's my responsibility."

"No, hell no!" said Jesse firmly. "You know I'm not going to let you do that, Captain. I'll go down."

"Truthfully, I am glad you offered Jesse. I am not the spring chicken I used to be. Go below and bring up the scuba gear," said Curt to the first mate.

"It will probably not be a big deal," said Jesse, rising from his pickle-bucket seat.

"What about all those sharks?" asked Ross looking overboard.

"They're too small to be a threat. My concern is that there may be larger ones around as well. Big tigers or hammerheads."

"I probably shouldn't mention this now, but I have a recurring nightmare involving a night dive and a 12-foot tiger shark that does not end well," said Ross.

"I don't want to hear that right now, Ross."

"Just keep your eyes open down there," said Curt.

"Oh, I will."

The first mate returned from the laboratory with a mask and a single-tank scuba rig. He opened the tank valve and checked the pressure gauge. He hung a swim ladder off the rear deck while Jesse stripped down to his shorts and put on the tank.

"No fins?" asked Jesse.

"You won't need those," said Curt. "You're only going about 8 feet under the boat to the prop. Be careful when you go along the hull. There's gonna be lots of barnacles down there, and they will cut the crap out of you."

"Oh yeah, been there done that," said Jesse seriously as he spat into his dive mask and spread it evenly on the inner surface of the glass to prevent fogging.

"For your peace of mind, I have the boat key in my pocket," said Curt.

"Thanks, Captain!" said Jesse. Wouldn't want anyone starting up while I was down there. That would be one big food processor."

Jesse inserted his knife into the scabbard that hung from his dive vest, put the regulator in his mouth to check air flow, said a brief prayer, and rolled off the deck.

"Listen, everyone," ordered Captain Curt. "I want all eyes watching out for Jesse and keep an eye on those sharks."

"SHIT!" shouted Ross as he looked over the railing at the spot where Jesse splashed in. "A butt-load of sharks are heading right for Jesse."

Captain Curt ran toward the wheelhouse and emerged with a 30-06 rifle. Curt quickly chambered a round and headed toward the railing.

"JESSE!" screamed Ross at the water.

"Stand back," ordered the captain as he searched the ocean's surface behind the boat. "Not sure this will do any good, but it might scare them away." Curt sighted down the rifle and squeezed off two shots that struck the surface near the group of sharks.

Jesse took a moment to adjust his buoyancy compensator so he would neither sink nor float. He took a quick assessment of the underside of the boat and the propeller. Startled by muffled rifle shots, he saw two speeding bullets cut through the water some distance away from him. He immediately pulled himself back to the surface.

"What's going on!" gurgled Jesse through his regulator as his head broke the surface of the water.

"Get the hell out!" screamed Ross, extending a hand to Jesse, who now hung from the dive ladder. "Sharks right behind you!"

"It's OK," said Jesse, pulling out his regulator.

"You sure about that?" asked Curt.

"If they wanted to eat me, they could have done it easily. They're just curious."

"If you say so," said Ross, breathing easier now. "That scared the crap out of us!"

"I appreciate the concern, but I think I soiled my shorts when that rifle went off," said Jesse. "The main line is wrapped around the shaft tighter than a tick on a pig's butt. It will take me a little while to get it out. If you happen to see a big tiger or hammerhead, just pound on the deck with something. I'll easily hear that and come up."

"We'll keep our eyes open," said Curt. "You do the same."

"Aye, aye, Captain," replied Jesse as he touched two fingers to his forehead in a navy salute, put his regulator in, and dropped down again.

Realizing he might never again have the opportunity to observe this many large sharks from underwater, Jesse paused momentarily to take in his surroundings. The sun's rays, refracted through a constantly changing sea surface, danced across the bodies of those sharks near the surface. The intense indigo below him revealed that the vessel had drifted over deeper water. As sunbeams knifed down into the depths, he wondered if this was how looking into a black hole might appear. At that moment, surrounded by sharks and suspended between a constantly changing, fractured surface and a featureless, seemingly depthless ocean, Jesse recalled why he so loved the sea.

By chance, a shark rocketed from the depths and disappeared when it left its watery realm very near, and in full view. He was a bit surprised by the very audible sound the shark produced upon re-entry. Curiously, when the shark "splashed down," it was joined by several other sharks as they swam together for a short distance. Two sharks broke away from the group and swam together, pressing their bodies against each other as they swam as one.

"Well, I'll be darned," gurgled Jesse as he realized what he had just witnessed. "It's mating behavior! That explains why they rushed toward me when I splashed in."

"OK, enough of this." Jesse changed position to have a better view of the hull and the propeller. He could see the rope that was wrapped tightly around the shaft. The remaining line, with leaders and potentially several sharks attached, disappeared as it angled off into the briny deep. Jesse could see a single leader, still attached to the main line and just under the boat, that held a decent-sized yellowfin tuna swimming slowly in circles. *That will be supper tonight! Glad that's not a hooked shark.* Although unconcerned about being bitten, a hooked shark could be a serious entanglement problem for him.

Jesse pulled himself under the vessel, bumping along against the bottom. Wincing, he had neglected to heed the barnacles attached to the hull as they lacerated his hands and arms. *Not a good start*! *Bleeding and surrounded by sharks*.

He began cutting away the tangled line, pieces raining down and disappearing into the deep. Although not overly concerned about this endeavor, he nevertheless paused every few moments to check his surroundings before returning to work. After some fifteen minutes of cutting and close to being finished, he made a curious observation: all the spinner sharks had suddenly disappeared!

That's strange! Jesse turned away from his work to check his surroundings. Thanks to the incredibly clear water, Jesse could just make out in the distance a dark object near the ocean surface. He made a mental note of the size of the unknown object and went back to work. Turning to look again, he realized that the object was distinctly larger, indicating that it was heading toward him. With renewed enthusiasm, Jesse began quickly cutting away at the remaining line.

Rick was the first to see it on deck. "Look!" he cried as he pointed in the direction of the huge dorsal fin that was cutting through the water.

"Jesus, it's huge!" said Ross. "Is that a shark?"

"That's a big freaking shark!" answered Curt in disbelief. "Signal to Jesse!"

Curt had given Rick a hammer, and he began banging on the deck. Everyone else on board began stomping like they were possessed as the fin drew ever closer.

"Shark, shark," screamed Ross from the railing into the ocean, hoping Jesse would hear. He removed his tennis shoe and pounded it Khrushchev-like against the deck.

The dark shape and huge dorsal fin heading straight for the ship suggested a shark of mammoth proportions. Some distance from the boat, the ominous shape sank beneath the surface but continued to approach the vessel, heading directly under the boat.

Curt stepped to the railing, gun still in hand, aimed just ahead of the dark object, and pulled the trigger. The hammer clicked, but there was no discharge.

"Shit! This piece of crap!" exclaimed Curt as he frantically tried to free the jammed rifle cartridge.

"Oh my God!" screamed Ross, as he was the first to notice the cloud of blood spreading from under the vessel.

CHAPTER 22

Cherie pushed through the glass door of the Dauphin Island Police Station and approached the receptionist's desk. A neatly dressed, large woman behind an equally kept desk sat at an electric typewriter. Pictures of family members, a small collection of porcelain figurines, and an autographed photo of Auburn University's coach, "Shug" Jordan, populated one side of her desk. The other was taken up by a typewriter and a large police radio that crackled with occasional reports from Deputy Murphy.

Aside from her receptionist duties, Dorothy Stratford also served as the secretary, dispatcher, bookkeeper, and accountant for the Police Department. In short, she was the entire office staff. Dorothy's carefully styled, vibrant red hair framed her kind face. Always impeccably dressed, her neatly tailored outfit exuded professionalism and efficiency. Even though the D.I.P.D. was small, she insisted that "We don't have to act small."

"May I help you, young lady?" asked Dorothy, looking up from her work.

"Yes Ma'am. I have an appointment with Chief East."

"You must be Dr. Belon?"

"I am. But please call me Cherie."

"Sure. He's on the phone at the moment," said Dorothy after noticing that the light on his phone line was on. "He should be off momentarily. Please take a seat."

"Thank you."

"Can I get you some coffee?"

"No Ma'am." Cherie took a seat on the couch in the small reception area. "I think I've had too much caffeine already this morning."

"I'm not sure that is even possible for me. So you're from the Centers for Disease Control?"

"Yes Ma'am."

"I heard about the Captain of the Crimson Tide. So sad," said Dorothy, shaking her head. "I hope you have some time to enjoy our little island paradise."

"It has mostly been work, but I got to spend time shark fishing with some of the students from the Oceanography Lab. It was great fun."

"There is some really good fishing around the island, although most people try to avoid catching sharks. My favorite is whiting, the best-eating fish in the ocean in my opinion."

"I love to make blackened redfish," said Cherie. "It was a specialty of mine back home."

"Let me guess, Lafayette, Louisiana?"

"Close… Baton Rouge."

"Oh no! You're not an LSU fan, are you?" asked Dorothy jokingly.

"Well, my degrees are from LSU, and most of my family are alumni, so I guess I have to be. I will pull for the Tigers, but truthfully, I would rather read a Michael Crichton novel or go to a good movie than watch football."

"I see Chief East is off the phone." Dorothy picked up the receiver and pushed the button for the Chief's line. "Dr. Belon is here for your appointment. Yes Sir. I'll send her back."

Dorothy replaced the phone on its cradle. "His office is the second door on the left."

"Thank you, said Cherie, getting up. "It was nice chatting with you."

"Likewise!"

Chief East stood as Cherie entered his office.

"Dr. Belon." The Chief extended his hand. "I appreciate you coming by. Have a seat."

"Thank you!" Cherie shook hands and sat across from the Chief. In sharp contrast to Dorothy's workspace, the Chief's desk was strewn with papers, unwashed coffee cups, one of them used as a pencil holder, his half-eaten lunch on a *Beauchamp's Sub Shop* wrapper, and a stuffed, albino squirrel, pink eyes glaring, guarded it all. A large bird cage containing a noisy blue and gold macaw stood near a window that looked out into the wooded lot behind the Police Station.

"My apologies for keeping you waiting. This has been one hell of a week for the DIPD," said the Chief while massaging his right temple, where a dull headache had persisted for the last two days.

"No problem. Wow! What a beautiful bird."

"That's Breaker. You can have him if you want."

"Uh…you're joking, right?"

"I am dead serious."

"Well, I would love to have a pet, but I can't care for one at this point in my life. Are parrots affectionate?"

"Breaker, if you'll pardon my French, is a real son-of-a bitch."

"Son-of-a bitch, son-of-a bitch,….AWWWKKK."

"See there!" said East as he pointed toward the cage with disgust. "It's like he knew we were talking about him. He can be affectionate one moment and then bite the crap out of you the next. I made the mistake of putting him on my shoulder once. You know, like a pirate. We could not get him off me. He dug his claws into my shoulder and pulled my hair out with his beak. Hurt like the dickens."

Cherie covered her mouth with her hand, trying to hide her amusement. "So why do you have him?" said Cherie with a chuckle.

"Long story. He was part of an exotic bird show at the Mobile Zoo. Someone who worked there thought teaching him a vocabulary of inappropriate words and phrases would be funny. He would say terrible things during shows, and some folks were very offended by it. They threatened legal action. I think the final straw was when he began saying unkind things about the Director of the Zoo. Made me think it was probably a disgruntled employee responsible."

"AWWWKKK…gimmee a damn cracker…AWWWKKK."

"I can understand why they would want to get rid of him, but it's not the bird's fault."

"No, it's not," said East. "It's exactly the same situation when a pit bull attacks someone. The dog's owner is legally liable, and, sadly, the dog gets put down."

"So, how did you come to own him?"

"Hell, I don't own that bird; he owns me," corrected East as Cherie giggled again.

"They didn't know what to do with him. I am friends with a fellow who works in the Animal Husbandry Department there, and he called me and asked if I would take it. Maybe try to rehabilitate it. If not, they may have to destroy it."

"Oh, that would be a shame."

"I could not let them kill it, and I thought it would add some color to the Police Department. The bird was over 20 years old when I took it. I figured, heck, he can't have much longer to live, so I'll let him enjoy the last few years of his life in exile on Dauphin Island."

"That was very nice of you."

"Stupid is more like it! I got played by my supposed friend at the zoo. That's a blue and gold macaw. Do you know how long these birds can live in captivity?"

"I do not."

"Over 100 years! Winston Churchill had a pet Macaw when he became Prime Minister that was famous for imitating Churchill's profanity-laced rants against the Nazi's. That bird is still alive today, in 1989!"

"There must be something about that species and expletives," mused Cherie jokingly.

"I know this, Breaker will still be cussing like a drunken sailor when I'm pushing up daisies," exclaimed East.

"AWWWKKK….Piss on George. Piss on George."

"That would be the Zoo Director, George Thompson," said East with an embarrassed sigh. "I am so sorry for this. He's generally not this talkative at this time of the day. He's probably just trying to impress you. I'll put the cover back on his cage and he'll shut up." East got up from his desk, covered the cage, and sat back down.

"No apology needed and, truthfully, I am impressed by how well that bird speaks despite the content," said Cherie, laughing.

"Yeah, he's a real charmer."

"I'm guessing that you'd like an update on the Crimson Tide investigation?" asked Cherie.

"Well, that's not why I asked you to come by, but since you mentioned it. Are there new developments?"

"Not really. The consensus at the CDC is that whatever caused the death of Captain Armstrong was not an infectious agent. They have concluded that this is not a public health issue, but most likely a criminal one."

"And what is your opinion?""On the record, I have to agree with the official CDC determination."

"And off the record?"

"Off the record?" Cherie, apparently struggling with an explanation of her concern, paused for a moment and looked down.

"Chief East, do you follow sports?"

"Oh yes. I'm a huge Alabama football fan."

"Have you ever had a feeling that you just know your team is gonna win, even when the odds are not in your favor and there is no logical reason for your feeling?"

"Doc, could you hold just a moment?" asked East as he noticed the light on his phone blinking. "Yes? No. Tell him I'm in a meeting. No. We tried that before, and it won't work. OK. Hold my calls unless it's an emergency. Thanks, Dorothy. Sorry about that, Doc. My deputy is new, and he requires more hand-holding than I like to give."

"No problem."

"So, it's a hunch?" asked East.

"More like an educated guess. I fear there is something else going on that we have been unable to track down."

"Before you continue," said East, "let me say that I, too, have concerns about the investigation. The official report from this office was an undetermined cause of death."

"Yes, I know. I reviewed the report. The scuttlebutt around the island is that it was a drug deal gone bad."

"I've heard everything from drug deal to alien abduction," said East, rolling his eyes. "I don't know about the alien thing, but that was no drug deal. The pieces just don't fit. Tom Armstrong was a respected community member, financially well-off, had no debt, and was happily married. Just doesn't fit the profile of a failing shrimper turned drug runner. Also, the Crimson Tide was actively shrimping when something happened. The deck was covered with mostly unsorted catch, one of the nets was still hanging and had not been emptied, and someone was in the middle of preparing a meal. No one does a little shrimping and starts preparing a meal if they are heading out for a drug pick-up. You go out and get in as fast as you can. You certainly don't provision and buy ice for a two-week trip. Most puzzling of all, why would the bad guys stuff the Captain in the chiller vat? You simply toss the bodies overboard far out at sea, and they will never be found."

"But how did the body end up in the chiller?"

"I think something happened to Tom that impaired him in some way, and he accidentally fell in. My understanding is that it was fortuitous for the CDC?"

"It was. Chilling the tissues resulted in them being beautifully preserved. I know that sounds morbid, but it's the truth."

"So, what bothers you about this mess?" asked East. "And could you please put it in terms a simple man like myself can understand?"

"There are just too many pieces that don't fit together. When we examined the body, we found extensive tissue destruction. Cells disrupted, fluids leaking from cells, destroyed capillary beds, massive edema, etc."

"That's a bit too technical for me."

"It was like he had exploded inside."

"OK!" said East, surprised. "That's disturbing!"

"There was tissue destruction and body fluid loss the likes of which I have never seen before. The damage was in every organ. And most troubling of all, the presence of damaged tissue all over the body suggested that whatever killed the Captain spread very quickly."

"But couldn't some toxic substance cause that?"

"You're correct. But we've checked for every known toxic agent: cyanide, ricin, nerve gas, even radioactive material. All results are negative."

"So, it's biological?"

"That would seem to be the case. However, bacteria or viruses just don't spread that quickly. Additionally, we've screened for all the usual suspects, hemorrhagic fever, bubonic plague, Ebola, etc., and came up with nothing."

"Please don't be offended by this, but you're very young and I'm guessing you haven't been at the CDC for long."

"No offense taken," said Cherie matter-of-factly. "You are correct. I am less experienced than everyone in the Infectious Agent Division. In fact, there's a twenty-year difference between the next youngest agent and me. But I think that is where my strength lies. I'm not biased by past experiences with disease investigation. While my training equipped me with the newest techniques for disease detection, we are also trained to "think outside the box," to use a cliché. It's predicted that new diseases will emerge as the human population swells. Those new diseases will not fit the profile of those that we've known from past outbreaks. The present investigation feels like exactly that situation."

"That ain't good!"

"There is also one other thing that I've not made public."

"What's that?" asked East, furrowing his brow.

"Someone boarded that vessel after it ran aground on the island."

"I am impressed," said East earnestly. "The Coast Guard came to the same conclusion after going through the bunk rooms, and I concurred. Someone went through the personal belongings of the crew. But what brought you to that conclusion?"

"There was a motorcycle track across the dunes near the boat and footprints down to the beach. But I cannot explain the fact that we have had no other reports of infection on the island. If this is a biological agent, and I pray it is not, we should have seen other similar occurrences."

"Doc," said East darkly, "you are not going to be pleased by what I am about to tell you."

CHAPTER 23

"Oh shit!" exclaimed Curt as he kicked off his shrimper boots and began stripping off clothing. "Someone get me a mask and the spear gun from the dive locker!"

The first mate disappeared into the laboratory, returned quickly, and handed Curt a mask and an old, but effective, spear gun. Curt jammed the butt of the spear gun into his gut and pulled the rubber bands back to "cock" it. He took two steps and was about to plunge overboard when he heard…

"Sounds like y'all are having a square dance up there!" said Jesse sarcastically as his head popped out of the water on the port side of the boat.

The entire crew rushed to the port railing.

"THERE'S A HUGE SHARK!" screamed Ross as he extended a hand to Jesse. "GET OUT! GET OUT!"

"Calm down and take this gear." Jesse removed the scuba tank and handed it up the ladder to Ross. He climbed the ladder and sat down on deck to catch his breath.

"We were all having heart attacks up here!" said Ross, still freaking out but relieved to see Jesse. "What the hell happened?"

"I think I saw it coming before you all did. At first, it looked like a huge shark, but once it got close enough, I could see it was a killer whale."

"A freaking killer whale!" exclaimed Chris. "Gnarly!"

"No way!" said Ross. "Killer whales are unheard of in these waters."

"It was after a yellowfin tuna that was hooked on one of the leaders under the boat," said Jesse excitedly. "I put the boat propeller between me and the tuna and got a front-row seat to the most amazing predator-prey interaction I have ever seen. The killer whale charged right past me and slammed into the tuna. Cut it in half right before my eyes! I was so caught up in the excitement of the moment that I had no concern for my personal safety at all. It scarfed the tuna down and took off."

"Damn!" said Ross. "I would have soiled my britches!"

"The whale was so focused on the tuna that I don't think it even noticed me."

"Lord, we are just thankful that you are OK." Curt, who had not yet recovered from the adrenaline rush of confronting a large marine predator, sat on the boat deck and leaned back against the railing. "I was about to go in after you."

"I am sorry, Captain. I heard you guys signaling, but I was reluctant to get out of the water with a large animal closing in. The good news is that I got all the line cut away. Oh, and something else. I now know why spinner sharks "spin". It's mating behavior."

"Really?" asked Ross. "How so?"

"A spinner came rocketing to the surface near me, and when it splashed back into the water, a group of sharks rushed to it," explained Jesse with a gleam in his eye. "After that, two sharks broke away from the group and swam side by side. The male held onto the fin of the female with its mouth and kind of wrapped its body around the female. They were mating."

"Is that how other sharks mate?" asked Rick.

"We don't know much about shark behavior. With that one observation, I probably just increased our knowledge of shark mating behavior by 100%. I've got to spend more time underwater and less in the lab," said Jesse in a moment of reflection.

Curt, recovered from the excitement, sat on the steel deck and slipped his shrimper boots back on. "What's the plan now, Jesse?"

"Let's pick up the radar buoy and retrieve the broken longline. There are a bunch of hooks that have been fishing out there that probably have spinner sharks on at least some of them. That is, if that killer whale hasn't eaten them all."

Curt returned to the wheelhouse, started the diesel, and headed in the direction of the radar buoy. Picking up the buoy went without mishap, and the crew began hauling in the longline. Jesse and Ross pulled the line in while Chris and Rick handled the leaders and recorded data. Leaders with sharks on them were removed from the mainline and clipped around the ship's railing until several were retrieved. To draw blood, sharks had to be directed into a metal-framed, canvas stretcher suspended by an overhead boom and winch that was lowered into the water. Hoisting the sharks to just above the railing, all hands were required to help control the animals while Jesse drew blood.

"A little higher," said Jesse to the first mate as he used the winch to raise the stretcher containing the last adult spinner. "It's a female and the hook time is 144 minutes."

"Female, 144 minutes," repeated Chris as he recorded the information on the datasheet.

"Everybody hold tight to the caudal fin!" ordered Jesse as he obtained a blood sample and cut the leader close to the hook. The first mate lowered the shark back into the water. When the stretcher hit the water, it opened up, and the shark took off like a rocket.

"Whew!" sighed Ross. "That's too much like work."

"Seriously!" said Chris as he plopped down on top of an ice chest. "I thought marine biology was supposed to be like Jacques Cousteau. You know French wine, red sock hats, and weenie-popper, bathing suits."

"French wine and sock hats are fine. But anyone wearing a *Speedo* on this boat is going to get chucked overboard," said Jesse, not entirely joking. "That was harder than usual. Every shark, despite being hooked for over two hours in some cases, acted like they were just captured. When they struggle in the stretcher like that, it makes it so much harder on us. But not harder on them, given that every one of them took off like a bat out of Hades!"

"Where have we seen that before?" queried Ross.

"I know," replied Jesse. "Bionic sharks."

"How many total did we get, Chris?" asked Ross.

"Nine sharks, all spinners, 3 females and 5 males, and one shark that was just a head," said Chris.

"It was nice of that killer whale to leave us the head," said Jesse. "I am surprised that he didn't eat more of them, but after that tuna and most of an adult spinner shark, he was probably stuffed."

"I know one whole shark is my limit when I eat at *Duffs, All You Can Eat Endangered Species Buffet*," said Ross, laughing as the mood on the boat changed.

"I prefer the Manatee myself," said Rick.

"Hey, we don't kid around about Manatees!" said Jesse. "Now, Dolphin, that's some good eating."

"Have you tried the puffer fish at Duff's?" asked Ross. "It's soooo good, and the buzz you get is better than three shots of tequila."

"You lost me on that one," said Chris, confused.

"Puffer fish is a very expensive delicacy, called *fugu*, that's served in some places in Asia, primarily Japan, if I recall," said

Jesse. "There's an extremely powerful toxin in some tissues that can quickly kill you if you get too much."

"Why in hell would someone want to risk that?" asked Chris. "It can't taste that good."

"Oh, I forgot to mention that in the correct dose, the toxin produces an intense euphoria," explained Jesse.

"Euphoria?" asked Chris, puzzled.

"They get high," said Ross.

"Really?" said Chris. "So, they get *fu-gu-ed* up."

Everyone laughed. "You could say that. They also believe it helps with their *manhood*," added Jesse while doing the two fingers in the air universal sign for quotes.

"Sorry, but there ain't no high worth that kind of risk!" said Ross, "although, if you're dead, you won't have a manhood problem!"

"OK, where to now, Jesse?" asked Captain Curt as he returned from the wheelhouse.

"Captain, eight sharks are a good sample here, so let's go to the 100 Fathom station and make a set."

"That should work out good," said Curt. "We should be there around 1:30. I'll have David put out sandwich fixings in the galley for lunch."

"Thanks, Captain," said Jesse. "Too bad about that yellowfin, I was looking forward to having some sushi."

Captain Curt wound up the diesel on the *Up-Chuck* and pointed the vessel toward the next long-lining location. While underway, Jesse and the crew cleaned up the back deck, repaired all the broken leaders, and got everything ready for the next set. The crew went below to have lunch, and Jesse went to the wheelhouse to speak with Captain Curt. Curt sat back in the captain's chair, steering the vessel with his feet while eating a sandwich.

"Did you get something to eat?" asked Curt.

"I'm not hungry at the moment. I'll grab something later," said Jesse as he took the unoccupied chair in the wheelhouse. "Where's David?"

"He's in the rack. Since he'll be taking the first set tonight, I told him to get some rest."

"These long swells don't help my appetite at all," said Jesse. "They're coming from that hurricane down south. It's amazing to me that waves created way down in the southern Gulf travel all the way up here."

"Hope it stays away from Dauphin Island," said Curt.

"Me too."

Curt laid down his sandwich, picked up his binoculars, and focused on a shrimp boat that was headed toward them.

"That looks like the *Miss Marie*." I wonder where Brett is going? Shrimpers shrimp at night and sleep during the day. He should be anchored up, not heading in."

"Do you know all the shrimpers around here?"

"Oh yeah. It's a pretty small group."

Curt took the VHF microphone off the hook and tuned to channel 9.

"Miss Marie, Miss Marie, this is R/V Charles Regan, reply 68."

"Roger, Charles Regan," came the reply. "Going to 68."

Curt reached for the radio and turned the channel selector to 68.

"Captain Brett, why ain't you on anchor? You heading for the hill? Come back."

"I'm done, buddy," answered Brett. "I ain't shrimping in this! Come back."

"What are you talking about? There should be plenty of shrimp out here. Come back."

"I'll pass close on your starboard side," answered Brett. "Take a look at my nets."

"Do you know what he's talking about, Captain?" asked Jesse.

"Beats me."

The vessel slowed as she passed close by. The first mate stood on the rear deck and spread open the netting that hung high above the deck from the now vertical outriggers.

"Good God!" exclaimed Curt when he saw the netting. What did you hit? Come back."

"I didn't hit anything. Sharks have been shredding my nets for the past two nights. We've tried everything. I lost thousands of dollars on this trip. Come back."

"Sharks?!" replied Curt. "I've seen them bite a few holes in trawls, but nothing like that." Come back."

"After one drag, the net was toast. Bit all the way through the chaffing gear. Changed them out, and the same thing. Totally wrecked all my nets. Come back."

"Damn, I am sorry, Captain," said Curt. "If I can help in some way, let me know. Come back."

"Much obliged, Captain! Be safe. Over," replied Captain Brett as the *Miss Marie* slid past on its way to the dock.

"You too. Over and out."

"Geez," said Jesse. "What a trip this has been, and we ain't even halfway yet."

"Look at it this way, we're pre-disastered. All the shit has happened on the first leg of the trip. Smooth sailing from here on!" said Curt as he reached for his sandwich, knocked his coffee cup off the dash, and tried to catch it as it shattered on the floor of the wheelhouse.

"Damn! OK, now we are pre-disastered!" exclaimed Curt, laughing as he took another bite from his cheese and bologna sandwich.

CHAPTER 24

Under a threatening sky, the *Up-Chuck* plowed past Dauphin Island lighthouse and into Mobile Bay as Captain Curt eased back on the throttle. Curt's prediction had come true, and the remainder of the trip went without major problems.

"Looking kind of stormy, Captain," commented the first mate.

"That squall line is about to come through," said Curt. "Probably hit us about the time we get to the dock. Jesse, how many sharks did we get this trip?"

Jesse stood against the railing just outside the wheelhouse door, watching a waterspout develop on the distant horizon, snaking and writhing down out of a black sky.

"Well, despite all those snafus early on, we did pretty well." He pulled a small notebook from his back pocket and did a quick tally of the numbers. "Let me see, 7 sharks at the shallowest station, 22 at the deeper station, and 18 at the deepest. A total of 47 sharks. That's not too shabby."

"You see that waterspout, Jesse?" asked the mate, pointing toward the western horizon.

"I saw that," answered Jesse. "I think waterspouts are fascinating!"

"What's the closest you've ever been to one?" asked the mate.

"Once, when we were anchored in Bon Secour Bay. I was inside the cabin of the smaller research vessel, *The Flying Tiger*, when I heard a loud whirring sound. I looked out, and a waterspout was fifty feet off the stern of the boat. Scared the crap out of me!"

"Never been that close," said the mate.

"It probably wouldn't have done anything except rock the hell out of the boat and maybe tear off an antenna or two," said Curt.

"Here is the weird thing," added Jesse. "Where the water spout touched the surface of the bay, which was glassy calm, it created a circular patch of choppy water. To the seagulls that were flying over, it looked like the disturbed water that a fish school would create. The gulls began diving into an apparent school of fish. When they hit that fast-moving air, just above the water, they were thrown out like children flying off a spinning playground ride. It was chunking birds in all directions."

"That is weird," said Curt. "That was some intense wind shear, huh?"

"For sure! It was comical, thinking back on it, but at that moment, I was just trying to pull anchor and get the heck out of there. Fortunately, it moved away from our boat."

Curt throttled back slightly as the *Up-Chuck* steamed past the Bay light house and into Mobile Bay. He leaned forward in the captain's chair as he noticed a Coast Guard vessel just inside the mouth of the bay. "What's going on over there? Looks like the coasties are checking somebody out." He turned up the volume on the VHF and switched to channel 16, the emergency and information channel. It took a moment before the recorded message repeated:

"Coast Guard Station, Dauphin Island, Alabama. All vessels near the mouth of Mobile Bay. Navigational hazard. An unmanned vessel circling just north and west of the Fort Morgan Peninsula. Avoid area if possible."

"Somebody's boat took off without them!" joked Curt when they drew close enough to observe the pilotless fishing boat cutting tight, fast doughnuts. "If he'd had his cut-off lanyard around his wrist, it would have shut the motor down when he went overboard, and he could have swum back to the boat."

"Are they gonna try to jump on it with it running like that?" asked Chris, who came forward to see what the commotion was about.

"Probably not. The coasties will stand by and wait for it to run out of gas, and then tow it to shore," said Curt. "Those outboards, even the big ones, get really good gas mileage, so it could circle for a while before it runs out. I hope they found the fellow who was tossed out."

Jesse took the binoculars and zoomed in on the boat. Even at a distance, the powerful binoculars provided incredible detail. "It's a nice little center-console fishing boat with a 90 HP Johnson. With that smaller motor, and if it had a full tank, the Coast Guard could be there for hours. That's a weird color combination. It's a white hull, but the inside of the boat is red. Well, it's at least partially red," corrected Jesse as the angle changed and he could see the interior of the boat more clearly. "No, that must be fish blood splashed all over the inside of the boat. Somebody was having a really good day fishing, I guess. OK, I gotta put these down, it's making me a little queasy!" Jesse, his head spinning a bit, took a seat in the wheelhouse.

"If they were catching ladyfish or tarpon, they bleed like a stuck pig when you put them on the deck," added Curt. "Jesse, you're the fish biologist. Why do they do that?"

"Never thought about it. Hemophilia perhaps? That's a joke by the way."

"Not much of one," countered Curt. "OK, crew, we'll be at the dock in about fifteen."

"Aye aye, Cap'n!" said Chris with a salute.

*****

Captain Curt nudged the ship up to the Oceanographic Lab dock, and Jesse and the first mate secured it to the pilings there. The gangplank was pulled from the shore onto the deck to begin the tiresome job of unloading the gear into the Lab vehicle. With almost all equipment off the boat, a CDC vehicle pulled into the crushed oyster shell parking lot.

"Well, well, well," said Ross teasingly to Jesse as Cherie stepped out of the vehicle. "Somebody just couldn't wait to see you. Wish I had a cutie like that to meet me."

Jesse climbed down from the upper deck and walked across the gangplank to meet Cherie.

"Hey!" said Jesse, smiling and waving as he approached Cherie, coming along the dock. A few raindrops spattered on the weathered wood decking.

"Hey to you, too!" said Cherie, returning Jesse's smile. "Glad y'all are back safe."

"Hi Cherie," shouted Ross from the deck of the boat.

"Hi Ross." Cherie waved. "Y'all had a successful trip?"

"It was good, except for the part when we thought Jesse was dead."

"What?" exclaimed Cherie, turning back to Jesse.

"It was no big deal," insisted Jesse. "We had some strange things at the beginning of the trip and at the end, but the in-between part was very productive," said Jesse, who could not keep the goofy grin off his face. "I'll fill you in later. How are things with you?"

"I have more information to fill you in on. Can we meet later?"

"For sure. We're just about finished unloading. What say we meet at my place at 6:00?"

"That sounds good."

"Just a warning. I might not be the best conversationalist. I'm pretty sleep-deprived."

"No worries. I mainly need to bounce some things off of someone I can trust."

"You can bounce anything you want off of me!" replied Jesse, immediately turning beet red with embarrassment after recognizing the double entendre. "Uh, that did not come out right."

"Jesse, it's OK," replied Cherie with a giggle, and placed a hand on Jesse's arm. "I'll bring something for dinner."

"That would be great because I've got nothing at my house. And just a warning, Bongo will be there."

"Then it should be exciting!" said Cherie as she walked away. "See you there."

"See you."

CHAPTER 25

Jesse left the dock in the El Camino and swung by Gino's to pick up Bongo. Jesse was comfortable leaving him there because Gino's wife, Doris, and the kids were crazy about the dog, and because the backyard at Gino's was fenced down to the water. This gave the kids and the dog freedom to run on the dock and to swim in the sound. When Jesse arrived, he parked on the street in front of Gino's modest home. A stack of crab traps and Gino's old F-150 sat in the side yard. As he got out, the sounds of laughing, screaming, and barking indicated that the family and Bongo were in the backyard. Gino and Marie sat in the shade of a sprawling live oak near the water's edge, keeping an eye on the kids who were swimming. Bongo was having the time of his life as he repeatedly ran down Gino's dock and belly-flopped into the Mississippi Sound.

"Hey, sharkman!" shouted Gino, beer in hand, as Jesse rounded the corner of the house.

"Hi guys." Jesse swung open the gate and walked across the grassy lawn. "Did that crazy dog behave himself?"

Upon hearing Jesse's voice, Bongo sprinted across the yard and body-slammed Jesse.

"Hey, big guy!" said Jesse as he wrestled with Bongo, who was now shaking, slobbering, and slinging water all over him. "Ok, fella, calm down!" He fell to the ground, rolled over on his back, and Jesse scratched him on the belly. He then leaped up, sprinted for the dock, and belly-flopped into the sound again.

"Well, that was a short hello," complained Jesse as he wiped his wet hands on his jeans. "Just long enough to soak me."

"I really appreciate you guys keeping him." Shaded by a sprawling live-oak tree, Jesse sat at the picnic table across from Gino. "I know he can be a handful."

"We love Bongo, and he was a good boy," said Doris.

"How did the shark researchin' go?" asked Gino.

"Minor problems, as usual, but we caught about 40 sharks."

"That seems like a good many. Did you catch anything you could eat?" asked Gino, always the commercial fisherman.

"As a matter of fact, we had a good-sized yellowfin tuna, but we lost it. I was gonna bring you some."

"Ooo, damn! That's too bad. I love fresh tuna. When are you going to finish that degree, or are you planning on being a professional student?" asked Gino half-jokingly.

"It's progressing, just not as quickly as I would like.

"How's it going with your new girlfriend?" said Gino suggestively.

"Gino, that's too personal!" demanded Doris.

"It's OK, Mrs. Patronus. I am used to it. He's talking about Dr. Cherie Belon, the CDC agent who's been on the island for a few days. We've become good friends. As a matter of fact, we're having dinner at my place tonight."

"See, I told you, didn't I?" said Gino smugly.

"We were going to invite you for dinner tonight," said Doris.

"I really appreciate it, but I've become intellectually invested in the Crimson Tide mystery that she's working on. I would love to take a rain check if you would let me."

"Intellectually invested? Is that what you young folks now call casual sex?"

"GINO! That's enough!"

"Sorry, hon," said Gino sheepishly. "But what's to investigate? Wasn't that some drug-running thing?"

"It's still uncertain what happened, but I'm pretty sure it wasn't drug-related. She's trying to figure out if it was some kind of disease."

"That was terrible," said Doris, shaking her head. "That poor man."

"The troubling thing is that someone appeared to have been on board the boat after it ran aground. Cherie and I went out to look at the spot where it was beached and found footprints leading to the boat. It looked like someone was on a dirt bike, got off, and walked down to the boat."

"You guys need to talk to Crazy Joe," said Gino.

"Who the heck is Crazy Joe?" asked Jesse.

"He lives in that big swamp on the west end. He knows everything that goes on down there." Gino took a big gulp of his beer.

"Maybe he was the one who went on board?" asked Jesse.

"No way in hell. First of all, Joe doesn't have a dirt bike. I don't think Joe owns anything except an old pirogue. Second, he's got no use for anything that would be on that shrimp boat. If you meet him, you'll understand what I am saying."

"How would we go about talking to him?"

"Well, you're gonna need to have plenty of mosquito repellent. That swamp is full of mosquitoes. You have to go after dark. He's never in his shack during the day. I guess he is always out looking for food. He only eats what he catches around the island."

"You've been to his shack?"

"Only once, several years ago. I was running wide open near the west end and hit a submerged log. Almost knocked the entire lower unit off my outboard. I was stuck there. I saw Joe in his pirogue and flagged him. He came over and paddled me to the beach so I could walk back to town for help. He saved my butt. Later, I took a butt-load of crabs to his shack and left them there. It's hard to believe he has lived there for all these years."

"I'll ask Cherie if she thinks it's worthwhile to talk to him, but, knowing her, she will insist on it. She's the type who leaves no stone unturned. How would we find him?"

"You want to go on foot or are you gonna use your boat?"

"I am not comfortable running the Gulf side at night. We would have to swim to the shore in the dark, and if it's rough, we might not be able to get close enough to swim in. Also, we might not be able to get back to the boat again if we anchor off the beach. We'll have to walk."

"Drive out to the end of the road. Then walk the beach on the Gulf side for about four miles. There's a big rusted-out navigational buoy that washed up on the beach in a hurricane years ago."

"I know where that buoy is," said Jesse

"About 200 yards further west, there is a freshwater creek that runs into the Gulf. Follow that creek into the swamp, and you'll find his shack. There's a pretty well-worn path, so you shouldn't have trouble following it. Take a flashlight and watch out for gators."

"I'm not liking the sound of this little adventure at all, but I'll let Cherie decide if she wants to pursue this. Changing the subject, have you heard about anyone being shark-bitten around the island lately?”

“Now that you mentioned it, I know two different commercial fishermen who have been bitten in the past few days. Both were mullet fishing and got nailed while taking a shark out of their net. Nothing serious, just sliced them up some.”

“You haven’t heard of anybody getting attacked while in the water, just swimming or wading, have you?”

“Not a one. Why do you ask?”

“Something weird is going on, and I don’t know how to explain it.”

“How do you mean?” asked Doris.

“Without going into a lot of boring detail, the sharks I am catching for my project…”

“Must be nice when you can fish, get paid for it, and get a P… H… and D,” interrupted Gino, spelling the letters slowly.

“Will you hush and let him finish!” scolded Doris.

Jesse continued. “The behavior of the sharks around the island has changed over the past few months. To put it simply, my project is looking at how sharks behave when captured. For instance, how quickly they tire out when caught. Lately, they’ve shown a behavior change. They just don’t tire out like they used to back in the early part of the summer.”

“So, you think that fishermen are catching them and handling them too casually because the shark should be tired out, but they aren’t?” asked Doris.

“Exactly. They grab the shark to release it or maybe to take a picture, and bingo, it bites them. I even have blood chemistry data that supports this.”

“That’s interesting,” said Doris. “Why have they changed?”

Jesse sighed and shook his head. “I can’t explain it. It keeps me up at night.”

“I guess you and Cherie will be up tonight, huh?” said Gino, laughing.

“That’s enough, Gino!” said Doris with a cold stare. “He is such an ass!”

"No problem. We go at each other all the time. Well, folks, I guess I'd better get that crazy hound and head to the house. I need to try to straighten up before Cherie gets there."

"Jesse, do you have a problem straightening up these days…OUCH!" Gino winced as Doris punched him on the arm.

"No dinner for you tonight!"

CHAPTER 26

Jesse cleaned his cottage as best he could and secured Bongo on the back porch. Fortunately, Gino's kids had just about worn Bongo out, and he lay down in his bed and fell fast asleep. Jesse even had time to catch a short power nap and felt very much refreshed. A knock at the door, and he found Cherie standing at the top of the stairs holding a sack of po-boy sandwiches.

"Come on in, Cherie."

"Hi Jesse, I hope you like *Beauchamp's* po-boys." Cherie held up a white paper bag with a New Orleans Saints logo on the side. "I used to eat at Beauchamps back home, but I haven't had one in a while. I was excited to find that there was one on the island."

"Ooh, I love their po-boys."

"Which kind do you like best? I got oyster and shrimp."

"I love them both. Let's cut them in half and have one of each."

"Perfect!"

"I would give you the grand tour of the place, but there's not much to see." Jesse led the way as they went into the small kitchen, where he opened the refrigerator door. "Sorry, my drink selection is kind of limited, but I've got some Cokes and ice water. Oh, and I have milk," added Jesse as he opened the carton, took a whiff, and recoiled in revulsion. "Whew-we! Correction, I don't have milk. It appears to be a carton of dirty gym socks."

"I'll just have a Coke," said Cherie, laughing.

Jesse removed Cokes from the fridge, and the two sat at the small kitchen table. He cut the sandwiches in two, and they ate them over the paper wrapping spread on the table.

This is a really nice cottage." Cherie looked around the kitchen and out the window that faced the bayou. "You couldn't ask for a better location."

"It's very Spartan, but I enjoy the seclusion here. No one ever comes out this way unless they're looking for me. This swamp runs all the way out to the west end of the island. The best feature is the porch that looks out over the Mississippi Sound. I get some spectacular sunsets and sunrises. If you want to hang around for an hour or so, we can watch it from the porch, although Bongo is out there and he is going to be glad to see you."

"That would be nice. What's in the aquarium?" Cherie pointed to a large tank that sat upon a heavy stand and took up most of one wall in the kitchen. Colorful coral rock strategically placed on the bottom created a small reef surrounded by sand and gravel. An aerator made a low hum as it pumped air into one corner of the tank, creating a plume of fine bubbles that rose and broke the water's surface.

"Not a lot at the moment. A couple of small fish and a large electric ray that we caught recently."

"An electric ray! Seriously?" Cherie rose from the table and bent over to look into the tank. "Where is it?"

"He's right there." Jesse stood beside her and pointed at the partially buried ray in the sand.

"Wow! I would never have seen him if you hadn't pointed him out."

"They are masters of camouflage. They hide in the sand, stun small fish and crustaceans with their electric organs, and then scarf them down. I named him Sparky."

Cherie giggled. "Original name. Are they dangerous?"

"Well, that one shocked Bongo repeatedly when we caught it, and he survived. However, it was not pleasant for him. I've been shocked by them a few times and I've suffered no serious damage…no serious damage…no serious damage." Jesse grimaced and jerked his head sideways each time he repeated the phrase in a mock nervous twitch.

Cherie held her hand to her mouth and laughed.

"But in all seriousness, for one that size, if you took a shock directly to the chest, it could throw your heart into arrhythmia."

"Like a heart attack?"

"Kind of. It would probably feel more like your heart was not working efficiently. If you already have a heart condition, it could kill you. It would certainly get your attention. This tank is small for him, but I won't keep him long. I enjoy observing fish behavior."

"Very cool!"

"Let's finish our sandwiches," Jesse said as they returned to the table.

"These po-boys are so good. It takes me back to my childhood in Baton Rouge."

"Do you go back there often?"

"I visit a couple of times a year. Unfortunately, the neighborhood has changed so much that it is hardly recognizable. Hurricanes, urban sprawl, and economic downturns all took their toll on the area."

"I guess few places stay the same anymore," said Jesse sadly.

"What about you? You've never told me much about yourself."

"Well, it wasn't always easy for me. I was born a poor black child."

"Uh…what?!"

"Sorry, I couldn't resist. Have you ever seen the Steve Martin movie called *The Jerk*? That's a line from the movie."

"I know Steve Martin from *Saturday Night Live,* but I haven't seen that movie."

"It's a dumb movie, but I enjoy zany humor and Steve Martin is one of the zaniest. He's my favorite comedian."

"I agree. He's crazy."

"I'm from a small town in Alabama called Sweetwater, about two hours north of Mobile, way out in the country. It's barely a wide spot in the road, a single stoplight, a cotton gin, and a quick-stop store. Not much happens there. My dad was the postman there, and my mom was a school teacher at Sweetwater High. We weren't poor, but didn't have a lot of money for "frivolities", as my dad used to call them."

"What did you do for entertainment in Sweetwater?"

"Hunting, fishing, playing sports, skinny-dipping in the Tombigbee River, nothing terribly exciting."

"It actually sounds pretty nice to me."

"We had some good times. I can say this: Sweetwater hasn't changed much since I was a kid. It seems that time has stood still there."

"How did someone from small-town Alabama end up working on a PhD in Oceanography?

"I don't tell a lot of people this, but it was Jacques Cousteau."

"You mean the marine biologist?"

"Yes. He did the television series called the *Undersea World of Jacques Cousteau* back in the 60s. I was in front of the television every Monday evening when that show came on. For an 8-year-old who had never seen the ocean, it was fascinating."

"Ok, yeah, I vaguely remember that show. Wasn't his boat called the *Calypso*?"

"That was it. The *Calypso* was nothing like our research vessel. For example, you would not believe what is involved if you wanted to take a shower on the *Up-Chuck*."

"I can imagine. So, what was it that Ross said about you being dead?"

"He was exaggerating, as you might have guessed, but I know it spooked them. What happened is we got the longline caught in the propeller of the boat. I went under the boat to cut the line out."

"This doesn't sound good," said Cherie, shaking her head.

"Well, there's more. While I was down there, a killer whale approached the boat and scarfed down a yellowfin tuna that was caught on our longline. I saw it bite the tuna in two. The crew thought it was me when they saw blood in the water. That whale was so focused on the tuna that it totally ignored me. I was never in any real danger."

"Really? No real danger? But they call them killer whales!"

"Because they kill and eat fish, seals, dolphins, and whales, but there has never been a case of a killer whale attacking and eating a human in the wild. By the way, they aren't actually whales; they are more closely related to dolphins."

"OK. But next time, let someone else go in the water."

"I will," said Jesse, sensing Cherie's concern.

"Changing the subject, I spoke with Chief East yesterday."

"What about?"

"He was concerned about an apparently accidental death on the island. A fellow was killed while driving his car when he ran off the road and struck a cypress tree. There was massive blood loss. Far more blood loss than you would expect from the injuries he suffered."

"Does he think there is some connection with the Crimson Tide death?"

"He doesn't know. That is why he wanted to talk to me."

"Did the body show the same kind of tissue destruction that was present in the Crimson Tide. Did you get tissue samples?"

"No one thought it was anything other than an accident, and, unfortunately, the body was cremated."

"Crap! What are your thoughts on it?"

"The massive blood loss that Chief East described is troubling. I told him to contact me if there were any other unusual fatalities on the island and to limit his exposure to any victims. And Jesse, you also need to be aware of anyone around you who might show signs of illness."

"I will. So, if that accident was caused by some infectious disease, wouldn't those who handled the bodies be infected?"

"Possibly. I've already contacted the EMTs, the Coroner's office, the funeral home, and the family of the deceased. None of them are ill. I asked them to limit their exposure to others if possible and immediately report any unusual health problems. That's about all I can do at this point. This is so frustrating." Cherie stared at the kitchen floor in troubled contemplation.

"Hey, you're doing a great job!" Jesse reached across the table and gently touched her on the arm.

"You don't know how much I appreciate that, Jesse! We get little encouragement from our supervisors."

"Wait!" exclaimed Jesse suddenly. He struck the side of his head with his palm as if dislodging a thought. "Something just occurred to me. As we came in this morning, the Coast Guard was trying to stop a boat that was running full speed in a tight circle. Whoever was at the wheel must have fallen overboard. It's not unusual for a boat with an outboard to go into a tight circle like that if no one is there to hold it on a straight course."

"That's strange, but what's your point?"

"I put the binoculars on it, and the inside of the boat was covered in bright red blood. I just assumed it was fish blood."

"You think the individual on the boat died suddenly and fell overboard?"

"It's a possibility. There is no chance of finding that body, however. The sharks in these waters are gonna make fast work of it, particularly if he went overboard bleeding like that."

"I'll get in touch with the Coast Guard when we get back to see if a body was found. I also need to warn them about blood exposure."

"You might find this interesting as well. I was talking to Gino Patronas earlier, and he said that we should talk to Crazy Joe."

"I don't know either of those people."

"Gino is a friend of mine, and Crazy Joe is a hermit who lives in the swamp that stretches all the way to the end of the island. It's a continuation of this bayou that surrounds us here. You will eventually meet Gino; he's a real character. Few people have ever met Crazy Joe. Gino said that he knows everything that goes on out on the west end. He might have seen the person who went on board the Crimson Tide."

"If he could have seen something, then I want to talk to him."

"I knew you were going to say that. After sunset, we'll see if we can find him. We'll have to walk some distance down the beach, and Gino said to use plenty of mosquito repellent."

"I've got my tennis shoes on so I'm ready to go when you are."

"Let's catch that sunset," said Jesse as they rose from their seats and walked to the porch, "and then we can go find Joe."

CHAPTER 27

Many of the locals on the island knew about Crazy Joe, the hermit who lived in the deepest part of the swamp that covered most of the west end. Where he came from or why he chose to eke out a living in that mosquito-infested, swamp was anyone's guess. The oldest residents recall seeing him wading the shallows barefoot, using his toes to feel for oysters, shucking and downing them on the spot. Joe was a descendant of the *Biloxi* tribe of Native Americans that once populated a portion of coastal Alabama and Mississippi. Decimated by smallpox, Joe may have been the only remaining member of his tribe.

Joe was small and thin, with a full head of dark hair, a black flashing eye, and chestnut brown skin. A mishap with a bull gator left him with a scar across his cheek and a milky, sightless left eye. During summer, he could be seen in tattered clothing and no shoes, sporting a hat fashioned from Palmetto fronds. During winters, which were relatively mild on the island, he wore buckskin leggings and an old bear-skin robe of indeterminate origin. Joe's most prized possession was a weathered pirogue that he had fashioned from a downed cypress tree. A tree in which he had sheltered when Hurricane Frederick made landfall on the island. Using a hand line, he could be seen paddling the Mississippi Sound or the Gulf of Mexico, landing catfish, croaker, and seatrout.

Despite having only one functioning eye, Joe saw everything that happened on the west end of the island. His awareness of the island led to him enjoying celebrity status among the locals when he quickly paddled his pirogue to the rescue of a child who had been carried into deep water by a rip current. He pulled the child into his pirogue, carried her back to shore, and paddled away without a word. Like the Mad Potter of Biloxi and Prince Mongo of Memphis, Joe was one of those peculiar individuals that communities in the southern U.S. tolerated and even proudly embraced in some cases.

With windows down, the damp night air rushed into the El Camino, and the gentle strains of Jimmy Buffett's *Tin Cup Chalice* filled the cab as they headed toward the road's western end. Ancient live-oak trees deep in shadow whizzed by along the north side of the road while sparkling gulf waters, interrupted only by the lights of an occasional offshore gas rig, stretched out to the south. The sunset they had watched together was now just a faint splash of magenta on the western horizon.

"So how long do you think it will take to get there on foot?" asked Cherie as they headed toward the road's western end. Cherie put her feet up on the hard metal dash and reveled in the cool, salt air that caressed her bare legs and arms.

"I am guessing about an hour and a half. There is an old navigational buoy on the beach about four miles west of here." Jesse pulled off the road and parked the El Camino on the shoulder. "A short distance beyond that is a creek that runs from the swamp into the gulf. We'll have to follow a path along that creek to find Joe's shack."

With flashlights in hand and covered in mosquito repellent, the two walked across the dunes and down to the harder beach surface, just out of reach of the surf, to begin their trek. Ghost crabs, startled from their nocturnal foraging by the illumination, darted along the upper beach and dove into their netherworld burrows. Shallow, long-period undulations coming in across the gulf created small waves that broke suddenly right at the shoreline with a barely audible "whump".

Look at that!" Jesse pointed toward the water's edge. "The bioluminescence is always strong at this time of year." From each breaking wave, a blue-green glow could be seen stretching along the water's edge into the distance.

"Oh, that is so beautiful! Those are bioluminescent dinoflagellates. I've read about them but never seen them," observed Cherie excitedly.

"There is something about the waters around Dauphin Island that creates the strongest bioluminescence I have ever seen," said Jesse. "It's amazing. Billions and billions of tiny microorganisms get jostled around each time a wave breaks and, just like a firefly, they flash that bluish light. It's the mechanical disturbance of their cell membranes that triggers them to glow. There's an enzyme called luciferase that reacts with a substrate called luciferin and a byproduct of that reaction is…" Jesse stopped and cleared his throat when he realized he had drifted off into nerd mode. "You want to wade in the shallows here? It's very cool to splash around in blue-green glowing water."

"Is it safe?"

"Oh sure. Just do the stingray shuffle so you don't get nailed by a ray."

"What's the stingray shuffle?"

"If you ever got scolded for dragging your feet when you were a kid, that is exactly what you want to do here. Walk like Frankenstein. That way, you won't step on top of a stingray that is buried in the sand. If you drag your feet and your foot encounters a stingray, it will flush it out of the sand, and it will quickly dart away. If you stepped on top of one, it's gonna stab you with the barb that's on its tail, and believe me, it's excruciatingly painful, and we would have to go to the clinic."

"Stingray shuffle it is."

Kicking off their shoes, the two walked down to the water's edge.

"I am very comfortable in the water, but something about being in the water at *night* unnerves me." It was clear that Cherie was excited and anxious as she stayed close to Jesse and unconsciously took him by the hand.

"It's perfectly safe. We're only going to be about knee-deep." Jesse was now equally excited, but not for the same reason.

The bioluminescence did not disappoint, and hand-in-hand, they carefully stepped into the water. Like an artist's brush stroke, Cherie swept her hand across the surface of the water, leaving a blue-green streak of light. She kicked and watched her legs and feet glow.

"I've never seen anything like this. This is amazing!"

Jesse playfully splashed Cherie with blue-green glowing water. Cherie retaliated with a torrent of water that soaked Jesse's shirt.

"Ok, you win." Jesse good-naturedly held his hands up in surrender. "We don't need to get soaking wet before making that long walk down the island."

"Look, look, look!" said an increasingly excited Cherie as she drew closer to Jesse. An unidentified sea creature shrouded in ghostly blue-green light swam slowly by. "What do you think that was?"

"It was definitely a fish, probably just a small shark. Sharks are very active just after sundown, foraging for food in the shallows. All our splashing probably attracted it. It likely thought there was a struggling fish."

Jesse's attention was drawn up the beach as a larger glowing organism could be seen moving in their direction.

"Here comes something big. Let's move closer to the shore."

Standing now in ankle-deep water, a large object moved into view, its pectoral fins undulating like an oversized butterfly.

"See how flat it is," said Jesse, pointing. "It's either a very large stingray or perhaps a devil ray. It could also be a small manta ray, but mantas are not common around here."

"This definitely goes in my memory journal," said Cherie, completely mesmerized by the experience.

"We'd better head toward Joe's shack. We don't want to be out here too late."

CHAPTER 28

It was pushing midnight when they arrived at the creek leading to Joe's shack. Jesse had chosen to remain barefoot but thought it best to put his shoes back on before going into the bayou. He sat on a driftwood log, brushed sand from his feet as best he could, and laced up his sneakers.

"Not meaning to frighten you, but there are a couple of things to be aware of in the bayou. There are plenty of gators here, so when near the water, keep your eyes open. The other thing is cottonmouths. This time of year, they can be rather belligerent and don't like giving up their ground. Just watch where you are stepping."

"Gird your loins!" said Cherie nervously, smiling. To Jesse's delight, Cherie took his hand again as they headed down the path.

The change from the wind-blown expanse of the ocean and open beach to the suffocating atmosphere of the bayou was like entering an alien world. Everything about this environment was strange and threatening, particularly at night. Beards of Spanish moss adorned the limbs of ancient, gnarled live oak and cypress trees that clung to the banks of the blackwater creek. A thin fog hung motionless in the air, giving their flashlight beams a laser-like appearance. Nocturnal flying insects, pursued by the occasional bat, fluttered through the light. The humidity and smell from centuries of decomposing organic material permeated the air. A cacophony of frog calls and buzzing insects seemed to come from everywhere.

"I love frog choruses. It reminds me of night-fishing on the Tombigbee River back home."

"I had no idea it could be so loud! It's almost too loud to have a conversation."

"I've been in some swamps back home where the frog calls were so loud it hurt your ears. Listen!" Jesse paused, cocked his head, and pointed to the east, a faraway look in his eyes. "That's my favorite frog call."

"Which one?" Cherie cocked her head and listened. "There are so many."

"It sounds like a plunk on a loose banjo string. Hear it?"

"OK, yeah, I hear it now."

"It's called the banjo frog. I hear them around my cottage on some evenings."

"You really know a great deal about the animal world," said Cherie as they continued along the path.

"I know a little about a lot of things," countered Jesse. "What's the old saying, Jack of all trades, master of none?"

"I don't think that applies to you, Jesse."

"Well, I appreciate the compliment."

As they plunged deeper into the bayou, the path became narrower and drew closer to the water's edge, requiring them to step over large cypress knees, aerial roots protruding from the ground. With a croak and a plop, frogs by the hundreds escaped into the water as they approached. Further along, they found themselves standing on the edge of a shallow lake, the obvious source of the creek.

"This is incredible frog habitat! They are everywhere."

"And, no gators so far," said Cherie.

"Shine your light across the surface of the lake," suggested Jesse as they stood on that Venusian shore. "You see all those red dots out there?" Jesse shielded his light to reduce the glare.

"I do, what are those?"

"Those are gator eyes. This swamp is teeming with them."

"Holy smokes! How many do you think are out there?"

At that moment, Jesse turned to face Cherie and looked into her shining eyes. He reached across with his left hand and placed it firmly on her right arm.

"Cherie," said Jesse softly, "I need to tell you something very important."

Jesse's heart was racing, and he could feel the blood pulsing through Cherie's arm. He drew very close. The scent of gardenias that always accompanied Cherie was strong despite the odor of the surrounding swamp. Jesse spoke quietly into Cherie's ear.

"I need you to be very still."

With one fluid motion, Jesse pulled his knife from its scabbard with his right hand and, using his left hand, simultaneously pulled Cherie away from the cottonmouth that lay curled, ready to strike at her feet. Cherie, unsure of what was happening, shouted. Jesse flung the knife, and the blade pierced the head of the viper, pinning the creature to the ground. It thrashed wildly, attempting to free itself.

"Oh my God!" Cherie was now in Jesse's arms, trying to come to grips with what had just happened.

"Are you OK?"

"I think so. You saved my life!" Cherie was now breathing heavily and perspiring. The thought of how close she was to the viper sent chills down her spine. Jesse released her and bent over to examine the writhing snake.

"Not really. If it had bitten you, we would have had to get you to the clinic, and that long walk back would have been very unpleasant for both of us. The bites are very painful and, without medical attention, cause tissue necrosis, but it would likely not be fatal. My grandfather was bitten on the leg by a large cottonmouth. He survived with no medical attention, although he had a limp for the rest of his life. Besides, vipers often use a "dry strike". They don't inject venom because they don't need to waste it on a large animal like a human. They want to get your attention to let you know that you need to move away."

"You hit that snake dead center on the top of the head! That was amazing."

"It was a big target and a short distance. I've practiced that knife throw at least a thousand times in preparing for competition. However, I've never thrown at a big cottonmouth. Hated to kill it, but I was not going to take a chance in this situation. It's too remote out here for us to risk injury."

Jesse withdrew his knife, severed the head, and wiped the blade on the mossy earth.

"We can stop here for a bit if you need to collect yourself. It can't be much further."

"I'm OK," insisted Cherie. "I'd rather get away from that snake. Let's push on."

A few additional steps along the path brought them to a clearing near the bank of the shallow lake. Items scavenged from the waters around the island were neatly arranged around the clearing: driftwood, old lumber, pieces of corrugated fiberglass, plastic buckets, bottles of every kind, weathered articles of clothing, old tires, barnacle-encrusted fishing rods and reels, and piles of oyster shells. Among the twisted branches and hanging

Spanish moss, Joe's shack emerged from the mist like an apparition. The organic appearance of the small abode suggested that it had grown out of the swamp itself. Set upon large stones, it was constructed from weathered, rough-hewn cypress boards. Rusted pieces of corrugated metal formed the gabled roof. A wisp of thin, blue smoke rose from the stovepipe that sat on the roof. A single window, apparently salvaged from an abandoned shrimp boat, revealed a dim light coming from inside. Above the brightly painted blue front door, hung a large, bleached alligator skull. Other trophies adorned the exterior: deer antlers, a large sea turtle shell, the toothy snout of a sawfish, shark jaws, and an assortment of stark white skulls of various species.

"You think this is the place?" whispered Jesse jokingly under his breath, unsure of how they would be received by Crazy Joe.

"I suppose. He seems to have an interest in comparative anatomy," observed Cherie.

Jesse smiled as they cautiously approached. As they drew closer, the care with which the collection of animal skulls had been prepared and placed became apparent. Every bone intact, cleaned of all tissue, and arranged along the weathered wall of the shack.

"Wow!" Jesse's light panned across the menagerie that hung before him. "This is amazing. These skulls are museum-quality work. He put a lot of effort into this."

"It's impressive if you are into skulls."

"He's even got them arranged by groups." Jesse was now paying no attention to Cherie at all. "Notice that the shark jaws and some large fish skulls are grouped, the sea turtle and alligator skulls are together, these are all mammal skulls, raccoon, possum, coyote, etc., and this dolphin, along with a weird-looking skull that I can't identify, are together. Whoa, look at this!" Jesse closely examined the unusual skull. "I think this is a freaking Manatee. I've never seen a Manatee skull before."

"We'd better see if Joe is inside," said a disinterested Cherie.

"You're right. Enough with the skulls."

They approached the door, Jesse stepped up onto a cinder block that served as a step, and knocked softly. "Mr. Joe, are you there? Mr. Joe." No response from the inside. "Gino Patronas told

us where to find you. We just wanted to ask you some questions."
Still no sound from the shack.

"Crap," said Cherie disappointed, "he's not here."

"Well, he's probably nearby. We'll wait for a little while, but I can't be out here all night."

"Neither can I," agreed Cherie.

"WHY ARE YOU HERE?" A deep, growling voice came out of the darkness, directly behind them.

CHAPTER 29

"AHHH," screamed both Jesse and Cherie as they quickly turned their flashlights onto the shadowy figure behind them. Jesse instinctively stepped in front of Cherie. There before them stood Crazy Joe, a twisted walking stick in one hand and a headless cottonmouth, the very one that Jesse had just slain, in the other. Joe was barefoot and shirtless, wearing tattered pants tied up with a length of rope. A small carved wooden figure of a dolphin hung from a leather thong around his neck. He was as dark as the black water that oozed from his bayou. All muscle and sinew, there was not an ounce of fat on his wiry frame. Jet black hair with threads of grey, a leathery face like a well-used baseball glove, he peered suspiciously at them with his good eye while his sightless eye glowed bluish, not unlike the bioluminescence they had just enjoyed. Joe cast an evil eye first at Jesse and then turned his gaze toward Cherie. Like storm clouds parting to reveal a clear night sky, a huge smile replaced the scowl when Joe saw Cherie.

"Oh man, you scared the crap out of us," said Jesse. "My name is Jesse, and this is Cherie."

"No," said Joe.

"What?" asked Jesse, confused.

"Your name is Shark, and she is Night Flower," Joe stepped closer to them.

"Ok." Jesse stepped back and cast a confused look toward Cherie. "Anyway, we are sorry for disturbing you out here, but Gino Patronus, I think you know him, gave us directions on how to find you."

"I know Crab," said Joe, still smiling and staring at Cherie. "He's a good man."

"We just wanted to ask you some questions. We won't take up a lot of your time. You're probably busy with…uh…swampy kinds of stuff. Ooof!" said Jesse as Cherie elbowed him in the ribs.

"Come!" He walked past them brusquely and impaled the snake on a spike nailed into the wall of his shack. "This is good food," said Joe, pointing at the snake. He opened the shack door and went in.

"Are you comfortable with this?" asked Jesse as they stood alone outside the shack.

"Absolutely! I didn't come all this way for nothing."

As they entered, Joe sat on the floor before a wood stove fashioned from a small steel drum. After feeding a few sticks of fat-wood onto the smoldering coals, the flames lit the room with a comforting glow. The contents of the room took both of them by surprise. Hand-crafted items lined the walls: a table made of burnished oak, a straight back chair, and a wash stand that the Amish would've been proud of. Heavy baskets woven from palmetto fronds and delicate ones from long-leaf pine needles hung from the walls. Fashioned from local clays, various-sized pots, bowls, and animal effigies sat on the table and floor, along with an assortment of animal wood carvings.

Joe pulled a wooden chair away from the wall and dropped it beside Cherie. He sat on the floor in front of them and crossed his legs like a Hindu swami.

"Sit."

Jesse sat on the weathered, wooden floor next to Cherie. As Cherie took her seat, she was surprised by the quality of workmanship in the chair upon which she sat. Fashioned from driftwood, a variety of individual pieces had been intricately woven together to mimic the twisted roots of the trees along the bayou.

"This chair is amazing!" Cherie ran her hand over the polished armrests of a genuine work of art. "This workmanship is stunning. Did you make this?"

"Yes," replied Joe, who was now grinning from ear to ear. He had yet to take his eyes off of Cherie. Joe got up, went to a corner of his shack, took something from a palmetto basket, and handed it to Cherie. "For you." Joe returned to his cross-legged spot on the floor.

"What's this?" said a surprised Cherie. Her eyes widened as she carefully held an exquisitely carved duck in her hands.

"Wow!" said Jesse, admiring Cherie's gift. "That's an exact copy of a hooded merganser."

"This is beautiful. But Mr. Joe, I can't take this." Cherie leaned forward to try to return the work of art to him.

"No." Joe pushed it back to her. "It's yours."

"Cherie, take the gift. We don't want to offend Mr. Joe," suggested Jesse quietly.

"Well, it's two against one," said Cherie as she turned the wooden bird over in her hands, admiring it from various angles. "Thank you very much. This is superb workmanship. I know exactly where I will put this back home."

"Mr. Joe, did you make all of these things?" asked Jesse as he motioned around the room.

"Yes," said Joe, still smiling and following Cherie's every move. "Time for food. Wait here." Joe gave Jesse a stern look, sprang from his seat, and went outside.

"I don't think Joe likes me much," whispered Jesse, feeling a bit jealous, "but does he ever have a crush on you? He has yet to stop looking at you."

"Oh, he's just being hospitable."

"Oh no, it's more than just hospitality."

"We should have brought something for him," said Cherie, still caressing her gift. "Jesse, if I bought you another one, would you give him your knife? I'll bet he could use it."

"Sure. I'm not personally attached to this one. I have several more at home, so you don't have to get me another one."

"Joe's an artist by anyone's standards. Look at these things." Cherie was still marveling over the room full of Joe's creations.

"He is talented. He's nuts, but talented."

Joe returned from outside and lit a piece of kindling from the stove.

"Come," said Joe as he carefully held the burning wood. "It's time for blue-fire."

Jesse looked at Cherie confusedly and shrugged his shoulders as they followed him outside. Taking the now-skinned cottonmouth from the spike, he threw it over his shoulder and walked across the clearing down a path deeper into the bayou. Jesse and Cherie switched on their flashlights.

"No," said Joe, pointing at their artificial lighting.

"Where are we going?" asked Jesse as they doused their lights. He received no reply.

They went deeper into the bayou to a place where the sounds of the night were even more intense. Jesse recognized several species of frogs by their calls, and one species he could not identify. Arriving at a small clearing, Joe stopped and removed a piece of scrap metal that lay across a small artesian well. Water from deep in the bowels of the swamp bubbled up and coursed away into the dark bayou. The ground around the spring was dry and well-packed, suggesting that this was a spot that was often used. Joe took a cross-legged seat on the ground at the edge of the spring as he directed them to sit on a fallen tree that lay on the other side. The light from the burning stick of wood danced across Joe's weathered face.

"Any idea what is going on?" whispered Cherie, leaning closer to Jesse.

"I haven't the foggiest."

Joe held the flaming wood just above the waters of the spring. Gas no longer held in check by the pressure of the overlying land and water, burst into blue flames with a "whoosh" and danced hypnotically across the top of the spring. Jesse and Cherie recoiled and gasped in unison.

"What the heck!" said Jesse.

"Blue-fire," said Joe matter-of-factly. "It's pretty, like Night Flower." Joe smiled at Cherie, flashing his perfect, white teeth.

The surreal scene spellbound Jesse and Cherie. Blue flames rose into the air, died, and rose again. Large balls of blue flame ignited, rose skyward, and then disappeared as the gas burned slowly away. Tongues of blue flame licked upward. Hundreds of tiny bubbles ignited with a barely audible "pop" just at the water's surface.

"It's a natural methane seep!" Cherie, transfixed, stared into the flaming waters. "I've heard of these but never seen one. It's not surprising. There's a reason for all those gas rigs around the island. They're tapping into huge reservoirs of methane below the ground. I am surprised that this one is still releasing gas at the surface. Eventually, this one will die out as the gas is removed."

"Blue fire," said Joe, smiling. "I am glad you like it."

There was nothing said between them for the next few moments as they watched the dancing flames, listened to the sounds of swamp creatures calling in the night, and smelled the wet earth of the ageless bayou. Joe continued to smile at Cherie.

"Mr. Joe," said Cherie, finally breaking the silence, "you've been very gracious, and Jesse would like to give you something."

Jesse stood, removed the knife and scabbard from his belt, and handed them to Joe. Surprised by this act of generosity, something that Joe rarely experienced, he stood and took the knife in both hands. Removing the knife from its scabbard, he held it close to his good eye and examined it along its length. The blue light glinted off the polished blade, and Joe's face beamed with approval.

"I hope you can use it. A man should have a good knife, and that one has served me well."

"You're a good man." Joe untied his rope belt and threaded the knife scabbard through it. He placed his hand on the hilt and struck a manly pose. Joe seemed to smile even larger, if that was possible.

"It looks good on you," complimented Cherie.

"Mr. Joe," asked Jesse, "I am just curious, why did you call me a shark?"

Joe placed his index finger against his nose and said, "shark".

"You mean you can actually smell the shark on me?" asked Jesse.

"No. Not on you...*in you*," said Joe, still admiring his knife.

Jesse looked at Cherie again, puzzled.

"Sharks have changed," said Joe.

"What did you say?" asked Jesse, shocked and unsure of Joe's pronouncement.

"Sharks are acting different."

"How do you mean?"

"Different," was all Joe said.

"Mr. Joe, if you don't mind, I have a couple of questions." Cherie removed her small notebook and pencil from her back pocket.

"About the boat?" asked Joe, his attention now torn between his new knife and Cherie.

"You saw the shrimp boat that was on the beach a few days ago?" asked Cherie, optimistic that Joe was aware of the Crimson Tide.

"Yes." Joe returned to his seat on the ground.

"Did you go on board?" asked Jesse.

"No."

"Did you happen to see anyone on a motorcycle near the shrimp boat?"

"Yes. A young man."

"Could you describe him?"

"Brown hair, white shirt, brown shorts, red motorcycle."

"Did he go on the boat?" asked Cherie.

"Yes."

"I knew it," said Cherie. "About how long did he stay on board?"

"Not a long time, not a short time."

"Did you see anything else?"

"Yes." Joe paused, his demeanor changing.

"What did you see?"

Joe paused, placed the knife back in its sheath, and closed his eyes. "Death," said Joe ominously. A frown replaced his smile, and darkness fell across his face. The wind picked up and sighed through the treetops. Brown cypress needles rained down around them and burned in reds and yellows as the blue fire consumed them. The calling frogs and denizens of the bayou suddenly fell silent. Like some lonesome night creature, a foghorn sounded from a distant gas rig.

"You saw death on the boat?" asked Cherie as a chill swept through her.

"No."

"Mr. Joe, I don't understand," said Cherie.

"I saw death here." Joe pointed a weathered finger into the blue fire that now burned with heightened abandon, the flames twisting and writhing. He seemed almost entranced as he leaned closer to the blue flames; the flickering light danced across his darkened face.

"You saw it in the fire?" asked Jesse, puzzled.

"Yes." Joe looked up into their faces. "More death is coming. You should leave the island."

"Wha…what do you mean?" asked Cherie nervously. "Are we in danger?"

"I cannot say. But now it's time for eating," announced Joe as he took the snake carcass and began to cut it into steaks for roasting.

The reptile repast was not to Cherie's liking, although, to be polite, she feigned eating some of the reptile while surreptitiously tossing it into the bayou. Joe consumed the snake like it was Prime Rib. Throwing caution to the wind, Jesse put a sizeable piece in his mouth and chewed away.

"This is mighty good cottonmouth." Jesse grinned while speaking through a mouth full of snake. "Don't let me leave without getting your recipe! Speaking of cottonmouth," whispered Jesse to Cherie, "that's exactly what eating this is like." Jesse swallowed hard, choking down the reptile.

"Mr. Joe," Cherie rose from her seat, "we are most grateful for the hospitality you've extended to us, but it's late and we need to be getting back to town. I want to thank you again for the beautiful gift. That was very thoughtful of you!"

Jesse stood and stretched, the muscles in his back feeling like an over-tightened rubber band. "Ohhh, pardon my groaning, but my back has been acting up lately. I have wrangled too many sharks and launched too many boats lately. I wish there was something I could do about it."

Joe sprang from his seat and caught a surprised Jesse from behind in a bear hug around his chest.

"Wha...what are you doing?" exclaimed Jesse.

Joe lifted a bewildered Jesse off the ground and bounced him in the air twice. An audible "crack" was heard on each bounce. He released Jesse.

"Whoa!" A wide-eyed Jesse stretched his back while turning at the waist. "The pain is gone. That feels so much better! I guess I'm gonna have to use you as my chiropractor from now on. Man, that feels better!"

"We can go now." Joe placed the scrap metal over the spring to extinguish the flames and left the clearing. They followed him back to the cabin, and Joe went inside but returned immediately.

"This is for you." Joe placed a coin in Jesse's hand. "Can you buy another knife with this?"

His mouth agape, Jesse held the coin up to the light. "This is a gold coin! I don't know coins, but this looks like a Spanish doubloon. Good grief, it's dated 1788!"

CHAPTER 30

"Can I see it?" Jesse handed the coin to Cherie. "It's probably just a Mardi Gras doubloon. One of those trinkets that they throw from the floats during parades."

"Feel how heavy it is. If you hit someone with that, it would knock them out. Mardi Gras doubloons are all made of plastic or aluminum. This is not aluminum. If this is real, it would be worth a lot of money."

"No use for money," said Joe, uninterested.

"Where did you get it?" asked Jesse.

"Found it."

"Where did you find it?"

"In the water. There were lots of them."

"Geez-Louise, you may have found a treasure. Could you take us where you found them?"

"Maybe. Can you buy another knife with it?"

"Joe, if this is real, I can buy a truckload of knives. But I can't accept it. What I will do is take it and find out its value for you. If it's real, I'll let you know how much it's worth, and you can do with it what you want."

"Money is not important. We can go now."

Joe escorted them back to the beach, where they said their goodbyes.

"Thank you, Mr. Joe," said Cherie, extending her hand.

Joe took her hand in both of his and held it carefully like a wounded bird. "Come back anytime you want." Joe smiled broadly.

"I'll come back and let you know what I find out about this coin," said Jesse.

"You and Night Flower," insisted Joe, still holding Cherie's hand. He was giving no indication that he was going to let it go.

"Yes, she'll come with me."

"Goodbye!" Joe released Cherie and disappeared back into the bayou.

The walk back to civilization allowed the duo to discuss the events of the evening. With the moon low on the horizon and the bioluminescence still strong, they puzzled over various things that had happened.

"Joe is definitely odd," observed Jesse while they plodded along. "He is a man of few words. Getting information out of him is like pulling teeth!"

"Living out there by yourself for most, perhaps all of your life, would tend to make you a bit odd," said Cherie. "With all that time on his hands, he's made some amazing things." Cherie held her cherished gift up to admire it with her flashlight. "Actually, I think he is a sweet man."

"He is sure sweet on you, that's for sure. If I had gone there alone, he probably would have fed me to the gators."

"No, he wouldn't!"

"I'm kidding. But I can tell you this, my back hasn't felt this good in weeks." Jesse was almost skipping along the beach. "Do you think you could perform that maneuver on my back, Cherie?"

"I could try, but I'm afraid there is too much difference in altitude between us."

"I wonder if Joe may have stumbled across the treasure that Jean Lafitte supposedly buried on the island 200 years ago?" Joe gripped the heavy coin in his shorts pocket, afraid to release it for fear it might somehow be lost again to history.

"I am going to predict that it's just a worthless trinket."

"Maybe." However, he had a hunch that this was no Mardi Gras bauble. "This entire evening has been freaky."

"Absolutely freaked me out when he said more death is coming," added Cherie.

"For real." Jesse picked up a piece of driftwood and tossed it into the ocean. "Was that a prediction about what was going to happen on the island?"

"I hope not," said Cherie, shaking her head. "But it could already be happening, and we just don't know it. The strange death and the boat with no one on board were disturbing. As strange as this excursion was, it was worth it. We now have confirmation of someone going on board the boat after it ran aground. We know it was a red motorcycle, and we have some details about the person. When I get back, I'll begin running down the people who have a motorcycle on the island. Chief East can no doubt help me with that."

"When I get back, I'm going to crash like a 747. I am exhausted."

"I wish I could take the day off, but I'll be at it again in about," Cherie glanced at her watch, "five hours. Oh boy! It's gonna be a long day!"

"He called me shark. How did he know that I work with sharks? Cherie, do I smell like shark sometimes?" Jesse was often concerned that he might offend folks after having to dissect sharks that sometimes smelled particularly strong.

"I've never smelled anything offensive on you, Jesse."

Jesse shifted into his marine biologist role, a persona that typically bored people. However, Cherie seemed to be interested in all things biological, one of the many things he loved about her. "Sharks concentrate an unusual compound in their blood and body fluids, and when the flesh spoils, it smells really bad."

"In fact, it's two compounds, urea and trimethylamine-oxide or TMAO."

"Exactly. Cherie, you never fail to impress me!"

"I learned about that in high school."

"It's even more impressive that you've retained it this long. All I can remember from high school is when Bobby McCormick up-chucked a sloppy joe right in the middle of Mrs. Budinger's lecture on the pancreas."

"That's disgusting!"

"Yes, it was, but it got us out of class, albeit briefly, while the janitor cleaned it up. Spoiled shark literally smells like the urinal at the Neptune Club. I once had to dissect over twenty rancid sharks, and it was nearly impossible to get the smell off my hands and out of my clothes. It had to *wear* off my hands."

"Bacterial breakdown of urea and TMAO in shark flesh releases volatile amine compounds with lovely names like cadaverine and putrescine," said Cherie. "Those are what smell so bad."

"I tell you when shark meat goes bad…it goes BAD!" said Jesse. "An interesting side-note. Scientists were unable to explain how sharks could survive with incredibly high levels of urea, concentrations that would kill humans, until it was discovered that TMAO cancels out the toxic effects of urea."

"I didn't know that."

It was only recently discovered."

"There are so many things about sharks that are just fascinating. But he didn't say he smelled sharks on you, he said he smelled sharks *in you*," observed Cherie. "What did that mean?"

"It means he's a bit nuts. But some of that stuff was strangely relevant to what's been going on. He said that sharks were acting differently around the island. You can't get him to explain anything, but I'll bet it's the same thing we've already observed. Bionic sharks; biting folks, fighting like mad, never tiring out. He's probably caught his share of sharks and noticed the change."

"I still can't get over the gift he gave me," said Cherie.

"The best thing about it for me was that fire-roasted, cottonmouth snake dinner. It's hard to find good cottonmouth these days."

"Oh yeah, that was great."

"I can now add that to my list of weird things that I've eaten."

"How many weird things have you voluntarily consumed?"

"Oh, the list is not extensive, but certainly more than the average person. Sea turtle, snapping turtle, iguana, various species of sharks, barbecued armadillo, eel, a bunch of supposedly inedible fish, rabbit, squirrel, groundhog, possum, raccoon, agouti, that's about all I can recall at the moment."

"I'm afraid to ask, but what the heck is an agouti?"

"Sounds delicious, doesn't it? An agouti is a very large rodent species that is common in South and Central America. I ate it in Costa Rica, prepared in a spicy stew. It was delicious."

"So, it's a big rat?"

"Basically."

Yeah, that sounds delicious!"

"There's our ride," Jesse pointed down the beach at the El Camino. "Your chariot awaits, my lady! With a sweep of his hand, Jesse executed a gentlemanly bow.

"You're too kind, Sir Jesse!"

CHAPTER 31

Marcel liked to open his shop before sunrise to catch those early morning fishermen angling for speckled trout and redfish in the backwaters around Bayou La Batre. Despite its remote location, *Marcel's Bait and Tackle* was prime, piscatorial real estate; close to the public boat launch and on a lonely stretch of road traveled by all those fishing out of Dauphin Island. The bait shop was typical of the cheaply constructed businesses in this part of Mobile County. Bare wood and a rusted tin roof, an array of metal advertising signs nailed to the storefront likely held much of the building together. After the bait shop had been wiped out by two hurricanes over the past few years and the unavailability of affordable flood insurance, it was the acme of folly to invest in anything other than a "no deposit, no return" building.

On weekends, Marcel did a brisk, early morning business, and although Wednesday mornings were always slow, he was a creature of habit and was not one to alter a routine once it was set. He parked his old International Harvester pickup truck next to the above-ground tank that supplied the single gas pump. As he switched off the engine, a loud backfire sent night creatures scurrying back into the dark waters of the bayou just behind the bait shop. Even though sunrise was still an hour away, the air was already uncomfortably hot and humid. The single streetlight buzzed its electric song as Marcel crossed the gravel parking lot. He chased a few toads away from the entrance to his shop, unlocked the door, and reached for the switch that turned on the bait shop sign. Perched on a creosote pole out by the road, the battered sign was the only thing that had survived the hurricanes that too often swept across lower Alabama, amusingly referred to as L.A. He switched on the lights inside the building. An assortment of fishing tackle hung from the rear wall, a shelf in the center of the room held various snacks, two large glass-fronted coolers, one for bait and one for drinks, and two chest freezers stood against the left wall. The cash register sat behind a low counter just to the right of the front door. A curtained door at the back right of the bait shop led to a covered porch where tanks holding live bait were kept. As he entered the establishment, he inhaled the strangely comforting aroma of live bait, boiled peanuts, and stale cigarette smoke.

Marcel knew that the first customers would start arriving in about half an hour, so he took the already loaded crock-pots of peanuts from the cooler--- one regular and one Cajun--- and plugged them in. Aside from bait and gas, boiled peanuts were a big seller for him. He switched on the slightly out-of-balance ceiling fan that wobbled and groaned into consciousness. Needing coffee, he prepared the first of several pots that his customers would demand that morning. His last duty for the morning was to remove any dead fish or shrimp from the live bait tanks, which required little time this morning. Satisfied that he was ready for all comers, he placed a three-legged stool on the weathered planks of the front porch, grabbed his red concertina, and began to play and sing while the day broke across the slash pines of south Alabama. Marcel was in his happy place.

Barely through the first lines of Hank Williams' *Jambalaya,* he spotted headlights coming down the road as a shiny Ford F150 pulled in and stopped in front. Marcel recognized the truck and the portly gentleman who climbed down from the cab.

"Good morning, Big-un", said Marcel as the overall-clad individual came toward him.

"Howdy, Marcel!" His thumbs hooked into the bib of his overalls. Big-un clenched a stub of a cigar in his teeth.

"You up mighty early this morning. You are aware that your boat has gone missing from the back of your truck? Must've fallen off back a-ways."

"Oh hell, I ain't fishing today." Big-un flipped the dog-chewed cigar across the parking lot and came up on the porch. "That worthless brother of mine got drunk last night and tore up a bar over in Bay St. Louis. I gotta go over and bail his fat ass out."

"I am sorry to hear that! Can't be a worse combination, family trouble and trouble with the law."

"And I'm getting my share of both these days. Darla says she's gonna run me off if I don't start paying more attention to her. I don't even know what that means. I wouldn't be too worried about it, but I'm the idiot that learned her how to use a pistol. That woman scares the crap out of me."

"You spending any quality time with her?"

"Hell yes! We go to the dog track every Friday night."

"You're the last of the romantics, Big-un!"

"I just stopped for some snacks and a Co-Cola. But I see you're mighty busy. Think you could find time to sell me some?"

"Yeah, yeah, I'm getting up." Marcel put his concertina down on the stool and stood with a groan. The screen door banged shut behind them as they went inside. "Get Darlene some of those Cajun peanuts. That'll put spice back in your marriage and fix things at home," joked Marcel.

"You a real comedian, you know that?" Big-un went to the drink box, got out a 16-ounce Coke, and took a jumbo-size bag of *Golden Flake* potato chips off the snack stand. "This will tide me over 'til I get there." Big-un put his selection on the counter, and Marcel rang him up.

"Appreciate it. And thanks for the free marriage counseling too," snarked Big-un as he started toward the door.

"You have a good day and drive safe."

"Ain't nothing good about today." Big-un loaded up and headed north on Dauphin Island Parkway.

No sooner had Big-un left than a grimy, early-model Chevy Impala stopped at the gas pump. Marcel glanced out the front window as he closed the drawer of the cash register. A short, stocky, dark-haired man in soiled clothes got out of the car and started toward the door. He paused on the porch and picked up Marcel's concertina before entering. Clearly, the man had no knowledge of music as he pumped the instrument and pushed random buttons to create an irritating cacophony. The stranger stared at Marcel through the storefront window and smiled eerily.

Who the hell are these yahoos? An uneasiness crept through him. Marcel placed his hand on the 9 mm Glock that he kept under the register as the individual came through the front door.

"Buenos días, mi amigo. Is beautiful musica, yes?" said the stranger in a thick Spanish accent as he continued pumping and fingering the concertina. "My English, not so good, but musica is un-i-ver-sal language."

"I've heard better," remarked Marcel coldly. "What can I do for you?"

The stranger stopped playing and placed the concertina on the counter. "Beer and food *por favor*."

"Beer is in the drink case over there." Marcel pointed toward the refrigerator. "The only food we have is snacks, candy, boiled peanuts, and some sandwiches in the cooler. Help yourself."

The stranger opened the drink case and looked around. Carta Blanca?" he asked inquisitively as he pulled his head out of the beer case.

"I don't know what that is, young fella. The only beers we have are *Budweiser*, *Dixie*, and *Pabst Blue Ribbon*." Marcel noticed the second stranger was out of the car and pumping gas.

The stranger loaded his arms with three six-packs of Budweiser and brought them to the counter. "Budweiser, King of Beers!" he said, smiling. He then gathered several packages of corn and potato chips, a handful of candy bars, and dropped them on the counter.

"Cigarillo?" asked the stranger as he held a pretend cigarette up to his lips and mimed smoking.

"What kind?" asked Marcel. He pointed to the cigarettes stacked neatly on a shelf behind him.

"Hmm," muttered the stranger eyeing the packages. He pulled on his chin in contemplation. "Ah, Cinco Marlboro." He held up five fingers.

Marcel turned his back on the stranger and removed the smokes from the shelf. "Where are you gentlemen from?" he asked and turned around to find the barrel of a pistol stuck in his face.

"You give monies," said the stranger, motioning to the cash register.

"Whoa, there, friend." Marcel held up both hands. "Let me open the drawer, and you can have it all." Marcel slowly moved his hand toward the register, pushed a key, and the drawer sprang open. Hidden by the now-extended cash drawer, he moved his other hand toward the Glock and felt the cold steel in his palm. Marcel took a fistful of bills from the drawer and placed them on the counter. The stranger grabbed the bills and, when he did, lowered his gun momentarily. Marcel quickly drew the Glock from its hiding place and fired point-blank into the gunman's forehead. The stranger fell against the counter, knocked the concertina onto the floor, and fell upon the instrument. Like a dying creature, the concertina produced a long discordant wail as blood pulsed from the wound out onto the dirty wooden floor. Marcel would remember the surprise on the stranger's face for the rest of his life…which would be only a few seconds more as the other individual came through the rear door and pumped three slugs into Marcel. Marcel fell behind the counter.

The second stranger stood over his motionless companion and kicked him. No response. "Muy estúpido." He pocketed all the cash along with several packages of Marlboros. Calmly, he went to the soft drink cooler and grabbed an orange Fanta. Near a stack of newspapers by the door, he took one, rolled it up, and stuck it in his rear pocket. Before leaving, he bent down and picked up the concertina. The morning sky was just beginning to lighten as he crossed the lot. As if nothing had happened, he paused, opened a pack of cigarettes, and lit one. He took a deep drag and blew the smoke skyward. The stranger noticed the large white above-ground gas tank on one side of the lot. These same tanks could be found all across Colombia, and as a child, he had always imagined what it would look like if one exploded. On a whim, he pulled the pistol from his pocket and fired the remaining rounds into the tank. Three pencil-sized streams of gasoline jetted out, pooling on the ground around Marcel's International Harvester, and flowing toward the bait shop. Disappointed with the outcome, the stranger tossed the concertina into the back seat of the Impala, climbed in, and started to drive off. The car suddenly stopped on the road and backed up. The window on the driver's side rolled down as the stranger flicked his cigarette across the lot toward the wounded tank. In no rush, he drove south down Dauphin Island Parkway. The window remained down, and he let the humid summer air flow through the old car. He would have loved to stay for the fireworks show, but he had important business to handle. Moments later, an explosion and shockwave shattered the early morning quiet of Bayou La Batre. He glanced into his rearview mirror to see a fireball and mushroom cloud rise into the gray sky.

The local newspaper from Bayou La Batre lay on the seat next to the stranger. The front-page news article read; *Centers for Disease Control Investigates Deaths on Dauphin Island?*

CHAPTER 32

Despite going to bed at an unbelievably late hour, Jesse couldn't sleep when the morning sun streamed into his room. Throughout the night, his sleep was broken by dreams of snakes, doubloons, and blue fire. Finally admitting defeat, he dragged himself out of bed, took a shower, and loaded Bongo into the front seat of the El Camino. He rolled the window down just enough for Bongo to stick his head out into the breeze.

"OK, no going crazy like last time," commanded Jesse as he got behind the wheel. The dog shook with excitement, rammed his head through the open window, and barked at everything they passed.

His stomach now beginning to growl, Jesse stopped at the *Ship and Shore* for a cup of coffee and a greasy sausage biscuit to go.

"You behave yourself." Jesse wagged a finger in the dog's face. "I'll be right back." He shut the car door on a confused, barking dog and walked toward the store.

The *Ship and Shore* was a crucial establishment on Dauphin Island. Like a diminutive *Walmart*, you could purchase groceries, clothing, hardware, beer, liquor, bait, seafood, and auto parts, as well as breakfast and lunch items. They also rented videotapes and videotape players. If you couldn't find it at *Ship and Shore*, you probably didn't need it. It was also a place for early-morning locals to gather to swap stories and discuss the news before the beginning of the workday. Retirees, commercial fishermen, shop owners, and Oceanographic Lab employees could be found conversing on the wooden benches along the storefront.

"What's up, Sharkman!" said Gino Patronus through a mouthful of Honeybun pastry. As always, he wore his yellow farmer johns and looked as though he had just finished pulling crab traps.

"Apparently, they allow anybody to hang out here," said Jesse, smiling.

"They won't let me go inside." Gino motioned toward the door with a half-eaten Honey-bun in hand.

"You think it's the smell?" joked Jesse.

"Can't be that if they let you in!"

"Hey, did you ever figure out who was poaching out of your crab traps?"

"Nah. But I caught some teenagers near my trap line acting suspiciously. I put the fear of God in them." Gino pulled a pack of *Lucky Strike* cigarettes from his shirt pocket, lit one, and took a long drag. "Can't say if it was them, but I can tell you this, no one's messing with my traps anymore."

"Hey, I really appreciate you and Doris taking care of Bongo when I was gone."

"No problem," said Gino.

By the way, how did you manage to talk that lovely lady into marrying you? Dude, she is way out of your league."

"Two things. First, you just gotta know how to sweet-talk the ladies, and second, alcohol."

"The alcohol part I can believe," quipped Jesse.

"So how was your meeeeting with that sweet young thing last night?" Gino over-enunciated to irritate Jesse.

"It went well. I appreciate you suggesting that we talk to Crazy Joe. We visited him last night. Your directions took us right to his place."

"What did he say?"

"Not a lot. He's a man of few words. But he did provide some information that might be important."

"Like what?"

"He saw the Crimson Tide when it ran aground, and he saw someone go on board. Said that it was a boy with brown hair on a red dirt bike. You know, anyone with a red dirt bike on the island?"

"There's probably a bunch of kids with red dirt bikes on the island. I'll give it some thought, however. Hey, what happened to your knife?"

"I gave it to Joe. He was so hospitable that we felt we should give him something."

"That was nice of you to do that. He can't have much in the way of modern conveniences if you could call a knife that." Gino crushed his cigarette out on the bottom of his shrimper boot and flipped the butt across the parking lot.

"He doesn't, but his shack is filled with stuff he has made; pottery, woven baskets, carvings. He is an amazing artist and craftsman. He gave Cherie a carving of a hooded merganser that is incredible."

"He let you go in his shack?" asked Gino in disbelief.

"Yeah, it was obvious that he was very much smitten by Cherie."

"That explains it. Crazy Joe trying to put the moves on your girlfriend, huh?"

"As I said before, Cherie and I are just friends.

"There ain't no such thing as *just friends* between a normal man and a beautiful woman," said Gino, waxing philosophically. "Are you attracted to her?"

"OK, I've got to go get some breakfast." Jesse turned and walked toward the front door.

"Yep, just as I thought," said Gino knowingly.

"Y'all have a safe day." Jesse entered the *Ship and Shore*, purchased a coffee and two sausage biscuits, one for himself and one for Bongo, and left without speaking to the group outside. He arrived at the Oceanography Lab and entered the building, the dog pulling him along the hallway on his leash.

"OK, this is going to be a learning experience for you. If you can behave yourself while I work, I'm going to give you a treat." Jesse had hidden the extra sausage biscuit in his pocket. Bongo recognized the word treat and perked up immediately.

"Whoa, whoa. Calm down!" commanded Jesse.

As luck would have it, the Director of the Oceanography Laboratory, Dr. Guner Gustafson, approached them in the hallway.

Oh crap! thought Jesse. *This is not going to be good.*

All the graduate students called Dr. Gustafson GG or G-squared. Having recently immigrated from Finland, Gustafson was an old-school physical oceanographer who believed any research not involving complex mathematics was nonsense. It was no surprise that he viewed Jesse's project as a waste of time. Bad breath and a permanent scowl were endearing traits compared to his tendency to rarely bathe. One might think that the smoke from the pipe he always held clenched in his teeth would hide his body odor, but it did not. Instead, the smoke and body odor together created an almost lethal environment. Riding in the rickety elevator in the oceanography lab with G-squared was like a slow trip to hell. Jesse experienced this only once, and after holding his breath the entire ride, he vowed never to take the elevator again.

"Mr. Gates, vat is zat creature doing in zis building?" Gustafson spoke in a thick Finnish accent in a most unsettling, imperative manner as he pointed with the stem of his pipe toward Bongo.

"Dr. Gustafson, we are going straight to my office, and I will be there the entire day. You will not see him again, I promise."

"I vill hold you to zat!" replied Gustafson, his tobacco-stained teeth showing behind his thin lips. "I understand you are speaking zis Friday at our zeminar zeries?"

Jesse paused momentarily, confused. *Oh no! I completely forgot.* "Uh, uh,…yes sir. I'm going to present… uh…some of my dissertation data." The sudden realization that he had a deadline looming completely jumbled his thoughts.

"I hope it iz vorthy of an Oceanography Lab Research Fellow," said G-squared haughtily. "We have plenty of GOOD students zat should have a fellowship." He walked away, leaving a trail of stench in his wake.

What an ass! The implication that he was not deserving of the fellowship he had been awarded made his blood boil. *How about I drop kick your nuts up around your… OK. Calm down Jesse. He's not worth getting all worked up over.*

Jesse climbed the stairs to the second floor of the Oceanography building, entered his office, and closed the door behind him. To calm himself, he sat for a moment in his chair, imagining that he was riding a motorcycle down a shady, country lane, winding through an autumnal forest, a cool wind in his face. An anger management technique, this imagined scenario often helped him sleep at night, sort of like counting sheep.

Settling in, he fed Bongo the remaining sausage biscuit. The dog lay at his feet and dozed. He turned on the IBM PC that took up the majority of the space on his desk. As the computer booted up, he removed all of the data sheets from his desk drawer, laid them out across the desk, and inserted a 3.5-inch floppy disc into the drive. Leaving Bongo asleep in his office, he went to the lab and quickly ran the blood samples obtained from the research cruise through the blood analysis protocol. He printed out the results and returned to his office.

He began sorting the data sheets by species: bull sharks, blacktip sharks, sharpnose sharks, spinner sharks, hammerhead sharks, fine-tooth sharks, etc. Entering these data would take a while, and he settled into a routine of systematically entering the numbers for each species. Although a tedious task, he kept reminding himself that it was one more step toward obtaining his degree and getting a real job. After punching in the last data sheet, he rose to stretch his back. Jesse turned from side to side, stretching his back muscles, expecting to feel that familiar twinge that had plagued him for weeks. "Man, my back is so much better after Dr. Joe's chiropractic treatment." Jesse reached down and massaged the angry red place on his thigh where Ross had injected him. "Wish I could say the same for my leg. Geez, that's sore!"

Bongo raised his head, glanced briefly at Jesse, and put his head down again, uninterested.

"Ok, now it's time to run the graphs for each blood parameter." Jesse rubbed his hands together as if he were about to dive into a sumptuous meal. The excitement of analyzing data that held the potential for discovery appealed to his nerdy nature. He opened up the graphing software, made several on-screen choices, and began plotting the data. The first graph that he created was for bull shark, blood lactic acid, and the graphic appeared on the glowing screen. The lines all showed an increase, as expected, except for several of the most recently collected bull sharks.

The door to the office swung open, and in walked Ross. "Hey dude, what's happening?" Fending off an over-excited Bong, he knelt, wrapped his arm around the dog's neck, and petted him vigorously with his other hand.

"Hi, Ross. Oh, just working up data that I should have taken care of months ago. Bongo get down!"

Bongo, finding that Ross had no treats for him, returned to his place at Jesse's feet.

"Did you speak with CC?" asked Jesse.

"I did. I apologized for not seeing her earlier, but I knew she was gonna be OK. I had to attend a meeting with G-squared about my degree progress. He is such a dick-head."

"Let me guess, he said you weren't making satisfactory progress?"

"Yeah, big surprise, huh?" Ross pulled up a chair and seated himself next to Jesse. "He tells everyone the same thing."

"He really doesn't understand field research, particularly biological research work," said Jesse. "He's old school physical oceanography and thinks fear is the best teaching tool. I saw him in the hall a while ago, and he tactfully reminded me that I have a seminar to deliver this Friday."

"Well, he got my attention. How bad was the smell?"

Jesse, never looking away from his computer screen, said, "Same as usual, like a skunk smoking shredded car tires in a pipe made of cow dung."

"Hey, speaking of physical oceanography, did you hear about the hurricane?"

"Oh crap!" Ross now had his undivided attention. "You know me, I never follow the news and haven't watched television in about two years. Please tell me it's not in the Gulf."

"It's not."

"Thank goodness," said a relieved Jesse.

"It's in the southern Gulf."

"Oh crap! It seems that hurricanes always head for the northern Gulf of Mexico." Jesse absent-mindedly reached into his pocket and felt the coin resting there. "Take a look at this." He handed the coin to Ross.

"Mardi gras doubloon?"

"I don't know. What do you think?"

"It's very heavy," Ross moved his open hand up and down, feeling the coins' heft. "Where did you get it?"

"A friend gave it to me," Jesse was not sure why he didn't elaborate on the origin of the coin, but chose to keep it under his hat. "I was going to try to get an expert opinion on it."

"I'm no expert, but it's probably just a Mardi Gras throw", he handed the coin back to Jesse.

"Yeah, that's what Cherie thinks." Jesse put the coin back in his pocket.

"Are you seeing anything interesting in your project?"

"Well, pretty much what I expected except for the last few weeks of data." Jesse stared at the screen and pulled on his chin in puzzlement. "Look at this." He traced the line across the screen with his finger. "Here's the normal response: lactic acid increasing over the entire 60-minute stress experiment. But look at these. In the same experiment, lactic acid increased very little for these sharks. I must have screwed up something during the experiment or the analysis. I may have to throw those numbers out."

"That's too bad," said Ross sympathetically.

"Cherie suggested that perhaps the response to stress in these sharks has changed, and these are valid numbers. I am checking all of the numbers over the past few months to see if there is any evidence of that."

While Ross looked on, Jesse proceeded to create on-screen graphs for the other blood parameters.

"It's the same problem for all the other blood parameters. The bull shark data from the last few weeks is completely different from previous experiments. Crap! If these are bad values, I'm never gonna finish this project."

He hit the print button for each of the bull shark graphs and heard the chatter of the dot-matrix printer as it spooled paper out onto the floor.

"Well, I guess I will run the other species; maybe there is better news there." Jesse began creating graphs for each blood parameter for each species. The computer screen lit up with graph after graph showing the same results.

"This is unbelievable. Every species and every parameter shows the same altered response. A month ago, all sharks were normal, about two weeks ago, a few were displaying the change, and now, all of them show it. And look at this! The sharks we captured during the longlining trip in shallow water nearest the island all show the altered response, and some of those in deeper water show it. The response is less common the further you go away from the island, and none of those captured in the deepest water show it. There has been a gradual change in the way these animals respond to stress, which has spread through the shark population over time, and it is apparently spreading away from the island. I have plenty of frozen blood plasma left, so I could re-run the analyses, but I don't think I have to. This strongly suggests that these values are real and the animals have changed."

"So, what does that mean?"

"I don't know. Their ability to withstand stress has increased dramatically over a very short time. This goes against everything we know about animal physiology. But you know, it would explain the behavior of that mako shark that almost drowned CC?"

"That's a good point," said Ross.

"It would also explain the fighting ability of a number of other sharks we tested," added Jesse. "Remember how they just never seemed to tire out? And did you hear about the number of fishermen on the island who have been attacked by sharks?"

"I heard about one person being bitten. Have there been others?"

"Yeah. There have been 4 or 5 just in the past few weeks, when typically, you should see one or zero attacks over an entire year. Fishermen are catching these sharks and, when they think they are tired out, like they should be, they whip around and bite them. That many shark bites is a crazy number."

"What do you think would explain this change?"

"I haven't a clue!" said Jesse. "But something has caused these animals to go from extremely stress-sensitive to almost completely stress-resistant."

"Like CC said, they've become bionic sharks!" said Ross with a grin.

"Yeah, you could say that. I've got to think about this some more. I have a meeting with Dr. Pearson later today to talk about my seminar this Friday. Maybe he'll have some insight."

CHAPTER 33

Cherie's room at the Palms Motel was comfortable but spartan. Oil paintings of beach sunsets, pelicans, and leaping dolphins, with price tags affixed, decorated the cinder block walls. A local artist had arranged to use the rooms at the Palms as their private art gallery. The single upholstered chair and a small table served as both a desk and dining area. A television perched atop a 1950s-style dresser, Cherie alternated the channels between the local station out of Mobile and CNN to stay abreast of any news regarding Dauphin Island. The double bed, which she had spent too little time occupying, was strewn with dirty clothes, notebooks, scientific papers, and CDC case reports. It had required only a few days for her to change her motel room into an extension of the CDC. But her doubts about the investigation were with her constantly, and at present, it was at a standstill. Her only lead came from Joe, and despite how impressed she was with the hermit, she began to wonder just how credible the information might be. At precisely 8:00 AM, Cherie picked up the receiver and dialed a number on the ancient rotary telephone.

"Dauphin Island Sheriff's Office. How can I help you?" came the friendly but professional greeting.

"Hi Dorothy," Cherie stifled a yawn as best she could. "Is Chief East in?"

"He is not. Is this an emergency?"

"No, Ma'am, it's Cherie Belon. I just had a quick question for him."

"Oh, good morning, Dr. Belon. Do you want me to try to reach him on the radio?"

"Uh… that's not necessary. Perhaps you could answer this question for me."

"I will try."

"If I needed to check on the registration for a motorcycle on the island, how might I go about doing that?"

"That would have to come from the Department of Motor Vehicles in Mobile. We do that sort of thing all the time. I can run it for you, but I will have to get the Chief's approval, which I am sure he will provide. I assume this is for the CDC investigation?"

"Yes Ma'am."

"What is the license number?"

"Unfortunately, I don't have one. I only have the description of a person, around 18 years old, who was on a red dirt bike on the beach at the west end of the island."

"Oh. That could be a problem. Those kids who ride the west end don't always register their motorcycles since some are not always street-legal. They are only allowed to ride them off-road."

"Great!"

"But that doesn't mean that it's not registered. Can I make a suggestion?"

"Absolutely."

"I could have the DMV search for all registered motorcycles of residents who live near the west end. If the person is riding those deserted beaches, they likely live out there near that end of the island. Also, they often ride together, so an individual who rides a registered dirt bike might know the person you are looking for. I have a friend at the DMV in Mobile, and they should be able to get me that information. They've got all those fancy computers over there. He can FAX the information to me right here in the office. It is amazing how technology has advanced. Used to, I would have to either drive to Mobile to pick up documents or wait until they arrived in the mail. What do you think?"

"That sounds great."

"I'll radio the Chief and OK it with him first. I'll give you a call as soon as I have the information."

"That will work. I owe you a lunch for this, Dorothy."

"No need for that. It's part of my job."

"Dorothy, one other thing. Could you see if the Chief is available for a meeting at his earliest convenience?"

"I'll find out when he's available. He can probably meet today, but you know how things can change quickly. Particularly these days."

"Would you leave a message at the motel desk since I will be out for a bit?"

"I can do that."

"Thank you so much. Talk to you later."

Cherie pushed the button on the phone to disconnect and dialed the number that Jesse had given her for the Oceanography

Lab. The phone in the student lounge rang for an uncomfortably long time before someone picked up.

"Hello."

"Yes, I was trying to reach Jesse Gates. Do you know if he is around?"

"I'm sure he's working in the lab; he's always there if not on the water. If you will hold for a moment, I'll send someone to check."

"I'll hold, thank you so much."

Ross poked his head through the partially open lab door to find Jesse hard at work as usual. "Jesse, someone wants to speak with you on the phone in the student lounge."

"Who is it?"

"Can't say. I didn't take the call. I was just asked to find you."

"Thanks, Ross."

Jesse left the lab and went to the student lounge, which was empty aside from one graduate student who sat on the sofa reading. He picked up the receiver.

"Hello."

"Hi, Jesse. How's it going?"

"Oh, hi Cherie." Jesse immediately recognized Cherie's Cajun accent. "Things are going OK, I guess. Have you recovered from our swamp adventure?"

"Not really, but my strategy is to just drink another cup of coffee and soldier on. That's all I can do right now. What about you?"

"I think we are both working too hard; you harder than I."

"The reason I called is that I am going to arrange a sit-down with Chief of Police East later today to discuss some things about the investigation. I hoped you might be able to join us."

"I have to present a seminar at 1:00 today, but that will be over, for better or for worse, by about 2:30, so I am free after that."

"Is your seminar today? I didn't know. I would love to come, but I can't make it at that time."

"I deliberately did not tell you because I know how busy you are, and I knew you would feel obligated to show up. On top of that, it's not going to go well, so I would rather spare you the embarrassment."

"I don't believe that. I'll bet it goes just fine."

"I wish I could share your optimism. I'm going to propose something that certain faculty members are going to find hard to accept. But we will see."

"When the Chief gets back to me about the meeting, I'll come to the lab. I assume you will be there?"

"Yes. After the seminar, I'll be in the student lounge licking my wounds, no doubt."

"I'll come by there, and Jesse, it's going to be fine."

"I appreciate the vote of confidence. I'll see you later today."

"I look forward to it."

Cherie hung up the phone, gathered up her backpack, and left. She stopped off at the front office and grabbed a cup of the free coffee that was barely palatable, but always available. Climbing into her vehicle, she swung out of the motel parking lot. After about three sips from a Styrofoam cup, she rolled the window down and dumped the remainder. *I've got to find better coffee than this.* Having had no breakfast, she decided to treat herself and headed for the Blue Crab Café. She parked, went in, and seated herself near a window.

"Good morning, young lady." A middle-aged, apron-clad waitress approached with a pot. "Can I pour you some coffee?"

"Yes, Ma'am, that would be great."

"You were here with Jesse a few days ago?" She turned her cup over and filled it.

"I was."

"Your name is, um… Cheryl?"

"Cherie."

"Well, I was close. I'm Marie."

"Nice to meet you," Cherie extended her hand.

"I saw you on television the other night. You're with the disease people from Atlanta."

"Yes Ma'am," said Cherie, chuckling. "The Centers for Disease Control. I was interviewed by a reporter about our investigation here."

"Do you mind if I sit down for a moment?" Marie slid into the booth opposite her without waiting for an invitation. "We are slow these days."

"No problem. Yeah, the place is pretty empty."

"Sad, ain't it? We are the only sit-down breakfast place on the island, and at 8:30 on a Friday morning, we should have most of the tables filled. Folks are worried about what is going on. That's what I wanted to talk to you about. How worried should we be?"

"Marie, I'll be honest. We still don't know what caused the death of the shrimp boat captain. However, if you take normal precautions, you should be fine. Wash your hands regularly, cover your mouth when you cough or sneeze, and stay out of large groups. If you want, I could give you some surgical masks that I have in the car."

"I'll take you up on those masks. Thanks!"

"No problem."

"You know, folks are putting things together that maybe they shouldn't. The dead shrimp boat captain and the fellow who died in his car. These things just don't happen on Dauphin Island."

"Chief East mentioned to me about that car accident. Very sad."

"I did not know the person, but I know the ambulance driver; he comes in regularly. He said that it was odd because the fellow was covered with blood, much more than you would expect, considering the accident. He also said that he believed the driver was dead before he crashed. Do you think it could be the same thing that killed the shrimp boat captain?

"I really can't say, Marie. I wasn't able to investigate that accident."

Maire and Cherie turned in unison and watched a grey Chevrolet sedan park in front of the restaurant. A dark, heavy-set patron got out and entered the restaurant.

"Sir, just sit wherever you like, I'll be right with you," called Marie as she rose from her seat to wait on the gentleman. "Let me take this order, and I'll be right back."

"Marie, you can go ahead and take my order if you don't mind?"

"Oh, child, I am so sorry. I totally forgot. What are you gonna have?

"Just toast and two scrambled eggs."

"I'll put this order in right now. Give me two seconds."

Marie attended to the patron and returned to her seat at Cherie's table.

"Boy, that was creepy." She leaned across the table and whispered to Cherie. "I don't like to talk about people, but that man has the coldest eyes of anyone I have ever seen. He gave me the willies!" Marie folded her arms across her chest and shivered slightly.

"Are you OK?"

"Have you ever had a bad feeling suddenly come over you for no obvious reason?"

"These days?" Cherie paused and put her coffee cup down. "I get them all the time."

"Well, that happened when I was talking to that strange-looking man," whispered Marie. "He doesn't speak English very well and, Lord, forgive me for saying this, he smells like he has not had a shower in a while. I've never seen a person with so much acne scarring on their face. He wanted something called *Weevos Rancheros*. You got any idea what that is?"

"He probably said *Huevos,* which means eggs in Spanish. I can't help you with the *Rancheros* part."

"Well, he's getting eggs. I at least got that part right."

CHAPTER 34

Chief East wiped his boots across the welcome mat that lay at the front door of the Sheriff's office, clearing the sand from the soles. His shirt soaked with sweat, he limped into the lobby, his war wound aggravated by a long walk down East Beach to investigate a report of a body lying in shallow water. After a grueling trek, the victim turned out to be a badly decomposed dolphin.

"You've got that look on your face," said East as Dorothy approached him coming in the door.

"And you look frazzled, Chief! What were you doing?"

"Just walked about a mile down the beach on a wild goose chase." East pulled his hat off and wiped his face with a handkerchief. "Thank the Lord for air conditioning."

"I got a call just as you pulled in. Mr. Theodore Barnes, out at Pelican Roost trailer park, reported that there is a terrible smell coming from his next-door neighbor's trailer." Dorothy handed him the address she had scribbled on a note. "He said he knocked on the door and no one answered. The mail has not been collected from the box either. The home belongs to Mr. Charles Walton."

"Are we talking natural gas, skunk spray, rotten fish?"

"Bad was all he said."

"It's probably nothing. Radio Sean and have him handle this. I gotta find some aspirin and sit down for a bit."

"Will do."

The Chief continued through the lobby, entered his office, and closed the door behind him. Dorothy picked up the radio microphone.

"Deputy Murphy, come in." A short pause before the reply.

"Come back, Dorothy."

"What's your location? Come back?"

"I'm parked at the bottom of the Dauphin Island bridge, putting the radar gun on folks coming onto the island. Come back."

"Could you swing by Pelican Roost and check out a report of a very bad smell coming from a trailer house? Mr. Theodore Barnes, a next-door neighbor, says that no one answers the door. There may be someone or something dead inside. It's trailer #23. Come back."

"I am on my way. Over." Deputy Murphy started the engine of his patrol car and eased out onto the blacktop. In a few minutes, he pulled into the gate of the trailer park. Pelican Roost was the only trailer park on the island and was home to mostly locals. Murphy drove the crushed shell road that wound through the park, around the giant live oaks festooned with Spanish Moss, and stopped in front of lot #23. A typical coastal trailer, it was a single-wide, no-frills, cracker-box, with a small covered porch at the front. An elderly gentleman in a wheelchair rolled down the ramp of the trailer next door and accosted the Deputy.

"Good morning, Officer," said the gentleman. "Thanks for coming out so quickly."

"No problem. Are you Mr. Barnes?"

"Yes sir."

"What's the problem?"

"My friend, Chuck Walton, lives in that trailer. He's a retiree and he's wheelchair-bound like me. I hadn't seen him for several days, and then I noticed a bad smell coming from that direction. I've knocked on the door several times, but no one answers. I'm worried about him."

"Does it smell like natural gas?"

"No, sir. It smells like roadkill."

"I'll check it out, sir." Deputy Murphy walked up the short ramp onto the porch, opened the screen door, and knocked. "Mr. Walton." He knocked again, harder this time. "Mr. Walton! Holy smokes, I smell it now. I wonder if there is a dead animal under this porch." He placed a hand against his nose and mouth to stifle the stench. Murphy shut the screen door, stepped off the porch, and peered in the front window. "Mr. Walton!" shouted Murphy again as he tapped on the window. Through the dirty glass and partially drawn curtain, he could just make out a seated person, silhouetted in the bluish glare of a television that was on.

"Can you see anything?" asked Barnes, who had wheeled his chair over in front of the trailer.

"I see him in there watching television. Does he have hearing aids?"

"No, sir."

"He is not responding, so that makes me think something is wrong. I'm gonna have to go in." The Deputy went back on the porch, and with one swift kick, the door flew open. A blast of hot, fetid air hit him in the face as he retched and drew away. "Oh Lord!" Murphy ran from the porch, bent over in the yard, and vomited.

"Oh no!" cried Mr. Barnes as he wheeled his chair toward the trailer.

"Don't go in there!" commanded Murphy between retches.

"I was afraid of this. He was my best friend, and he died in there all by himself." He began to weep softly.

Murphy composed himself as best he could, sat on the hood of his cruiser, taking deep breaths to clear the smell, and waited for the nausea to pass.

"Mr. Barnes, I have to go in there on the chance that he is alive. But I'm not optimistic. Do you have a towel I could borrow to use as a mask?"

"I can get you one." Wiping his eyes with his shirt sleeve, he wheeled back to his trailer, came out quickly, and handed the deputy a towel.

"Thank you, sir."

Murphy held the towel tight against his nose and mouth and entered the trailer. Walton sat in his wheelchair across the small, dimly lit, sparsely furnished living room. A television, a couch, and an overstuffed chair. Fearing the worst, he approached from the rear, reached out, and touched him on the shoulder. "Mr. Walton, it's Deputy Murphy." No response. "Oh Lord!" exclaimed Murphy as he came around the front of his wheelchair. House flies buzzed around a pallid face contorted in pain. Blood turned black from the stifling heat covered the body, the chair, and the carpet around him. Murphy unwittingly had walked through a puddle of black, congealed blood. In Walton's hand, he held a rosary and, in his lap, partially covered with blood, lay the slipcover of a VHS tape, *The Exorcist*, the movie he was apparently watching when he died. Murphy, feeling nauseous again, rushed out of the trailer.

"I'm sorry to tell you this, Mr. Barnes," the Deputy stood bent at the waist in the front yard, taking deep breaths, "but I'm afraid your friend has passed away."

Mr. Barnes silently wheeled himself back into his trailer and closed the door.

Murphy went to his cruiser, took the microphone from its hook, and radioed the Sheriff's Department.

"Dorothy. Come in."

"Come back, Sean," replied Dorothy.

"Get the coroner out to the trailer park. Mr. Walton is dead and appears to have been that way for a couple of days. Come back."

"Oh, my goodness! I'll call them right away. Does it look like foul play? Come back."

"Oh, it's foul alright!" Murphy gagged for a moment from the memory of what he had just experienced.

"Sean, are you OK?"

"I'm alright. Still recovering. The smell is so bad that I can only stand to be in the trailer for a few minutes. There is blood everywhere. Can't say much for his taste in movies. He was watching *The Exorcist* on video when he died. That disgusting movie probably killed him. Gave him a heart attack, no doubt. Over."

"Heaven help us! Standing by."

Dorothy rang the coroner's office and then Chief East's office. "Chief, that bad smell at Pelican Roost turned out to be a body. A Mr. Charles Walton."

"Son of a...!" Do I need to go over there?"

"Sean is handling it. The coroner is on his way now."

"What in blue blazes is going on around here?"

"I don't know. I forgot to mention that Dr. Belon called about a meeting with you this afternoon."

"Did she say what it was about?"

"No, but I'm sure it's about the investigation."

"Let her know that I'll make myself available at any time."

"I'll let her know. Would 4 o'clock be OK?"

"Yes, assuming no other folks drop dead on the island."

CHAPTER 35

Free Bird Parasailing Company was the only parasailing operation on Dauphin Island. Brothers Larry and Bart Owens pooled their funds, modified their 25-foot fishing boat, and purchased second-hand equipment from a failed company out of Panama City, Florida. Although hardly a tourist Mecca, they believed that parasailing would appeal to the adventurous island visitor, and indeed, they were doing a brisk business. The major selling point of their brand of parasailing was that you did not have to get wet at all. The brothers would launch their boat, the *Scream Machine*, at Billy Goat Hole on the island's eastern tip and take customers for a scenic, 30-minute parasail along the beaches. Thrill-seeking customers were strapped into their harnesses on the back of the boat, and the parachute was launched while the boat was underway. A winch released the tow rope as the parachute, and the passengers rose into the sky. The altitude of the parachute could be increased by releasing more line and, to some extent, by increasing the speed of the boat. Brother Bart, the operator of the vessel, enjoyed giving the guests a thrill by momentarily throttling back on the boat and allowing the parasail to descend toward the "shark-infested" waters. A moniker he made a point of using when explaining to tourists what to expect. He particularly enjoyed hearing the screams of younger, female parasailers when he dropped the chute suddenly and dipped their feet into the water.

On this occasion, the *Scream Machine* operation included Bart, his employee Tommy, who operated the winch, and three customers: two teenage girls and a 40-something male.

"OK, Aquanauts!" said Bart as he throttled back on the boat and stopped just offshore of the eastern tip of the island. He motioned with his hands to draw the group around him and, to give his parasailing safety speech, put on a serious face. "I need to go through a couple of things before lift-off. First, let me mention that your safety is paramount at *Free Bird Parasailing*. We've been in business for almost a year now, and we've only lost 12 people. That's almost a 90% success rate. However, we expect their bodies will wash ashore any day now. At least what's left of their bodies." *The expression on his customer's faces was always priceless,* thought Bart. "That was a joke, people... We've only lost 3 customers." Nervous laughter from the group. "So, you two ladies will go first, and then we will take uh… what is your name sir?"

"Paul."

"We can take Paul up last."

"I just want to get some aerial pictures around the island. I'd prefer not to get wet."

"No worries. That's a nice camera, Mr. Paul. I've never seen one like it."

"It's a new Nikon with a power winder. I just have to hold the shutter button down, and it continually takes pictures."

"Very cool! We will keep you dry on this ride. Is there any chance we could get some copies of the pictures?"

"Absolutely. I'll have duplicates made for you."

"Awesome!" said Bart. "OK, rule number one, you are forbidden to touch any of the buckles on the harness. We don't want you falling out. When you're up there, don't throw anything into the water. You should take any valuables out of your pockets and leave them on the boat. If you need to come down before the ride is over, give Tommy, my assistant, the universal stop signal, a fist held up like this." Bart demonstrated the stop sign. "If, for some reason, the boat stops, the parachute will slowly drop, and we will immediately winch you to the boat. No need to panic if that happens. If there are no questions, let's get you ladies strapped in."

Bart and his assistant put the harness on the young girls first and readied them for take-off. He throttled up the engine, and his assistant deployed the parachute. When the chute was filled with air, he activated the winch, and the line began spooling out. Screaming and laughing, the girls rocketed skyward. Bart pushed the *Pronounced Lynyrd Skynyrd* cassette tape into the player and cranked the volume on *Free Bird*, his company's namesake tune.

Slow-paced at first, the rock classic boomed from the large speakers that hung from the center console of the *Scream Machine*. In his attempt to entertain the guests, Tommy played air guitar through the fast-paced instrumental portion of the song. The long version of *Free Bird* was always followed by *Iron Butterfly's, In-A-Gadda-Da-Vida*. The two songs together lasted about 30 minutes and signaled the end of the ride.

"Let's give them a thrill," said Bart with a gleam in his eye as he throttled back on the engine. With more screams and laughter, the chute dropped, and the young girl's feet just touched the water's surface when Bart powered the boat forward again. He repeated the maneuver a couple of times before taking them to cruising altitude. They rode west down the island and had just started back east again when the 30-minute ride was over.

"We may have a little fog rolling in," remarked Tommy, looking offshore at an obscured horizon. He activated the winch and pulled the young parasailers to the deck of the boat.

"It shouldn't be a problem," said Bart. "The weather report said it would not be rolling in until later. We should have plenty of time to finish this parasail. Mr. Paul, are you ready?"

"Ready to go."

Tommy buckled Paul into the harness and positioned him for lift-off.

"Is there something in particular you wanted to photograph?"

"Just some shots of the island, but if we could get close to a gas rig, that would be great."

"I am required to stay a certain distance away from the rigs, but I can run offshore a little to get closer. I'll run along the island for a bit and then turn and run offshore before we winch you back in."

"As close as you can will be fine."

Tommy engaged the winch, Bart pushed the *"Skynyrd"* cassette back into the machine, and Paul rose into the air. After reaching altitude, Bart proceeded down the island until the song finished, whereupon they started the next song and began a slow turn toward the closest offshore gas rig. They ran south for several minutes and suddenly encountered a thick fog bank rolling in off the Gulf.

Bart looked aloft. "Crap, I can't see the customer anymore. That's not gonna be good for pictures."

"Did you hear that?" asked Tommy. "I thought I heard something. Turn the music off."

Bart ejected the tape. "I didn't hear anything. What did it sound like?"

"It sounded like a scream," replied one of the young girls.

"It was probably just a seagull," said Bart. "We are going to have to end Paul's parasailing. This fog is way too thick. He may be angry, but we'll offer him a free ride when the weather improves."

The fog continued to thicken, and Tommy began slowly winching Paul back in. "Man, this is thick as pea soup! I can't see squat. It's amazing how fast this crap rolled in."

Minutes passed as the winch continued to take in rope. Finally, the harness with Paul suddenly broke through the fog a short distance above the deck of the boat.

"OH MY GOD!" screamed one of the girls in disbelief. They ran toward the front of the boat and away from the sight before them. Clutching each other, they hid their faces and cried hysterically.

Tommy stopped the winch and drew back in revulsion. He gazed in horror at the bloodied, lifeless body that hung in the air just above the boat deck. Like one of the condemned from *Dante's Inferno*, his head was thrown back, and his bloody eyes stared skyward. A face contorted in white-hot pain, his mouth wide open in an apparent final scream when his soul slipped from his body. Blood and gore streamed out of his eyes, ears, and mouth. With blood soaked through his clothing, the body was framed by a macabre, blood-splattered parachute that billowed in the foggy breeze behind what was once Paul.

CHAPTER 36

"Sheriff's Department." Dorothy held the phone against her ear using her shoulder while standing in front of a tall filing cabinet, rifling through its contents.

"Yes, this is Steve Metcalf, and I'm calling from the Oceanography Lab."

"Yes sir. How can we help you?"

I was driving by the boat launch on the east end, and someone asked me to call the Chief. There's been an accident here at the launch."

"Can you tell me what happened?"

"No Ma'am, I cannot. There is a group of people and a very bloody person on a boat here. It looks like there's been a terrible accident. A police officer and an ambulance need to get down here immediately. Although I don't think the ambulance is gonna be able to do much good."

"Thank you sir. We'll get someone down there right away."

Dorothy put down the reports she was attempting to file and picked up the radio microphone. "Chief East, come in."

"Go ahead, Dorothy," came the quick reply.

"Just got a call from a Dr. Metcalf from the Oceanography Lab. Says there's been an accident at the Billy Goat Hole boat launch. Sounds serious. You need to get down there. Come back."

"Another one? Good Lord! Did you get any details? Come back."

"All he said was that there was blood everywhere. Come back."

"Oh Lord! That sounds disturbingly familiar. I am on my way. Call the ambulance immediately, and after you do that, give Dr. Belon a call. I left her phone number with you. Tell her to meet me at the boat launch. I have a suspicion that she is going to want to see this. Over."

"Can do and standing by."

East switched on his siren and lights, turned onto Bienville Boulevard, and headed toward the boat launch. In minutes, he pulled into the parking lot. Several onlookers gathered at the dock, were all focused on a boat that sat in the launch. He walked down the pier to the end of the dock where the boat was tied. A crumpled parasail lay in the water behind the boat, and a bloodied corpse, partially covered with a raincoat, lay face up on the rear deck. He stepped down onto the deck of the boat and knelt beside the corpse. The salty air mixed with the metallic tang of fresh blood caused East's stomach to roil. Using his nightstick to pull back the raincoat revealed a horrific face. He paused momentarily, hoping to see signs of life. No movement, no breathing. Despite the tortured visage, he thought the victim looked familiar. He covered his face again and stood.

"Folks, I need everyone to move off this dock immediately." East walked along the dock, motioning with both hands as if directing traffic. A distraught individual, looking very pale, approached East.

"Sheriff. I'm Bart Owens. My brother and I own *Free Bird Parasailing*."

East took a small notebook and pen from his shirt pocket and began taking notes. "I'm Chief of Police East. Can you tell me what happened?"

"Chief, if you don't mind, I need to sit down. I'm not feeling well."

"You want to sit on the boat?"

"Hell no! I want to burn that boat after what I saw." Bart took a long drink from the *Dixie* beer he held in his hand.

"OK. Let's sit in the shade," East motioned toward tables next to the water, and they walked off the dock.

"I am going to ignore the fact that you have an open beer, considering. Just take your time and tell me what happened."

"This fellow signed up for parasailing this morning. His first name is Paul. I don't know his last name, but I have all his information back at the office."

"Oh, Geez!" said East in a moment of realization. "That's Paul Stanford, he owns a restaurant here on the island."

"Not anymore." Bart sighed heavily, pulled the front of his t-shirt up, and used it to wipe sweat from his face and brow. "He said he wanted aerial pictures of the island and maybe some of a gas rig if we could get him close enough. We strapped him in and sent him up on the chute. No big deal. After a little while, I turned the boat south toward a gas rig, the nearest one to the island, but we didn't even get close before heavy fog rolled in. It was so thick that we couldn't see the customer at all. Because of that, I immediately told Tommy to start the winch and bring him down."

"Who is Tommy?" interrupted East.

"Tommy Carpenter is our employee; he's over there," added Bart, pointing back toward the dock.

"I will need to talk to him. Go on."

"Well, when we got him low enough, below the fog, we could see that he was covered in blood and looked the way you see him there." Bart grimaced and rubbed his eyes with both hands as if trying to wipe the image from his mind. "Dude, it was a gnarly sight. Other than the fog, there was nothing out of the ordinary. Although one of the other customers said she thought she heard a scream when the fog rolled in."

"About how long ago did this happen?"

"It was only about 30 minutes ago. We came straight in."

"I need to get the names of your other customers. I may need to talk to them."

"OK. That info is also back at the office," said Bart. "The parachute was covered in blood, and so I left it deployed until we got to the dock. When we slowed down to dock the boat, Mr. Paul fell to the deck, and the parachute fell into the water."

"Was he alive when you brought him down?"

"I don't think so. He said nothing, he wasn't breathing, and he wasn't moving. I was not about to get near him to check his pulse." Bart took another pull from his beer, his hand shaking as he set the beer down again. "Sorry, Chief, but I've never seen a dead person before. What do you think happened?"

"That is what we are trying to find out. Was Mr. Stanford behaving unusually?"

"No, sir, not at all."

"He didn't seem to be ill or distraught?"

"No, sir. Like I said, he wanted to get aerial pictures of the island and maybe a gas rig. He seemed perfectly fine."

Both East and Bart looked toward the white CDC vehicle that pulled into the parking lot and stopped. Cherie got out of the driver's seat and approached them. "Chief East."

"Dr. Belon, how are you?"

"I've been better."

"Tell me about it!" said East, shaking his head in disgust. "I think this may be what you've been looking for."

"I hope not." Cherie and East walked to the end of the dock. Cherie stepped down onto the rear deck where the victim lay. She pulled gloves from her pocket, put them on, and drew the raincoat back from the victim. "Oh my! Not good, not good. I guess he was dead when you got here?"

"He was. That's Paul Stanford. I know him, uh… that is, I knew him."

"You saw the other unusual case, the car crash. Does it look similar to that?"

"Well, if similar means bloody and bled out, then yeah."

"Did you touch him at all?"

"I did not. You've got me too worried to risk that. No one on the boat got near him."

"Good." Cherie stood and addressed the rubberneckers who stood in the parking lot. "Did anyone come in contact with this person or with blood?"

All answered in the negative. Bart, feeling somewhat better, returned to the dock.

"Cherie, this is Bart Owens, owner of the parasailing business," said East. "This is Dr. Belon from the Centers for Disease Control."

"Hello," said Bart.

"Mr. Owens, Chief East said that no one on your boat got near Mr. Stanford?"

"Yes Ma'am. Well, except for Tommy, my employee. He is the one who put the harness on him before he went up. But no one got near him after he died."

"I'll have to talk to Tommy. You're sure there was no one else?"

"Absolutely. Who would want to touch that?" said Bart grimly as he motioned toward the body. "We left him hanging in the harness, and he dropped to the deck right where you see him."

"There's the ambulance," said the Chief. "They took their sweet time getting here. Not that it matters."

"They will be of no use to this person," said Cherie.

"They will not. I'm gonna send them away and radio the office to get the coroner down here. Do you need me for anything, Doc?"

"It would help if you would tape off this area while I get pictures and blood samples. This is the first opportunity we've had to obtain blood from an apparent victim, and I need to do it immediately."

"No problem. You're not gonna work in those clothes, are you?"

"No, I'm gonna suit up. I've got protective clothing in the car."

"Doc, I am more than a bit concerned. Dorothy mentioned that you wanted to talk. This incident is going to keep me busy for the rest of the day, so we should try to meet tomorrow afternoon if that works for you?"

"Tomorrow afternoon or the next day will work better for me."

"I'll have Dorothy give you a call."

"Thanks, Chief."

CHAPTER 37

"Dorothy, I'm going to patrol the west end for a while." Chief East fumbled with his gun belt, attempting to buckle it as he strode through the lobby of the Police Department. "I'll be back in an hour or so."

"Having some trouble with that duty belt?" asked Dorothy accusingly. "Do not, I repeat, DO NOT stop at Wilson's Bakery again. You know you have to watch your weight, and a sack of beignets is the last thing you need."

"Dorothy, you know me too well!"

His enthusiasm for cruising now much diminished, East pulled onto Lemoyne Drive, drove three blocks, turned right onto Bienville Boulevard, and cruised toward the west end of the island. The two-lane road ran along some of the narrowest parts of the island, between the pastel pink, green, and blue summer cottages that lined both sides of the road, most of them owned by folks from Mobile and Birmingham with cutesy names like Paradise Found, My Little Heaven, and Sand Dollar Holler. In some places, both the Gulf of Mexico and the Mississippi Sound were simultaneously visible on the south and north, separated by a few city blocks of sand. The highest point on this end was maybe 10 feet. On a high tide and after a hard rain, the road would sometimes flood.

The Chief figured he had traveled a million miles behind the wheel of a police car, most of it up and down Bienville Boulevard, the main artery on the island. Although many would find it boring, the solitude of cruising allowed East to resolve various issues that troubled him, and at the moment, his mind was filled with issues. Training his new deputy, the string of deaths on the island, and the hurricane that was in the Gulf, to name a few.

If the island took a direct hit from that hurricane brewing down south, it would be total devastation. What a mess that would be! God, I need to think about retiring.

All anyone could do was to pray that it went somewhere else. However, as of this morning, the forecasters were still unable to predict landfall more precisely than the northern Gulf of Mexico and east Florida. He slowly cruised as far as the road went, turned around, and slowly headed back when Dorothy's voice came over the radio.

"Dispatch to Chief East, dispatch to Chief, come in."

The Chief took the microphone from the dashboard hook and replied, "This is the Chief. Come back."

"We have another accident reported down at the water tower. Somebody fell from the tower. Come back."

"Are you kidding me!? Damn it! What's next?"

"I'm sorry Chief. Sean and the ambulance are already there. Come back."

"Not your fault, Dorothy. I'm on my way. Over and out."

"Standing by."

The chief turned on the blue lights and siren and rushed to the scene.

"Deja vu all over again," said the Chief as he recognized the same EMTs he had spoken with after the previous accident. Sean knelt next to the spread-eagled victim who lay face down on the dunes that surrounded the tower. A bloody mess, the body had partially penetrated the sandy soil, such was the force of the impact.

"Hello again, Chief," said one of the EMTs. "No use even attempting to resuscitate after that fall." He pointed up to the stark white tank above. "We'll just load him up and take him straight to the County morgue. Same as that other fellow."

Damn, that was a long fall!" said the Chief, looking up. "What have you got for me, Sean?"

"Looks like he slipped and fell from that maintenance scaffold." Sean pointed upward at the tank that was at least 200 feet in height. "He's just a kid. I found his wallet on him. Gene Guidry, eighteen years old. Lives on Greeno Road, out on the west end. I believe that's his bicycle leaning against that tree over there."

"Damn," said Chief East sadly.

"Chief, I haven't seen that many bodies, but look how pale he is. It looks like he's been dead for a couple of days. He's lying in a pool of his blood. It appears that it came from his mouth, nose, ears, and even his eyes. Do you think the sudden impact could cause that kind of bleeding?"

"I couldn't say Sean. The coroner would have to make that determination."

"Chief, unless you need anything else, we'll take the body," said one of the EMTs.

"Sean, do you need anything?"

"No, sir. I took pictures of everything, so I think we are done down here."

The EMTs loaded the victim into the emergency vehicle and drove away.

"Sean, we need to do something about this mess here," said the Chief as he looked around, hoping to find something he could use to cover the blood. "Hell, just push sand over it."

The officers used their boots and pushed sand over the point of impact.

"That's good enough," said the Chief. "We just got that tank painted, and I'll bet dollars to doughnuts that he was up there painting graffiti on it."

"That's exactly what it was. Look at the side of the tank." Sean pointed to the bright red marks starkly contrasting with the brilliant white tank. "Can't tell what he was trying to write, but it was probably his girlfriend's name or some other such nonsense. Maybe this will keep kids off the damn tower for a while."

"Don't count on it, Sean. Kids nowadays don't have the same concept of reality that we had. They think they're bulletproof. I need you to go up there to take a look around."

"Let me take my duty belt off." Sean removed his belt and holstered weapon and handed it to Chief East.

"Take the camera and get some photos. Be careful and take your time."

"Oh, I will," replied Sean as he put the camera strap around his neck and began the long climb up the tower. In a few minutes, he had pulled himself onto the maintenance platform. The first thing he noticed was a can of spray paint lying on the metal grating. He shot a few pictures of the platform and the blotches of paint on the tank.

"What you got, Sean?" shouted the Chief, looking up.

"There is paint everywhere up here," called Sean, leaning over the railing. "I also found a can of black spray paint."

"Black?" shouted the Chief. "No red paint."

"That is peculiar," said Sean. "What the hell!"

"Sean, what is it?"

"Chief. This ain't red paint that's all over everything up here."

"Not paint? Then what is it?"
It's blood!"

CHAPTER 38

Jesse returned to his cottage for a quick bite, placed Bongo on the screen porch, and drove back to the Oceanography Lab to speak with his PhD advisor. As Jesse climbed out of the El Camino and crossed the lab parking lot, he ran into CC and Ross, who were in a conversation outside the door of the building.

"Hi guys! What's up?"

"Hey Jesse," said Ross and CC simultaneously.

"Did you hear about the dude who dove off the water tower?" asked CC.

"Seriously?"

"Did a swan dive right off the tower." She held her hand above her head and mimicked a free-fall. "Splat! He did a face plant right into the ground."

"Oh, good lord! Was it suicide?"

"I don't know.

"Freaking weird stuff," said Ross.

CC continued. "So, there was a fellow that died in a bloody car accident, another fellow was found dead in the trailer park on the island, and now this water tower thing. The news people are all over this cluster of deaths. My Dad called me from home and said it's in all the major newspapers, and he saw it on the national news. It's become a big story."

"All of this wonderful, free publicity for our tiny island! Business owners will be overjoyed." Jesse's words dripped with sarcasm. "Well, as much as I would like to continue this uplifting conversation, I've got to meet with my advisor." Jesse headed toward the door. "See you later."

He climbed the stairs to Dr. Gerald Pearson's office on the second floor. Pearson was largely responsible for his acceptance into the research program at the lab and was instrumental in his receiving a research fellowship, apparently against the recommendation of G-squared. For this reason, Jesse felt a great deal of anxiety about succeeding so that he might prove Gustafson wrong, but primarily to please his advisor. Although in his mid-sixties, he was the picture of health. A graduate of Florida State University, he was perhaps the most laid-back individual Jesse had ever met. He was one of the most well-liked professors at the Oceanography Lab, soft-spoken, slow to anger, gregarious, and friends with everyone. A distinguished individual, he stood well over 6 feet in height, with a full head of white, flowing hair, an aquiline nose, and piercing hazel eyes. Unlike some research advisors who exploited their graduate students, Jesse felt fortunate to have come under the tutelage of a man with apparently limitless patience and a mentor who gave freely of himself.

"Come on in Jesse." Pearson stood near a window that looked out upon the Gulf of Mexico, an open book in his hand, apparently engrossed in some complex, oceanographic conundrum. Always professionally dressed, he wore a light grey, linen sports coat, a white shirt, grey pants, and a light blue tie.

"I am sorry to bother you, Doc," announced Jesse as he entered the office. Despite the complete approachability of his advisor, Jesse always felt like he was very much out of his league when he walked through the door. The office, with floor-to-ceiling bookcases filled with volumes on every topic in oceanography, was like entering the "inner sanctum" of academia.

"No, no, it's not a bother." He closed the book and placed it on his desk. "Jesse, remember I told you that I will always find time for students. That is what they pay me for. But in addition, I enjoy our discussions. Take a seat."

"Thank you, sir."

"What's on your mind?" He leaned back in his squeaky office chair and interlaced his fingers across his stomach.

"Doc, I am perplexed." Jesse laid his research data across his advisor's desk. "The responses to the stress experiments that I've carried out over the past two years have been very predictable. Lactic acid increases, glucose decreases, etc." However, about two weeks ago, I found some sharks that displayed an aberrant response. When I say aberrant, I mean that they did not respond at all. None of the expected increases or decreases in blood parameters." Jesse removed the bull shark graph and handed it to him. Pearson put on his reading glasses and scrutinized the data.

"I would think that these are errors in your measurements. That kind of thing has happened to all of us."

"That was the first thing I thought. But look at this," Jesse handed him additional data sheets. "A few weeks ago, there were only a few that were out of the ordinary. A few days ago, there were more, and the most recent samples near the island all show the aberrant response."

With a puzzled look and an index finger to his temple, he examined each data sheet in turn. "All blood samples were taken uniformly? "

"Yes sir. Nothing has changed in the protocol; reagents are the same, syringes are the same."

"Have you retested your samples to double-check?"

"I have. Same results. And look at this." Jesse handed him the results from the longlining research trip. "There is a change in the response as you move further away from the island. All sharks were aberrant in shallow water, some in deeper water, and none of them in the deepest water. It appears that the change in these sharks is currently underway and has spread from shallow to deep water."

"This is peculiar. So, you are saying that these animals show little or no response to stress?"

"That seems to be the case. We first noticed this when we were collecting sharks a few weeks ago. The darn things just don't tire out. After taking repeated blood samples from the same individual, it's like nothing ever happened to them. We release them and they take off like a bat-out-of-hades. I'm convinced that this is real, but I cannot explain it. That is why I am here."

"I'm afraid I am at a loss, Jesse. You observed this in all species, not just certain ones?"

"I've seen it in all the species I've captured; bulls, blacktips, spinners, hammerheads, etc."

"Very strange!" Pearson sat for a moment in silent contemplation. "Hmm…you know, there was something in the newspaper about a shark. Where did I put that paper?" He got up, retrieved a copy of the Mobile Press-Register from the garbage, and leafed through the pages. "Here it is. Did you see this article about a huge tiger shark?"

"No, sir."

Pearson perused the article, reading aloud. "A local shark fishing club hooked a tiger shark they estimated to be over 500 pounds."

"That's not unusual. Tigers can exceed 1000 pounds."

"Here is the interesting part. After it was hooked, it towed their 26-foot fishing boat for…" Pearson looked again at the news article, "22 hours before they had to cut the line and release it."

"Twenty-two hours! That's insane! I would expect that shark to tire after 3 or 4 hours at most. That's the same thing we've been seeing in our collecting."

"I thought that seemed like a very long time and figured it was a typo."

"Crazy! Well, I'm going to present the results to the students and faculty at this Friday's seminar. I just wanted to let you know."

"I think that's a good idea. Perhaps someone will have some insight. However, you will be challenged on this."

"I welcome it."

"I know you do. That's what I like about you, Jesse! No fear in you."

"That may appear to be the case, Doc, but I'm just good at hiding the anxiety."

"This goes against what we know about shark physiology," added Pearson, "which isn't very much at this time. If this is real, you've documented some new phenomenon which could be really exciting. I wish I could be more helpful, but I've never encountered anything like this."

"No problem, Doc. Maybe someone will have some thoughts at the seminar." Jesse gathered up his data sheets and prepared to leave. "I do have another, off-topic question." He reached into his pocket, produced the gold coin that Joe had given him, and handed it to Pearson. "Have you ever seen anything like this?"

"Hmm. Where did you get this?"

"Do you know who Crazy Joe is?"

"I've heard of him, but that's about it."

"I spoke with him recently, and he gave it to me in return for a knife. Ross said he thought it was just a Mardi Gras throw."

"Wow! This feels like gold." He turned the coin over in his hand, switched on his desk lamp, and held the coin under it for closer examination. "It has some age on it, too."

"About 200 years, according to the date."

"Did he say how he came by it?"

"He said he found it in the water. He didn't elaborate. I don't know if it was in the swamp, in the Mississippi Sound, or in the Gulf. He doesn't talk a lot."

"I know a little about coins. I had a collection when I was a kid." He paused while he continued to examine the coin. "I am almost certain this is a genuine Spanish doubloon."

Jesse leaned forward in his chair. "Seriously! How can you tell?"

"First of all, notice how crude it is. Not like modern coins that are precisely minted. This coin was struck. It was made by taking a blank disc of gold, placing a die on top of it, and striking it with a hammer to imprint an image onto it. If memory serves, the image on this coin is King Charles III. That prominent nose of his is pretty recognizable."

"Any idea on its value?"

"I do not know precisely, but probably in the neighborhood of a thousand dollars."

Jesse almost fainted. "Holy smokes! Joe said there were lots of them."

"He could be sitting on a fortune and not even know it," added Pearson.

"I don't think he cares about money. But I told him I would find out its value and give it back to him."

"There's also the legend of Jean Lafitte, which I have never believed, said Pearson." The pirate who supposedly buried treasure somewhere on the island. If it's part of that treasure, the value could be even higher. There's a place in Mobile that appraises coins if you'd like to take it there."

"That would be great. What's the name of it?"

"I can look it up for you." He picked up a Mobile telephone directory and rifled through it. "It's called *Mobile Rarities,* and it's on Airport Boulevard. The owner is a coin expert."

"I don't get off the island much, but I'll try to get over there this weekend."

"He may not be able to tell you if it was from Lafitte's treasure horde, but he'll know if it is genuine." He copied the address on a note and handed it to Jesse.

"Thanks, Doc!"

"I'll give the shark question some more thought, but before you present this information to the faculty, be sure to double-check everything. You know Dr. Gustafson has very high expectations for all graduate students. I can imagine him being very critical if something doesn't sound right."

"I don't think he likes me very much," said Jesse.

"I'll give you a bit of advice that has served me well over the years. Don't take criticism of your science personally. It's not about you. It's about the quality of the science. If you avoid getting too emotionally caught up in your work, it will help you to examine it with greater objectivity."

"I will try that, Doc, but it's hard not to be emotionally attached to a project you've worked so hard on."

"I understand completely. I was in a similar situation when I was working on my PhD. And just between you and me," said Pearson as he leaned forward across his desk, smiled, and lowered his voice, "Gustafson is an ass."

They both chuckled, and Jesse added, "That seems to be the consensus among all the graduate students."

CHAPTER 39
Centers for Disease Control, Atlanta, Georgia, August 19, 1989

The black Mercedes navigated through the *Centers for Disease Control* lot and parked in a reserved space just outside the doorway of the administrative offices. The male occupant sat briefly, eyes closed, absorbing the last few notes of Luciano Pavarotti's *O Sole' Mio.* Turning off the engine, he pulled down the sun visor and used the vanity mirror to check his hair and adjust his power tie. At 38 years of age, C. M. Scheller II was the youngest person to ever hold the Director's position at the CDC. The stereotypical yuppie, he was tall, slim, and impeccably dressed. His hair, dark brown with splashes of gray at the temples, was perfectly coiffured in a style befitting a young executive. His unblemished complexion and perfectly trimmed nails were a testament to his obsession with appearance.

Scheller pushed the sun visor back into place, exited the car, bent down to brush a speck of dust from his Italian leather shoes, and walked through the revolving door of the CDC. A casual observer passing by the entirely unimpressive building would never guess that behind those steel and concrete walls were some of the deadliest pathogens known: anthrax, plague, and Ebola. Like the Spanish flu of 1918, which killed 50 million worldwide, an accident at the facility could alter the course of human history. And C.M. Scheller was the man controlling that power. But Scheller was the worst kind of administrator. A narcissist, he lacked empathy, craved attention and admiration, took credit when it was not deserved, and manipulated his subordinates. Scheller's proudest achievement, at least in his mind, was his infallible, cover-your-ass administrative style. Delegating responsibility and relying on a series of "fall guy" assistants and junior administrators gave him foolproof, deniable plausibility. "The buck stops on someone else's desk," a bastardization of Harry Truman's famous motto, was Scheller's mantra. His rapid rise through the ranks of the CDC was simply a step toward his ultimate goal. Using his family's political connections, he intended to become the next Secretary of Health and Human Services, assuming the right candidate won the upcoming election and secured the presidency. After that, as far as he was concerned, the sky was the limit.

"Good morning, Dr. Scheller." His secretary smiled and looked up from her work as Scheller stepped off the elevator onto the 12th-floor executive suite. "A reminder of your 9:00 Director's meeting. The agenda is on your desk."

Scheller walked past her desk without reply and glanced at his *Rolex Oyster* wristwatch. "Go in and tell them I will be there in a moment. They can wait. But first, bring me a cup of tea and the newspaper."

"Yes, sir," replied the secretary, rising from her desk. "What a jerk," she added under her breath after he closed his office door behind him. "How hard is it to say good morning?"

Scheller eased into his crocodile leather office chair, feeling the smooth hide in his hand. Besides the luxurious sensation, the idea that he sat on the skin of one of the most dangerous predators on earth was oddly satisfying. He chuckled. Taxpayers would be shocked to know what this chair cost them. Scheller's 12th-floor office offered a stunning view of the Atlanta skyline. Everything about his office radiated power: the mahogany paneling, the portrait of Napoleon on horseback, and his desk, a replica of the HMS Resolute desk in the Oval Office. He leaned forward and picked up the agenda for the day's meeting. A knock at the door. "Come in," Scheller said, never looking up.

"Here's your tea, sir, and the newspaper. You should look at the article on page 3." The secretary placed the tea and the Atlanta Constitution newspaper on his desk, turned, and left the room.

Without acknowledging her presence, Scheller continued scanning the agenda for today's meeting. *God, I hate these things! A total waste of time.* He took a sip of tea and found it unacceptable as usual. Disgusted, he tossed the agenda aside and picked up the newspaper. *What did she say about an article?* Leafing through the pages, he found a news item entitled: *Mysterious Deaths on Dauphin Island, Alabama.* Sheller's immediate reaction was one of curiosity, then disgust, and culminating with anger as he read:

A cluster of deaths on Dauphin Island, a quiet vacation spot off the coast of Alabama, has island officials perplexed and locals fearing the worst... Rumors among residents of this sleepy fishing village include alien abduction, simple accidents, toxic gas, and infectious diseases... Dr. Cherie Belon, a Centers for Disease Control Agent investigating the deaths, is quoted as saying, "The Centers for Disease Control has been unable to identify an infectious agent and, at this time, there is no indication of a threat to the community." There has been no official statement from the CDC, and, as of press time, no additional information from the CDC was available.

Scheller was furious. Removing the page with the article, he tucked it neatly into the pocket of his tailored suit, pushed away from his desk, and left the office. "Meeting room, now!" Scheller ordered as his secretary, holding a notepad and pencil, rose from her seat and followed behind him.

The meeting room where the six Associate Directors had patiently waited fell silent when Scheller appeared. The directors gathered monthly to report progress and/or problems within each of the six divisions of the CDC, with each participant reporting in turn. He took his seat at the head of the table, leaned back in his chair, fingers steepled beneath his chin, and began the meeting by calling for each director to report while his secretary recorded the details. Each individual in the room knew it was pointless to ask for direction or opinion from Scheller since his doctorate was in Business Administration, and he had received this appointment through political favors. The directors each described the progress they were making, the goals that had been met, and the expectation of progress for the coming weeks.

At Scheller's request, Dr. Randolph Stern, the Associate Director of the *Center for Infectious Diseases,* reported last. After all the directors had spoken, Scheller dismissed the attendees and informed Stern that he wanted to see him in his office immediately. They walked together back to his office, and Scheller closed the door behind them.

"Have you seen this?" Scheller handed Stern the news article as he took a seat across from his desk.

Stern paused for a moment while he perused the article. "I have not."

"It sounds like your department doesn't know what the hell they're doing."

"Director Scheller, if you find my performance unsatisfactory, I will be happy to tender my resignation without delay." Stern placed the news article back on Scheller's desk.

"That's definitely a discussion for another day. But what I want to know right now is what the hell is going on? That article makes the CDC sound like a bunch of damn rubes!"

"Sir, we are following established CDC protocols. We have one of our best field agents working on Dauphin Island, and we are doing all we can. You are well aware that after recent resignations, we are understaffed in the Infectious Disease Center at a time when we have four active investigations across the country. If you would like me to pull agents from one of those other investigations to send to Dauphin Island, just tell me which ones." Stern knew that there was no way Scheller would make such a decision. One that might ultimately reveal his incompetence.

"What I want you to do is use that damn PhD of yours to complete this investigation!" Scheller slammed a fist on his desk, rose from his chair, and walked to the large windows that looked out across the Atlanta skyline. He continued speaking with his back to Stern. "We have a responsibility to protect the citizens of this country, and it appears that you are not doing your job."

"I know very well the responsibility of this job." Stern was spitting fire with each word. "I've spent many sleepless nights worrying about just that. And I repeat, if you want my resignation, just let me know."

"Enough with the resignation threats!" Scheller wheeled around to face Stern. His spray-tanned face was now scarlet red. "So, tell me, Stern, what do you have at this point, if anything?"

"As I outlined in the last report, we have been unable to identify an infectious agent as yet. We've processed all tissue samples, and we've found nothing. After the report from the FBI, it looks more like the victim was exposed to an unidentified toxic substance and not a biological agent. And by the way, it's *Dr. Stern*! I don't care for being addressed by my last name."

"Whatever!" replied Scheller indignantly. "What FBI report are you referring to?"

"Director Scheller, have you read any of the reports that I've submitted?"

"I am very busy and don't have time to read everything that comes across my desk."

"Again, as described in the last report," said Stern sarcastically, "an unusual device was discovered onboard the Crimson Tide. Investigators found a suspicious metal cylinder in one of the fishing nets that had not yet been emptied. It was handed over to the FBI, and it appears to have been a device that was designed to deliver its pressurized contents."

"An explosive device?" Scheller returned to his desk.

"The FBI does not think so. There was no trace of the contents remaining inside, but the design suggested a weapon to deliver a gas or a toxic material of some kind."

"Are you saying that someone designed it to randomly kill whoever came across it?"

"Yes. A relatively sophisticated terrorist device, according to the FBI."

"Do they have a clue as to how such a device came to be on a shrimp boat off the coast of freakin' Alabama?"

"They did not report it to me. But since it was found in a trawl that had not yet been emptied, the obvious inference is that it was caught in the trawl accidentally and brought aboard. They were just in the wrong place at the wrong time."

"And you are still unable to identify a toxic agent?"

"We've never seen anything like it. It doesn't fit the profile of a biological agent, at least none we have ever encountered before. Given the widespread tissue damage, the only thing we can compare it to is highly radioactive material that disrupts practically every cell in the body. But there was no sign of radioactivity in the cylinder, none on the body of the Captain, and none anywhere on the shrimp boat. We assume the captain and crew were killed by whatever was released from the device. We are hoping that they will be the only victims of this. Dr. Belon, our field agent on the island, reports to me regularly. She found that there may have been another unidentified individual who went aboard the boat before the Coast Guard impounded it. She is putting forth every effort to identify that individual. She is working closely with the local authorities and the Alabama Department of Health. We are keeping close tabs on this."

"Does she know about the cylinder?"

"She does not. The FBI has asked us to keep this strictly confidential. That is why we have given little or no information to the press."

Scheller's phone rang. "That's my secretary." He picked up the receiver and put it to his ear.

"Director Scheller, my apologies for interrupting, but Dr. Belon is on the line. She needs to speak with Dr. Stern. It's apparently urgent."

"A call for you," said Scheller to Stern as he waved him from the room the way one might shoo away a bothersome insect. "See my secretary."

Stern rose and left, happy to be out of the room. He walked past the secretary and shook his head in disgust. "Thank you, Rose. I'll take the call in my office."

CHAPTER 40

"And in conclusion…" Jesse stood in a darkened lecture hall, a large screen behind him. He pushed the button on the slide projector, and an image of a colorful sunset appeared on the screen, signaling the end of his seminar and the beginning of the dreaded question-and-answer period. "…these data suggest that a change in the stress response has occurred in these animals, a change that has spread rapidly through the population. A phenomenon of this kind has hitherto never been reported. Thank you."

To the sound of applause, Dr. Pearson rose from his seat near the front of the room and turned to face the standing-room-only crowd of students and faculty that filled the conference room at the Oceanography Lab. "Thank you Jesse. Would someone get the lights, please? Are there questions?" Several hands went up, and Pearson called on Gustafson first.

Oh crap! thought Jesse as a knot formed in the pit of his stomach. *This is not going to be good.*

"Mr. Gates, did you do a statistical power analyziz, and if zo, vat vere the results?"

You old fart. I totally anticipated that question, thought a smiling Jesse.

"Let me return to the stress response slide." Jesse held the slide controller button down as images flashed in reverse across the screen. "As is clearly shown here…" Jesse used a laser pointer to indicate the statistical results, "… the sample sizes used in this study were greater than those estimated by *a-priori* power analysis."

"Zo you zampled more sharks than power analysis indicated vere required. You vasted your time and resources."

"I respectfully disagree," countered Jesse as he approached the seated Gustafson in a mildly intimidating manner. "When working with wild-caught, live animals, it is impossible to anticipate how many animals may be captured at a particular time and place. Unlike the physical sciences, where measurements, say of ocean temperature or salinity, are often limited only by the enthusiasm of the researchers themselves, in field biology, the availability of animals often limits measurements. A marine biologist may catch 200 animals on one day and zero the next. Given the difficulty in capturing these particularly intractable animals, if I only needed 50 sharks to satisfy power analysis and I caught 60, it would be unwise to make measurements on 50 and release the other 10. Furthermore, let's say you lose a portion of the blood samples before you can make measurements, or the measurements are incorrect due to instrument error. Those extra 10 sharks then become very important. I'm afraid that scientists outside of biology don't understand the difficulty in obtaining animals, and capturing sharks is one of the most difficult of all."

"Mr. Gates, are you familiar vith Occam's Razor?"

"Also called the Principle of Parsimony," replied Jesse somewhat condescendingly, "which says that the simplest explanation is likely the correct one. Everyone is familiar with Occam's Razor."

Gustafson's attempt to embarrass Jesse was unsuccessful to everyone in the room, and he was now scowling more than usual. "I zuggest that the zimplest explanation iz that you have made errors in your measurements and your elaborate hypothesis iz based on flawed data."

In outward appearance, a poker-faced Jesse showed no trace of the anger that was burning in his brain. *I've had just about enough of this bald son of a....* "To reiterate, if you had been paying attention," said Jesse forcefully, "you would have recalled that I tested blood samples in triplicate, recalibrated the instruments, and changed out all chemical reagents. The results were unchanging. If you have an alternate hypothesis, I would love to hear it."

With that statement, Gustafson got out of his chair and left the room.

"Guess he doesn't have one," said Jesse as guarded laughter spread around the room.
*****

As was tradition at the Oceanography Lab, the students and some faculty retired to the student lounge after the seminar. Calling the room a lounge was a stretch. A large couch, lounge chairs, and a coffee table were the dominant furnishings in the room, aside from the small bar that sat against one wall. As a meager attempt at interior decorating, a section of fishing net with various marine-themed decorations, a dried starfish, an inflated, lacquered porcupine fish, and pastel-tinted coral hung from the wall above the bar. While alcoholic drinks could not be sold legally in the lounge, a "donation" jar helped pay for the keg that was provided every Friday afternoon.

Not long after the seminar, Cherie found Jesse, Ross, CC, and several other graduate students engrossed in discussing the material he had just presented. A keg of beer had been tapped, officially signaling the beginning of TGIF, Thank God It's Friday, and the weekend. Cherie crossed the room and approached the group to find Jesse dressed unusually dapper: khaki slacks, a button-down, blue, short-sleeved shirt, and tan deck shoes.

"Man, did you put G-squared in his place?" said an over-excited CC. "He was fuming when he stalked out."

"I am so freaking proud of you!" said Ross as he high-fived a less-than-enthusiastic Jesse. "I'll bet he thinks twice before trying that crap with other students."

"No, what I did was ruin my future as a Marine Biologist," bemoaned Jesse. "He'll never sign off on my dissertation now or blackball me from getting hired anywhere."

"He has no choice but to sign off if Dr. Pearson and your committee approve it," replied Ross.

"We'll see," replied Jesse. He smiled as he spotted Cherie approaching.

"Hi Jesse." Cherie was surprised at Jesse's appearance as she had never seen him in anything other than shorts and t-shirts.

"Hi Cherie. It's great to see you."

"Wow, don't you look nice!" She held Jesse at arm's length as she looked him up and down.

"I appreciate that. They expect us to look professional when we present a seminar, and this is about as professional as it gets for me."

"Well, you look very nice."

"Hi Cherie," CC came forward and gave Cherie a big hug.

"Hi CC. I haven't seen you since the shark fishing trip. How have you been?"

"Very well, thanks."

"How did the seminar go?" Cherie posed the question to Jesse, but Ross chose to answer.

"Hi Cherie. The seminar went just fine, although Jesse is convinced it was a disaster. We were just talking about it."

"What makes you think it was a disaster?" asked Cherie, turning to Jesse.

"Some of the faculty believe that my research data has been corrupted in some way. If my PhD advisory committee shares that sentiment, then my degree is in jeopardy."

"I disagree," said CC forcefully. "You've documented something completely new. The numbers you have are real, I have no doubt."

Ross, a solo cup of beer in his hand, came to Jesse's defense as well. "I agree with CC. If my opinion counts for anything, this could be an incredibly important discovery. And by the way, you can dismiss G-squared's opinion since, number one, he is so clearly biased against anything in biology and, number two, is...uh...uh...he's a big pile of number two!" Ross started belly-laughing. "Get it, number two?"

"Yeah, I got it," deadpanned Jesse. "You should not be drinking beer this early in the day, Ross."

"Yes Mom," said Ross sarcastically.

"Who or what is G-squared?" asked Cherie.

"That's Dr. Guner Gustafson. He's the Chair of the Marine Science Department," said Ross with derision. "When he does not like a seminar, he lets everyone know by turning his chair around to face the back of the room while he busies himself with grading tests or reading scientific articles."

"Are you kidding? He did that during your seminar?"

"He did. I just ignored him. I can't let it get to me because of this anger management thing. However, when I know something like that might happen, I can prepare myself for it, although I can't help but be disappointed. Which is why he does it."

"And he calls himself a professional?" said Cherie disgustedly.

"Jesse put Gustafson in his place. The dill-weed stormed out of the seminar," said Ross.

"And probably took my degree with him."

"You know that's BS," said CC.

"It's OK if I'm not awarded a PhD. I always have my skills as a bullfighter to fall back on. I'll just change my name to Francisco Salvatore and take my red, matador suit to the cleaners."

The comment caught Ross in mid-guzzle, and he snorted beer on the floor in front of him. Cherie could not help but laugh. Cherie's laughter always made Jesse feel better.

"I would pay to see you in that suit," joked Cherie as she smiled. "Jesse, the truth will always win out. What does your major professor think?"

"After my seminar and the details of how I tested and re-tested the blood samples, he is on my side and quite excited about this."

"Jesse was even able to estimate the approximate date when the change in the shark population began," said CC.

"Impressive," said Cherie, smiling. "I am sorry I missed the seminar, but I do not doubt that this is going to be fine."

"I hope so."

"Changing the subject. Sheriff East and I are meeting this afternoon or tomorrow to discuss some issues, and I would like you to come along. Is that something you could do?"

"No problem."

"Have you met Sheriff East?"

"Well, uh, yeah. Not socially, however. He gave me a warning once for speeding."

"He's very nice and very competent. The folks of Dauphin Island should be thankful to have him as Chief."

"He seems like an upstanding guy! I was definitely over the speed limit, and he could have given me a ticket, but didn't."

"I don't know him, but I've only heard good things about him," added CC. "He's a veteran of some war, which earns my respect right there. I forget which war it was."

"Hey, did you find out anything about that coin?" asked Ross.

"Dr. Pearson gave me an address for a dude in Mobile that can identify it."

"Betcha it's worthless," said Ross, who was now slurring his words slightly.

"We'll know as soon as I can go to Mobile. But Doc said he believes it is genuine. In fact, he mentioned something about Jean Lafitte's treasure. There's a legend that it's buried somewhere on the island."

"You mean Lean Jafitte the pirate? What did I just say?" Ross giggled at having reversed the letters. "I think Lean Jafitte was Fat Jafitte's brother…ha, ha, ha." Ross laughed and stumbled slightly.

"CC," asked Jesse, "would you cut Ross off? He's had enough."

"Consider it done."

CHAPTER 41

"I appreciate y'all coming by on a Saturday." Sheriff East, Jesse, and Cherie walked along the corridor of the Police Station. "We rarely use this conference room, but there's a chalkboard, and I thought it might come in handy." Chief East went to the old window unit air conditioner in the small conference room, turned it on, and cranked it as low as it would go. The AC droned like a Mac truck on the interstate. "Sorry for the heat, folks. This unit is old, but it'll cool the room off quickly."

"Chief, I asked Jesse to join us because I value his insight. I believe the two of you have met?"

"Oh yes, we've met. 1968 El Camino, going 45 mph coming off the Dauphin Island Bridge onto the island. You still remember that the speed limit drops to 25 right there?"

"Yes sir. I have not forgotten." Jesse, amazed that East had remembered details of the encounter, extended his hand. "Jesse Gates, sir."

"Nice to see you, Jesse. It's funny how I can recall the most insignificant stuff but fail to remember names, birthdays, anniversaries, etc. I remember that stop because you were in that El Camino. We don't see that many classic cars on the island."

"Thank you for meeting with us, Chief." Cherie and Jesse sat down at the small conference table.

"Thank you for working so diligently on this," replied the Chief.

"I should mention that Jesse is a scientist and has been helping me with the investigation."

"You're a scientist?"

"Yes sir. I'm working on a PhD at the Oceanography Lab. But honestly, all I've done is helped with some tissue samples and chauffeured Dr. Belon around the island some. My contribution has been minimal."

"His help has been invaluable," countered Cherie. "He's just being modest."

"Dr. Belon, I've wondered why the CDC sent only a single investigator. They must think highly of you."

"I don't know about that. It's primarily a manpower issue. The Center for Infectious Diseases is spread pretty thin right now.

If things happen to get worse, they'll have to find people to send here."

"So, what do you have thus far, Doc?"

"I will give you the good news first. I think I've identified two individuals, one of whom might have been the person who went on board the Crimson Tide when it ran aground. Thanks to Dorothy's help running the registration on motorcycles registered to owners living on the west end, I have two names: Vince Lewis and Gene Guidry. Lewis lives at…"

"Gene Guidry?" interrupted Chief East. "An 18-year-old who lives on Green Road?"

"Yes sir. How did you know that?"

"Bad news. Gene Guidry died from a fall off the Dauphin Island water tower yesterday afternoon. That's why I couldn't meet sooner."

"What? Are you kidding me? He fell off a water tower?"

"Are you sure it was him?" asked Jesse.

"I'm afraid so. He had identification on him. I was going to tell you that the condition of the body was similar to the other recent deaths on the island. Massive blood and body fluid loss."

"I can't believe this!" Cherie shook her head in disbelief. "One step forward and two steps back! I need to get some blood and tissue samples."

"His body is at the coroner's office in Mobile. I told them to treat it as infectious and that you would want to examine it as soon as possible. I left a message at the motel for you to call me, but obviously, you didn't get it."

"Was he wearing tennis shoes by any chance?"

"I believe he was. Why do you ask?"

"I have photos of footprints that we found on the beach where the shrimp boat was grounded. They were footprints of an approximate size 9, a Converse brand tennis shoe. The tread pattern was distinctive."

"I am impressed! Doc, if you ever decide to go into law enforcement, I want you to come down here and work for me."

"She is awesome!" Jesse smiled and gave Cherie an appreciative look.

"I'm just doing my job. We also have reason to believe that the person who went on board the Crimson Tide had brown hair."

"Yep, Gene Guidry had brown hair," affirmed East.

"I've got to take a look at that body as soon as we finish here."

"Chief," said Jesse, "I've been out of the loop recently. How many deaths have we had on the island?"

"You know, that's a good starting point for discussion." The Chief picked up a file folder that lay on the table and went to the blackboard. "If we count the captain of the Crimson Tide," he paused to leaf through his file and wrote the names, "we have 1, Captain Tom Armstrong, 2, a tourist from North Carolina, Reginald Carter, 3, a retired trailer park resident, Charles Walton, 4, Paul Stanford, who owns a restaurant on the island. He was a good guy. And 5, just this morning, Gene Guidry, only 18 years old. Just terrible!"

"Wow!" Jesse shook his head in disbelief. "I had no idea that so many people had passed recently. Chief, is that an unusual number for Dauphin Island?"

"That's unheard of for the island. In my 15 years as Chief, we've never had this many people die in such a short time."

By the way", added Jesse, "you could probably include the fellow who disappeared from his fishing boat. When we were coming in a few days ago after a research trip, the Coast Guard was monitoring an unmanned boat that was running in tight circles in lower Mobile Bay. The boat was covered with blood."

"You're probably right," said East. "I knew about that incident, but I don't have information about him since the Coast Guard handled that case. Plus, the body was never found. So that makes six deaths. Doc, does any of this help your investigation at all?"

"Sorry, Chief," said Cherie, a blank expression on her face. "I'm still trying to process the fact that Guidry is dead."

"No problem." East took a seat at the conference table.

"Suppose he was indeed the individual who was onboard the Crimson Tide," said Cherie. "If true, we may have just identified the primary case, the individual who first brought the agent onto Dauphin Island. This could be a critical finding. Assuming Guidry was the primary case, all subsequent infections would be secondary or tertiary cases. Secondary cases are those that were infected by Guidry; tertiary, those infected by secondary cases, etc. Of course, this is all predicated on there being some agent which we still have not identified."

"So, if you document direct or even indirect contact between Guidry and the others who have died, that would be evidence that some kind of agent has passed between them?" asked Jesse.

"Yes, it would. This gives me an important starting point for establishing contact and may provide insight into how this thing is transmitted."

"Chief, were you able to identify any common characteristics surrounding the deaths of these individuals?" asked Jesse.

"Yes. But they don't seem important. For instance, all were male. Probably just a coincidence. All were relatively young and active, except for Walton. One odd observation that my deputy made was that Walton was watching a video of *The Exorcist* when he died. He said it probably gave him a heart attack."

"That movie is disgusting," observed Cherie, shaking her head.

East continued. "Guidry climbed up on the water tower, and something happened up there before he fell off. The medical examiner said he believed Guidry was dead before he hit the ground. There was blood all over the tank and the service scaffolding. Same as that tourist from North Carolina, uh…what was his name?"

"Carter," said Cheri.

"I am convinced that Carter was dead before he crashed," said East. "He had just swerved to avoid hitting a stray dog in the road. The fellow following behind him in his car said it scared the heck out of him when Carter almost lost control of his vehicle before he crashed into the bayou."

"So, you think he lost control, regained it, and then crashed his car?"

"According to an eyewitness, that seems to be what happened. After barely missing that stray, the witness said he drove down the road a short distance, then accelerated to high speed and crashed."

"And Paul Stanford also," said Jesse. "He parasailed into a fog bank and died suddenly. I wonder what the blood profiles look like for these victims?" said Jesse, thinking out loud. "It may tell us nothing, but I could do the blood work fairly easily."

"Jesse is a physiologist studying stress in sharks," said Cherie to East. "I am open to anything at this point, but you absolutely cannot handle potentially infectious blood in your laboratory."

"Was there enough blood in any of the victims to test?" asked East.

"I did get blood samples from Paul Stanford, but they were delivered to the CDC in Atlanta."

"Could they do blood chemistry on those?" asked Jesse. "I'm not sure what I'm looking for, but it might be interesting to know the commonly measured blood parameters and hormone levels."

"They have the equipment to do any blood parameter that we need. I'll request those right away," said Cherie.

"Chief," Dorothy softly knocked on the conference room door and stuck her head in. "Sorry to interrupt, but I just picked up the photographs you requested."

"Did you look at them?"

"I did not. Thought it might be too creepy for me." Dorothy handed the envelope of photographs to East.

"Thanks. This could be fortuitous, or it could be nothing," cautioned East. "Paul Stanford was parasailing to obtain photographs of the island and wanted some pictures of a gas rig. He had a camera around his neck. I've never seen a camera like this. It had an auto-wind feature so you could shoot pictures continuously just by holding down the shutter button. I was told that he intended to have the pictures framed to hang in his restaurant. On a hunch, I decided to have the photos developed." He sat down, opened the envelope, and paged through the photographs. "Oh dear!" He looked away and steeled himself. "These first pictures are of his wife and kids. Damn it. Paul was a good man." He took a deep breath and continued. "OK, here are several pictures of the island from the air." He passed the photos to Cherie and Jesse. "Nothing to see on these. Here's where the boat turned south toward a gas rig that you can see in the distance. Here's a closer shot of the gas rig as they headed south. That's the #14 gas rig, I believe. The fog is closing in on these pics. Look at this! A bird of some kind is headed right for the camera. Jesse, do you recognize that bird?"

"It's a laughing gull. Probably got confused in that fog bank. I wonder if it struck him? Those are one of the most common gulls around the island. Probably scared the crap out of both him and the bird."

"Well, he continued taking pictures because he shot every picture on this film roll. These are the last several." East quickly rifled through them as he described each and passed them on. "Fog, fog, fog, blurry picture, blurry picture, leg of his pants looks like."

"Why is he taking these random photos of nothing?" asked Jesse.

East suddenly paused. "Oh crap!" He turned away in horror and placed the final photos face down on the table under his hand.

"Chief East, are you OK?" asked Cherie. "What is it?"

It took a moment for East to reply. "Something must have jammed the shutter button down because the camera just kept taking photos of nothing. However, some of these are horrendous. Doc, are you sure you want to see these?"

"If it might help this investigation, then I have to see them."
"Jesse?"

"I've probably seen worse than what is in those photos, Chief."

The Chief handed the photos to Cherie. The images showed first a human hand and a parasailing harness covered in blood, and then blood-spattered clothing. The next image appeared to be of blood captured in mid-flight as it was propelled through the air. Worst of all were images of Paul's face, some blurred, others crystal clear. One showed his face, blood-covered, and frozen in absolute torment. The final photos were uniformly red as the camera lens seemed to be covered in blood.

"I was wrong," admitted Jesse. "I've not seen worse."

"Jesus help us!" said Cherie as she laid the final photograph down. "Could you excuse me for a moment? I need a drink of water."

"Sure, Doc," said East. "There's a water fountain in the lobby. It's not that cold, but it's wet."

Cherie pulled her chair back and left the room.

"What in the world happened to this poor man?" Jesse picked up the photo again. "Blood is coming out everywhere, even his freaking eyes…Good Lord!" Jesse grimaced and handed the image back to East.

"Like the other victims," said East, "death was preceded by massive blood loss."

Cherie returned with a cup of coffee in hand. "Dorothy is such a nice lady!"

"She's a peach!" said East. "Frankly, she keeps this place from falling apart. I couldn't get along without her. Doc, we were just talking about the fact that there was massive blood loss before the death of each of these victims. I already knew this and reluctantly assumed it was because of the trauma caused by the accidents. The EMTs mentioned to me that they could find no injury that could account for the amount of blood loss they saw. It seems to me that in some, maybe all of these cases, an otherwise healthy person experienced massive blood loss, and their death was, in part, caused by that blood loss."

"That may be the case," added Cherie, "but it's all circumstantial evidence, and we still haven't identified an infectious agent. The CDC is not going to move forward until we have something more concrete. I am very worried that we are dealing with a new kind of hemorrhagic fever, like Ebola or Dengue Fever. Those viral diseases cause blood loss, but not the kind we have seen in these victims. But what I have to do now is examine the body of that poor kid, and confirm that he was onboard the Crimson Tide. "

"Request that blood analysis as well," reminded Jesse.

"Oh, yes. They can likely have that in a matter of hours, and Chief, is it OK if they fax that to the Sheriff's Department?"

"No problem, just let Dorothy know."

"I'll phone in the request as soon as we finish here. I am anxious to re-examine the contact tracing that I've done with Guidry as the primary case. The most difficult part is going to be interviewing the parents of that kid, assuming that's necessary."

"That's going to be hard," cautioned East. "Those folks are grieving, and the last thing they would want to hear is that their deceased teenager may be responsible for this mess."

"That is not how I would approach it. There's no need to tell them that he may have been the primary case. As a matter of fact, we need to keep our discussion here confidential."

"Absolutely," agreed both Jesse and East.

"Jesse, would you be willing to go with me to speak to the family if I need to?"

"Of course I will. But I am not good in these situations. I never seem to say the right things, so I just keep my mouth shut."

"I would not ask you to speak with them, but I could use the moral support."

"Just let me know when you want to go."

"Can I offer a suggestion?" asked East. "Since most people on the island attend church, it might be helpful to approach their pastor for guidance on how to proceed. The pastor may even accompany you to provide some comfort to the family."

"That's a good idea," said Cherie.

"Doc, I can't continue to ignore this. I'm going to contact the Alabama Department of Health for help."

"I understand. God help us if an unidentified infectious agent with a 100% rate of mortality reaches the mainland!"

CHAPTER 42

Cherie and Jesse left the Sheriff's Department and, like stepping into a Turkish sauna, they were immediately enveloped by the humid, island atmosphere. They stood together on the front steps of the building, attempting to adjust to the change.

"Whew, that sun is brutal." Jesse used his t-shirt tail to wipe the condensation off his sunglasses before putting them on. "I love warm weather, but this humidity is ridiculous. I don't see how folks survived in the South before AC."

"A few years back, I ran across an article, I think it was by a sociologist from LSU. He argued that the availability of air conditioning was the single most important technological development, responsible for moving the southern U.S. from an agricultural economy to an industrial one."

"There's a lot of truth to that," said Jesse. "It changed the South."

"Jesse, do you want to ride with me to the coroner's office in Mobile? I need to examine the body of that young man as soon as possible."

"Of course. I am committed to this investigation now. But I have one condition."

"And what might that be?" asked Cherie.

"That we take tonight off."

"What did you have in mind?"

"We go out for dinner. We do something fun. Mainly, we forget this investigation for a few hours."

"Why Jesse, are you asking me out on a date?"

"Yes, I am."

"I don't know, I have so many suitors vying for my attention." Cherie gave Jesse a coquettish look.

"I don't doubt that. But none of them are bullfighters, I'll bet."

"Good point. I will agree to go out with you, but I also have a condition."

"Uh oh!"

"You have to let me pay for it," insisted Cherie. "I know what it's like to be a graduate student, and I have a real job."

"I can't let you do that. It just wouldn't feel right."

"OK, then how about this? I'll pick up something from the grocery store, and we can cook it at your house."

"I can live with that. It happens that I make an excellent shrimp creole, and I have frozen shrimp at home. You really won't have to buy much at all. I'll give you a list. Afterward, we go for an early evening cruise on board the R/V Bongo and watch the sunset. The seas are very calm tonight. What do you think?"

"That sounds wonderful!"

Under a cloudless sky, the two crossed the parking lot toward their parked cars.

"Let's get this over with. The Chief called ahead and arranged for me to examine the body."

"Do you mind if we swing by a business called Mobile Rarities on Airport Boulevard? My advisor gave me the address of an expert there who can provide information about the old coin that Joe gave me."

"No problem. So you showed it to your advisor?"

"I did. He used to collect coins as a kid, and he's pretty sure it's the real thing."

"Well, that would be exciting!"

"Your vehicle or mine?" asked Jesse.

"Let's take the Crown Vic to keep this official. Biohazard suits and masks are in the car. I'm going to hand out some more suits at the coroner's office. I've already given some to Emergency Services for the EMTs to wear. We will need to wear them when we inspect the body."

"I assumed that we would."

They climbed into the white, unmarked Ford Crown Victoria, Cherie behind the wheel, and made the 30-minute drive to the coroner's office. Housed in a repurposed church built in the 1930s, the grand façade, wrought iron balconies, decorative moldings, and arched windows showcased the French architecture that characterized downtown Mobile. But like many other structures in this troubled part of the city, it had fallen into disrepair. A building, once full of life but now a repository for the dead, was unsettling for Jesse. Cherie parked the car on the street in front of the building.

"Whoa, this was an impressive building." Jesse paused on the sidewalk and looked up at the imposing structure. "I expect to see Quasimodo hanging from the church spire?"

"It was beautiful at one time." They gathered up their biohazard suits, footies, and particle masks and entered the building.

"May I help you?" asked the man at the front desk.

"Yes, thank you. I am Dr. Cherie Belon. Sheriff East called ahead regarding the young man who was brought in yesterday."

"Oh yes. From the CDC," said the individual as he extended his hand. "It's nice to meet you, Dr. Belon. I'm Steve Fontenot, the Assistant Medical Examiner."

"Fontenot? Are you from Louisiana?"

"I am. Hammond, Louisiana. That accent of yours places you down in Cajun country."

"I'm from Baton Rouge," replied Cherie, "but most of my family lives down around Chalmette, as Cajun as it gets."

"And this is Jesse Gates." Cherie turned to introduce Jesse. "He's a scientist from the Oceanography Lab and is assisting me in the investigation."

"Nice to me you," replied Jesse as they shook hands. "I assume it's Doctor Fontenot?"

"It is, but please call me Steve."

"And call me Cherie."

"Cherie, I'm gonna cut to the chase. What the hell is happening on the island? This is the fourth or fifth body we've received over the past several days."

"Unfortunately, we still do not know for sure. I hope that examining this poor kid will give us some important clues."

"We can do that. He's in drawer #22."

"I hope you still have the clothes he was wearing?" asked Cherie.

"We do. They are bagged separately. I can show those to you. Let me get my bio-suit, and I'll take you back."

"Glad to see that you're using those," said Cherie. "I have more of them in the car to drop off.

"No need. We just received a shipment of suits and masks, so it's all good. We're taking no chances here. Everyone is required to wear them and we disinfect our vehicles, tables, gurneys, the whole damn building, just about.”

They left the front office and walked into a hallway where Cherie and Jesse suited up. Cherie took some photographs from her backpack and dropped them into the pocket of her suit. Steve disappeared and returned wearing his.

“This way folks.” Steve led them down the hall through a door into a refrigerated, climate-controlled room. Rows of numbered, stainless-steel drawers lined one wall of the room, and three stainless autopsy tables sat at the room’s center. “We can accommodate 30 cadavers here, and you can see that Mr. Guidry is in #22. We can’t take many more.”

“Who are all the others?” asked Jesse.

“Mostly murders, accidents, one suicide. Just a word of caution, you don’t want to be downtown after dark.”

“Don’t worry, we’ll be back on the island by this afternoon,” said Cherie. “Are you aware that there is a rumor on the island that this kid committed suicide?”

“I was not,” said Steve, “but the autopsy revealed internal organs that were liquified like nothing I have ever seen before. I thought he had died days ago, but I’m told that we received the body within hours of his death.” Steve pulled open drawer #22 and unzipped the body bag.

“Gird your loins,” said Cherie quietly.

They steeled themselves as the body was revealed. Like all the other victims, the pallid face and contorted expression suggested a painful, sudden death.

“There was an incredible amount of blood loss but no major external injury.” Steve ran a gloved hand around the abdomen, showing the minor contusions and scrapes on the greenish skin. “I’ve autopsied a few people who died after falling from a great height, and in every case, the spleen ruptures upon impact, and there is massive internal bleeding. Not in this case. All the organs have been affected, not just the spleen. The official report is that the fall killed him, but I am quite sure that he was dead before he ever hit the ground.”

“Brown hair,” noted Cherie.

"I've seen the very same condition in other bodies that I've recently examined from the island," noted Steve. "Blood loss and organ destruction."

"Steve, I am particularly interested in seeing the tennis shoes that he was wearing."

"I have them here." He removed a bag from the drawer and took out a pair of blood-splattered, black *Converse* tennis shoes. He handed them to Cherie.

Cherie removed from her pocket the footprint photographs she had taken at the beach where the Crimson Tide had grounded, and compared them with the sole of the Converse. "Look at this Jesse. The pattern is the same."

"Are they size nine?"

"They are." She handed the shoes back to Steve.

"May I ask why these are important?"

"There's a confidentiality question involved, so I can't provide details. But I can say that you have provided possibly the most important evidence in our investigation thus far."

"Always glad to be of assistance," said Steve. "Is that all you need?"

"Yes," said Cherie. "You've been a great help."

"Let me know if I can do anything else."

The two left the coroner's office and headed for Mobile Rarities. As Cherie drove, she reflected on the significance of what they had learned.

"Although it's circumstantial evidence, I believe it's safe to assume that Guidry was the initial case. I've done some contact tracing of him when I learned that he owned a dirt bike and lived on the island's east end. I know he had a large circle of friends."

"That's not good."

"It's not. But, looking on the bright side, it's summer, and he could have been in school and possibly infected his entire class and his teachers."

"So, you've decided it's an unknown infectious agent?

"Everything is pointing to that conclusion. Once I finish contact tracing, I'll have a better idea."

CHAPTER 43

Cherie and Jesse arrived at *Mobile Rarities* and parked in the lot behind the building. The innocuous, one-story structure could have housed any number of common businesses. However, as they entered, it was clear that the contents of this establishment were anything but mundane. As if stepping into another world, the space was filled with all manner of exotic and bizarre items. Some near the door included a taxidermy kangaroo with a spider monkey riding its back, a knight in armor, a human skeleton, a chair made entirely of tennis balls, marble gargoyles removed from local buildings, a headless Elvis statue, Mardi Gras costumes, and a pickled item in a glass jar labeled "Big Foot Hand".

Jesse picked up a preserved Alligator head and grinned. "I want this for my birthday."

"Sure, how much is it?"

He turned the head over, searching for a price tag, and found it in the mouth of the scaly reptile. "Here it is. It's only $175. That's a bargain for a head of this quality."

"Being from Cajun country, I know the benefit of having at least one alligator head in the home. You know the saying, "The head of a gator brings good luck later.""

"I've never heard that expression before."

"Jesse, I just made that up."

"Ha! You got me! But I am impressed. That's pretty good Cajun poetry."

"You know the Cajun word for alligator is ko-ko-dree."

"Interesting."

Something caught Cherie's eye, and she moved along a cluttered aisle to a large bell that stood on a wrought iron stand. "Wow, look at this. A bell this ornate must have hung in a church steeple somewhere. Look, it says it was cast in 1853." She rapped the bell with her knuckles, producing a single, pure note. "Beautiful!"

"Well, you know the old saying, ring a bell so you won't go to hell."

"That was pretty sad."

"Yes, I know."

"I've always been fascinated with bells." With an expression of pure joy on her face, Cherie ran her hands along the religious images cast into its surface. "Think about all the times this bell has called people to worship. The times it rang for christenings, baptisms, and weddings. On Christmas morning, on Easter, and for all kinds of special occasions. It probably rang when the Civil War ended. Guarantee you it rang for the end of the World Wars." Lost in contemplation, Cherie paused for a moment as Jesse came to her side and stood silently by.

Although she was not aware, Jesse gave Cherie a loving look. "Beautiful indeed!" said Jesse, not referring to the bell. "

"When I have a house, I want a big bell on a post out in the yard. One that I could ring whenever I want."

In agreement, Jesse remarked, "We could have a bell one day," and then turned red with embarrassment. Hoping Cherie had not noticed, he quickly added, "Your words could be lyrics to a song. Maybe I'll compose one."

"I would love that!"

At the back of the store, hunched over a desk behind a long glass display case, sat the proprietor. Known only as Leo, he was wizened, with thin, white hair encircling his bald head. He wore a white shirt and a khaki vest with multiple pockets holding cigarettes, his eyeglasses, and an assortment of small tools he used in his trade. At first glance, he might have been mistaken for one of the shop's curiosities. But behind his aged appearance were twinkling eyes that reflected a wealth of knowledge gained from many years of trading in artifacts from bygone eras. A caretaker of the past, his love of historical objects and the stories he could draw from them kept him returning to the shop for the past 47 years. He mumbled to himself as he held a recently purchased curio close to his face for a detailed examination. The ash from the cigarette held in his thin lips fell onto the desk in front of him. He squinted through thick glasses and looked up as Jesse and Cherie approached.

"Hello," called Jesse as they made their way deeper into the bowels of the shop.

Leo removed the cigarette from his mouth, looked up, and croaked a reply. "Back here."

"I hear him but don't see him," said Cherie.

"Come on back."

"Oh, there you are," said Jesse. "Man, you've got some amazing stuff in here."

"Oh, I've got far more at home and in a storage warehouse. After all these years of being in the business, I've acquired quite a lot of merchandise."

"I'm Jesse Gates, and this is Cherie Belon."

"Nice to meet you. I'm Leo." He extended an arthritic hand that Jesse found to be surprisingly strong. "What can I do for you?"

"Mr. Leo, I was told that you have some expertise in old coins."

"I do. I've probably handled every kind of coin ever minted in the U.S. and many from other countries."

"Then I've come to the right place." Jesse removed the doubloon from his pocket and placed it on the glass-topped display case. "What can you tell me about this?"

Leo carefully picked up the coin and held it to the light. He drew a jeweler's loupe from his vest and peered at it closely. He gasped as he turned the coin over to examine every detail. "How did you come by this?"

"A friend asked me to find out if it was real. We thought it might be a Mardi Gras trinket."

"Oh…no, no, no. This is no trinket." Leo removed a small plastic case from a drawer. "You need to keep it in this coin case to protect it, definitely not in your pocket. I cannot believe this coin just walked into my shop." Leo went back to examining the coin, clearly thrilled that it was in his hands.

"So, it's real?"

"Very much so. What you have here is an 8-escudo, King Charles III, gold doubloon. Do you see the "So" stamped here on the coin?" Leo used a fine pointer to indicate the location of the mint mark.

Jesse leaned forward. "Yes sir, I see it."

"That means it was minted in Santiago, Chile. That is one of the rarest mint marks. Aside from rarity, coin condition is very important, and I would give this coin an AU grade, almost uncirculated. Only uncirculated coins would have a higher grade. Rarity and condition are the two most important characteristics in determining value."

"So, how valuable do you think it is?"

"I can give you an estimate, but at auction, it is hard to say how much it could bring."

Cherie looked at Jesse and smiled. "This is very exciting."

"Retail value would be somewhere in the $3000 range."

"Holy smokes!" Jesse swooned for a moment and braced himself against the display case. "You mean I've been casually carrying around a coin worth three grand? That's more money than I make in a year."

"As I said, it could bring more at auction. But it could also bring less. It just depends on how badly someone might want it. So, what are your plans for it? I would love to make you an offer if you're interested in selling."

"It's not mine to sell."

Leo picked the coin up again and re-examined it with his loupe. "You know this could grade as uncirculated."

"Although this probably makes no difference," added Jesse, "the coin was found on Dauphin Island, and some have suggested that it could be part of Jean Lafitte's pirate treasure that is supposed to be buried there."

"Without a provenance that connects it to Lafitte, it would not alter the value. Possibilities have no value. However, if that could be established, there is no telling what it might bring. Collectors will pay crazy kinds of money for anything associated with pirates."

Could you call the owner to see if he would like to sell?"

"I can't. He doesn't have a phone." Jesse amused himself momentarily with the thought of how ridiculous it would be to speak with Joe on the phone.

"I'll tell you what, I will give you $3000. That's straight-up retail. I wouldn't normally do this because there is no meat left on the bone, but I'm not buying it to resell. I would love to have this coin for my collection. What do you say?"

"Can I discuss this for a moment in private with Cherie?"

"Sure thing."

Jesse and Cherie turned to walk away as Leo said, "You don't have to move an inch. I'm deaf as a post without these." He pulled out his two large hearing aids and placed them on the counter. "I was a gunner in the war, completely destroyed my hearing." You could almost hear Leo's arthritic joints creak as he shuffled his bent body back to his desk and sat down heavily.

"Take it!" said Cherie. "I'm a pretty good judge of character, and he is being honest. Think what we can do for Joe with that money."

"No argument here." Jesse gave the thumbs-up sign to a smiling Leo.

CHAPTER 44

The late afternoon, south Alabama countryside swept by as they motored along Dauphin Island Parkway, headed for the island. "Can you freaking believe that? Three thousand dollars? Jesse was beside himself with excitement. He unconsciously patted the large wad of cash in his pocket.

Equally as excited, Cherie smiled back at Jesse. "We will have to find out what Joe's needs are, but it seems he needs everything. Clothes, shoes, food. Although his cabin is quite comfortable. Maybe a better wood stove. What do you think… Jesse?"

"I'm sorry," said Jesse, whose mind was elsewhere as visions of doubloons clouded his thoughts. "What did you say?"

"I said that Joe would appreciate most anything we bought for him."

"I agree. But I think we need to do it slowly. It would be a huge shock, after all those years of frugality, if we dumped $3000 worth of stuff on him."

"You're right."

"How about some music?" asked Jesse. "We can get the rock station out of Pensacola from here, but it will fade out before we get to the island."

"Sure."

Jesse switched on the radio and tuned to the Pensacola station. "Oh poo, it's news at the moment. Wait, it's something about the hurricane." Jesse turned up the volume."

…and Hurricane Allison is expected to strengthen as it passes over the warm waters of the Gulf of Mexico. Landfall is projected to be in the late afternoon on Thursday, somewhere along the northern Gulf between Galveston, Texas, and Apalachicola, Florida. Coastal residents are advised to evacuate low-lying areas.

"Oh, crap! We are right in the middle of the projected landfall, and Dauphin Island is a terrible place to be in a hurricane."

"If there is a lockdown on the island to prevent the spread, I honestly don't know what we are going to do," said a very concerned Cherie. "How can you force folks to stay on an island that's in the path of a hurricane?"

"Let's pray it doesn't come to that."

Cherie suddenly braked the car as a mule-drawn wagon appeared around the curve ahead. The wagon, riding on old automobile tires, was loaded with produce and rumbled along, half in and half out of the road. An old black man sat atop the weathered wagon, reins in hand. "That's something you don't see every day."

"You don't. But once you get away from the city, there are still lots of poor folks around that live like it's 1889 instead of 1989." As they passed, Jesse turned completely around in his seat to get a good look at the old man's wares. "That's some good-looking produce. See if you can find a safe place to pull over, and let's see what he has."

Just ahead, Cherie pulled the Crown Vic onto a wide spot on the side of the road and waited until the wagon caught up to them. They got out and walked back along the kudzu-covered roadside, the smell of kudzu and honeysuckle flowers scented the air. Jesse flagged the man as he approached, who pulled back on the reins and stopped. The old man adjusted a frayed straw hat he wore, pushed the pole brake on the wagon, and gave the two a suspicious look. Seeing the government license plate on the vehicle, the man spoke first.

"Sir, I'm sorry. I'm coming from the Bayou La Batre farmer's market and heading home. I got a little out in the road back there, but this old wagon and my old body cain't take a lot of bouncing."

"No, no," said Jesse, waving his hand to negate his concerns. "We just wanted to buy some produce. Could you sell us some?"

"Oh!" The old man grinned broadly. "Yes sir. I'll be glad to." He pulled a blue handkerchief from the back pocket of his faded overalls and wiped his face and hands. He slowly climbed down from his perch. "Not as agile as I used to be."

Cherie approached the mule cautiously and extended her hand to let the creature take her scent.

"Do you need some help?" offered Jesse, seeing the old man struggle to climb down.

"That's very kindly, but I got it." The old man paused for a moment and turned toward Cherie. "Mam, watch out there, Daisy don't like strangers too much.

"Hello, Daisy," said Cherie softly as she slowly stroked her neck and shoulders. "That's a good girl." Daisy lowered her head and allowed Cherie to rub her jowls and between her eyes.

"Well, if that don't beat the dogs a-trottin! That mule won't let anyone but me do that." The old man took a carrot from the wagon and handed it to Cherie. "Feed her this carrot if you want to really make friends with her."

"Thank you." Cherie offered the carrot to Daisy, and she ate it, crunching loudly. "That's a good girl." Cherie continued to stroke her on the shoulders.

"Did you do well at the farmer's market today?" asked Jesse.

"Just middling, unfortunately. Folks ain't coming out 'cause it's been so hot. So, what do you good folks need? I've got the sweetest watermelons you'll find anywhere. Got beans, sweet taters, silver queen corn, maters, cucumbers, merlotons, squash."

"We're going to make shrimp creole, so I need two bell peppers, a couple of tomatoes, and some celery. I'll take a watermelon and 4 ears of silver queen also."

"Yes sir. Got all of those." The old man began filling the order, dropping the items into a paper sack, all except the watermelon. "That's all you need?"

"I think that will do it. How much do I owe you?"

"That will be $1.50 for the watermelon, 60 cents for the corn, 40 cents for the tomatoes, 50 cents for the celery, and 40 cents for the bell peppers." Without hesitation, he said, "That's $3.40 total."

"Man, you totaled that up fast."

"I'm pretty sure that's correct, sir, but I can write it out for you if you would like."

"No, no, I wasn't doubting you. I was just impressed by how fast you added that up. I have to count fingers and toes to do that."

"I've been selling for fifty years, had a lot of practice."

"$3.40, you said." Jesse pulled some cash from his pocket and placed a bill into his weathered hand.

"Oh!" I'm so sorry, sir, but I cain't make change for this." The old man held the bill out to give it back to Jesse.

Jesse picked up his produce. "That's the smallest bill I've got."

"Oh." Disappointment clouded his face as he assumed he had just lost a sale. "Well, sir, you go ahead and make that shrimp creole for that young lady. Next time you are in Bayou La Batre on a Saturday, you can just bring it by. I'm there every Saturday until the weather gets cold." Again, he held the money out to return it to Jesse.

"Don't worry about it," said Jesse. "Just keep the change."

"What? But… that's… that's crazy!"

"You have a great day!" Jesse smiled, gave a thumbs-up, and headed to the car.

"Wait. But, sir…"

"Have a good day! Bye, Daisy." Cherie gave the mule a peck on the cheek, and Daisy brayed and stamped her hoof in reply. Cherie and Jesse left the old man standing by the side of the road, bewildered and staring at the bill in his hand. They loaded up their government vehicle and got in.

Cherie turned out onto the rural highway and headed south. She glanced in her rearview mirror and something caught her eye. "Look back there." She pointed a thumb directly behind her.

Jesse turned around in his seat to see the old man dancing a jig on the side of Dauphin Island Parkway. "Ha, ha, I think we made that man's day," said Jesse, laughing.

"What did you do?"

"I gave him a hundred-dollar bill. I don't think Joe would mind."

"I know Joe wouldn't mind." They rode for several miles with no conversation between them.

"Jesse Gates, you are a genuinely nice guy."

"Well, I try. And you've become a very special person to me as well."

Cherie momentarily took her eyes off the road and caught Jesse gazing longingly at her. With an overwhelming urge to kiss him, Cherie realized that she had never felt this way about anyone.

"Is it hot in here to you?" She reached for the controls to turn down the air conditioner.

"A little."
*****

Jesse glanced at his watch as they approached the Dauphin Island Police Department and pulled into the parking lot. Cherie parked next to the El Camino. Jesse got out and loaded their purchases into his car. "So, it's 3:45 now, you want to come to my house at about 5:30? Shrimp creole doesn't take very long to prepare."

"Do you have everything you need?"

Jesse leaned down to speak to Cherie through the driver's window. "I do. I don't eat extravagantly, so we'll have shrimp creole over rice."

"Sounds good to me. I love shrimp. If I think of anything else, I'll pick it up on the way over."

"I have beer, water, and Coke at my cottage."

"I'll get a bottle of white wine. That's what you normally have with seafood."

"OK. See you in a few." Cherie drove away, and Jesse climbed into the El Camino.

CHAPTER 45

Jesse stood over his kitchen stove and sautéed the "trinity" of Creole cooking: green pepper, onion, and celery. He poured a small amount of white wine into the mix as the steam rising from the cast-iron skillet filled the cottage with a comforting aroma. From the living room came the strains of George Benson's *Breezin* playing on the stereo. He had set the kitchen table with two mismatched plates, one with a picture of a young Elvis standing at a microphone, the other with a fish motif. The place setting looked ridiculous, but the alternative would be paper plates, and that would be worse. He was inexplicably nervous. Other than the occasional football game with friends, Jesse had never entertained anyone at his cottage to whom he felt such a strong romantic attachment. He wanted the evening to be special, but his social awkwardness left him feeling inadequate. Jesse did not truly understand nonverbal communication. Body language was a complete mystery to him. Being a scientist, he was better at massaging numbers than massaging someone's neck. Ultimately, he planned on making his feelings for Cherie known, but the fear of rejection was palpable. Unknown to him, Cherie was already aware of his feelings, which she shared.

Jesse heard Cherie's car pull into his driveway. He went to the door to meet her. "Hey," he called, smiling and waving from the top of the stairs that led up to his cottage. Cherie got out, a manila envelope in one hand and a paper bag in the other. "Do you need help with anything?"

"Hi Jesse. No, I got it." Cherie came up the stairs, and Jesse's heart skipped a beat as she approached. She was a vision of loveliness. Gone was the ball cap she often wore, and her hair was pulled back in a ponytail, tied with a blue ribbon. A face that required no makeup, she wore only light pink lipstick on her full lips. A thin, floral skirt hung close to her body, and a bright blue halter top left Jesse breathless.

"Wow!" said Jesse. "You look beautiful."

"Thank you. You look nice too. I didn't bring much to wear for social engagements." Cherie made it to the top of the stairs, wiped her shoes across the welcome mat, and reached up to kiss Jesse on the cheek.

Jesse reeled. The beauty that stood before him and the hint of gardenia blossoms surrounding her was almost more than he could bear. "I've never seen you in a skirt before," was all Jesse could think to say.

"I threw this old thing in my luggage as an afterthought."

An awkward moment passed between them as Jesse could not stop staring and smiling like a schoolboy. Cherie motioned toward the door. "Should we go in?"

"Oh, uh, yes, I'm sorry. Come in." The couple made their way to the kitchen.

"Wow, that smells good."

"I hope you enjoy it. The secret ingredient is to use Chili Sauce to put a little zip in it and then add a little Tabasco for added heat. I also use bacon drippings to cook with, and we can sprinkle bacon bits on top of the serving."

"I picked up a bottle of wine." Cherie produced the bottle and put it on the kitchen table. "The selection at Ship and Shore is kind of limited. Oh, I forgot." She handed the manila envelope to Jesse. "Dorothy called me at the hotel, and I picked this up for you. It's the hematological data on Mr. Stanford from the CDC. The fellow who died parasailing."

"Boy, that was fast!"

"They had already worked it up. I just had to request the hormone levels be included."

Jesse took the envelope and started to open it, and then paused. "No, I'm gonna stick to my promise about not discussing the investigation." He tossed the envelope on the kitchen counter. "I'll leave it for later. Probably nothing relevant anyway."

"Where's Bongo?" asked Cherie.

"I took him over to Gino's. He can be such a pain in the butt, particularly when I am trying to cook. They've agreed to keep him for the next several days. I haven't been taking care of him like I should, and he will be happier over there. Plus, I thought you would welcome some peace and quiet."

"I admit that I could use some relaxation. How's Sparky getting along?" Cherie walked to the aquarium, kneeled in front of the glass, and peered in.

"He's doing really well. Eats like crazy. You might have noticed that there are no other fish in the tank now. He zapped them all and ate them."

"Oh! That's too bad." Cherie stood, came back to the table, and picked up the wine bottle. "You want to try some of this?"

"Sure." Jesse retrieved two glasses from the cupboard. "Oh darn! I don't have a corkscrew."

"I anticipated that. I bought one from *Ship and Shore*." Cherie pulled the instrument from the paper bag.

"*Ship and Shore* has everything." Jesse took the corkscrew and twisted it into the bottle. He struggled with it a bit before the cork popped out and then poured wine into each glass.

"Cheers," said Cherie as they clinked their glasses together and took a sip.

"Cheers." Jesse swished the wine around in his mouth before swallowing. "I don't know much about wines, but it tastes OK to me."

"It's not very good," admitted Cherie, "but it will do. Jesse, you mentioned maybe going out to watch the sunset from the boat. Is it OK if we just hang out here?"

"Absolutely. We can watch the sunset from the deck. There's a light breeze from the north that will keep the mosquitoes at bay, so it should be quite nice out there. The shrimp creole is ready. Let's eat, and then we can relax for a bit."

Cherie took her seat at the small dining room table. "I love the Elvis plate."

"Somebody gave me that as a gift. I think you're supposed to hang it on the wall, but as you can see, I haven't done much interior decorating. If I did, it would likely look a lot like Joe's cabin; stuffed animals, fish skulls, and snake skins." Jesse placed a serving of rice onto Elvis and ladled the shrimp creole over it. "I hope this is OK."

"The place could use a little of a woman's touch. I would be glad to help any time you would like." Cherie daintily placed a small portion of shrimp Creole in her mouth. "Oh my! Jesse, this is absolutely delicious. An excellent Chef AND a bullfighter. That's pretty impressive!"

"Thank you Ma'am. Oh, I forgot the French bread." Jesse got up and retrieved a plate of toasted bread.

Cherie shoveled a much larger portion into her mouth. "This is so good!" she mumbled through a mouthful. She placed her hand over her mouth in embarrassment. "Oh, excuse me. I got carried away."

"No problem, I'm glad you are enjoying it."

"Speaking of Joe, what do you think we should buy for him?"

"I've been giving that a lot of thought. If I were living "off the land" like Joe, I would want the tools that would make it easier to capture food. Let's get him a quality cast net, some good fishing rods and tackle, some crab traps, flounder gigs, and maybe a gill net."

"All good ideas," agreed Cherie. "What about some real tools for his craft work? He obviously enjoys woodworking. Perhaps a hammer, nails, a hand saw, chisels, knives, and a locked trunk to keep them in. And clothing. I could guess his size pretty closely. Some winter and summer clothes. A warm coat, a raincoat, and some shoes. And cookware. Some pots and pans, and various utensils."

"I wonder how attached he is to that pirogue he uses?" Jesse got up and served both himself and Cherie seconds. "

"Pardon me for eating like a horse, but this is the best meal I've had since I arrived on the island."

"Cherie, you don't know how happy it makes me to hear you say that. I love cooking, and I love it even more when it's appreciated," Jesse continued. "We could get him a small portable boat of some kind. That's a big-ticket item. Maybe get that for him after we get some of the other things."

They finished eating, and Cherie collected up the dishes and went to the sink to wash them.

"Cherie, you don't have to do that. I'll take care of it later."

"It's no problem. You cooked, and I don't like leaving dishes unwashed. But you know what I would really like you to do for me?"

"Just say the word."

"I would like to hear you play the guitar."

"Uh, sure. Let me go get it." Jesse left the kitchen, switched the stereo off in the other room, and returned with an acoustic guitar in hand. By the time he returned, Cherie had finished the dishes. "I'm no entertainer, but I'm pretty good on guitar and my singing voice is not terribly offensive."

"That's not what Ross and CC said."

"They were just being kind. Why don't we go out on the deck? The sun is just beginning to set."

"OK." Cherie grabbed the bottle of wine and the glasses, and Jesse brought the guitar. Jesse sat on an old chaise lounge with his guitar in his lap. Cherie set the bottle on the deck and took the lone patio chair. They faced the setting sun as the sky turned golden.

"If you've ever wondered why there is such color in the sky during sunsets, it's because of something called *Rayleigh Scattering*. The rays of light travel through a greater amount of atmosphere at sunset than when the sun is overhead. That causes more scattering of the blue and purple wavelengths. Therefore, more of the red and orange wavelengths are left for us to see. I especially like the sunsets when there is an interesting mix of clouds and clear sky."

"Never thought about it. I just enjoy the show."

"My Dad bought this guitar for me when I was 16." He held the guitar out for Cherie to see. "If the house were on fire, the first thing I would get out, after my family and Bongo, would be this guitar. I used to play it in bed and have fallen asleep with it in my hands."

"It's beautiful. Is it valuable?"

"No, not really. Other than sentimental value." Jesse ran his hand along the neck of the guitar and thought of the joy he felt the Christmas morning when he received it. "Do you have a request? Not that I could necessarily play it."

"Something soft maybe?"

"Soft, hmm." He placed his index finger against his temple and paused for a moment. "Let me think. Oh. Here's one you might like." He began playing the instrumental opening to "Same Old Lang Syne" by Dan Fogelberg. "Do you recognize it?"

"I do indeed."

"My voice can't hold a candle to Dan Fogelberg's, but I'll give it my best shot."

Cherie sat back in her chair and closed her eyes while Jesse sang. There was an obvious change in her physical bearing as the anxiety seemed to drain from her body. As he played, Jesse occasionally glanced over to gauge her response to his music. The golden glow of the dying sun played across her angelic face. She was radiant. Jesse could not believe that he had met someone as beautiful as this. As Jesse sang the final line and ended the song, he glanced over to see a single tear as it coursed down her cheek.

Surprised by her reaction, Jesse immediately stopped playing and quickly stood. "I am so sorry. I've upset you." He put the guitar down on the chaise lounge.

Cherie wiped the tear from her cheek. "I can't believe you picked that song. My Mom used to play it on the piano and sing when I was a kid. It was one of her favorites."

"I'll stop playing." Jesse had completely misinterpreted her reaction and was mortified.

"Please don't stop! That was beautiful and brought back such wonderful memories. I've never told you, but my mom passed away when I was a teenager. Not a day goes by that I don't think about her."

"Oh, I'm so sorry. If she were anything like you, she was a very special lady."

"Yes, she was." Cherie rose from her chair and approached Jesse. She took him by the hand and drew him near. The closeness of this captivating creature, the smell of gardenia, and the wine created a storm of desire that he knew he could not control. She put her other hand against his cheek and looked up into his eyes. She smiled timidly. He had an overwhelming desire to kiss her. Was this the right thing to do? Alarm bells were going off in Jesse's head. Ring… ring… ring. *Wait, what is that?* thought Jesse. He suddenly realized he was hearing actual bells.

"The phone is ringing," said Cherie, disappointedly, as she turned away from Jesse.

"What?" Jesse shook his head as he was suddenly snatched out of the moment. "I never get calls at this hour."

"You should probably get that. It could be important."

"You're right." They went into the kitchen, and Jesse removed the phone from the wall where it hung. "Hello. Yes." A confused look as Jesse paused and listened. "Could you repeat that, please? OK. Yes, she is. One moment." Jesse placed his hand over the receiver. "It's someone with a heavy accent. Wants to speak with you."

"Oh. OK." Jesse handed the phone to Cherie. "Hello. Yes, it is. What?" As the conversation continued, concern spread across Cherie's previously serene face, and the tension that she had been saddled with for the past several days seemed to return. Jesse could tell that this had something to do with the investigation.

"Yes. And what is your name again? OK. Yes. I can be there in about 10 minutes. Yes. OK. Goodbye."

"What was that about?"

"It was someone named Hector Fernandez. He got your number from Sheriff East. He said he urgently needed to speak with me." Cherie sat down at the kitchen table. "He claims that he has important information about the investigation, and we are in grave danger."

"That's not good. Did he provide details?"

"No. I'm going to meet him at the Neptune Club."

"I'll go with you. No way you're going alone in the middle of the night to speak to some shadowy figure that says we are in danger."

"You're the best Jesse."

"Yeah, I know. But you have to promise me something."

"What would that be?"

"Another date without the interruption."

"Nothing would make me happier."

CHAPTER 46

As usual, the Neptune Club was smoke-filled, loud, and busy on a Saturday night, but Jesse and Cherie had no trouble finding the mysterious individual. Dr. Hector Fernandez sat in a corner booth with a bottle of *Dos Equis* and a half-empty basket of fried crab claws in front of him. He stood as they approached. "Dr. Belon. Thank you for meeting," spoke Hector with a Spanish accent. Without smiling, he extended his hand to shake. "I am Dr. Hector Fernandez."

"Uh, yes. No problem," said Cherie as he took his hand. "Cherie Belon, and this is Jesse Gates, a friend."

Jesse looked Hector over with a suspicious eye and did not like what he saw. Unlike his vigorous appearance of barely a year ago, he now looked old and tired. His previously black hair was now completely grey, and, although never a physically imposing individual, he was thin, gaunt, and generally unhealthy-looking.

"Please have a seat," said Hector, motioning to them. "Please excuse my English. I still learn."

They slid into the corner booth opposite Hector.

"Cerveza…um…beer for you?"

"No thanks," replied both Cherie and Jesse.

"Could you please tell us what this is about?" asked Cherie.

"Dr. Belon…" began Hector when Cherie interrupted.

"Please call me Cherie. I only use my title in professional settings."

"Forgive me, por favor, in my country, titles are important. We have only little, um… opportunities, not like Americans, and if have a degree, the title becomes you… um… becomes your name."

"And what is your home country?" asked Jesse.

"I come from Colombia. I was Ministra de Arquelogia… um…Minister of Archaeology for the country of Belize. You know Belize?"

"I know it is in Central America, but that is about all," said Cherie.

"Wasn't it a British protectorate until recently?" asked Jesse.

"Yes. My wife and I live there in 1982 when I was Minister after it got freedom from United Kingdom. I am PhD from the

Center for Mesoamerican Archaeology at The University of Colombia. I study pre-Columbian archaeology. I study long time, Mayan archaeology." Hector struggled to find certain words. "Um… Mayan art, pottery, textiles, I know very well."

"What does all of this have to do with the events here?" asked Cherie, cutting to the chase.

"A long story, maybe hard for you to believe. The deaths on Dauphin Island, you study those. The death, they come from my work on Mayan archaeology in Belize."

"The deaths on the island are connected to archaeological work in Belize?" asked Cherie incredulously. "How is that possible?"

"Please, I explain. My wife, Eliana, and I work near the Mopan River in Belize. We got great discovery. Many treasures. We also found death!" It was evident that Hector was having difficulty telling this story as his voice trembled and he repeatedly clenched and relaxed his fist. Beads of sweat glistened on his forehead. "Please excuse me," he paused to take a drink from his beer, "I have much hard time. Do you know, um… paludismo?" Hector held the back of his hand to his forehead as though checking for fever and wrapped his arms around himself while shivering. "Paludismo?"

"I'm sorry, I don't know what that means," said Cherie. "Jesse?"

"I don't know either."

"Um…el mosquito bite and sick come," explained Hector.

"Oh goodness, you mean malaria?" said Cherie.

"Yes, malaria," repeated Hector. "But I am now not sick, just tired."

"I am so sorry. Just take your time," said Cherie.

Hector began again. "In archaeology digging we find seis, uh…" Hector held up six fingers and thought for a moment… "six, Mayan codices have much information about Maya. Muy importante… um… very important we find. Very much money."

"I've heard of the *Dresden Codex*. Wasn't it one of just a few codex's…uh… or is it codices?" asked Jesse, thinking out loud.

"Yes, yes, very important codex."

"And you found six more?" asked Cherie. "That's incredible!"

Hector reached into a satchel that sat next to him to reveal a tattered and burned page from one of the codices. "Very sad! Have now only this." Hector placed the piece of paper on the table in front of them.

Cherie picked up the partial document to more closely examine it in the dim light. "Wow! This is beautiful. It reminds me of Egyptian hieroglyphics."

"Beautiful, yes, and deadly. These things come from rainforest in Belize." Hector pointed at various images on the codex. "My wife, she found was a…" Hector paused, searching for the correct word… "a recipe. I think is word. We not know what the recipe makes. We now know that it was a recipe for dead, um, for kill enemies. Maybe use for kill *Toltec* people."

"It was a recipe to make something that was used to kill people?" said Cherie. "Freaking incredible! It was a bio-warfare agent. Oh my God!"

As Jesse scrutinized the document, his expression changed from scientific curiosity to concern. "Well, ain't that special!" As if radioactive, he used only an index finger and thumb to gingerly place the codex back in front of Hector and then wiped his hands with a napkin.

"Bio-warfare?" said Hector. "I do not know this word. Bi-o-war-fare," he repeated more slowly. "The Maya make much war."

Cherie was having trouble believing this tale. "That would have to be the first bio-warfare agent in history. You're trying to tell me that an ancient, Mayan bio-weapon is now killing people on Dauphin Island?"

"I think this very much!" The steeled look on Hector's face was not one of a man prone to flights of fantasy. "I come to America, I watch, I wait to find this terrible thing. When I read about deaths here, I call police here. I ask if they die with much blood. He say yes. I know that I find."

"I think I'll have that drink after all," said Jesse as he looked around the room to find a waitress. "Do you want something, Cherie?"

"No, I'm fine. Dr. Fernandez, you can understand how incredible this sounds. Do you have evidence?"

"Dr. Belon, I ask you question. Fishing boat come on land on island?"

"You mean when the Crimson Tide ran aground?" asked Jesse.

"That is name, yes, Crimson Tide," repeated Hector. "I read about in newspaper. It say dead people on Dauphin Island. They die with much blood."

Cherie's jaw dropped as the comment took her completely by surprise. "No one knows about the connection between the Crimson Tide and the deaths! How did you know about that?"

"My wife make recipe to kill Americans."

"What?" asked Cherie in disbelief.

Hector put his hand to his forehead, closed his eyes, and slowly shook his head. The pain of the events was very visible as he struggled to find the right words. "Please excuse, I say this story only few times. It is very hard."

"No problem," said Cherie, "take your time."

Hector opened his eyes and began. "To our research in Belize come many armed men…terrorists. Their leader is name Arturo. Kill everyone. We try escape but were captured. They break all priceless things that took us years to find. They used the paper codices, to smoke marijuana! Dios mio, what a terrible loss!" Hector sighed deeply and took another pull from his beer. "Arturo say there is muy dinero…uh…ransom is word, ransom for us so he keep us many months. It is too bad, Eliana's notebook gave how to make the recipe. She write in notebook that recipe can be drug."

"I've heard about hallucinogens, such as peyote cactus, being used by native people in their religious practices," added Jesse. "In fact, I had an accidental encounter with a naturally occurring hallucinogen not too long ago."

"You've never mentioned that," said Cherie, turning to Jesse.

"It was no fun, but that's a story for another time," replied Jesse. "Dr. Hernandez, please continue."

"Do you know coca and ayahuasca?" asked Hector.

"Everyone knows about coca, which is used to make cocaine," said Jesse. "But I've never heard of… Hiawatha… what did you call it?"

"Aya-huasca," said Hector slowly, accentuating the syllables. "Many peoples in rainforest use ayahuasca to talk to ancestors, talk to God. To make, you must long time cook leaves from ayahuasca plant."

"So, a codex describing a recipe for some kind of drug was a reasonable assumption," said Cherie.

"Yes, yes," said Hector, pleased that they understood despite his broken English. "Arturo, tell my Eliana make recipe from coca leaves, mushrooms, blood from *guarachaco*. All the pieces of recipe I do not say. Arturo easy make because Eliana make notes."

"You say they used blood from what?" asked Cherie.

"Please excuse. Blood from guarachaco…um…I cannot find word." Hector hooked his thumbs together and flapped his hands like wings. "What is?"

"A bird of some kind?" asked Jesse.

"Noche bird."

"A night bird?" said Jesse quizzically. "Oh, a bat!"

"Yes. Was blood from bat and other things I cannot say."

Cherie cringed. "Bats harbor dangerous viruses like rabies and Ebola that could be transmitted to humans. There is no telling what they made."

"So, Arturo recognized the possible value of a drug that he might be able to produce from common items found in the rainforest," said Jesse.

"Yes. He would be the only one to have," said Hector. "Arturo very smart, very evil."

"Think about it," observed Jesse. "He would be the sole supplier. Any money from the drug could be used to fund his terrorism."

"Excuse please," Hector motioned to a waitress who happened to walk by. "Another Dos Equis, por favor? And something for my friends if they like."

"I'll have the same," said Jesse. "Much obliged."

"None for me," said Cherie.

Hector drained what was left of his beer and sat back. Some of the tension seemed to have gone. "Arturo used Eliana's writing to make the…um…mezcla…how do you say in English?" Hector, thinking out loud mimed mixing something with his hands. "Mixture, yes, the mixture. His men eat. Bad, very bad! Pain, blood comes to everyone. Blood all over. All who eat died rapido, fast. Oh, terrible death!" sighed Hector and rubbed his eyes with the heels of his hands.

Jesse, wide-eyed, turned to Cherie. "My Lord, they drank this concoction, and it killed them. Does this remind you of anything?"

Cherie nodded in agreement. "Definitely."

"More people die later, days, weeks. Some die never eat the mixture. Disease kill almost everyone." Hector's eyes welled with tears, and his voice broke as he continued. "Mi hermosa esposa… Eliana, she… die."

"Oh no," said Cherie. "You poor man."

Hector, broken by the recollection of the tragic events, paused to compose himself. "But Arturo not die," Hector spat the words out. "He escape into rainforest. Some men escape also."

"How did you survive?" asked Jesse.

"Afortunado…uh…lucky, gracias a Dios", said Hector, looking skyward. "Arturo keep me in dirty cage for long time. Like animal. Bad water, bad food. My clothes are *putrefaccion*," said Hector while pulling at his shirt. "Do you know this?"

"You mean rotted?" asked Jesse.

"Yes, that is it. Clothes rotted. One hombre give some food and save my life. No touch anyone. I no catch. When hombres go, I use fingers, dig day and night, and I escape. Very bad, very long walking. Sisters care for me and then in hospital for long time but after, I come to America."

"Have you told the FBI about this?" asked Jesse.

"Yes, they write down. They do nothing. They think I…loco maybe." Hector traced circles around his temple using his index finger.

"That doesn't surprise me," said Cherie.

Hector's body language and tone changed to a man with a mission. "They know Arturo at FBI. They say he kill many people in Guatemala, Belize, Honduras, and in United States."

"You mean to say he is in the U.S.?" asked Cherie.

Hector sighed heavily. "More worse. I think this diablo here on island!

Suddenly, a disturbing thought came to Cherie. "Dr. Fernandez, what does Arturo look like?"

"Long time since I see. He is short, *macho*, like…uh… *Arturo*…uh…like bear." Hector doubled his fists and flexed the muscles in his arms like a bodybuilder. "Hair black and have many espinillas on his face." Hector dotted his cheek with his index finger. "The English name I do not know."

"Pimples?" asked Jesse.

"Yes."

"Oh my God!" said Cherie. "I think I saw this person at the Blue Crab Café. Does he wear his hair in a long ponytail?" Cherie pulled her hair back to show Hector.

"Yes! When you see?" asked Hector now with fire in his eyes.

"It was, uh, let me think… three days ago. He was driving an old, four-door Chevy. What color was it?" said Cherie, thinking out loud. "It looked like it had not been washed in years. I think it was white. "

"Otros hombres?...um…how do you say this?"

"Were other men with him?" asked Jesse.

"Yes, that is what I say."

"He was alone," said Cherie. "But why would he come here?"

"Arturo hate America. Hombre who give me food say Arturo want kill all in America. I ask how he do this? Hombre say he use mezcla. He put in marijuana, bring to U.S."

"You mean he put a deadly agent in marijuana to smuggle it to the United States?" asked Jesse.

"Yes. Smuggle. Arturo loco, monstruo…um… a monster. He has no feelings for others."

"He sounds like a psychopath," observed Cherie.

"Yes, psychopath. I never see evil like this hombre. He has cold blood when he kill."

"Dr. Fernandez," said Cherie, "we knew that the disease was brought to the island on board the Crimson Tide, but had no idea how it came to be on that ship. Based on what you are saying, the boat must have been smuggling drugs, marijuana, that had been infected in some way."

"Yes. I read about Crimson Tide and dying on island and I learn this."

"But that makes no sense," said an adamant Jesse. "The Coast Guard said there was no evidence of drug smuggling. Plus, the Captain was well respected in the community and was financially doing quite well."

"I don't know," said Cherie. "The lure of huge amounts of drug money has turned many upstanding citizens into criminals."

Jesse shook his head in disagreement. "I just cannot accept that the Captain of the Crimson Tide was smuggling drugs."

"Where it came from is academic," said Cherie. "Based on what you are saying, we have a bioterrorism agent, most likely a virus, infecting the people of Dauphin Island, that has already taken the lives of five. You said that some people did not die right away, that they died days or weeks later?"

"Yes. One *hombre* he die when jaguar come."

"A jaguar attacked him?" asked Jesse, confused.

"No. Jaguar come into camp. I see this. He see jaguar, much afraid. Jaguar run away. *Hombre* scream, blood come, he die."

"So, he was frightened by a jaguar and suddenly died?" asked Jesse.

"Yes, I see this. He died with much blood."

Cherie rose from the table. "Dr. Fernandez, thank you for this information. I have some urgent phone calls to make." Cherie removed a pen and paper from her pocket. "This is my phone number at the hotel where I am staying, and this is Jesse's number. Please call me or Jesse if there is anything we can do or if you have other information."

"Could you tell us where we can find you if we need to get in touch?" asked Jesse.

"I stay in *tienda*. Um…what is word?" Hector held the tips of his fingers together to form an upside down "V" shape."

"A tent?" asked Cherie.

"Yes, that is word."

"Many tents," added Hector.

"At Dauphin Island Campground?" asked Cherie.

"Yes, Dauphin Island Campground. I ask you be very careful. Arturo never stop." A darkness fell across Hector's face. "I vow before God; I find this man and I kill him!"

Jesse and Cherie said their goodbyes to Hector and left the Neptune Club.

"What do you think about this?" asked Jesse as they drove toward his cottage.

"I think he's telling the truth." Cherie pulled into Jesse's driveway and stopped the car. "There are too many parallels between Hector's story and what's been happening here. I think my worst fears have been realized. This has to be a viral agent, but I don't understand why we did not find it in our electron microscope images."

"I agree." Jesse sighed deeply and turned in the seat toward Cherie. "I've been worried, but it's more than worry now. What are you going to do?"

"I'm going to try to call my supervisor tonight. I may not be able to reach him, but as soon as I can, I'm gonna let him know about this. I'll have to put together a detailed recommendation based on contact tracing and the information provided by Hector. I'll be working on this all day tomorrow. It's going to be his call about an island lockdown."

"Well, since tomorrow is Sunday, I'm going to church. I haven't been attending regularly, and I think I need to put this before God. I'll call you tomorrow after church." Jesse opened the car door, started to get out, and paused. "Cherie, this is scary stuff. Will you promise me that you will be very careful?"

"I promise." Cherie took Jesse's hand, leaned over, and kissed his cheek. "Thank you for being a friend."

"Sure, no problem," Jesse said, surprised. "Call me if you need anything."

"I will."

CHAPTER 47

"Fourteen tickets for the 9:00 showing of *Jaws,* please." The President of the *Jaws Fan Club* approached the ticket booth in front of the *Ocean Cinema* theatre.

He wore a *Jaws* t-shirt and a hat upon which sat a stuffed shark. His entourage waiting near the door was similarly attired. One had a cardboard shark fin upon his back, another was an apparent shark attack victim, and another peered through the bloody teeth of a papier mâché shark's head that he wore. Three attendees were convincingly dressed as the principal characters of the movie, Captain Quint, Marine Biologist Cooper, and Sheriff Brody.

"Only 14 this time?" asked the man in the ticket booth.

"Yeah, a few members weren't able to make it tonight.

"Very good. How many total members do you have now?"

"We have 21 active members, including our newest member. He's the one dressed as a shark attack victim."

"Cute! That will be $56."

The young man handed him three twenty-dollar bills.

"Out of $60. Here's your change, enjoy the show."

The *Ocean Cinema* was the only theatre on the island and had been in operation for many years. A relic of the 1950s, time had not been kind to the aging establishment. Faded, crushed velvet seats, stained carpeting, a peeling ornate ceiling, and an out-of-date projection system were a testament to the fact that the "OC" was on its last legs. In truth, Terry Broussard, the owner and Mayor of Dauphin Island, had been trying to sell the theatre for the last two years. Making little money due to rising costs and dwindling customers, there were too many days when he made no money at all. Rarely were there more than 10 people in attendance, and he was throwing in the towel.

The Ocean Cinema only showed second-run movies. Terry couldn't afford to screen current films because the customer base was simply too small. However, there was one movie that had a loyal fan base and consistently drew more customers than usual. The "Jaws" Fan Club consisted of teens and 20-somethings who believed the film was the pinnacle of cinematic artistry. Instead of just watching the film, they turned it into an event similar to the "Rocky Horror Picture Show," which was the nationwide craze at the time. Members brought various shark-themed items, wore shark accessories, and dressed as characters from the movie. One member often arrived dressed in a full-body, white shark costume, which made it difficult for him to sit and get out of theater seats. Terry thought the fan club members were certifiable, but he was glad that "Jaws" ticket sales helped keep the theater afloat over the past year. That's why he showed the movie on the first and third Saturdays of every month.

With great fanfare, the group entered the theater and gathered around the snack bar. The excitement among the members was palpable. Harold and Connie, who managed the snack bar, handed out overpriced popcorn, Raisinettes, and sodas. One of the members, imitating the oboe score from the movie, started the official Jaws Fan Club pre-attack chant, slow at first, gradually picking up pace and ending with a blood-curdling scream by everyone.

"Duh, duh……. duh, duh……, duh, duh, duh, duh, duh, duh, duh, duh, AHHHHHHHHHH!"

Someone yelled "feeding frenzy!" and all members simultaneously placed an erect hand to their foreheads to simulate a shark fin, the official fan club salute. After which, the "shark school" moved, *en masse,* into the theatre.

"Here we go again," said Connie, who had worked this performance at least 20 times.

"It just keeps getting better and better," replied Harold sarcastically.

In truth, Connie was a little envious. She would've loved to participate, but being a cousin of the owner, it was assumed that she would help out at the theatre. The extra income, although small, was also nice. Most island residents held two jobs, and Connie was no exception, teaching at Dauphin Island Elementary during the day and working at the theatre at night.

The other employee, Carl the OC projectionist, moved to the island 12 years ago from Mobile after serving time in federal prison for drugs and counterfeiting. Carl had the clever idea of using a color photocopier to make copies of $100 bills. He would then use fake money to buy drugs, believing that most drug dealers wouldn't notice, and even if they did, they wouldn't report it. Luckily for the police, Carl bought the drugs during a citywide sting by the Mobile Police Department, and the officers quickly recognized the poor quality of his fake $100 bills.

Carl was able to post bail, and during his arraignment, brilliantly pleaded "not guilty," arguing that he did not know the money was counterfeit and that since it was counterfeit, the drug purchase was never legally consummated. In addition, Carl came to court very high on horse tranquilizers and said to the judge during the trial that "drug laws in America are stupidiculous" and they should "megalize larijuana". The judge bought none of it and charged Carl with contempt of court in addition to the drug charges and counterfeiting. After his release from the slammer, he moved to the island and started a rudimentary fishing guide business that he was pretty good at. In large part, Carl had straightened his life out, providing the few island tourists with a chance to land sharks, redfish, and seatrout. Carl liked to tell folks, "I think all the time. Even when I'm not thinking, I'm thinking about thinking."

Carl loaded the film reel that held the commercials for local businesses: Trey Murphy's Used Car Emporium, Island Pizza, and Patronus Seafood. Two cameras were required to show a feature; one would project a film while the other was loaded with the next reel. As the first reel ran out, a seamless transition to the second reel and camera would occur. Carl would then remove the first reel and place reel number three onto that camera. A feature-length film would require 5 to 7 reels. The two, large, 50's era cameras produced a lot of heat, and combined with the soundproofing in the small projection room, it was uncomfortably hot. An exhaust fan in the rear of the room helped, and Carl had found a way to make the job tolerable. While the film was running, he would prop his chair against the wall right in front of the exhaust fan and smoke a joint. As the smoke was exhausted to the outside, he would put on his headphones and let the music of *Hall & Oates*, his favorite group, wash over him, being careful not to miss the next reel change.

Carl took a deep toke on his joint, blew the smoke out the exhaust fan, and loaded reels #1 and #2 onto the cameras.

"Showtime, kiddies," said Carl to himself.

He dimmed the house lights and flipped the switch to start the film as the fan club erupted in applause and cheers. Leaning back against the grid of the exhaust fan and cranking the volume of his "Walkman", Carl obtained a buzz and quietly sang along with *Rich Girl*.

The fan club members were seated front and center, each prepared to perform their parts. After many viewings of the movie, most members had memorized the entire script, and those members in costume would recite the lines along with their character on the screen. The fan club endeavored to make the event interactive, criticizing and arguing with characters, and screaming in unison during the most dramatic parts. Indeed, some members seemed to be genuinely frightened by the most intense scenes. The newest fan club member had something special planned for his inaugural Jaws screening: a smoke bomb that he thought would be a nice effect for the most frightening portion of the movie.

Connie and Harold sat atop the snack bar counter and waited for the spectacle to begin. They could clearly hear the movie and the excited responses of the fan club, and, after many showings, they knew exactly when the loudest screams would occur. It was so predictable that they would take advantage of the responses to pass the time by incorporating the screams into their *repartee*.

"Harold, does this shirt make me look fat?"

"AHHHHHHHHHHHHHHHHHH!" came the screams from the Fan Club.

Harold jumped from behind the popcorn machine to startle Connie. Connie, pretending to be frightened, opened her mouth in a mock scream timed to the screams from the fan club.

"Man, they really are into the movie tonight!" observed Harold. "That was the loudest and longest scream I think I have ever heard from that crazy group."

"And they just keep screaming," said Connie. "That's a new twist. Too much chocolate and caffeine, most likely."

As the film continued through some particularly dramatic scenes, the theatre fell strangely quiet.

"That's odd," observed Harold, puzzled. "They should be whooping and hollering right now."

"Did they all leave out the emergency exit? Harold, see what's going on in there."

"OK." Harold swung his legs over the counter, crossed the lobby, and stuck his head through the cracked door. "What the hell? There is smoke all over," said Harold.

From the flickering light of the film and through the smoky haze, Harold could barely make out ghostly silhouettes of Fan Club members in various positions, some slumped over in their seats, some sitting against the wall, and others lying on the floor.

"Harold, what is it?"

"Something ain't right. Nobody's movin' and they're not saying a word," Harold drew his head back into the lobby. "The place is filled with smoke as well."

"Do you think it's some new fan club thing?" asked Connie.

"I don't know," said Harold, confused. "This is weird. It's the scene where the kid gets eaten. They should be screaming their heads off."

At that moment, Carl burst through the door of the projectionist's room and ran into the lobby—a look of terror on his face.

"Wha…wha…what's going on in there?" asked Carl breathlessly. "I think they're all d… d… dead."

"Oh, hell no, Carl," said Harold. "You must've got ahold of some bad weed."

"You look in there!" insisted Carl, pointing at the theatre door, trembling. "Something has happened in there and it ain't good."

"Calm down, Carl," insisted Connie. "Go turn up the house lights, and we'll take a look. They'll probably all jump up and scare the crap out of us."

"I ain't going back up there," said Carl as he backed away from the double doors of the theatre.

"Carl!" yelled Connie. "Turn up the house lights!"

Carl ran toward the projection room door, tripped over the lobby carpet, got up, and ran up the stairs.

"That is one stoned dude right there," observed Harold. "Connie, you stay here. I'll go check this out. This is some kind of joke, I'm sure."

"Works for me."

The house lights came up, and Harold pushed through the theatre doors, anticipating a group scream from the fan club. Smoke swirled through the flickering camera light while the film's dialogue was in strange contrast to the total quiet in the theatre. From the back of the theatre through the smoky haze, Harold could barely discern the occupants, but as he approached, he knew this was no joke. The carnage was unbelievable. Blood and vomit covered the front rows and the occupants of the theatre.

Harold backed away in disbelief and bolted out of the theatre just as Carl returned from the projection room. "Oh my God! Oh my God! Call the Sheriff…NOW!" commanded a visibly shaken Harold as he swooned and sat down on the floor of the lobby.

"What did you see in there?" asked a wide-eyed Connie.

"It looks like a freakin' mass murder. There's blood everywhere."

"Oh my God!" Connie ran to the phone behind the snack bar and quickly dialed the Sheriff's Department.

"I'm getting out of here!" said Carl as he crossed the lobby at full speed and ran toward the exit.

A mad rush for the exit ensued, with Carl leading the way. They burst through the doors, surprising the ticket booth attendant, who shot them a perplexed look.

"What the heck?" asked the attendant.

"Something terrible has happened in there! We called the Sheriff. You should get out of the building," said Harold.

"I'm gone!" said Carl as he headed toward his truck, intent on putting as much distance between him and the OC as possible.

"Carl, wait!" said Harold. "The Sheriff will want to talk to you. It will look suspicious if you ain't here."

Carl stopped and turned to Harold. "I'm freakin' out man," his voice cracking. "I was loading reel three and happened to look out the projection window to see 'em all going nuts in there. I've never seen 'em act like that. Are you sure it's not just some fan club BS?

"Not unless they all committed suicide, ala Jonestown," replied Harold. "That fan club does not strike me as the mass suicide kind of crowd."

"I can't let the fuzz know I am stoned. I can't go back to prison. I've had enough trouble with the law in my life.

"Calm down, man!" implored Harold. "You believe the Sheriff's gonna think that we had something to do with this? That's crazy."

"Not us, me!" said Harold, wringing his hands nervously.

"So you snuck past me and Connie, went into the theatre, killed all these people, and then went back into the projection booth?" asked Harold. "You're just being paranoid."

"You're probably right," said Carl nervously. "It's the weed talking, I guess."

"Chief East is on the way," said Connie. "I also called Terry. I told him that he needed to come to the theatre immediately, that it was an emergency, and I got out."

CHAPTER 48

Mayor Broussard arrived at the Ocean Cinema to find both Dauphin Island police cars, lights flashing, and the entire police force consisting of Chief East and Deputy Murphy. The officers were busy cordoning off the theatre while Terry's employees stood in a group in the parking lot. A single mercury-vapor streetlight harshly illuminated the lot and attracted a cloud of flying insects that dove crazily in and out of the light. Terry skidded to a halt in the crushed oyster shell parking lot and quickly got out. Chief East came across the lot to meet him halfway.

"What the hell is going on, Bobby?" asked Terry. "Did Carl do something?"

"No, Carl is fine, but we got us a hell of a situation here, Mayor." The Chief wiped his brow with his palm, pulled his hat off, and fanned himself with it. "Damn, it's humid tonight! We got 14 dead people in your theatre."

"What! Yeah, right. Real funny Bobby."

"I wish I were joking."

"How did..., what?" muttered Terry, unable to speak.

Chief East's professionalism kicked in. "After receiving a call from Connie of a disturbance, we went into the theatre and found fourteen victims, all male, of what, we have no idea. There is blood everywhere."

"Oh, my Lord!" exclaimed Terry. "Are my employees OK? Is Connie alright?"

"They're fine. Just shaken up."

"Heaven help us!" Terry, feeling suddenly nauseous, placed both hands on his knees in a partial crouch and tried to catch his breath.

"We've taken statements from each. They all corroborate. Carl is stoned as usual, but we are going to overlook that. He said it looked like they exploded. Your employees say no one entered or left the theatre during the movie. There was no evidence that anyone came in through the emergency exit, as it was locked from the inside. We are leaving the theatre just as we found it, and Sheriff's Department investigators from Mobile are on their way. They're better able to handle this kind of thing. I am at a loss as to what they are going to find. Dr. Belon from the CDC is already on the island, and I'll contact her as soon as we secure the scene."

"What the heck is going on, Bobby? The captain of that shrimp boat, dead. That kid who fell from the water tower. Paul Stanford died. He had no damn business going up on a parasail like some teenager. And now this. Do you think there might be some connection?"

The Chief bit his tongue, not wanting to make public what he already suspected. "I don't know what could have caused the bloody scene that I saw in that theatre. The folks who make the big bucks will have to figure that out. A toxicology report should rule out some kind of mass suicide."

"There is no way that they did that," said Terry. "I knew some of them, and they were happy, well-adjusted young adults. Oh God! Think about their families."

"I'm sorry," said the Chief, now distracted by his concern that all the deaths were connected. "What did you say?"

"I said I can't believe this was some bizarre suicide. They were well-adjusted young folks."

"I don't think it was suicide; however, we can't rule anything out right now. But, time will tell. For now, I'm restricting any entrance to the OC until this can be cleared up." As if stepping out of his official role, Chief East took his hat off, tossed it onto the front seat of his cruiser, and leaned against the car door. His expression changed to reveal an intense sadness. "Terry, it was awful in there. I've seen some terrible things in 'Nam, but nothing like what was in that theatre."

"Are you going to tell the families?" asked Terry.

"I have to. As soon as possible. The news people are gonna be all over the island by morning, and I can't let family members find out like that."

"Good evening, Mayor," said Deputy Murphy as he approached the two.

"Hi Sean. But it ain't good."

Sean's approach snapped Chief East back into the moment as he pushed away from the car.

"I think it was some kind of toxic gas leak," said Murphy. "Harold said there was a lot of smoke in the theatre when he found them. Maybe something leaked out of one of those holes that the gas companies keep punching all around the island."

"But why didn't it kill everyone in the theatre or, for that matter, everyone on Dauphin Island?" asked Chief East. "And why did the victims exsanguinate all over the theatre? I know of no naturally occurring gas that would do that."

"I don't know," said Sean. "I also don't know what exsang…, exsanguish…, that word means."

"It means bleed out," said East.

"Chief, if we're done, I need to talk to my employees," said the Mayor.

"Sure. Go ahead," said the Chief as Terry walked away.

"What do we do now?" asked Deputy Murphy.

"I need a cup of coffee," said the Chief. "It's going to be a long night."

CHAPTER 49

Cherie held the motel room phone to her ear and dialed the home of the Associate Director of the Infectious Diseases Center, hoping he would be available at this hour on a Saturday evening. The phone rang several times before someone answered. Dr. Randolph Stern sat at his desk, working through a stack of reports he had neglected for the past two months. A master of multitasking, he held the phone to his ear with one hand and rifled through some of the many documents on his desk with the other. In his mid-forties, he was thin, of medium height, and with dark brown hair. He had a kind face and wore black horn-rimmed glasses that sharply contrasted with his pale complexion, a result of too much time behind a desk. He clutched a barely lit pipe in his teeth, a terrible habit he knew, but one he couldn't kick and that lately had become one of the few pleasures he allowed himself. The stress of this job was evident in the lines on his face and the premature gray at his temples. He resented having to work from home on a weekend, but it was the only way he could keep up with the mountain of paperwork he was saddled with.

"Hello," said Stern as a bad feeling suddenly came over him.

"Dr. Stern, this is Cherie Belon."

"Uh oh," replied Stern. He removed the pipe from his mouth and placed it in an ashtray on his desk. "This can't be good."

"I apologize for calling your home on a Saturday night, but the situation on the island has taken a terrible turn. I have just come from a theatre here where we have 14 dead people, all exhibiting the symptoms that we've seen in several other people."

"Oh God! Here we go! Give me the details."

"Rapid loss of body fluids, hemorrhaging from the mouth, eyes, nose, and ears. Loss of bladder and bowel control. Death was fast, and from the stricken expressions on the faces of the deceased, it was incredibly painful. Precisely the same as previous victims."

"My God!" Stern picked his pipe up again and began to nervously fidget with it.

"I sent a FAX to your office earlier today with a summary of what we've discovered regarding contact tracing as of this morning. I am 99% certain that a young man, Gene Guidry, brought the infection to the community on the island. He went aboard the Crimson Tide when it was grounded and somehow became infected. Additionally, I've established that he had close contact with 3 of the 4 initial victims, and even more importantly, he was a member of the *Jaws Fan Club*."

"The *Jaws Fan Club*? I'm not following."

"Sorry sir, it's been a long night. The 14 victims in the theatre were all fan club members who were there for their regular meeting. He must have infected them."

"They all died at the same time?"

"Yes. They appeared to have died within minutes or seconds of each other."

"They died that fast! My God! If this is an infectious disease, it behaves like none we've ever encountered."

"Dr. Stern, the characteristics of this thing are frightening. It is fast-acting, at present undetectable, and 100% fatal. I've never seen anything like this."

"Good lord! The worst-case scenario. This has to be an Ebola variant of some kind."

"I can't say, but I'm convinced it's a virus and probably a completely new one. We've received information supporting a virus and about where this thing originated. I outlined all of this in the report I faxed."

"You said, we, you've recruited someone to assist?"

"Yes sir, I have. There is a PhD student on the island named Jesse Gates who is helping. He is close to finishing his doctorate at the Oceanographic Center. He's the individual who reported the Crimson Tide when it ran aground on the island. His assistance and insight have been invaluable."

"Do you think that is wise in an investigation like this?"

"Sir, we are being extremely careful. Jesse is more like a consultant for the investigation. He has also been very helpful in introducing me to some of the locals. I should add that we've become friends and would not do anything to put him at risk."

"I trust your judgment."

"Regarding risk reduction, we've begun handing out surgical masks, and I've posted CDC flyers all over the island about social distancing, hand washing, and good hygiene in general. I am trying to get ahead of this thing. Even if I am completely wrong, preparing for the worst is the best strategy in a situation like this.”

“I agree. You said you may have information about its ultimate origin?”

“Yes, sir. You may find this unbelievable. A Dr. Hector Fernandez contacted us, and we met with him earlier this evening. He was an archaeologist employed by the government of Belize. While working in Belize, near the Mopan River, Dr. Fernandez’s team of researchers discovered a new Mayan site and several ancient Mayan documents. One of those documents was a description of how to make a compound that was apparently used as a bio-warfare agent by the Maya.

“What? A Mayan bio-warfare agent?”

“Yes sir, and it gets worse. That document fell into the hands of a psychopathic terrorist named Arturo. He was able to recreate the compound and, in doing so, killed most of his men. Dr. Fernandez witnessed the deaths of several people who demonstrated the same symptoms we are seeing now on the island. Sadly, his wife was also infected and died. As luck would have it, Arturo and a few of his men escaped and were able to somehow get the agent aboard the Crimson Tide. I believe the captain was smuggling drugs, probably marijuana, and Arturo purposely infected a shipment of marijuana. Drug smuggling was the primary means of generating funds for his twisted Marxist movement. I must say that the captain of the Crimson Tide does not fit the profile of a drug smuggler, and Jesse doesn’t believe he was smuggling pot. On that point, we disagree.”

“Good Lord, I don’t like where this is headed!”

“I have no way of knowing how Guidry, the primary case, became infected, but I could envision him finding marijuana on board and taking some for personal use. That would have been the last joint he ever smoked.”

“Dr. Belon, I have some very unsettling information that you do not have. For national security reasons, I was told by the FBI that I could not disclose what I am about to tell you, so I have to insist that you keep this confidential.”

“Of course.”

"A strange cylinder was discovered in one of the unemptied trawls on the Crimson Tide. The FBI is certain that the device was engineered as a weapon of mass destruction. They suspect it was designed to deliver a noxious agent, perhaps a gas of some kind. The level of sophistication of the device makes the feds very nervous. I can't explain why they did not want me to disclose this, but I hoped that perhaps this would have ended on board that shrimp boat, making it a moot point."

"Nothing about this investigation surprises me," said Cherie.

"Your assistant was correct. The captain was not smuggling drugs. They were just in the wrong place at the wrong time and by chance trawled up one of perhaps multiple cylinders. Its contents were released when it was brought aboard and killed everyone on the ship. Based on what you have told me, it must have been a weaponized virus."

"Wow! If Arturo wanted to infect Americans, all he had to do was place a device in a bale of pot and smuggle it into the U.S. This investigation just gets more bizarre."

"While I don't know anything about the details, I've given it a lot of thought," said Stern. "I could imagine a device that was triggered to release its contents when the bale of pot was opened, maybe it was on a timer, or perhaps it was shock-sensitive. Like nitroglycerine, you bump it too hard and it goes off. The entire bale of pot would have been infected."

"But if there was no pot on the shrimp boat, how did the cylinders come to be on the boat?"

"I think the smugglers had to dump their load of pot. Perhaps they dumped it ahead of being boarded by the Coast Guard, or maybe they just got cold feet and tossed it? After floating around for a bit, the bales broke open, the cylinder separated from the pot and sank to the bottom, and the Crimson Tide trawled it up."

"Wow, talk about bad luck! Was the lab able to identify what was in the cylinder?"

"They assured me that it was empty when discovered. No trace of anything."

"Great," said Cherie, disappointed. "The main reason I am convinced it is a virus is because of something Dr. Fernandez mentioned. One of the things listed on that Mayan codex was bat blood."

"Bat blood?"

"Yes. It was combined with various other ingredients, some of them psychoactive, to produce the bio-agent."

"Good God! Bats harbor so many strains of dangerous viruses that there is no telling what it is."

"This may sound harsh," said Cherie, "but it was fortunate that the Crimson Tide and its deadly cargo ran aground on the island. It will be far easier to contain this thing here than if it reaches the mainland. Which brings me to my next point. It's time for a complete quarantine and lockdown of the island. I can meet ASAP with the authorities on the island and state officials and make the announcement tomorrow."

"I agree. This is an unprecedented national emergency. I am authorizing you to announce a lockdown. When we end this conversation, I will make the calls to mobilize the rapid response team. That theatre has to be quarantined, and all those who have been in contact with any of the deceased must be quarantined as well. I am going to put in an emergency call to the Secretary of Health and Human Services. He needs to be aware of the situation. I'll have our Emergency Response Team in place on the island before sunrise. I'm also going to request assistance from the Coast Guard to control the waterways, as well as the National Guard to patrol and control the island itself. There is only one road on and off the island, so that should be easy. Controlling boat traffic will be harder."

"Do you have to OK this with the CDC Director?"

"This rises to the level of an emergency requiring an immediate response, which gives me authority."

"One final item that will complicate things. There is a hurricane in the Gulf of Mexico, and it's thought that landfall will be along the northern Gulf. That puts us right in the middle of the projected area. "We can't hold folks here if the island goes underwater."

"Oh Jeez!" said Stern, punctuated by a long sigh. "Are there predictions as yet regarding when it will make landfall?"

"Sometime on Thursday, probably the late afternoon or evening."

"Great! It just keeps getting better. By the way, you are doing an exceptional job under terrible circumstances. I wish I had about 25 of you."

"Thank you so much."

"Expect that response team to be there in about 6 hours, and please be careful."

"Yes sir, I will. Goodbye."

CHAPTER 50

Jesse lay in bed and listened to a storm as it drove rain against the windows of his cottage. The house shuddered as a squall line out of the western Gulf moved across the island just before midnight. Unable to sleep and always the scientist, he had timed the lightning flashes through his bedroom window with the arrival of thunder to estimate the storm's distance. It was moving fast. However, a summer squall was hardly the cause of his restlessness. The events of the day, Mayan bio-warfare, a psychopathic terrorist, the hurricane in the Gulf, and a gnawing sense of dread had sabotaged his slumber. But above all was his concern for Cherie. Lately, she was on his mind all the time. He kicked himself over the last thing he said to Cherie after she kissed him; *Sure, no problem. Call me if you need anything. Gates, you are a complete idiot! That's the best you could come up with! How freaking lame can you get!*

Jesse finally crawled out of bed just as the sun peeked over the horizon and prepared himself for the day. *I've got to have some coffee.* He proceeded into the kitchen, prepared a cup of Sanka, and made some dry toast. On the counter where he had left it the evening before, lay the manila envelope containing the blood data from the latest victim. Jesse picked up the envelope and smiled when he thought he detected the faintest hint of gardenia blossoms. Yawning and stretching, he perused the numbers in the amber, early morning light that streamed through the windows. Examining each parameter, he compared the numbers from memory with normal human values. Puzzled at what he found there, he began to doubt his ability to recall typical human blood values. *I believe these values are unusually high,* thought Jesse. *I'll have to check them when I get to the lab.* He went to his bedroom, put on his Sunday clothes, stuffed the manila envelope into his backpack, and drove to *First Baptist Church, Dauphin Island,* to attend the 9:15 service. The congregation was surprisingly small, given that the sanctuary was normally filled.

Jesse always felt spiritually rejuvenated after church, and this morning, Pastor Cummings had preached from *Psalm 91; He is my refuge and my fortress. Surely, He shall deliver you…from the perilous pestilence.* He thanked the Pastor as he left and commented that the message was "Precisely what the congregation needed."

Pastor Cummings nodded and replied, "Thank you, Jesse. Right now, we all need to be in thoughtful prayer."

The comment and the concerned look on the Pastor's face were troubling.

Jesse arrived at the Oceanography Lab a little before noon, to find few cars in the parking lot. The building was typically deserted on Sundays. Entering the laboratory, he settled in to work on his research project. After spending over two hours on data analysis, he realized that he was getting nowhere.

Suddenly, CC burst through the door. "There you are! Have you talked to Cherie this morning?"

"Hi CC. No, I haven't seen her. I came straight here after church. I'm still trying to make sense of my research project. Shouldn't you be taking it easy after our little mishap?" added Jesse earnestly.

"I'm fine. So, you haven't heard?"

"I've heard more than I want, but what are you talking about? Oh crap! Cherie's been called back to Atlanta, hasn't she?"

"Whoa! You are really smitten, aren't you?"

"Just tell me," said Jesse impatiently.

"Nope. She's not going to be leaving anytime soon, I don't think." CC hopped onto the desk in front of Jesse and sat down.

"You've got that look on your face. What's going on?"

"A bunch of folks died at the *Ocean Cinema* last night," said CC with a bit too much enthusiasm.

"Are you kidding! What happened?"

"They are not sure. Blood all over the theatre. Dead bodies everywhere."

"No way!"

"I heard about it on the radio this morning. There are news people and police all over the island. I don't think they know what caused it, but folks want answers."

"Oh Lord! Do they think it is connected to the other deaths on the island?"

"I don't know. But I'm headed down there now. You want to go?"

"No, I've got too much stuff going on with this research project right now."

"I'll bet Cherie will be there. I heard they've brought more folks in from the CDC. She could probably give us some inside information about it."

"Actually… I do need to call Cherie. Let's go down to the student lounge, and I'll give her a call."

"OK."

Jesse tried to reach Cherie on the phone, but there was no answer.

"Well, maybe we should drive down," admitted Jesse, "this stuff can wait."

"Let's roll!" said CC enthusiastically. "We'll grab Ross. He's in his office. Oh, by the way, there was a news item on TV about that gold doubloon."

"What?" Jesse stopped short as they were about to leave the lounge. "Only a couple of people knew about that. How did the news people get wind of it?"

"Well, a dude from a pawn shop in Mobile was interviewed about it and was on TV. He mentioned that it could be part of a larger treasure on Dauphin Island. I think they said the treasure was from some French guy."

"Why would he have done that?"

"I can tell you exactly why. He's drumming up business for his shop. What's the big deal? Everybody on the island knows you found it?"

"I just don't want or need the attention right now. And how did everybody on the island learn that I found it? And by the way, I did not find it; it was given to me."

"Well, Ross told me, and he may have mentioned it to others. Did you tell him to keep quiet about it?"

"I didn't."

"Not that it would have mattered," said CC, grinning.

"Exactly."

The three left the Oceanographic Lab and climbed into the El Camino. Jesse motored off campus and, in a few minutes, pulled into a vacant lot down the street from the OC. Police cars, news vans, CDC vehicles, and a few rubberneckers lined the two-lane road up to the barricade that kept unauthorized individuals from getting closer than about a block. The three approached the barricade where a Mobile County Sheriff's Deputy wearing a surgical mask stood guard. In the distance, the OC could be seen covered with plastic sheeting, while large, white plastic tunnels allowed hazmat-suited CDC employees to move from the OC into a large van parked just outside. Another tunnel led to a large, mobile containment facility that took up most of the OC parking lot.

"Good grief!" remarked Ross. "It looks like the carnival is in town."

"This does not look good at all," remarked Jesse. "I hope Cherie is OK."

"She's a professional," said Ross. "She knows what she's doing."

"That doesn't prevent me from worrying."

"Officer, can you tell us anything about what's going on?" asked Jesse to the young deputy. "We are scientists."

"First, y'all need to put these masks on." The Deputy reached into a box of surgical masks and gave one to each. "Here are some extras for you to give to others. I've been here since late last night, so you probably know more than I do. I know there are victims of something in there. I was told to tell folks that there will be a radio and televised press conference at City Hall at 4:00 today. They instructed me to tell everyone that they should watch on television or listen to the radio because only news people will be allowed at the conference. Maybe your questions will be answered then."

"Thank you, sir," replied Jesse.

"Damn!" said Ross. "If they are handing out masks, the crap must be about to hit the fan."

"Let's go back to the lab," said CC. "We can catch it on the local news broadcast out of Mobile or maybe CNN."

"CNN?" asked Jesse. "What's that?"

"The 24-hour news network. You know, Cable News Network, CNN? We just got cable installed in the lounge."

"Never heard of it."

"You really need to get out more!"

"I am struggling to finish this project and graduate, and things are not going so well right now."

"I know, and I'm sorry," said CC sympathetically. "But sometimes taking a break lets you tackle a problem with fresh eyes. It works for me."

"You may be right," replied Jesse. "But that press conference is hours away, so I'm going to work on this project data until then."

"Suit yourself," said CC.

Jesse returned to the lab and tried to concentrate on his project with little success. Stretching his legs, he crossed the lab to switch on the boom-box radio that someone had left there. Tuning to the classical music station, the strains of Mozart's *The Magic Flute* floated across the room. *That's interesting.* Although not an opera aficionado, he was familiar with the piece. The opera appeared to be a simple fairy tale, but was, in reality, a clash between the forces of darkness and light with a strong moral message. The magic flute, played by the prince, could change sorrow to joy. *Maybe that flute will work its magic on me.* Jesse chuckled. Returning to his desk, he placed his head down across his folded arms and breathed a troubled sigh.

He sat up in his chair and looked around, confused. *Oh crap!* The drool on his cheek and the puddle on his desk revealed that he had fallen asleep. Momentarily in a panic, he glanced at his watch and found that only a few minutes had passed. Although a short nap, he felt much refreshed. Wiping the drool from his face and desk, he turned his attention to the graphs in front of him. His data revealed that the change in shark behavior began a couple of weeks ago. All sharks before that time demonstrated the typical stress response, but with each subsequent group of sharks collected, the "normal" behavior had declined gradually until most of those fish recently captured displayed the altered "bionic shark" behavior, as CC had so eloquently termed it. A plot of the percentage of bionic sharks in his samples over time showed a classic, textbook S-shaped increase; few in the beginning, a rapid increase, and then slowing to reach 100% change. Additionally, he was able to project backward in time to determine that the altered response first appeared in early August, and all sharks around the island were altered in about 12 days. However, he could find no reasonable explanation for the change.

Screw it! Disgusted, he side-armed a wadded piece of paper at the trash can and missed. He sighed deeply, rose from his chair, and began to pace around the room. His thoughts now turned to Cherie and the CDC investigation. Remembering the blood data from the CDC, he took the manila envelope out of his backpack, reached for a reference book on stress physiology that he kept at his desk, and checked the blood values for humans.

Good Lord! All of the stress indicators are through the freaking roof. Cortisol and adrenaline are 10 times higher than normal! He scratched his head. *What the heck does that mean?* He reached across his desk and picked up the stack of electron microscope images of liver tissue that he and Cherie had taken from the Captain of the Crimson Tide. Absent-mindedly leafing through the highest-magnification images, he was disappointed in the consistently poor quality of each. With the idea that he might use the topic of liver function for one of his required graduate school seminars, he had checked out a textbook from the library on the *Structure and Function of the Liver*. He took the textbook and cracked it open. Beautiful electron-microscope images of liver cells appeared on the page.

My images normally look like that, thought Jesse as he opened a desk drawer and removed electron microscope photographs of shark muscle tissue that he had processed and photographed last year, admiring their quality. He placed a row of shark muscle tissue images across his desk alongside the puzzlingly poor human liver images. Taking a magnifying glass from his desk drawer, he enjoyed scrutinizing the clearly defined details of the cells, his skill with the electron microscope proudly on display. Jesse then focused the magnifying glass on the human liver images, disappointed at the lack of fine detail. The photos taken at the highest magnification, in particular, were like images taken in a dust storm, with all the cellular structures clouded by particles. He looked at each image in turn and compared them with the textbook images. He looked back at the high-quality images and compared them again to the liver images. A puzzled look spread across his face. Leaning back, he stared at the ceiling and pulled on his chin in contemplation as soft classical music filled the room.

"What the heck!?" exclaimed Jesse as he excitedly leaned forward. "Holy smokes!" He rose from his desk with a start, toppling his desk chair over behind him in the process. Tossing the images, textbook, and magnifying glass into his backpack, he hurried out of the lab.

CHAPTER 51

Reports of the tragedy at the OC spread fast around the island, and when CC and Ross walked into the lounge, a group of graduate students and Professors had already gathered to watch the news conference. Conversations among the crowd included theories about the deaths, the upcoming Jimmy Buffett concert in Mobile, various students' oceanographic research projects, and how great the surfing would be if the hurricane made landfall near the island. Cherie's efforts to protect the public were having an effect, as several people were already wearing masks in the room.

"If we had a keg and a steel drum band, we could start TGIF early," quipped Ross as he and CC approached the television that sat at one end of the lounge.

"I could use a beer, although it's not five o'clock yet," said CC.

"Quiet, everyone! They're talking about the hurricane," said one of the Professors. "Turn it up."

The volume came up, and a perfectly coiffured WMOB local news anchor appeared on the screen.

"And now we go to our intrepid weatherman, Bob Simpson, to give us the latest on Hurricane Allison. What's it looking like, Bob?"

Bob stood in front of a large map of the Gulf of Mexico. A spiral graphic of Hurricane Allison covered much of the southern Gulf and the Yucatan Peninsula. Bob wore an ugly, plaid, polyester leisure suit, his trademark "Weatherman" attire.

"Thanks, Vic. Here we are, folks, trying to reason with hurricane season. Not to trivialize this, because we have a serious situation way down south," said a stone-faced Bob as he pointed at the satellite photograph on the screen. "Take a look at the eye of this sucker! Small and very well-defined. This is the same storm that almost destroyed one of our hurricane hunter planes out of Biloxi. Barometric pressures of 910 mb and 185 mph wind speeds have been reported. It's Category 5 folks! If you're not aware, that's the highest category. Hurricane-force winds extend out 70 miles, so this is a beast of a storm. At the moment, the storm is slowly inching its way northwest. However, this low-pressure system that is swinging down from the north will likely cause it to accelerate and drag it further east as it moves across the open Gulf.

We expect some weakening of the system as it moves into slightly cooler waters, but it is still gonna be a very dangerous storm when it makes landfall. Where it makes landfall, we don't know, but you can be sure of this: there will be major damage and loss of life. Everyone from Galveston to Apalachicola needs to keep an eye on this. We will have complete coverage at 5:00. Bob Simpson, WMOB News. Back to you, Vic."

"That's good advice, Bob," said the news anchor. "Everyone needs to be weather aware and watch this storm closely. Now we turn to a developing story out of the small community of Dauphin Island. Our WMOB News Reporter Brenda Vale is live on the scene in Dauphin Island."

The scene changed to show a petite news reporter standing in front of a police barricade with the OC mostly covered in white plastic sheeting in the background.

"Thanks, Vic. Tragedy struck this small town last evening when a group of young people died mysteriously inside the Ocean Cinema theatre, the building draped in white, seen behind me." Brenda turned, and the view changed to a long shot of the theatre.

"Information is still forthcoming as to the cause of death, but island residents are reeling from the reports. At present, there are 14 people confirmed dead, all of them in the theatre. We've been told that they were all members of the Jaws Fan Club. As you can see, Police have cordoned off the area as investigators from the Mobile County Sheriff's Department and officials from the Centers for Disease Control attempt to determine the cause of death. We are fortunate to have with us here, a resident of Dauphin Island, and projectionist at the Ocean Cinema, Mr. Carl Renfield. Thank you for speaking with us, Mr. Renfield."

The camera pulled back and panned right as Carl came into view.

"No problem," said Carl, looking a bit bewildered. A shot of Brenda and Carl from the waist-up filled the screen.

"That's Carl!" exclaimed Ross. "He's a fishing guide on the island. Look at his eyes. Man, he's stoned."

"He's always stoned," said one of the other graduate students.

"Hush!" demanded CC. "I want to hear this."

"We understand that you were present in the theatre when the deaths occurred?"

"Yes Ma'am," said Carl. "Like I done already told Chief East, they was watchin' *Jaws* for about the hunderth time. I was changing the film reel and looked out the camera window into the theatre. They just exploded."

"Exploded! What do you mean by that?" asked the news reporter incredulously.

"It was freaky, man. They was jerking and screaming, and blood was going everywhere. And then they all just stopped," said Carl as he jerked his body and flailed his arms. "Have you ever seen something that you wish you had never seen? That's what I got stuck in my head," lamented Carl as he repeatedly smacked his forehead with his palm as if to dislodge the offending image from his memory. "Some say it was some kind of gas because of all the smoke in there, but I don't believe that," added Carl.

"There was smoke in the theatre?" asked Brenda.

"The room was full of it. It was like some kind of horror movie with "Jaws" on the screen, smoke in the room, and them folks exploding."

"If Carl was there, you can be sure the theatre was filled with smoke!" joked Ross.

"And what did you do then?" asked the reporter.

"I ran out of there like a scalded monkey. It weren't no gas that killed 'em. I think some of that concession stand food was what poisoned 'em all. That stuff ain't real food. I saw where somebody found a Twinkie that was a hundred years old, and it was just as good as one made today in 1989. You can't put that stuff in your body and…"

The cameraman panned left to reveal a smirking Brenda trying to remain professional.

"Thank you, Mr. Renfield," said Brenda as she moved away from Carl. "Well, there you have it. I'll be monitoring the situation here, and we will keep our viewers informed. This is Brenda Vale, WMOB. Back to you, Vic."

"Exploding people and 100-year-old Twinkies. That's Carl, alright," quipped Ross as laughter spread among the graduate students and Professors.

"Thank you, Brenda," said Vic as the scene changed back to the newsroom. "Please stay safe. We now take you to WMOB's Clark Morris outside the Dauphin Island City Hall."

The scene revealed a group of reporters and Police Officers at the front of the one-story City Hall building. A microphone stand placed at the top of a short flight of exterior stairs was surrounded by Chief East and several other official-looking individuals. The news reporter faced the camera with his back to the gathering.

"Thanks, Vic. We are moments away from a news conference regarding the mysterious deaths, last evening, of 14 citizens inside a local theatre. We are told that Dauphin Island Chief of Police Robert East and officials from the Centers for Disease Control in Atlanta will be making a statement."

The camera panned across the gathering of news people as Clark continued speaking.

"Hey, there's Jesse!" exclaimed Ross. "I thought he was in the lab."

CHAPTER 52

Jesse quickly drove to City Hall and located Cherie. He was able to get her attention as she stood among the officials gathered around the microphone in front of the City Hall building.

Looking very weary, Cherie came down the stairs when she saw Jesse. "You aren't supposed to be here."

"I pulled my scientist credentials and they let me through. I guess you heard?"

"Everyone has heard. I was worried. Are you OK?"

"I'm fine. Just tired. I need to talk with you in private for a moment." Cherie lowered her voice and walked to the side of the City Hall building away from the group. "Under the circumstances, a public meeting is a bad idea, but I guess it is the fastest way to get the word out." The frustration and fatigue were evident in her voice. "Everyone at the CDC is going crazy. My supervisor approved a quarantine and total lockdown last night, and it has been approved all the way up to the President. No one goes on or off the island. The National Guard will block the road coming onto the island, and the Coast Guard will blockade the waterways."

"Oh geez," groaned Jesse. "This is turning into a nightmare."

"It's already a nightmare for a lot of families on the island. Fourteen dead is what it finally took to authorize the lockdown. It's a shame that those kids died. I am so distraught over this. I don't know what I could have done differently."

Jesse took Cherie's hand and looked her straight in the eye. "Exactly! There is nothing you could have done differently. There is no need to feel guilty about it."

"I feel more disappointed than guilty."

"Have you told Chief East about our meeting with Fernandez and this Arturo fellow?"

"I did. I am unsure if he believes it, but his plate is so full I don't think he can process anything else."

"Sounds like your plate is full as well. You really need a break. Can you get away for a while?"

"I can't get away until this evening."

"Can you come to my house later? I've got something extremely important to show you."

"I can't come until after about 6 tonight. We are probably going to be working late, but I'll take a dinner break at that time."

"Come to the house and we can eat there. I'll have something for us."

"Uh-oh!" said Cherie. The news conference is starting; I have to go. I'll see you at 6, and Jesse, I want you to immediately start limiting your exposure to people on the island. We don't know what's going on, but I am convinced that this is an undescribed viral infection."

"No problem, I tend to be something of an academic hermit anyway. And, by the way, I think I've figured out what is going on," said Jesse knowingly.

Cherie cast Jesse a puzzled look as she hurried back to the podium.

"Test, test. Is this thing working?" Holding a hastily penned address in his right hand, Chief East stood on the top step and tapped the microphone. A loud feedback squeal from the speaker drew a groan from the news people who had gathered.

"Sorry folks. First of all, if you are not wearing a surgical mask, you are required to put one on immediately. Masks are available free at the table over there." East pointed toward the CDC personnel sitting at a table, where boxes of surgical masks were stacked. "Also, everyone needs to spread out to keep their distance from each other. I'm Dauphin Island Police Chief Robert East. To my right is Mobile County Police Chief Charles Everly, next to him is Captain Louis Thomas of the U.S. Coast Guard, and this is Dr. Cherie Belon from the Centers for Disease Control. Oh, my apology, to her left is Alabama National Guard Captain Richard Wallace. It's out-of-the-ordinary for me to address an ongoing investigation publicly, but this is an unusual situation."

East began to read. "At about 8 PM last evening, we received a report of a problem at the Ocean Cinema Theatre. Deputy Murphy and I arrived a few minutes later and, upon investigation, found that 14 people had died in the theatre." Gasps and hushed expletives went through the group. "We are withholding the names of the deceased until notification of next of kin. Due to the seriousness of the situation, we immediately contacted the Mobile County Police Department, the Alabama Bureau of Investigation, the Alabama Department of Health, and the Centers for Disease Control, whose personnel were already on the island. The CDC Rapid Response Team arrived early this morning from Atlanta to secure the building and the surrounding area. We are unsure of the events surrounding this tragedy. It's too early in the investigation to draw conclusions, but there appears to have been no foul play. At this time, I would like to turn the mike over to Dr. Belon from the CDC."

Cherie moved to the microphone.

"Thank you, Chief East. First, for those of you who lost loved ones last night, our hearts and prayers go out to you. I am Dr. Cherie Belon, a Public Health Microbiologist for the Centers for Disease Control in Atlanta. As Chief East just stated, it is still early in the investigation, and we are still gathering data. Public health is the primary concern of the CDC, and we are vigorously investigating these deaths. What we know at this time is that there are similarities between the fatalities last night and recent deaths that have occurred on the island. We are asking all residents to limit social contacts and are also implementing restrictions on gatherings of more than 5 people. Likewise, we encourage folks to practice good personal hygiene, wash their hands regularly using hand sanitizer, and cover their mouth when sneezing or coughing. Finally, the CDC will provide surgical masks free of charge, which we are requiring everyone to wear if you must go out in public. Those masks will be available at all government buildings, the police station, the fire station, and at most businesses on the island. Finally, if you or anyone you know had contact with any of those who died last evening or those who died previously, we would like you to come forward to speak with us at the CDC as soon as possible. Rest assured that Chief East, law enforcement, and the CDC are working day and night to protect the people of Dauphin Island, and we will keep everyone informed of any developments.

"We will now open this up for questions," said Chief East as he moved back to the microphone. "But to repeat, we will give no details regarding the identity of the deceased."

Several hands shot up in the crowd, all of them from members of local news organizations.

"Yes," said Chief East, motioning to a reporter near the front of the group.

"Thank you, Chief East. I'm Trent Strong, WMON, Montgomery, Alabama. You said there was no indication of foul play. There has been a rumor of a mass suicide. Could you respond to that?"

"I said there appears to have been no foul play," corrected Chief East. "There is nothing at present to support mass suicide. A toxicology report is forthcoming, but I am willing to bet the farm that it will come back negative. I knew the families of some of these young people, and they did not fit the profile. At least the ones I knew were well-adjusted, happy individuals. Also, the employees at the theatre confirmed that they were there to see a movie and have fun. I am no expert on the psychology of mass suicide, but a bunch of young folks dressed in silly costumes, cracking jokes, and buying almost $100 worth of overpriced concessions, that kind of behavior does not say mass suicide to me. No sign whatsoever that they had suicide on their minds."

"Were these people members of a cult?" asked the same reporter.

"Hell no!" answered the Chief angrily. "It was an innocent fan club, that's all."

"You, sir," said East, pointing to another individual.

"Chuck Stuart, WLOX Biloxi. Dr. Belon mentioned that there were similarities between the deceased and other deaths on the island. Could you speak to that?"

"That would be best answered by Dr. Belon," replied Chief East as Cherie stepped toward the microphone.

"I cannot go into a lot of detail at this time, but the condition of the bodies of those recently deceased on the island has been similar. All the victims showed rapid loss of blood and extensive tissue damage. These pathologies were also observed in the case of the Crimson Tide."

"So, is it a communicable disease of some kind, like the plague?" added the news reporter.

"Although we have yet to identify an infectious agent, we cannot rule out a disease of some kind, and that is why we are taking extra precautions. All the expertise of the CDC has been turned to this investigation. Thank you."

Cherie stepped away from the microphone, and Chief East returned. "Thanks, Dr. Belon. I am turning the microphone over to Captain Wallace."

"Thanks, Chief. Ladies and gentlemen, I'm Captain Richard Wallace of the Alabama National Guard. The National Guard is responsible for protecting the citizens of the state of Alabama. We are also responsible for responding to natural disasters. Due to the seriousness of the situation, we are announcing, effective immediately, a quarantine and lockdown of the island. I'm sorry to inform you, but you will not be allowed to leave."

"What! You can't do this!" shouted a National Public Radio reporter, followed by groans and displeased murmurs.

"Yes sir, we can!" countered Wallace. "As of 2:15 AM this morning, local law enforcement and the National Guard were given emergency authority by the Governor of Alabama." Captain Wallace held up a document and waved it at the reporter. "The National Guard has already set up a checkpoint at the approach to the Dauphin Island Bridge. The Dauphin Island Airport has likewise been shut down. Additionally, we will have patrols on the island to assist local law enforcement. Finally, the Coast Guard will be patrolling the water around the island, but I will let Captain Thompson comment on that."

"Yes, thank you." Thompson approached the microphone. "The Coast Guard has been given emergency power via an executive order from President Bush to patrol all the waters around the island 24/7. Let me be clear, we will turn back anyone attempting to arrive on or leave the island. Let it be known that with our radar system, we can monitor the movements of every vessel and object down to the size of a rubber duck. If you attempt to leave, you will be subject to arrest or worse. So don't try it."

Continued shouts of confusion, concern, and anger interrupted the conference, and some reporters hurried away to phone in their reports.

"THIS IS BULL SHIT!" shouted a particularly belligerent National Public Radio reporter. "You'll be hearing from our attorney!"

"So, you've blockaded the entire island?" commented another journalist. "It's like the Cuban Missile Crisis!"

"I've got a deadline to meet," shouted another. "How am I supposed to file my report?"

"Folks, please… please!" Cherie took the microphone, attempting to calm the group. "I understand your frustration, but your news deadlines pale in comparison to our responsibility as public servants to protect every one of you and, in fact, the entire nation. Let me try again to make the potential seriousness of this situation clear. And this is not hyperbole. So, I am gonna lay it out for you. My job at the CDC is to consider worst-case scenarios. Those 14 deaths," Cherie said, motioning toward the OC, "and the previous five victims, suggest that we have an infectious agent that has a 100% mortality rate. That's bad, really bad. However, as bad as that sounds, it may be even worse. Whatever this is, it kills with amazing speed, appears highly infectious, and is presently undetectable. We likely have island residents who don't realize they are infected. The virus seems to emerge quickly and kill quickly. That combination of characteristics causes public health personnel like me to lose sleep. If this finds its way to the mainland, the number of lives lost would be staggering. We have to stop it on Dauphin Island, and we will do whatever it takes to accomplish that."

As Cherie's words sank in, the mood changed from anger to concern. The WMOB reporter raised his hand.

"You, sir," said Cherie.

"So infected residents are like walking time bombs? Is that a fair description?"

"Your words, not mine," replied Cherie.

"Yes?" Cherie pointed to another reporter.

What happens if that hurricane makes landfall here?"

"Captain Wallace, could you respond?" asked Cherie, stepping away from the microphone.

"Yes. Thank you for that question. Obviously, that will make our job much harder. We hope and pray that we will not have to evacuate, but an evacuation plan is being developed as we speak. If evacuation is necessary, all occupants on the island will be relocated to Riley Air Force Base in south Mobile County. There are about 2500 people on the island, including residents and visitors, and Riley is adequate for over four thousand. We have commandeered buses from local schools and Universities as well as military buses for the evacuation. All of your needs will be met."

As cooler heads prevailed, another reporter asked a question. "Mike McCallum, WFLA Pensacola. The theatre was filled with smoke or gas when the victims were found. There is talk that it had something to do with the deaths. Could you comment on that?"

"Chief East, could you address that question?"

"Yes," replied East, moving back to the microphone. "There was no gas release. The smoke in the theatre had nothing to do with these deaths. Investigators found a discharged smoke bomb in the theatre, an innocent firework that you can purchase anywhere. One of the individuals set it off during the movie. It has likewise been sent for testing, but it seems very unlikely that someone would have weaponized a 25-cent smoke bomb to use against a bunch of young people. There is also…"

"WHERE IS MY SON?" screamed a distraught, middle-aged lady as she rushed forward and was met by a Mobile County Police Officer who held her back. "What have you done with my son?" pleaded the lady as she collapsed sobbing in the officer's arms.

"Could somebody assist Mrs. Burgess?" implored the Chief as two masked CDC employees assisted the broken individual. "We are done here," declared Chief East as he gathered his notes and disappeared into City Hall.

"Crap!" said Ross as the mood in the student lounge changed from amused interest to deep concern.

CHAPTER 53

Chief East left City Hall through the rear entrance. To avoid irate citizens and news reporters, he took a circuitous route back to the Police Station. He momentarily sat in the parking lot and massaged his leg, hoping to relieve the pain that shot down the back of his thigh. He could always count on his war wound flaring up during stressful situations. Finding little relief, he got out of the car and limped into the station. Dorothy looked up from her work as he entered.

"I heard the news conference," said Dorothy. "That was awful…Mrs. Burgess. I felt terrible for her… and you."

"It comes with the territory, I guess. That's why we get the big bucks."

"Yeah, right."

"Oh crap! You've got that look on your face again."

"Sorry, Chief," said Dorothy. "Got a call about a vehicle way out at the west end of the island. They did not want to give their name but said that there was a body in the car. I've already dispatched Sean out there."

"Let me guess. Looks like a week-old corpse and covered with blood?"

"No, they didn't mention anything about that."

"Well, that's good news," said East sarcastically. "Just your garden variety murder or stroke perhaps."

"Sorry, Chief, but there's more."

"Oh great."

"I also got another call. It appears that two people died while watching that Alabama football game that was on earlier. One died while Alabama was trying to score on a 4th and goal from the 2-yard line. Covered in blood."

"Are you kidding me!?"

"His wife was hysterical, so I had to get someone out there immediately. The CDC now handles these unexplained deaths, so I called them and the Mobile Sheriff's Office. You don't have to deal with that, but you should run out there and check on Sean."

"I'm on my way." East began to limp out to his cruiser.

"Wait, take these." Dorothy handed him a Coca-Cola and two Tylenol. "I saw you out there, in the car, in pain. These will help."

"Thank you, Dorothy. You are a blessing! We couldn't function around here without you."

"It's an old Chevy Nova." She picked up a green Post-it note and read from it. "White, rusty, parked on the shoulder at the end of Sailfish Way. It has a New Mexico license plate. Must be a tourist."

"That's probably the first tourist we've ever had from New Mexico."

"And maybe the last."

East swallowed the two pain-relievers and washed them down with Coke. "I hope those kick in soon. Damn it! This place is falling apart."

"You need this also," Dorothy held out a surgical mask.

"No damn way I'm wearing that! If this person is like the others, I'll put it on."

"Promise me you will do that."

"I promise."

The Chief limped back out of the station, climbed in his cruiser, and headed for the west end. He pulled off the road behind Deputy Murphy's cruiser. Sean stood at the door of the vehicle, Billystick in hand, and was about to smash the driver's side window when East arrived. Sean stopped when he saw Chief East.

"Another one like all the rest?" asked East as he limped over to Sean.

"I don't think so. He's slumped over in the front seat, and there's blood running onto the floor, but not like the others we've dealt with. I found two bullet casings on the road here by the door." Sean removed the two casings from his shirt pocket.

"Damnit Sean, you picked them up! Now your fingerprints are all over them."

"Sorry, Chief," said Sean sheepishly. "The door is locked, and I was about to bust the window."

"Did you try the other side?"

"Uh, no. Guess I should do that, huh?"

"That would be the smart thing, Sean." East shook his head in frustration and sighed. "And don't use your bare hand. Get some of those paper towels out of my cruiser."

Sean returned with a handful of towels, and they went to the other side of the car. He tried the door and it swung open. They knelt outside the vehicle for a better view.

"Definitely not the same as the others," said East. "There are two obvious bullet wounds in his head."

"Could have been suicide," observed Murphy.

"Sean, think about what you just said. He shot himself twice in the forehead?"

"I am not following you, Chief?"

"No way he survived that first shot. How did he pull the trigger on the second one?"

"Didn't think about that."

"Clearly, you did not. I want you to tell me what else you see and write it down in your notebook."

"Am I being tested?"

"No, I just want you to practice your skills of observation."

Sean removed a small notepad and pencil from his shirt pocket and began taking notes. "Well, the deceased is relatively short, thin, dark complexion, full head of grey hair." Sean scribbled in his notebook. "Tan pants and a white button-down shirt. He is lying across the front seat. Two bullet holes in his forehead, two large exit wounds in the back of his head. Blood all over the front seat and on the floor."

"Do you see anything significant about the blood splatter?"

"Not really."

"Look at the blood and tissue across the top of the seat back on the passenger side. His head was turned looking out the driver's side window when the shots were fired. Someone approached him from that window and fired two shots point-blank. The force spun his head around and knocked him across the front seat. You see the stippling around this entry wound?" East reached into the car and pointed with a pencil. "These small dark spots?"

"Yes sir."

East grimaced as he stood and straightened his sore leg. "Those are powder burns," said East with a groan. "The pistol was against his head or within a few inches. The perpetrator stood outside the car, placed the gun against his forehead, and fired two shots rapidly. You could probably determine which shot was first by the amount of stippling because the first shot would have pushed his head away from the gun before the second shot was fired. Not sure why you would want to know which shot was first, however."

"There might be footprints below that window."

"On asphalt? Another odd thing," continued East, "the window must have been down when the shots were fired because the window isn't broken. The perpetrator shot him, opened the door, rolled up the window, and locked the door behind him. That's strange behavior. I wonder if he took anything from the car."

"Are you writing this information down!?"

"Oh, sorry," Sean scribbled in his notepad. "Damn Chief! How do you know all of this stuff?"

"Many years of law enforcement, that's how."

Chief East bent down and looked in the front windshield of the Ford. "There's a Spanish-language newspaper on the dash. That's strange, although the plates are from New Mexico. There is also a Dauphin Island Campground parking permit hanging from the rear-view mirror."

"Somebody camping on the island."

"Must be. Sean, go over to the campground and check into this. They should have the license plate on file for this vehicle. Find out who it is and get back to me."

"Yes sir. You want me to go now?"

"Yes. We're not going to investigate this. We've got an army of law enforcement on the island. We'll let them handle it."

CHAPTER 54

Another stupid American! Concealed from view in a grove of cypress trees, Arturo had watched the remote cabin for several days and now knew the routine of the old man who lived there. *This is going to be the cleanest kill I've ever made.* Chuckling softly, he replayed the scene in his mind; *I'll surprise him as he walks to the mailbox, one bullet in the skull, then toss the body into the swamp and let the alligators take care of the evidence.* The brutality of this execution appealed to him in an almost erotic way. Stifling a laugh, he imagined the old Gringo's surprised face as the bullet hit him. The same shock he had seen on countless victims.

This man doesn't realize how his death will help bring about the Marxist rebirth that's coming. Wipe the slate clean and start all over. Arturo had stolen a quote from Karl Marx but believed, in his twisted mind, that he was the originator. *There's only one way to stop the convulsions of the old society and the bloody birth pains of the new: revolutionary terror.*

After living out of his car and driving the back roads of Dauphin Island for days, Arturo had selected this particular cottage for its remoteness. Strangely, the abode also reminded him of an abandoned cottage he fled to as a young boy in Colombia. A place of refuge from where he could escape the constant abuse and beatings he had received at home. Begging in the streets of Bogota, severe punishment would greet him if he failed to bring home enough to cover his stepfather's ever-growing appetite for cocaine and *Viche*, a cheap, local moonshine. At age 14, his life changed forever when a local drug dealer offered him a job and a place to stay in return for his services. Using money he made from his first drug delivery, he purchased a cheap revolver and six bullets, found his step-father passed out in his filthy hovel, and unloaded the gun into him, pulling the trigger repeatedly long after the bullets were gone. Like swatting a fly, there was no great unburdening, no weight lifted from his shoulders, no remorse. Although he could not know it at that time, his cold detachment and complete disregard for human life would serve him well for the rest of his "career".

"Who the hell are you?" asked the old man as Arturo suddenly appeared. Seeing this stranger, he backed away and quickly put his hand into the rear pocket of his loose-fitting trousers. "Get off my property!"

"Yes, Señor, my car is not so good and…" he stopped mid-sentence and brought his pistol up to carry out his plan.

But Arturo had underestimated his victim as the old man quickly produced a weapon and squeezed off two rounds. The pistol shots sent a group of herons squawking away from their roost in the cypress trees. Arturo, caught completely off-guard, dove for cover. He clutched his shoulder when he felt the sting of a bullet that grazed him. The old man sprinted up the driveway, firing his weapon behind him as he ran. A bullet pushed up a cloud of dust in the drive just ahead of Arturo as he rose to pursue his quarry. Arturo shot once but missed. Gasping, the old man ran to the rear of the cottage and took cover behind his pickup truck. He fired once more and pulled the trigger again with no discharge. Arturo took cover again after the pistol shot, but upon hearing the "click" of an empty chamber, he knew the old man was no longer a threat.

Arturo rose and dusted himself off. "Señor, why you so angry? We go in casa, we talk. I only wish to use your…uh…telefono and maybe a drink of aqua." Arturo gestured with his pistol as he casually walked toward the old man.

The old man crouched behind the truck, gasping for breath and trembling. "Get off… my property you… son of a bitch. I'll shoot your nuts off!"

"Oh, I think you are not telling the truuuuth," replied Arturo in a sing-song fashion. "I just want to be your amigo."

The old man ran toward a small dock where a boat was tied. Taking his time to aim carefully, Arturo fired, striking the old man in the leg. He fell onto the dock in a heap.

Arturo slowly approached, stood over the old man, and then knelt next to him. He noticed a Marine Corps, *Semper fi* tattoo on the old man's arm. "You are soldier? *Federales?*" He straightened his back and saluted mockingly.

"Damn you to hell, you piece of shit!" groaned the old man through gritted teeth. He clutched his bleeding leg and writhed in pain.

"Senor. Why you make this so hard?"

"Lousy bastard, I ain't afraid of you. I make turds bigger than you," growled the old man. Held at gunpoint, Arturo placed a foot on the old man's wound and ground it against the weathered planks of the dock. The old man howled and grabbed him by the ankle. Arturo put the pistol barrel against his temple and shot point-blank. The blowback from the explosion sprayed blood and tissue across Arturo's expressionless face.

Emotionless, Arturo wiped the gun barrel with his shirt and inserted it into the waistband of his trousers. After searching the body, he found a set of keys and a wallet containing $38.

"John Wayne Riley," read Arturo with some difficulty as he examined the victim's driver's license. "John Wayne!" smirked Arturo. "Tough guy."

He dragged the lifeless body to the edge of the dock and rolled it into the water. Using a paddle he found in the small boat, he pushed the floating body under the dock. Arturo hurried down the long dirt driveway to retrieve his old Chevy. He parked it behind an outbuilding, concealing it from anyone who came to the house. Remembering the pistol the old man carried, he found it where his victim had fired his last shot. He picked it up and wiped it clean with his shirt. "Qué sorpresa!" exclaimed a surprised Arturo as he held an exquisitely engraved 1911 Colt 45 automatic with inlaid rosewood grips. Arturo removed his revolver from his waistband and replaced it with the Colt. He then walked to the end of the dock and heaved the old Smith and Wesson into the bayou. Climbing the stairs to a screened-in back porch, he entered the cottage through an unlocked door and found the bathroom where he washed the bullet wound on his shoulder. Rummaging through a medicine cabinet, he found a tube that he thought was an antibiotic. He closed the cabinet and grinned when his reflection in the mirror revealed the splatter of blood across his face. He licked the dried blood from his lips and ran water to remove the rest. "Dios mio!" Arturo winced and threw the tube across the room as the toothpaste he mistakenly applied to the wound burned like fire. Finding a package of gauze and tape, he bound the wound and went in search of food. White bread and lunch meat from the refrigerator sufficed to ease his hunger, and a can of *Budweiser* slaked his thirst. He wandered through the house, pulling open drawers and searching for valuables and cartridges for the Colt. In a hall closet, he found several boxes of ammunition, various military-style rifles, and a Vietnam-era uniform. Firmly believing himself to be a soldier of the coming revolution, he put on the sergeant's jacket, which was two sizes too large, brandished the Colt, and posed in front of a full-length mirror. Taking several boxes of cartridges for the Colt, he also found ammunition for an AR-15 that he requisitioned.

Uniformed and armed, Arturo entered the living room. Along the fireplace mantel and on the walls appeared an array of *Band-of-Brothers* style photographs; soldiers in jungle fatigues, M-16 rifles in hand, sitting in fox-holes, posing with locals. Arturo thought he recognized the old man in several photographs. He lit a cigarette and took several deep drags while perusing the photos. He removed some loose photographs from the mantle. Turning on the television and taking a seat in an overstuffed recliner, he amused himself by burning holes through the photographs with his cigarette, obliterating the faces of each soldier. His attention was drawn to the television screen as a piece about Dauphin Island was reported by a buxom news anchor. Arturo sat up in his recliner. Although he did not understand some of what was being said, he recognized the person being interviewed and had recently come to understand what "CDC" stood for.

CHAPTER 55

Jesse and Cherie sat together at his kitchen table, eating po-boy sandwiches. Cherie was so very tired that she could barely think straight. While not always the most sensitive individual, Jesse could tell she was struggling.

"Cherie, I want to preface this comment by saying that you are always beautiful in my eyes, but right now, you look exhausted, and that worries me. I think you should go in there and take a nap if you are planning on working this evening. You can use the couch or my bed. I just changed the sheets on it today."

Cherie looked up from her sandwich and smiled. "That's very kind of you to offer, but I'm fine. When we finish here, I'm going back to the motel and crash for a while. Although I could use a cup of coffee if you have some."

"No problem."

Jesse rose and began preparing coffee. Cherie went over to the aquarium and looked in on Sparky.

"How's he doing?"

"Oh, he's great. He eats everything I put in the tank."

"He's grown some since I saw him last!"

"He has. He lost a little weight at first, but after adjusting to his new surroundings, he's turned into a butterball. I'll keep him a few days more and then release him."

"Aww…I'll miss him."

"Me too. But he needs to be back with his buds doing the Sparky dance and electrocuting little fishes."

"The Sparky dance?"

"Ooo… you're gonna love this!" he said, grinning. Jesse went to the refrigerator and took out a piece of frozen shrimp. He ran water over it for a few seconds to thaw and then dipped the juicy morsel in the aquarium water.

Cherie watched closely as the electric ray sat motionless, partially buried in the sediment. "Nothing is happening."

"Wait for it."

The ray stirred momentarily, and then suddenly, he erupted from the sand and began a curious wiggle dance back and forth across the aquarium. The ray would swim up to one end of the tank and fall back to the other end, shaking as it went.

Cherie giggled. "Well, isn't that interesting!"

"I think it's a searching behavior. He probably does that in the wild when trying to pick up the scent of stunned prey. A word of caution. While Sparky is performing, you never, never want to put your finger in the tank like this…Yeowwwww!!" screamed Jesse through a tortured expression. His entire body went completely rigid. "Ca… ca… ca… can't ge… ge… get, my, my, h… hand out."

"Jesse!" shouted Cherie and grabbed him by the arm.

Jesse turned and smiled. "Just kidding."

"Oh, you…" Cherie swatted him on the shoulder, and they both had a good laugh.

"I'll bet that woke you up, didn't it?"

"Yes, but I still want that coffee." Cherie returned to her seat. "So, what did you want to tell me?"

"I may have made some really important observations regarding the investigation."

"I'm all ears."

"There are two things that all of the victims had in common," said Jesse as he spooned instant Sanka into a cup. "They were all male, and the death of each one was preceded by something frightening or startling."

"The fact that they were all male could just be a coincidence," said Cherie. "I don't follow the second thing."

"Think about it. The tourist from Birmingham almost struck a dog before he crashed his car. Guidry, the primary case, was at the top of a water tower, and the coroner says he was dead before he hit the ground. The parasailing dude…what was his name?"

"Um…Paul Stanford."

"Yes, Paul Stanford. He was struck by a laughing gull before he died. Trailer-park guy…sorry, but I am just terrible with names."

"Charles Walton."

"Yes, Walton. He was watching a horror movie when he died. The boat we came across that was running in circles with no one on it? I could easily imagine the fellow experiencing some highly emotional event that caused him to go overboard. And those 14 victims at the OC. Chief East said that someone set off a smoke bomb in the theatre. Think about that. You are watching a horror movie in a theatre, and suddenly, the room fills with smoke. That would be frightening."

Jesse handed Cherie a cup of coffee. "You take it black, don't you?"

"That's fine," said Cherie. "Recall also that Dr. Fernandez mentioned that one of the terrorists suddenly died when a jaguar came into camp."

"That's right," agreed Jesse. "I forgot about that one."

"So, they were all frightened or startled by something before they died. What are you suggesting?"

"I'm suggesting that an emotional event and the appearance of the virus are linked. All those in the theater could have been carriers of the virus. It erupted when the fan club members were frightened by the smoke, the darkened theatre, and that movie."

"But my contact tracing revealed that most of the fan club members, before attending the movie, had no contact with Guidry, the primary case, or with those who encountered Guidry." Cherie closed her eyes and yawned. "I'm sorry. This day is beginning to catch up with me. "If your hypothesis is correct, they all should've been infected ahead of the fan club meeting." Cherie paused to puzzle over her observation.

"That's true. That would be hard to explain," admitted Jesse.

"Unless…" She paused again as she grappled with a new thought. "Unless there was some kind of infectious chain reaction. One or a few carriers of the virus fell ill during the movie and infected the others in the theatre, who subsequently died. The virus burned through everyone in the theatre as it spread from person to person like a nuclear reaction. We know that the symptoms appear very quickly because we saw photographs of the disease progression when it killed Paul Stanford. Also, Dr. Fernandez witnessed it kill one of the terrorists who was healthy one minute and dead the next."

"You're right. It was painfully obvious that Stanford died within minutes, if not seconds," said Jesse. "The disease could spread to all those in close contact with them at the time."

"You are suggesting that an emotional event is required for the agent to kill?"

"Yes. Without that, the agent lies dormant."

"That's scary!" said Cherie. "We may have hundreds, maybe thousands of residents on the island that are walking time bombs, ready to explode at any time."

"That is a disturbing but accurate description," said Jesse. "And I'm the guy with the anger management issue. But there is more, and this is more hopeful." From his backpack, he removed the electron microscope photographs of the liver tissue taken from the captain of the Crimson Tide, along with a magnifying glass and images of shark muscle tissue that he had processed and photographed previously. "You recall the electron microscope images that we took?" Jesse rose, retrieved images from his backpack, and placed them on the table in front of Cherie.

"Yes."

"They were very cloudy, and I assumed it was because of a mistake that I made during tissue preparation." Jesse handed Cherie the magnifying glass. "This is unorthodox, but use this and focus on the spaces outside of the tissues, where there is no cellular structure."

"Okay." Cherie bent down and brought the glass into focus on an extracellular area. "What am I looking for?"

"What do you see?" asked Jesse.

"It is all very…fuzzy. That is the best I can do to describe it."

"Now do the same thing with these images of shark muscle tissue that I prepared last year."

"It looks very clear. Can't see anything."

"Exactly. Now look again at the Crimson Tide images, but this time, look VERY closely."

Cherie brought the glass into focus again and studied the image closely. "Looks like it is covered with dust particles."

"Yes," agreed Jesse. "Like a cloud of particles. What you see there, I believe, is the infectious agent. We did not notice it initially because these virus particles, or whatever they are, are smaller than any that have ever been observed. We thought the terrible images were an artifact of preparation. The virus is everywhere, clouding the entire image. I'll bet the images they've made at the CDC look exactly like this."

"Holy smokes!" exclaimed Cherie, still perusing the images. "I'm awake now."

"Also, unlike other viruses that would typically be attached to the outer cell membrane, or perhaps concentrated in some discrete regions of the cell, this thing is found in all tissues and body fluids. It's extremely small, like a gaseous agent or sodium cyanide, and it's carried very quickly throughout the body. That's how it kills so fast."

"Wow, you've given this a lot of thought."

"I tend to be a bit obsessed when it comes to problem-solving, one of my many endearing personality traits, along with my anger-management problem."

"Thank God for your obsessiveness."

"Which brings me to my final point. This morning, I checked the data from the CDC regarding the blood chemistry of Paul Stanford. His values were so far off from what I thought were normal that I doubted my memory and had to go to the lab to check my reference material. All of the stress indicators in Stanford's blood, adrenaline, cortisol, lactate, etc., were orders of magnitude greater than anything that has ever been recorded for a human and perhaps for any mammal. It was like there was a *fight-or-flight* "storm" raging in his body."

"So, the virus caused an overproduction of stress hormones as it took over and killed its victims."

"That is one explanation, but there is another. What if the *fight-or-flight* response is the trigger for the virus to erupt from where it lay dormant?"

"That's an interesting thought, but isn't that a purely academic distinction?" asked Cherie. "What difference would it make? Wait…if the stress response initiates the virus to erupt and burn through the body, then we can prevent eruption and the development of the disease by inhibiting the stress response."

"Exactly," said Jesse. "It wouldn't clear the virus from the body, but it would keep it in check and give the CDC precious time to develop a treatment. It could also slow or even prevent any further transmission. Preventing the stress response is a relatively easy thing to do. There are a number of medications that would probably do the trick. Of course, we would have an island full of stoned folks if this works."

"That's better than an island full of corpses," said Cherie.

"Absolutely."

"I have a question. Does any of this help explain the fact that all the victims were male?"

"Good question! Are you familiar with the hormone oxytocin?"

"I am. It's sometimes called the love hormone."

"That's true. They call it that because it's important in social behaviors and in mother-child bonding. Females typically have a depressed stress response when compared to males. Part of the reason for this is due to oxytocin. Oxytocin may inhibit the stress response and is 3 to 4 times higher in the blood of women."

"So could we administer oxytocin to males as a prophylactic?" asked Cherie.

"That might work, but I wonder about the side effects of large doses of oxytocin on males, particularly on children. But we need a way to test this hypothesis before we do anything."

"That's my area of expertise," said Cherie. "We need a small colony of lab mice and some blood from one of the victims."

"I'm guessing you'll have to go to Atlanta to do that."

"No. We have containment facilities already set up on the island. If I can get approval for a small number of mice from Dr. Stern, I could test it easily."

"Would it be risky to do it here?"

"The CDC is finally taking this seriously and has moved our rapid deployment, biosafety-level 4 facility here. It's required for handling blood and tissue samples that could be contaminated with the highest-risk microbes. I just need to approve it with Dr. Stern and have the mice brought down from Atlanta. I'll call him tonight. If he agrees with your hypothesis, I feel certain he will approve the experiment."

"I hope this tells us something," said Jesse

"Me too. If I can reach Dr. Stern and get approval tonight, we could have the mice delivered by afternoon tomorrow. They have a gigantic mouse colony at the CDC. I could do the injections late tomorrow and maybe have an answer by late Monday or early

Tuesday. This will not be an exhaustive experiment. It's gonna be quick and dirty to hopefully answer this question."

"Sounds good. Is there anything I can do?"

"I'll keep you posted on the progress."

"Would it be possible for me to go into the unit with you?"

"Uh…well, it's a restricted facility. There is no way I could get approval."

"Not even as just an observer?"

"I would have to do it under the radar."

"If not, that's OK. I don't want to get you in trouble, but it sounds like it would be interesting."

"Let me give it some thought."

CHAPTER 56

Cherie said her goodbyes and left to return to her motel room. A wave of fatigue came over her as she drove. The sound of tires on the road's shoulder immediately brought her back to awareness. *Wake up!* She slapped herself on the cheeks and sat up straight. As she motored along Bienville Boulevard, she took no notice of the old grey Impala parked on a dirt side road. After she passed, the occupant took a Marlboro cigarette from a pack and tapped it against the dash. The cigarette lighter's flame momentarily illuminated the occupant's coarse features and pockmarked face. With headlights off, he slowly pulled out onto the boulevard.

The house always felt incredibly empty with Bongo gone and without Cherie, so Jesse retrieved his guitar and softly played the opening chords to a new song he was composing. He watched Sparky nose around in the bottom of the aquarium, looking for any morsel he might have missed. Lately, fish-watching or playing guitar were the only times when he could put aside the worries that kept him up at night.

The phone rang and Jesse started. *Is that Cherie? I hope nothing is wrong.*

He put down his guitar and took the phone from the wall. "Hello."

"Uh, yes. This is Chief of Police East. To whom am I speaking?"

"Oh! Hi Chief. Uh…this is Jesse."

"Jesse Cage?"

"Uh…no, Jesse Gates." Jesse was momentarily confused.

"I meant Jesse Gates, sorry."

"No worries. Is everything OK?"

"As OK as it can be, considering. I don't want to alarm you, but we had another death on the island earlier today."

"Oh no. Was it the same as the others? Another bloodbath?"

"Not this time. It was a murder."

"Good Lord!"

"This isn't supposed to happen on Dauphin Island," said East, exasperated. "At any rate, the reason I am calling is that investigators found a note on the body with two phone numbers on it. I called the first number, but no one answered. The other was yours. Any idea why this person would have those numbers on him?"

"Oh no! That's Dr. Fernandez. The archaeologist from Belize that Cherie and I met with. We gave him our numbers in case he needed to get in touch. The other number would be for her hotel room."

"I'm going to need to get a statement from you and Cherie first thing tomorrow."

"No problem. Cherie just left here to go to the motel and…. uh… Chief, could you hold for just a moment? Someone's knocking on my door. That's probably Cherie now."

"I'll hold. I need to speak with her."

"I'm coming," announced Jesse. He put the phone down and went to the front door. Jesse switched on the front porch light and, as he turned the knob, the door exploded from the weight of the individual who threw himself against it. Ripped from its hinges, the door slammed into Jesse as he was tossed backward against the far wall. His ears rang. His head spun. Warm blood trickled down his forehead. He shook his head, trying to make sense of what was happening. As a shadowy figure stepped across the broken door and into the room, Jesse realized that his analytical abilities would do him no good now. Back-lit against the moonlight, the silhouette of the intruder was of a stocky, muscular individual, a pistol held in his hand.

"What the hell?" said a surprised Chief East when he heard the loud crash over the phone. "Jesse…Jesse!" East slammed the phone down and rushed out of his office.

Jesse pushed through the pain that wracked his body and, on rubbery legs, stumbled toward the back of the house and into the brightly lit kitchen. His mind still cloudy, he reached for the knife that always hung from his belt and found it missing. The intruder came into the room, the light glinting off the chrome-plated pistol aimed menacingly at his head. Jesse gasped as he recognized the shabbily dressed individual from Hector's description. It was Arturo.

Expressionless, Arturo approached him slowly. Taking a rolled newspaper from his back pocket, he quickly looked at the newspaper, then at Jesse, and then again at the newspaper, all the while keeping the gun aimed at Jesse's face. Satisfied with what he saw, he asked, "Where is money, where is gold?" He foisted the crumpled paper at Jesse, where he saw his picture and an article describing the sale of the doubloon to Mobile Antiquities.

It was now clear. Arturo found the news article and was intent on taking the money from Jesse.

Jesse held up his hands and backed away, trying to collect his thoughts. "The money isn't here. It's in the bank. I've got about twenty dollars in my wallet. You can have that."

While keeping Jesse in the sights of his chrome-plated pistol, Arturo opened Jesse's refrigerator, reached in, and removed a beer. He cracked the can open and drained it with one gulp. He crumpled the can in his hand and tossed it across the room. "Where is money, where is gold?" repeated Arturo.

"I don't have it here. I put it in the bank." Jesse's head injury was not helping as he struggled to recall the Spanish word for bank. *What is it? What is it? Oh yes, it sounds like bank.* "En el banco" said Jesse, using his best Spanish accent. "Es en el banco."

"No, en la casa!" demanded Arturo. His cold black eyes fixed on Jesse, he dismissively waved the Colt and approached.

Jesse continued backing away until he was against the kitchen counter. That's when he felt an unfamiliar object pressing against his back and realized what it was. When he was thrown against the wall, his knife had shifted on his belt and was now hanging at the small of his back. Thankfully, Arturo had not noticed it.

"I have Denaro," said Jesse. He pointed to the wallet in his back pocket. Slowly, Jesse reached to remove his wallet. Arturo pulled the trigger. Jesse believed he was dead. The slug struck the kitchen wall just behind him. The shock wave from the bullet burst Jesse's eardrum as pain swept through the side of his head. A metallic taste in his mouth, the acrid smell of gunpowder filled his nostrils. In one fluid motion, executing a throw that he had practiced countless times, Jesse pulled the six-inch blade from its scabbard and threw it as hard as possible. The blade flashed through the air and found its mark. The knife went completely through Arturo's forearm, its bloody tip emerging through the eye of a skull tattoo that was there. Blood poured from the wound.

Arturo screamed. The force of the blade pushed the pistol away from Jesse as it discharged a second time, right into the aquarium. The glass shattered as 50 gallons of aquarium water spilled onto the linoleum floor and Sparky landed with a thud. The anger that he had lately been able to control was now on full display as it swept through his body like a prairie fire. There was no stopping it now, and Jesse embraced it completely. The next few moments would determine life or death, and he was going to go down fighting. He was now an uncontrollable demon. A fury that could not be contained, blood laced with adrenaline, pulsed through his body. He flung himself at his assailant and body-slammed Arturo with every ounce of force he could muster. Arturo, taken completely by surprise, stepped back, slipped on the wet floor, and fell backward against the kitchen table, breaking it into splinters. Jesse landed atop Arturo and struck his injured arm, the gun skidding across the floor. Jesse struck him with two blows to the face. Arturo's head snapped back, but he quickly recovered and punched Jesse in the side with his good hand. Locked in mortal combat, they rolled across the wet floor. Jesse's hand fell across a heavy metal salt shaker that he gripped like a brass knuckle. He punched Artruo in the face again. Blood spurted from his broken nose, and salt burst from the shaker, pouring into Arturo's eyes. He screamed like a wounded animal. Jesse punched again, and the salt shaker flew from his hand. Using brute strength, Arturo inched across the floor, reaching for the pistol that lay a few inches from his fingertips. Jesse punched him again, but he pulled closer to the gun. Arturo's hand closed around the handle of the gun. Desperate to find anything he could use as a weapon, Jesse grabbed the struggling electric ray and slammed it against Arturo's chest.

"Gird… your loins… you… son-of-a-bitch!" shouted Jesse. He struggled to hold the ray in place as the electricity coursed into Arturo and up Jesse's arm.

Arturo's face went completely white as Sparky repeatedly discharged its powerful electric organs right into his chest, throwing his heart into arrhythmia and paralyzing the muscles that controlled breathing. Arturo's face was frozen in fear. His lips moved imperceptibly, but no sound could be heard. Frothy, red spittle bubbled from his mouth and nose before Jesse released the ray that fell back to the floor. "Sorry, buddy," said Jesse to Sparky weakly as he collapsed exhausted across Arturo's lifeless frame. He lay there a moment, panting uncontrollably. He tried to sit up but found his right arm was completely numb. With some difficulty, he managed to remove himself from atop the stinking pile of humanity that lay in bloody water on his kitchen floor. A siren wailed in the distance. Jesse sat, trying to focus on what had just happened, adrenaline still coursing through him. He reached and knocked the pistol a safe distance away from Arturo. Suddenly, like Nosferatu rising from his coffin, Arturo sat up out of the bloody water and seized Jesse with both hands around his neck. Despite the injury, the loss of blood, and the induced heart attack, Arturo's grip was like iron. Arturo's battered face was inches away from Jesse's. His fetid breath was in his nostrils. Jesse could do nothing. He pounded on Arturo's arms, driving the knife blade deeper into his flesh. He clawed at Arturo's cold eyes and face as he began to lose consciousness. Through the curtain of darkness that was descending upon him, he imagined he saw Cherie standing in his kitchen, smiling. It was strangely comforting that his last thoughts on earth would be of Cherie, but also disappointing that he had never fully expressed his love for her. He knew it was the end as the strains of The Allman Brothers Band, *Blue Sky* played across his fading consciousness. Jesse smiled weakly. As his vision waned, the image of Cherie strangely morphed into one of Crazy Joe standing behind Arturo, his walking stick in hand. Joe raised the stick like a Scottish claymore and brought it down on the terrorist's head with an audible "thud". Arturo's iron hands relaxed, and Jesse collapsed.

"Bad man!" said Joe.

"Thank God!" said Jesse weakly.

CHAPTER 57

With siren wailing, East skidded into the drive at Jesse's cottage. He bailed out of his cruiser, pulled his service revolver, and raced up the stairs as fast as his injured leg would carry him.

"Jesse!" said Chief cautiously when he found the front door ripped from its hinges.

"Back here, Chief," croaked Jesse.

Chief East cautiously stepped over the door and went to the back of the house. He kept his revolver drawn, lowering it only after he found Jesse slumped against the wall, covered in blood, and holding a dish towel to his ear.

"What the hell happened?"

He looked up forlornly. "Had a disagreement with an uninvited guest," deadpanned Jesse.

"That was some disagreement." Chief East holstered his gun and went to Jesse. "Are you OK?"

"I've been better, but it'll heal."

"That's some bad bruising on your neck, and you're gonna have a hell of a shiner tomorrow. Let's get you out of this water." East helped Jesse up from the floor and sat him in the only unbroken chair in the room.

"Damn! Is that a knife stuck through his arm?"

"Yes sir. I would appreciate it if you would pull it out and put it in the sink over there."

"I can do that. It's gonna hurt like a bastard when I do."

"I hope so."

East stooped over Arturo and pulled the knife out. Arturo moaned and struggled weakly against the bonds that held his arms and feet. "I heard the crash over the phone and knew something was wrong. I rushed over immediately. Who is that and what happened?"

"That must be Arturo. The terrorist that Dr. Hernandez told us about. As I went to answer the door, he crashed through it. Almost killed me when it slammed me against the wall. He had a gun and demanded money and gold."

"Gold?" asked East, puzzled.

"Yeah. I had a gold doubloon that Joe gave me, but I sold it."

"Oh yeah, I heard about that."

"Arturo had a newspaper article about the doubloon with a picture of me. He discharged his gun right next to my ear, and I think it ruptured my eardrum. That was his mistake. It set me off like a Roman candle. I've got an anger management problem that I normally can control."

"Well, you certainly anger managed all over that dude!"

Jesse attempted to stand, failed, and sat back down again. "Oh… my head's swimming a bit." Jesse continued, "When he fired his gun, I got the drop on him with my knife, and we had a little throw-down on the kitchen floor after that."

"You tied him up?"

"No, Joe did that."

"Joe who?"

"Crazy Joe, the fellow who gave me the coin. That scum bag had his hands around my throat and was choking me. He has a grip like iron. I was a goner until Joe showed up and knocked him out. He saved my life."

"Damn! You are one lucky man."

"I guess Joe had been keeping watch on my house. Probably because Cherie visits me occasionally, and it's pretty clear that Joe has a crush on her."

"Thank God he was watching. Where is he now?"

"I guess he went back to the bayou."

"Well, you sit tight, and I'll get you some help."

"No thanks," said Jesse. "That's not necessary."

"You need to have someone look at that ear at least," insisted East.

"I'll have it looked at tomorrow if needed."

"Jesse, you are one tough dude! I'm going to use your phone. I better call the EMTs to get this scumbag some assistance, although I should just let him bleed to death."

"I need to clean up this mess and get someone to help me fix that door."

"I'll get someone over here to help you."

"Thanks, Chief." Jesse grimaced and adjusted the towel he held to his head. "Chief, I would appreciate it if you did not mention this to Cheri. You can tell her that Arturo is no longer a threat, but don't tell her I was involved."

"I'll do the best I can with that," said East.

"One last thing, Chief?"

"What's that?"

"Would you go to my bedroom and get a pillowcase? I need you to carefully scoop up Sparky without touching him…" Jesse pointed to the ray gasping on the floor, "and release him in the bayou back there. You should have seen Arturo's face when he met Sparky."

"What?"

"I'll tell you about it later."

CHAPTER 58

"Our little island paradise is going to Hell in a handbag, Dorothy!" Chief East slumped in his desk chair, a glazed look on his face as he stared at a pile of unfinished reports that seemed to grow larger by the hour. Having just uncovered Breaker's cage, the profane parrot hopped around inside, squawking out a continuous stream of obscenities. "Dorothy, would you give that bird something to eat? Maybe that will shut him up."

"I'll get him some fruit; he loves apples." She stood at the office door, impeccably dressed as usual, wearing a particle mask and holding a notepad. "I know it seems like everything is falling apart, but we just have to soldier on."

"Yeah, I'm trying."

"What was that call about last night?"

"A home invasion and attempted robbery."

"Who was it?"

"The invader is a scum bag named Arturo, wanted by the FBI. He broke the door down at Jesse Gates's house and tried to rob him."

"Good Lord! That nice young man who is helping Dr. Belon?"

"Yeah. Arturo's a terrorist who bit off more than he could chew when he tried to rob Jesse. Jesse stuck him with that knife he carries with him all the time, and Crazy Joe knocked him out."

"Oh, my goodness! Is Jesse OK?"

"Lots of bruises and a damaged ear, but he refused medical treatment, so I guess he's OK.

"Thank God!"

"I took Arturo to Doc Nolan last night to get him bandaged up. Lucky for him, the knife missed a major artery. He's in lockup back there. Sean has been here since early this morning because of him. The FBI is coming to pick him up this morning. That report is gonna be hell to write."

"Do you think that this fellow may be connected with the murder of Hernandez?"

"I'm sure of it. Ballistics on the weapon should answer that question. Which reminds me. I've got to ask Jesse about the weapon since we didn't find it. I wonder if Joe took it?" added East, thinking out loud.

"A terrorist on Dauphin Island! Thank goodness Jesse's OK!" Dorothy glanced at her notepad. "Do you want these messages now or should I come back?"

"Go ahead and give them to me."

"You want the good news or bad news first?"

"There's good news? Give that to me."

"The hurricane is going to make landfall east of Dauphin Island."

"Damn! That's the good news?"

"That's better than a direct hit. The intensity will be much less since we're west of the projected landfall. They expect some minor flooding, maybe loss of power, and hurricane-strength winds, but an evacuation will not be necessary."

"Oh, thank God! I did not look forward to being quarantined at an abandoned, run-down military base. What else you got?"

"My phone has been ringing off the hook with reporters from several news agencies who want an interview. We even had someone from the *New York Times* requesting a statement."

"Screw those reporter requests. I got no time for them."

"OK. Got a report of a boat on fire just west of the Dauphin Island bridge. My sources say that someone was trying to get off the island early this morning and was chased by the Coast Guard. They struck a bridge piling and burst into flames."

"The Coasties will handle that one, if there is anything left to handle."

"I have two more reports of people dying during that University of Alabama football game. Same bloody mess. Both males."

"Damn, it's dangerous to be an Alabama fan these days. I assume you alerted the CDC?"

"They took care of it."

"Thank God they are here!" said East. "You know Jesse suggested that emotional events might be the trigger for this bacteria, virus, disease, whatever the hell it is. I am beginning to wonder if he might be correct."

"Gimme a damn cracker! Gimme a damn cracker!" squawked Breaker.

"SHUT UP YOU SACK OF CRAP!" shouted East.

"Sack of crap! Sack of crap!" replied Breaker.

"Chief, my phone is ringing again. Let me answer it and then I'll get Breaker some fruit."

"Forget the phone. Let the recorder take it."

"OK." Dorothy left and returned quickly with slices of apple. She placed them in the food tray and Breaker grabbed a piece, manipulating it with his thick, grey tongue.

"Thank you, Dorothy!" said East. "What else you got?"

"A surfer died out at the west end. Kids are out there riding those big waves that are rolling in from the hurricane. He literally died on his surfboard. Sean interviewed the witnesses and got their names. They said he was fine one minute, and then he suddenly collapsed and fell off his board. They said the water was bright red where he disappeared."

"Damn it! Those kids are supposed to be on lockdown. I've a mind to go arrest them all."

"In that big surf and with all that blood in the water, no one wanted to retrieve the body and it was gone by the time Sean got there."

"Hell, I don't blame them. But it will eventually show up. The current runs to the west. It will wash ashore on a beach somewhere between here and Mexico unless the sharks get it first. Call the CDC and the Coast Guard and let them know about this. The body will have to be handled appropriately. Also, tell them that we need more law enforcement out at the west end. Those waves will continue to roll in for a few more days and those kids think they're bulletproof."

"I'll do that." Dorothy scribbled notes on her pad. "Do you have any idea what they are doing with all the deceased?"

"They've got a big refrigerated semi where they are holding them. I'm told that they're taking photographs of the deceased and using those for identification by next-of-kin. The best they can do under the circumstances. It seems likely to me that all the bodies will have to be cremated. If they are infectious, that's the only safe thing to do.

Dorothy flipped the page on her notepad. "Three calls came in regarding missing persons. I think you know one of the families. I've got the details here if you want them."

"I do not. I know that sounds callous, but we can't do a thing right now. Call the Guard and let them know. Call the Mobile County Sheriff's Department also."

"Chief, I understand better than anyone. Finally, the worst news of all."

"Oh crap, what is it?"

"The CDC called and reported that an oil rig worker died out on one of the platforms. Same as those on the island, he bled out."

"Shit! That means this thing has escaped the island. That is really bad news."

"Do you know who it was?"

"Yes. His name is Frank Peron."

"Frank Peron?! Brother of Charlie Peron, who lives on the island?"

"That's him."

"I've arrested Charlie more than once. Most of the time, for being drunk and disorderly. It's not very Christian of me to say this, but the world would've been better off if it had been Charlie who died instead of Frank. He's a waste of skin."

"Frank left the island just before the quarantine."

"Charlie's still here?"

"Yeah. My understanding is that he is on a different work schedule and he's still on the island. He lives in a run-down house on Phillips Avenue."

"I wonder if he knows about this?" asked East.

"He may not. They don't have a phone, so I can't call."

"I guess I should run out there and let him know."

"Radio me when you get out there," requested Dorothy.

"I will." East got up, put on his hat and service revolver, and left the building. After a few minutes, he stood on the front porch of the Peron brothers' house, knocked repeatedly, but no one answered. He returned to his cruiser, reached in, and removed the microphone from its hook.

"Dorothy, do you have your ears on, over?" East stood outside the door of his patrol car with his elbows resting on the car roof.

"Come back, Chief," replied Dorothy.

"I'm here and tried the door, but no answer. His truck and old boat are gone. Over."

"You think he's fishing somewhere? Over?"

"Definitely not. The Guard won't let anyone launch their boat. And as far as I know, they don't fish. Over."

"Could he be trying to get off the island? Over."

"He might be. Radio Sean and tell him to keep an eye out for him. Over and out."

"I will do that. Standing by."

CHAPTER 59

"What in the world happened to you?" asked Cherie as Jesse climbed into her vehicle. They had agreed to meet outside the CDC compound, where Cherie would escort him into the restricted area. The guarded compound was located in a large vacant lot near the approach to the Dauphin Island bridge. An abandoned marina, a victim of Hurricane Frederick, was on one side, a sea wall against the waters of Mobile Bay on the other, and Dauphin Island Parkway, the only road on or off the island, was frontage. Hastily assembled, the restricted area consisted of a collection of tractor-trailers, CDC vehicles, a field hospital, a morgue, and a portable biohazard unit. Large air ducts snaking into the unit circulated air through nano-pore filters to prevent the escape of the high-risk pathogens held inside.

"I fell," replied Jesse rather sheepishly.

"Fell into what? A wood chipper?"

"Uh…" It only just occurred to Jesse that he should have thought of a better excuse for his appearance. "I was on my bicycle and had a spill. I'm OK."

"I didn't know you had a bike. You've got to be more careful," implored Cherie as she came close to examine his black eye and bruised neck.

Jesse quickly changed the subject. "You should come to my place as soon as possible tomorrow. The weather is predicted to continue to worsen throughout the day, so we need to be settled in before that."

"I'll be there as soon as I can," said Cherie. "Ross and CC are also coming?"

"Yes, they'll be there early also."

Cherie drove up to the guard, who stepped forward to request identification. Cherie rolled the window down and smiled.

"Oh, hello, Dr. Belon," said the guard as he leaned forward and looked into the vehicle.

"Good morning."

He stepped back and waved the vehicle through. Cherie drove slowly through the compound and parked near the level-4 biohazard unit.

"Are you sure you want to do this?" asked Cherie as they climbed out.

"Absolutely!"

"Jesse, I am violating some serious guidelines by allowing you to enter this facility. You have to promise me that you will do exactly as I say."

"I promise."

"I could lose my job over this, so your presence here has to be kept completely confidential."

"Of course."

"OK, then gird your loins!" Cherie swiped her identification card through the wall-mounted reader and swung the door open. Positive airflow into the biohazard unit created a low "whooshing" sound as the door swung open. They entered a small, sparsely furnished room.

"This area is technically not BSL-4. However, when we enter that room, there is no turning back." Cherie motioned toward an interior door with a yellow biohazard sign hanging on it. "You can still back out if you want?"

"No, I'm good."

Cherie swiped her card again, the door slid open, and they stepped in. The room was small, with a low bench and lockers on one side and various-sized surgical scrubs hung from a rack on the other.

"Give me a second. I have to record my name and time of entry into the log book." Cherie opened the log and recorded the information. "I hope you are not self-conscious because we have to take off all clothing and personal items, jewelry, watches, etc., and leave them in these lockers. Back in Atlanta, we have separate rooms for males and females, but space is at a premium in this portable unit. We'll have to put on scrubs to wear under the protective suits. There should be scrubs here that will fit you. You'll need to put on these socks as well."

"Take off all our clothing? Even underwear?"

"I'm afraid so. Nothing that goes in the BSL comes out, except our naked bodies. So, no street clothes allowed."

"OK, I promise I won't look," said Jesse.

With their backs to each other, they changed out of their clothes and into green surgical scrubs. Unbeknownst to Jesse, Cherie caught a brief glimpse of the injuries on Jesse's back in the polished surface of a stainless-steel cabinet. She gasped quietly.

"How fast were you going when you crashed?" asked Cherie without turning around.

Jesse pulled the scrub over his head. "Crashed what?"

"Your bike, of course," said Cherie, now suspicious that he was not being completely truthful.

"Oh…uh…too fast. Are you dressed?" asked Jesse.

"I am. You can turn around."

"You look beautiful. Green suits you."

"Yeah, right. I'll bet you say that to all the CDC agents before you enter the hot zone of a BSL-4 facility that contains a deadly virus."

"Only the beautiful ones," said Jesse, grinning.

"That's sweet, but we've got to get serious now."

"OK."

"The next room through this door is the suit room." They entered the room. Protective suits hung along one wall, and coiled hoses snaked down from the ceiling. She pulled one of the suits from a rack of several. "You'll need one of the larger ones."

"Looks like a space suit," commented Jesse.

"We take every precaution when working with high-consequence pathogens."

"I would hope so. High-consequence pathogens: I've never heard you use that term before. Sounds ominous."

"The consequences have never been higher. These suits are positive pressure and must be hooked up to this air supply." Cherie directed Jesse to a pair of coiled hoses hanging from the ceiling. "Those are air hoses that we would normally use to inflate the suits to check for leaks. We don't have to do that because these are new suits and I've already gone over them carefully to ensure there are none. When we enter the next room, the hot zone, we'll connect to the air hoses there. Positive pressure inside the suit means that if there is a puncture, the pressure will prevent anything in the room from entering the suit. However, if there is a leak in your suit or if it is punctured, we will evacuate immediately and enter the chemical disinfection room."

"I will be careful."

"Before you suit up, you have to put on two pairs of surgical gloves and duct tape them to your wrists over the sleeves of your scrubs. Same with your socks. Use two layers of duct tape.

We will also wear surgical masks. It seems like overkill, but there is no such thing as overkill when working with these deadly agents. Remember, you are only an observer. I don't want you to touch anything in the room."

"No problem there."

After making sure the suits were properly zipped up, the two opened the door, entered the hot zone, and hooked up to the air supply. Her voice somewhat muffled, Cherie spoke to Jesse through the clear face mask. "This container holds liquid nitrogen, where we have frozen samples of blood and plasma from some of the victims." She pointed to a small metal vessel that sat in one corner of the room. "These are the plasma samples from one of the victims that I used for the experiment." Cherie pulled open a small refrigerator and removed a rack of vials. "OK. Here's how I set up this experiment. I have 60 mice total. That's a reasonable number under these circumstances. Half male, half female. A control group of 10 male and 10 female mice will not be infected. Nothing will be done to them. Those mice are in these cages here on the other side of the room." Cherie turned and walked to where the control mice were happily scurrying around in their cage bedding. "There are 40 mice in the experimental groups, two groups of 20 mice each. Again, half male and half female." She turned and walked to where the cages of mice sat on a stainless-steel table. "All mice in the two experimental groups were given a mild sedative before infection. Since I received plenty of mice, I was able to try to get some data on the idea of using a sedative to block the appearance of the agent."

"Good idea. Which sedative did you choose?"

"Diazepam, which you may know as Valium. It's a common anti-anxiety drug."

"I've heard of it."

"While they were sedated, all 40 mice were given an injection of plasma from one of the victims of the agent. That was…" Cherie glanced at the digital clock on the wall. "…about two and a half hours ago. The sedative will be worn off by now for one group of 20 mice. However, the other group of mice has the sedative in their drinking water, so they should still be protected from the virus if your idea is valid."

"So let me get this straight. These mice are infected and have been continually sedated." Jesse pointed to a cage. "These are infected but are no longer under sedation. And those across the room have never been sedated or infected."

"That's correct."

"Awesome! I am anxious to see how this turns out."

"Can you see a difference in behavior between the sedated mice and the unsedated?

Jesse approached the cages and examined them. "That's obvious. The mice in these cages are behaving just like the control mice. Actively interacting with each other, burrowing around in the cedar chips. These guys over here are zonked. Looks like they've smoked too much pot."

"That's right. If what you suggested is correct, then the virus should not erupt from the sedated mice when they are stressed. Also, if female mice are not susceptible, then the virus should appear only in males in the infected, unsedated mice."

"Experimental research like this has always impressed me. Most of my shark research has been descriptive. It's very difficult to conduct classic, control, and experimental research on wild-caught organisms, particularly in the marine environment. It's pretty much impossible to do that when you are studying sharks."

"So, Jesse, it's time for your contribution. How do you suggest we stress them?"

"We just need to frighten them. Some mechanical stimulus, a loud sound, an image of a predatory bird like a hawk or owl. Any of those would work…"

KABOOM! A lightning strike very near the CDC compound sent shock waves through the room.

Cherie started and let out a frightened squeal.

"Geez, Louise!" said a thoroughly frightened Jesse. "That should have done it. Was that fortuitous or what! I wonder if that is from the hurricane. I think it's too early to be storming here on the island."

Cherie, not listening, was paying close attention to the mice in the experimental cages. "Look!"

All the unsedated, infected male mice began to shake right before their eyes. Their shaking progressed to convulsions as they lost equilibrium and stumbled over each other. Blood ran from their noses, eyes, and mouths. In heartbreaking shrieks of pain, each mouse, a bloody mass, expired within minutes.

"Heaven help us!" said Cherie as tears welled up in her eyes. "It hurts me to see them suffer like that. Look at the sedated mice; not a single male or female has died. And none of the unsedated female mice died. That's pretty solid evidence that what you've been saying is correct. Oh, wait, correction. One of the female mice has died. It seems that females are not completely protected after all… Jesse?" Cherie turned toward Jesse, who had crossed the room.

"Cherie, was this supposed to happen?" With a confused look, Jesse stood next to the control cages and pointed to the uninfected male mice. "The males are all dead! And some of the females are dead too!"

"What in God's name?" Cherie gazed in horror at the carnage in the control cages. "Those mice were never infected. Oh no! Something has gone terribly wrong. We've got to get out NOW!"

Cherie went directly to a wall panel, flipped up a cover, and pressed a switch on the wall. The door to the decontamination room slid open. "Go!" commanded Cherie, motioning Jesse toward the exit. The two disconnected their air hoses and entered the room. Cherie pressed a switch, and the door slid shut. "I will start the chemical shower, and we will be sprayed down with disinfectant. Use these brushes to scrub every inch of the suits. I'll scrub the places you can't reach, and you do the same for me." Cherie depressed the switch, and the room was instantly filled with a spray of brown disinfectant raining down from nozzles in the walls and ceiling as the two scrubbed down.

"This is not the normal protocol, but I'm going to start the cycle again. This thing is too infectious to take any chances."

"OK."

After returning to their street clothes, they conferred outside the facility.

"What happened in there?" asked Jesse as they climbed into Cherie's car to leave the compound.

Cherie was agitated, a worried look on her face. "Damn it! That should not have happened. The controls had to have been infected by aerosol from the infected mice. Never have I seen a disease agent that infects that easily and that rapidly. By chance, we discovered that the virus can be transmitted through the air, even though air exchange is tightly controlled in that unit. That's an important and very frightening finding. If this virus can infect from across the room of a BSL-4 unit, the potential for spreading the agent every time someone coughs or sneezes is very high. Higher than any agent we have ever seen."

"Good news and bad! Like everything else in this investigation."

"And Jesse, please say nothing about this, even to Ross or CC."

"Don't worry, mum's the word."

"I've got to get in touch with my supervisor immediately. He'll be anxious to hear the results of this experiment.

"How quickly do you think he can act on this?"

"I think it will be fast. We can start distributing diazepam to all adult residents. That will at least give us time to find a treatment or vaccine."

"OK. I'm going to head home. I've got to do some cleaning after last night. My cottage is a wreck after…" Jesse cut himself off when he realized what he was about to reveal.

"What happened last night?"

"Oh…um…my aquarium sprang a leak," said Jesse, thinking fast. "Salt water all over the kitchen floor."

"Oh no! Is Sparky OK?"

"He's fine. I released him yesterday." Jesse got out of the car and came around to the driver's side. "Cherie, if you need me for anything, just let me know. I'll either be at my cottage or at the laboratory."

"What I need is for you to be extra careful. This is a dangerous and highly contagious virus. There's no way to predict how many people are already infected. Please promise me you will take precautions."

"After what I just saw in there. You can be sure that I will be careful."

CHAPTER 60

Dorothy put down her cup of coffee and headed to lockup, where Sean was keeping watch on the prisoner. Although she could use the phone to call the jail, her curiosity to see the face of an infamous terrorist got the better of her. With only three cells, the jail was rarely used for anything other than the occasional DUI offender. Separate from the Police department, it was connected by a hallway with a security door. As she approached the jail, she noticed the security door standing open. *That's odd. Sean knows better than to leave that door open.* A sense of dread came over her as she peered around the corner.

"Oh my God!" Sean lay face down inside the empty jail cell. With her heart in her throat, she rushed to help. "Please, Lord, let him be alive!"

Finding him unconscious, she hurried to the phone and then went to the police radio. Dorothy pleaded into the microphone. "Chief East, Chief East, emergency, emergency, come in!"

"Come back, Dorothy."

"Arturo has escaped! I found Sean unconscious in the jail, and the cell empty. The ambulance is on the way. Over."

"What? Oh, my Lord!" Chief East made a U-turn on Bienville, switched on the lights and siren, and floored the accelerator. "How bad is he? Over."

"He's alive but bleeding. Chief, the ambulance is here. Meet us at the clinic. Over."

"On my way. Over and out."

Chief East rushed to the clinic and burst in. The surprised receptionist, who was straightening up the waiting room, looked up and recognized him. "He's being examined now. You can go back there, but you've got to put on this mask." She handed the Chief a particle mask. "He's in the first room on your right."

"No problem." He put on the mask and went to the examination room, where he found Sean in bed with Doc Nolan shining a small flashlight in his eyes and Dorothy looking very distraught. "How is he, Doc?"

"Hi Chief. He has a nasty bump on his head, but his pupillary response is normal. Doesn't appear to be any brain injury."

A large white bandage wrapped around his head; Sean looked like a Hindu swami.

"Just in case, I've given him something to reduce cranial pressure and a painkiller. We have to keep him here for observation at least until tomorrow."

"I'm… sorry, Chief," said Sean thickly, barely able to speak. "He was on… the floor covered with… blood. As… God… is my witness… I thought he was dead."

"Don't worry about it, Sean," the Chief placed a hand on Sean's shoulder. "We'll catch him. With all the police and military presence here, the scumbag will never get off the island."

"Chief, Sean's parents are on their way," said Dorothy. "If it's OK with you, I'll stay with him until they arrive, which should be any time now. I'll head back to the Police Station when they get here."

"No problem. I'm going to the office to alert the FBI."

"I've already done that, Chief. I called them, the National Guard, the Coast Guard, and the Mobile County Sheriff's Office. I did not call Jesse Gates, however."

"I'll let him know as soon as I get back."

"One other thing," said Dorothy quietly, "Sean's service revolver is missing. Arturo must have taken it."

"Great!" Chief East turned to Doc Nolan. "He's going to be alright, isn't he?"

"I think he'll be fine. Head injuries are never something to be taken lightly, but I see nothing that looks serious."

"Thank goodness. Dorothy, I'm going to the office to send out another APB and call Jesse. He needs to know as soon as possible since that scum bag likely holds a bit of a grudge against him.

"I'm going to see if I can tell which way Arturo went."

"I'll be there as soon as Sean's parents arrive."

"That's fine. Thanks, Doc," said the Chief as he left.

Chief East returned to the Police Department and went to the jail cell. A puddle of blood on the floor and bloody footprints, it wasn't easy to tell which prints were Arturo's and which were the EMT's. He followed the trail out of the jailhouse, down the hall, and into the Police Department. Most of the prints led to the front of the building, but one set of faint prints took a different direction, leading to the conference room door. East heard a soft rustling and drew his revolver. Cautiously opening the door, gun at the ready, he looked around the room and found papers rustling and an open window; the window where Arturo had made his escape. "Damn it!" East closed the window and stood for a moment in thought. *If I were Arturo, which way would I go?*

East returned to his office, picked up the phone, and dialed Jesse's cottage.

"Hello."

"Hi Jesse, it's Chief East."

"Hi Chief. How are you?"

"I've been better. I've got bad news."

"Oh crap!"

"Arturo escaped this morning. He somehow managed to overpower my deputy."

"Oh my God! Is he OK?"

"He's at the clinic with a bad concussion, but he'll survive."

"Thank goodness he's alright!"

"I've alerted all the law enforcement folks on the island. Unfortunately, he took Sean's revolver."

"Wonderful!"

"By the way, how are you doing?"

"I'm OK."

"Jesse, I've been puzzling over something. We didn't find the pistol that Arturo used when he broke in. We know it was a 45 because we found the spent casings. Do you have a thought on what happened to it?"

"Well, some of the events are fuzzy. Particularly after he almost strangled me. The last time I recall seeing it was when we were on the floor, and I pushed it out of his reach."

"Do you think Joe could have taken it?"

"I guess it's possible, but that doesn't seem likely to me. Material things don't seem to be important to him."

"If you see him, could you ask about it?"

"I will, but our paths never cross. I could go out there and see if I could find him, but I'm pretty much staying hunkered down until this hurricane passes. Have you heard any updates on it?"

"It's predicted to make landfall tomorrow somewhere around Destin. Thank God we will not get the brunt of it although it's going to be really shitty weather for the next few days. Are you aware that the National Guard has set up an evacuation area out by the bird sanctuary?"

"I do. We're going to stay here."

"So, you're all set?"

"Yes sir. The El Camino is gassed up, although I'm not sure what good that will do since we can't leave the island. My windows are taped, and I have plenty of non-perishable food and fresh water. I've also got a battery-powered radio and a propane camping stove. The cottage here is well constructed, so the wind should not be a problem. I just worry about flooding. Since the cottage is raised up about ten feet on stilts, water won't be a problem for the house. There's an old Indian shell midden on the property that is several feet above sea level. I'll park the El Camino on top of it. Hopefully, that will keep it out of the water."

"Sounds like a plan. Have you spoken to Cherie?"

"Yes. I'm going to meet her later today. She's gonna ride it out here along with Ross and CC."

"Sounds like a hurricane party."

"Not much of one. We're serious graduate students, and partying is not real high on our priority lists these days."

"Well, I've got some other phone calls to make and patrolling to do. Let me know if you have a thought about that missing pistol."

"I'll do that Chief."

"Y'all stay safe."

"You too. Goodbye."

Jesse hung up and went to the kitchen to double-check his "hurricane list". Convinced he had everything he needed, he turned his attention to the mystery surrounding the missing pistol. "Where was I when I saw it last?" he said, thinking out loud. He got down on the floor on hands and knees. "Hmmm, I wonder?" Jesse rose and went to the old refrigerator. It took some effort, but he managed to slide the appliance away from the wall. "Well, son-of-a-gun!" The exquisitely engraved Colt lay amongst the dust and kitchen detritus. Jesse started to pick it up, but stopped. "I better give Chief East a call."

CHAPTER 61

Crouching behind a low brick wall at the rear of a service station, Arturo watched an olive-green military truck as it rumbled by. He chuckled as he thought about how he had so easily fooled that stupid deputy. Tearing out a few stitches, expressing blood from the wound, and smearing it on his face fooled the gringo into opening the cell. When he entered, Arturo kicked his legs from under him, causing him to hit his head against the bars. *Those stupid gringos thought they could hold me. Can't they see it? Don't they understand? What's a few meaningless peasants' lives in exchange for the destiny to which I have been called? To establish a new world order.* The wound in Arturo's arm throbbed with every heartbeat, and every heartbeat was a reminder of the man who had done this to him. The thought of revenge gnawed at him like a festering wound. *He will pay, oh yes, he will pay.*

Only minutes after his escape, he knew he had to act quickly. Spying a used car lot a few blocks away, he quickly crept through underbrush and drainage ditches toward the lot. Crawling on hands and knees through standing water, clouds of mosquitoes swarmed around him, attacking his flesh, while gnats targeted his wounds. Years spent eking out an existence in the rainforests of Central America had given Arturo an almost superhuman threshold for pain. Suddenly confronted by a large, dark snake, he recoiled and reached for the pistol he had taken from the unconscious guard. Fortunately, the serpent quickly swam away. Although unaware, a bite from the venomous cottonmouth he flushed from its daytime hiding place could have led to a painful death.

The used car lot appeared to be closed, and Arturo was able to sneak onto the lot unnoticed. Crawling between vehicles, he bypassed several as he looked for an inconspicuous automobile with which he was familiar. "Maravilloso," exclaimed Arturo quietly as he found a brick-red 1980 Ford Fiesta. A locked door was no barrier to Arturo. Removing the heavy service revolver from his waistband, he struck the driver's side window with the barrel. The window exploded with a low "whump" as fragments of safety glass fell into the lot and onto the seat. He ducked down and listened intently.

Trey Murphy sat at his desk in the back office and perused the *Mobile Press-Register* classifieds. His cowboy boots propped on his desk, he held the folded newspaper in one hand and a cigarette in the other. Low on inventory, he searched the pages for cars that he could clean up and/or repair. The classifieds were "scraping the bottom of the barrel" in the used car game, but the next dealer auction was two weeks away, and his "rolling stock" was low. Although his island world was crumbling around him, he was determined to maintain a semblance of normality.

Reading every ad, he ran his finger down the columns trying to identify possible purchases… "Nope… nope… nope… Here's a possibility. 1985, Pontiac." Trey grabbed a pencil and notepad and wrote down the information. He picked up the phone to call, but paused as he thought he heard a sound from the lot. Replacing the telephone on its cradle, he walked across the lobby and unlocked the front door. He stepped out into an overcast day, grey clouds scudding overhead pushed along by the winds of the approaching hurricane.

"Is someone there?" called Trey. He held the door open and looked across the yard, shielding his eyes with his newspaper. For some reason, diffuse sunlight coming through grey cloud cover always bothered his eyes more than direct sunlight. He walked out into the lot. A gust of wind caught the door and slammed it shut, startling him. "Crap! I got to fix that door."

"Oh, that's just great!" exclaimed Trey disgustedly when he spied the broken window. "How in hell did that happen?"

Walking along the line of cars to the old Ford, his boots crunching on broken glass, he examined the largely missing driver's side window. "Damn it. I'll bet one of those big-ass National Guard trucks picked up a rock and…" Arturo came from behind and struck him in mid-sentence. Trey fell to the pavement, unconscious. For good measure and pure enjoyment, he struck him again across the face.

Wasting no time, he unlocked the car, opened the door, and slipped into the front seat. A common automobile in Colombia, Arturo had hot-wired and stolen many of these small cars, giving them over to his drug dealer employers. He reached under the dash, pulled the wires connected to the switch, and identified the three needed to start the vehicle. Twisting two wires together and touching the starter wire to the bundle, the engine turned over several times before coming to life.

Arturo was unaware there was a quarantine, but was glad the streets were deserted. However, taking no chances, he backed the car up, pulled out into the road, and quickly turned down a small side street. Having driven the length of the island multiple times, it had not taken very long for him to learn most of the streets. He would take all the back roads to return to his secluded cottage, where he would plan his next move.

Weaving his way through the less populated areas of Dauphin Island, he realized that he would have to pass through one of the island's small business districts to make it back. About five blocks of Bienville Boulevard included a gas station, a bait shop, a motel, and *The Blue Crab Café*, a restaurant where he had dined on his first day on Dauphin Island. He pulled up to a stop sign and looked both ways along the street before making his turn toward the west end. Although all of the businesses were closed, several cars sat in the parking lot of the *Palms Motel*.

Arturo's attention was drawn to a car parked at the motel that he thought he recognized. He rolled by slowly, hoping to avoid drawing attention to himself. Leaning forward in his seat to get a better view, he realized where he had seen the car before. "That's the car that belongs to that little *chica*!" growled Arturo. He turned the old Ford into the lot and parked next to the vehicle with the CDC logo on the door.

CHAPTER 62

Dauphin Island was a ghost town as island residents, already on lockdown, took shelter ahead of Hurricane Allison. Jesse stood on the front porch of his cottage and looked south toward the Gulf of Mexico. A steel gray sky hung heavily over the island, and dark clouds gathered ominously in the distance. Although the Gulf waters were not visible from his cottage, Jesse had been on board an oceanographic vessel caught in Hurricane Barry in 1983 and could easily imagine the sea conditions this storm would produce. He braced himself against the porch railing as a gust of wind struck him full-on, moaning ominously around the cottage. Humid and salt-laden, the air smelled of seaweed and swamp as cypress needles and live oak leaves sailed through the air. A precursor of what was to come, the storm was predicted to make landfall the following day in the early afternoon, and Dauphin Island was already under a hurricane warning. "I hope Joe's okay," he said, thinking out loud.

Jesse was about to retreat into the cottage when he spotted Ross's pickup truck coming down the drive, CC behind the wheel. He waved from the porch and watched as she parked on top of the shell midden next to the El Camino, and they got out.

"It's about time you got here." He descended the stairs to help unload.

"It took us a little while to load up some stuff," Ross motioned toward the *Dixie* beer and bags of snacks in the truck bed. "Damn! What happened to you?" Ross leaned in to get a closer look at Jesse's battered face.

"My God, Jesse, you look rough!" added CC.

"I had a little accident."

"That was more than a little accident!" said Ross.

"It looks worse than it is. I'll tell you about it later."

"Can you believe it?" asked CC. "Ross stocked up on beer days ago when he first heard about the hurricane."

"And it's a good thing I did because I'll bet you can't find any beer on the island now."

"And apparently, he's already had a few," added CC.

"It's five o'clock somewhere," countered Ross, grinning broadly. "Frigate birds!" Ross pointed skyward as the graceful birds glided past.

"You rarely see those over land," said Jesse as he reached into the truck bed to help unload. "That storm has blown them in from offshore. Ross, do you think three cases of beer will be enough?" added Jesse sarcastically as he hefted a case from the back of his truck.

"That's enough for me. I don't know what you guys are gonna do."

"Where's Cherie?" asked CC. "I thought she would have been here by now."

"I don't know. I called the motel earlier, but no answer. She's probably working at the CDC compound."

The three carried the food and beer up the stairs and deposited the items in the kitchen.

"Is your refrigerator on the fritz?" asked CC, puzzled by the fact that the appliance had been pulled out from the wall.

"And what happened to your aquarium?" asked Ross.

Jesse was a poor liar, so he decided to tell them about his encounter with Arturo. After relating the entire event, CC and Ross were dumbfounded.

"What the hell!" said CC, wide-eyed. "That explains all the bruising."

"I just found the pistol, and Chief East is coming by to pick it up." Jesse paused as he turned an ear toward the sound of an approaching vehicle. "That must be him now." He looked out the front door to see Chief East pull up and park in front. Jesse went to the porch to greet him.

"Hi, Chief," said Jesse as he approached.

"Hello, Jesse." East grabbed his hat against another gust of wind. "Dorothy said you found the pistol?" He climbed the stairs and entered the cottage.

"Yes sir. I must have knocked it under the refrigerator during that melee. I haven't touched it. Thanks for the assistance getting this door put back on its hinges. And thanks for letting me know about the escape."

"You need to be very much aware until we catch him, and we will get him. He won't be hard to recognize after that beatdown you put on him. His face looks like it wore out three bodies."

Jesse chuckled. "Yes sir, I am being vigilant."

"Whose car is that outside?"

"Two of my friends are here to ride out the hurricane. They're in the kitchen."

"Oh! Do they know about Arturo?"

"They do. I figured I'd better tell them. By the way, I left the gun right where I found it, figured you might need prints or something."

"That was the right thing to do. The investigators will dust it for prints. Seems unnecessary given your story, but it's routine."

They walked into the kitchen. Ross and CC stood together, still trying to process the information that had just been revealed to them.

"Chief East, this is Ross Jenkins and Christina Carrigan. Fellow graduate students," said Jesse as they exchanged pleasantries.

"So, you still insist that it's not a hurricane party?" queried Chief East, half-joking as he pointed to the cases of beer on the kitchen counter.

"That's Ross's propensity to over-compensate. CC and I rarely drink."

"Hey, what if we get stranded here for weeks?" said Ross. "I'll need that beer to keep me sane."

"Based on hurricane projections, I doubt you'll have any trouble," said East. "And by the way, I know the man who built this cottage. It's made of cypress, and there is hurricane strapping all over this thing. This is probably one of the safest places on the island."

"Good to know," said Jesse. "There it is Chief." Jesse pointed out the gun, and East threaded a pencil through the trigger guard, lifted it, and then dropped it into a large Ziplock bag.

"Wow! That's some weapon." East held the bag up near his face to examine the gun more closely. "Look at that engraving! That's a 1911 Colt 45. Not your run-of-the-mill murder weapon."

"Could I take a look, Chief?" asked Jesse. "I know a little about weapons, and that gun is intriguing."

"You can," said East. "Don't pick it up, but you can take a look." East put the gun on the counter, and Jesse and Ross gathered around it to look.

"I don't understand men's fascination with guns," said CC.

"That's beautiful engraving," said Ross. "It must be valuable."

"It is," said East. "A 1911 Colt, even an old, beat-up one, is worth a lot. I'll bet dimes to doughnuts that it's stolen."

"Chief," asked Jesse, "did you notice there are initials engraved on this gun?"

"I did not!" East stepped closer to look. "Good eyes!"

"It's J.W.R., probably the person he stole it from, wouldn't you think?" asked Jesse.

"Most likely. Well, folks, I've got to get back on patrol. We've got everyone on the island looking for this guy, but until we catch him, you need to be careful. Jesse, do you have a gun?"

"I have an old single-shot 20-gauge that I squirrel hunted with back in Sweetwater. I've been keeping it loaded by the bed since the break-in."

"Good idea."

"By the way, Chief, have you seen Cherie lately?" asked Jesse.

"Not since the news conference at City Hall."

"OK, I was just wondering. She's not at the motel, and I was a bit concerned. She's probably at the CDC compound."

"I'll swing by her motel room and the compound to see if I can find her. I'll let you know if I do."

"Thanks, Chief!"

"Don't hesitate to call me if you have any problems."

"Nice to meet you, Chief," said CC and Ross.

"Same here," said East, Y'all be safe."

"You too Chief," said Jesse as East left.

"Jesse, does Cherie know what happened?" asked Ross.

"She does not. I told her I had an accident on my bicycle. I don't like lying to her, but she has enough crap to deal with as it is. I would appreciate it if you did not mention this to her."

"We won't say anything," said Ross. "We need to tell her that the shit-head has escaped? She probably needs to know that."

"Absolutely," said Jesse. "I would have told her already if I could get in touch."

Jesse went to the kitchen sink and began washing dishes that he had ignored for too long. "Sorry for the mess, guys. I should have cleaned this place up, but I've been preoccupied."

At that moment, the phone rang.

"CC, could you get that?"

"Sure." CC took the phone from its receiver. "Hello. Oh, hi Cherie. We've been wondering where you were. Yes, he's right here. Jesse, it's Cherie." CC gave Jesse a puzzled look as she handed him the phone.

"Hi, Cherie. What's up?" Jesse leaned against the wall next to the phone as they spoke.

Watching from across the room, CC noticed Jesse's face drop as he listened.

"OK," a long pause as Jesse listened intently. "Yes," another long pause. "Yes. I will do that. OK." Jesse hung up the phone. Deep in thought, he paused for a moment before turning to Ross and CC. "I've got to pick up Cherie. She had…uh…car trouble."

"You need me to go with you?" asked Ross.

"No!" replied Jesse. "You guys just stay here. This shouldn't take long."

"Is there a problem?" asked CC, who sensed something was amiss.

"No. Everything is fine… everything is fine," repeated Jesse. His mind in another place, he sleepwalked to his bedroom and pulled open a dresser drawer. He reached into the back and removed a wad of cash. *Thank God I took this money out of my account.*

Jesse stuffed the money into his pants pocket, put on a light, waterproof jacket, and left the cottage. He got in the El Camino, hooked up the RV Bongo, and drove away.

Ross and CC watched from the porch as Jesse departed.

"That was very odd," said Ross. "Why did he take the boat?"

"Definitely odd, and I have no idea. Did you notice how concerned he looked when speaking to Cherie?"

"I didn't pay attention to the conversation, but taking his boat out while we are under a hurricane warning is just crazy."

"Something is not right," said CC.

CHAPTER 63

Chief East placed the Colt on the seat beside him and drove away. After travelling south for several blocks, he turned east toward the police station. This portion of Bienville Boulevard was just a few blocks from the Gulf waters that were now white-capping as hurricane-driven waves crashed along the beachfront. East slowed the cruiser as he spotted three teens at the water's edge, surfboards in hand. "Damn it! Someone is supposed to be patrolling out here!" He pulled off the road, took a bullhorn from the back seat, and strode partway down the beach.

Even with the bullhorn, East had to shout above the sound of wind and waves. "ALL BEACHES ON THE ISLAND ARE CLOSED. IF YOU AREN'T OFF THIS BEACH IN FIVE MINUTES, I'M GOING TO IMPOUND THIS VEHICLE AND ARREST EVERYONE OF YOU."

Like a scene from a Keystone Cops movie, their reaction was immediate as they quickly grabbed their gear and ran toward the truck parked just down the way from his cruiser. Normally, he would have waited until they arrived and given them a good tongue-lashing, but he had other things to take care of. He brought the bullhorn to his mouth again. "IF I COME BACK AND FIND YOU HERE, YOU ARE ALL GOING TO JAIL! GIVE ME A THUMBS UP IF YOU UNDERSTAND!" All three of them indicated they understood, and East drove away.

East swung by the CDC compound and found it practically deserted. A few National Guard vehicles rolled in and out, but he could find no one from the CDC. Heading for the Palms Motel, he pulled into the lot and parked in front of the office. Finding the office door locked, he looked in through the front window. The geriatric proprietor was asleep in his desk chair, his chin on his chest. He rapped softly on the window. "Sam, it's Chief East." No response. "Sam!" He knocked louder this time. The individual sat up quickly, startled by the sound. After blinking and looking around the room in confusion, he saw Chief East peering through the glass and got up.

"Just a minute," he said, coming to the door and unlocking it. "Sorry Chief. I haven't been sleeping well lately."

"No problem, Sam." The chief stood outside the door, giving the proprietor plenty of distance. "Nobody on the island is sleeping well. Are your folks doing OK?” asked East, genuinely concerned as he had known the proprietor for many years.

“We’re OK, considering. How about you?”

“It could be better, but you don’t want to hear about that.”

“What can I do for you Chief?”

“I’m trying to find Cherie Belon’s room. She works for the CDC.”

“Oh, yes. Nice young lady. She’s in 103. It’s six doors that way,” said Sam as he pointed. “Her car is gone, so she may be out.”

“Thanks, Sam.” He walked the short distance to the room and knocked repeatedly with no response.” Removing his hat, he pressed his face against the window, trying to see between the heavy curtains. He walked back to the office and leaned in to speak to Sam through a partially opened door. “Sam, she doesn’t answer. Something doesn’t feel right. No one has seen her today, and I’m concerned for her safety. Do you think you could let me in?”

“I think that requires a warrant, but I’m willing to bend the law a bit for you. Let me get the key.”

Sam came forward with a large set of keys, and the two went back to the door.

“I’ve got too many doggone keys on this ring. I know one of them is the master.” Sam's hands shook as he tried several keys. “This Parkinson’s ain’t helping either.”

“It’s a bitch, I know. My Dad had it before he passed,” said East.

After several failed attempts, he found the master and cracked the door open.

“Dr Belon, it’s Chief East, are you here?” said East through the crack in the door, hoping to avoid an embarrassing encounter. He swung the door open a little wider. “Dr. Belon?”

“Ain’t nobody here,” said Sam.

They both stepped into the room. Cherie’s CDC papers and personal effects were strewn across the bed and floor.

“Whoa! She is one messy lady,” said Sam.

“I don’t think so,” said East. “A broken cup and spilled coffee, an overturned chair, and papers that someone walked across. Damn it! It looks like there may have been a struggle. Sam, I think she is in trouble.”

“You must have a reason for suspecting something.”

"I do. Did you hear about the escape from the jail?"

"I did not?"

"A scumbag terrorist named Arturo. He is wanted by the FBI and is a really bad dude."

"Good Lord, Chief! Hurricanes, people dying, terrorists. It feels like Armageddon has come to the island."

"Tell me about it! He'll be easy to spot. A Colombian, black hair pulled back in a pony-tail, pock-marked face, short, stocky. He has a black eye, a bruised face, and a bandaged arm. If you see anyone matching that description, call Dorothy immediately."

"I will. You don't think he has that young lady, do you?"

"Truthfully, Sam, I don't know. Hell, I don't know anything anymore! I'm just going day-to-day."

"Sorry Chief."

"It is what it is. Seems I've been saying that a lot these days."

"If you happen to see Dr. Belon return, would you give Dorothy a call immediately?"

"I will. I hope she's OK."

"Me too. Thanks, Sam."

"Chief East, come back!" Dorothy's unmistakable southern drawl came over the airwaves as East walked back to the cruiser. He quickened his pace and reached through the passenger side window to retrieve the microphone.

"Go ahead, Dorothy. Over."

"Trey Murphy is at the clinic. Someone attacked him at his lot and stole a car. I wonder who that could have been?" she said sarcastically. "Over."

"Shit!" exclaimed East. "That's three blocks from the police station. Is Trey OK? Over."

"I don't know. They had to helicopter him to Mobile for treatment. Don't know how they are going to do that with the quarantine we are under. Over."

"Son of a bitch!" East kicked the tire of his cruiser with his good leg. "Do they know what kind of car was taken? Over."

"Yes. It was a red 1980 Ford Escort. Connor Blake, Trey's employee, is at the lot if you want to go by to speak with him. I can tell him you're on your way. Over."

"I guess I should do that. Let him know. Thanks, Dorothy!" Over and out."

East hung the microphone back on its hook and climbed into the cruiser. He backed out of the lot and started to drive away when he spotted a red Ford parked a few spaces down from Cherie's room. *Damn! That's a red Escort, and it looks to be about the right year.* He pulled back into the lot, removed his service revolver from its holster, and slowly made his way toward the automobile. Confident that the vehicle was unoccupied, East holstered his gun and examined the car. He stooped down and peeked into the driver's window. Shards of safety glass from a broken window were scattered across the front seat and the floor mat. Empty Marlboro cigarette packages and beer cans were strewn about the interior. Dried blood on the steering wheel and the seat confirmed East's suspicion. He was now sure that Arturo had taken Cherie.

He returned to his cruiser and radioed Dorothy.

"Dorothy, you got your ears on? Over."

"Come back Chief. Over."

"I just found the stolen car. It's parked at the Palms Motel. The motel where Dr. Belon is staying. Over."

"Oh God!" A pause as Dorothy struggled with what she knew he was suggesting.

"Dorothy, are you there? Over."

"I'm here Chief. Over."

"I'm going by the car lot, and then I'll be back at the station. Over and out."

"Standing by." Dorothy replaced the microphone, bowed her head, and said a prayer.

****

Chief East limped into the office carrying his hat in one hand and the Ziplock bag containing the Colt in the other.

"Any word on Dr. Belon?"

"The stolen car was parked near her room at the motel, and there appears to have been a struggle in her room. I believe Arturo took her car and her car." East placed the Ziplock bag on her desk and slumped into a chair in the lobby. "Alert all of the enforcement folks on the island for them to be on the lookout for her white Crown Vic."

"As a matter of fact, I just got a call from a person named Christina Carrigan."

"I just met her at Jesse's cottage. What did she want?"

She said that right after you left, she got a phone call from Dr. Belon."

"Oh, thank God. She's OK then?"

"Maybe not. That's why she called. Cherie asked to speak to Jesse, and then he left immediately. Said Cherie had car trouble. CC was concerned by Jesse's behavior after he spoke to her. She said he looked very troubled when he left. Much more than a little car problem would merit."

East fanned himself with his hat. "Damn, it's hot in here."

"Even more concerning was that Jesse hooked up his boat and took it with him."

East stopped fanning. "What!? He's going out in this slop?"

"She said something just wasn't right about the whole thing."

"Ain't nothing right about nothing on this island. I'm not sure what to do with that information. If he leaves the island on his boat, he won't get far. The Coast Guard will stop him."

You look beat, Chief," said Dorothy.

"I'm OK. That's the gun that Arturo threatened Jesse with." East pointed to the gun.

"I'll put it in the evidence locker," said Dorothy.

"Wow, some gun!" Dorothy leaned over to get a better look. "That's gotta be a presentation piece. A gun given to someone who retired from law enforcement or the military."

"Yeah, that's what I figured, too. It's got J.W.R. engraved on it. Know anyone with those initials?" The chief did not expect an answer from Dorothy.

"As a matter of fact, I do. John Wayne Riley."

"What?!"

"He and his wife used to come to bingo night. When his wife passed, he stopped coming."

"Damn!" East sat up at attention.

"He's a Vietnam vet. An ex-marine. He lives on the back side of the island near. I've got his address."

"Dorothy, you are a Godsend! Get that address for me quickly." East hurried to the weapons locker, took a 12-gauge riot gun and a box of shells, loaded the gun to capacity, and started out the door.

"Chief, should I alert the other agencies on the island?"

"Not yet. I'm going to check his place first. I pray this is nothing. I'll radio you when I get there."

"I hope he's OK!"

"Me too." East limped to his cruiser, put the riot gun on the front seat, and climbed in. Gravel and dust flying, he rocketed out of the police station lot and headed toward the address that Dorothy had provided for him. He arrived in minutes. The chain across the dirt driveway that normally stopped unwanted visitors was down. He parked his cruiser on the highway, retrieved the 12-gauge from the front seat, and chambered a shell. Staying close to the forest edge, he cautiously walked along the long, dusty drive that curved toward John Wayne's secluded house. The cartridge casings strewn along the drive were the first sign that something was amiss. East stooped down for a closer look and noted that some of the casings had been run over by a vehicle, either coming or going. He continued walking. As the house came into view, it appeared that no one was home. Hidden behind a large live oak tree, he watched the house for several minutes. John Wayne's old Ford pickup sat at the rear of the house, but there were no lights on in the home, no sound, and he observed no activity.

East climbed the stairs quietly, cautiously. Standing to one side, he used the barrel of his 12-gauge to knock on the heavy cypress door.

"Mr. Riley." East paused, listening for any signs of occupancy. "Mr. Riley, it's Chief of Police East." East knocked again more vigorously. No reply. "Damn it!"

East descended the steps and walked to the rear of the house. He stopped to examine the truck and found more shell casings on the ground. *That's a bullet hole.* He ran his hand across the truck fender where a large caliber bullet had penetrated. Kneeling, he examined the tires on the truck, noting that these mud tires did not match the tread pattern of the vehicle that had run over the shell casings in the driveway. Similar tire tracks led across the yard to an old storage shed where an automobile had been parked.

Noticing that the rear door was ajar, he was about to climb the stairs when he caught a whiff of an unmistakable odor. From his military service and years of law enforcement, he knew a decomposing body when he smelled one. Across the small swamp, he noticed an unusual number of gators floating at the surface. East walked across the yard and stepped onto the dock, where he found a puddle of dark, coagulated blood. The smell here was overpowering, and he held his hand over his nose and mouth. Through the cracks between the weathered dock boards, he could see the swollen face of a large man. "Shit! I'll bet that's the homeowner. I'd better check out the house."

East returned to the stairs and cautiously approached a partially open door, his weapon ready. He pushed the door open with his riot gun. "Yeeeowwwww," a large, yellow feral cat screamed, streaked out the door between his legs, and disappeared into the palmettos. "Damn it!" East leaned against the porch railing, his heart racing, trying to catch his breath. He walked in cautiously and did a cursory search. No occupants, a trashed kitchen, blood in the bathroom sink, and broken pictures on the floor. Although difficult to positively identify, one of the photos could have been the man who was now floating in the bayou.

East left the house and walked back to his cruiser. He climbed in and picked up the microphone. "Dorothy, have you got your ears on? Over."

"Go ahead Chief. Over."

"I'm here at the address you gave me. Contact the county investigators. Tell them we need crime scene investigators out here. Come back."

"Oh no!" Dorothy paused to gather herself. "Is it Dr. Belon? Come back."

"No. It's John Wayne Riley. Come back."

"I'll have the investigators out there ASAP. Come back."

"I'll wait here until they arrive and then head back to the station to fill you in. Over and out."

"Standing by."

CHAPTER 64

As Jesse drove away, a wave of helplessness swept over him. Dauphin Island's hurricane-shuttered houses and deserted streets deepened his foreboding. When he answered the phone and heard the chill in Cherie's voice, he instantly knew something was wrong: Arturo had kidnapped Cherie. How could this have happened? A rush of intense emotions filled his mind with worst-case scenarios. *What if she's hurt? Is she in pain? What if I can't rescue her?* He couldn't help but feel responsible. Jesse's heart raced, he broke out in a cold, and his hands trembled as he steered the El Camino toward the most secluded boat launch on the island. His instructions were clear: come alone, bring the money, put the boat in the water, and wait. If he failed to follow these orders, Cherie would die.

Jesse knew precisely what Arturo planned to do. He would force Jesse to help him escape the island. And as long as Cherie was in danger, he would do whatever Arturo wanted, even if it meant going to sea in a hurricane. Jesse shuddered. Recalling too well the look of pure evil in Arturo's eyes, there was no doubt that Arturo was going to kill them both, and he knew of no way to prevent it.

Jesse arrived at the dock and backed the RV Bongo down the boat ramp. Though relatively sheltered, getting the boat in the water was going to be difficult. Launching with no help could be trying even in a light breeze, but in this weather, it was almost impossible. Gusts of wind from the north and waves refracting around the protective peninsula tossed the boat wildly as Jesse struggled to launch. As far as he could see, the Mississippi Sound was covered with white-capping waves, and not a single boat was in sight. *Nobody is stupid enough to go out in this mess.* After several failed attempts to launch and a thorough soaking, he finally secured the boat to a dock piling. The boat pitched and strained against its bonds like a living organism as waves passed beneath it. In these conditions, it would take all of Jesse's boating skills to reach the mainland--- assuming that was where Arturo wanted to go. But there was no guarantee they would reach land at all. He turned his VHF radio to the NOAA weather station and waited for the looping message to report on sea conditions in and around Mobile Bay. He was not reassured by the report. Hurricane warnings extended across much of the northern Gulf of Mexico with winds at thirty-five miles per hour and gusts up to sixty.

He sat on the dock in troubled contemplation, staring at the wind-driven trash and dead fish that had collected in the boat basin. His thoughts were not unlike this jumble of debris. Almost completely overwhelmed by the situation, he closed his eyes, trying to anticipate a situation that he might turn to his advantage. *Think, damn it, think!* He stood up and paced along the dock, a habit that often helped him focus his thoughts. *Any attempt at rescue on land would be futile. There's no way I can overpower him while Cherie is in danger. The best chance will be after he is on the boat, when he is in my world. That's it. Yes. On the boat! That's where it will have to happen!* A plan was beginning to develop. He knew it was a risky one, but at least it was a plan. Requiring help from above, he said a silent prayer.

Jesse did not have long to wait. He steeled himself as Cherie's white Crown Vic slowly came along the road and stopped a distance away from the ramp. Jesse could see Cherie at the wheel and Arturo in the passenger seat next to her, peering warily around the area. He could also see the stolen service revolver, held against Cherie's head. At the sight of Cherie, Jesse began to feel the anger welling inside him as he clenched his fists in rage. *Stop it!* Through sheer willpower, he held his anger in check. The beast that lay hidden inside him would do nothing but further endanger Cherie, and that could not happen!

Convinced that no ambush awaited him, Arturo ordered Cherie to pull the car to the top of the boat ramp. The passenger door opened, and Arturo got out, pulling Cherie across the seat by the arm. Holding the gun at Cherie's head and nervously keeping watch on his surroundings, he walked toward Jesse. He looked like death warmed over. The beating Jesse had applied to his face, the bleeding bandage on his arm, along with his pockmarked complexion and greasy black hair, combined to produce a genuinely frightening visage. Arturo came forward while Jesse backed along the dock.

"Are you OK?" asked Jesse. It was clear that she was not. Haggard, pale, and her shirt torn, it was almost more than Jesse could bear. However, the fierce look in Cherie's eyes told him that she did not go down without a fight. *Stay calm. Stay calm.*

"I'm OK," replied Cherie.

"NO TALKING!" shouted Arturo as he shook Cherie violently. "I do all talking!"

Jesse gritted his teeth as he turned over in his mind what he would do to this scum bag if given the chance. He took a deep breath and exhaled slowly. *Stay calm. Stay calm.*

"You give money NOW!"

Jesse moved to put his hand in his pocket, and Arturo recoiled nervously, pulling Cherie in front of him like a human shield.

Jesse threw his hands up in surrender. "It's OK. Denaro! Denaro!" said Jesse as he pointed at his jacket pocket. He slowly placed his hand in his pocket and extracted a large wad of cash held together with a rubber band. He placed the cash on the dock and backed away.

With an evil sneer and without taking his eyes off Jesse, Arturo retrieved the cash. "Now Arturo is head honcho. You no hurt Arturo again." He nodded at the knife wound on his arm. "Take off shirt and pants!" He shook Cherie again, and she began to sob quietly.

"Yes sir, yes sir." Jesse quickly pulled his t-shirt over his head and stepped out of his shorts. "I don't have a weapon." He turned around completely so Arturo could see that he was unarmed.

"In boat!" commanded Arturo. "You take Mobile!" Arturo so badly mispronounced their destination that Jesse doubted what he had said.

"You want to go to Mobile?" asked Jesse, surprised by the absurdity of the request. "That's all the way up the bay. It will take us hours to get there in this slop. We won't make it before sundown."

"You take MOBILE!" growled Arturo as he brought the gun up to Cherie's head and pulled the hammer back.

Jesse held his hands up in surrender. "Please. Please. No problemo." He climbed into the boat and started the engine.

"Move!" commanded Arturo while gesturing for Jesse to move to the front of the boat.

Jesse followed orders, and Arturo awkwardly climbed in, keeping Cherie at gunpoint as he did so. He nearly slipped but steadied himself on the center console. He held Cherie close, and they stood together on the vessel's port side.

Jesse made note that Arturo was clearly uncomfortable onboard the RV Bongo. *He doesn't know his way around boats. That will work to my advantage.* "We all need to put these life jackets on, it is going to be rough." Jesse held out two life jackets at arm's length.

"No! GO NOW!" ordered a nervous Arturo, suspecting a trick. He waved the revolver menacingly, never taking his eyes off Jesse.

"OK… OK!" He tossed the life jackets onto the deck. *These will at least be available if we go down.* Jesse cast off the lines, quickly put the engine in gear, and throttled up. He slowly navigated the boat out of the slip and then out of the protection of the small basin. From this vantage point, Jesse could see across a wide expanse of the Mississippi Sound and Mobile Bay, and the conditions looked terrible. He checked his watch and assessed the situation as he slowly motored out into open water. *Five thirty-five. Running directly into this north wind, we're never going to make it.*

"Everyone needs to hold on!" announced Jesse as he pushed the throttle forward and pointed the bow out into open water. The vessel gained speed and began to rise from the water as it attempted to plane off. The R/V Bongo shuddered each time the bow pounded into the relatively small waves that covered this sheltered part of the bay. *This is nothing. When we round Oyster Point, that's when things are really going to get dicey. God help us!* Jesse knew that it would take all his boating skills and then some to keep the boat afloat.

The pounding was relentless, requiring Jesse's constant attention at the throttle. Their progress slowed to a crawl as conditions worsened. Adding to the discomfort, bow spray thrown into the air was blown back and rained down onto the boat, drenching its occupants. Jesse, wearing only his boxer shorts, shivered as he attempted to stay on course. He looked back to see Cherie holding onto the boat's railing and Arturo, now wearing a life jacket, holding onto Cherie.

Jesse made the turn around Oyster Point and directly into the near gale-force wind, steam-rolling down the length of Mobile

Bay. The seas suddenly changed from very uncomfortable to dangerous as they were met by mountains of water charging across the bay. Heading directly into these monstrous waves to reach Mobile was pure folly.

"HOLD TIGHT!" shouted Jesse over the roar as a particularly large wave loomed just ahead. The R/V Bongo wallowed in the deceptively calm wave trough. The massive swell lifted the bow, and for a moment, they stared into the churning, grey sky. A jagged bolt of lightning ran lengthwise across the horizon, followed by a low rumble barely perceptible over the shrieking wind. Jesse white-knuckled the wheel and throttled back as the Bongo climbed each wave. At each crest, the boat was blasted by wind and driving water, reducing visibility to almost zero and requiring Jesse to turn his face away from the onslaught. He knew that he had to "quarter" the wave crests or risk capsizing. Increasing power to maintain control, he charged down the back side of the wave and into the trough before climbing up the next. Over and over, this cycle repeated as Jesse grew increasingly fatigued and was near hypothermic. His legs flexed constantly to counter the boat's violent motion, thighs burning from the effort.

Each time the vessel crested a wave, water crashed over the bow, flooding the deck. The rear deck where Arturo and Cherie stood was awash, indicating that the bilge pump was unable to keep up with the water that was pouring over the railing. After an hour of slow progress, they were now in the middle of the bay and in a desperate situation. *I'm gonna lose the boat if I maintain this heading. This crap has gone on long enough!* Just before the R/V Bongo climbed the next wall of water, Jesse turned and looked Cherie in the eye and shouted;

"GIRD YOUR LOINS!"

In that instant, a moment of complete recognition, Cherie knew that Jesse was about to take control of the situation, for better or for worse. She nodded knowingly.

The moment they reached the wave crest, Jesse turned the wheel hard to port and gunned the 200-horsepower outboard. The stern dug deep as water crashed over the side and into the boat. Now listing perilously, the port side suddenly rose and fell over the wave crest. Both Arturo and Cherie toppled overboard.

Please, Lord, watch over Cherie! Jesse prayed as he fought to keep the Bongo afloat.

Taken completely by surprise, Arturo bobbed to the surface and found himself alone in a boiling sea. He cleared the stinging seawater from his eyes to reveal the stern of the Bongo moving quickly away from him. He searched in vain to find his hostage, but she was nowhere to be found. In desperation, he pointed his gun and emptied the chamber. Jesse started as a bullet plowed into the center console, barely missing him. Arturo let the now-empty revolver fall to the sea floor.

"PLEASE, AMIGO!" shouted Arturo. "COME BACK. COME BACK!" Arturo waved his good arm frantically. "YOU TAKE ALL MONIES!" Arturo bobbed to the top of a crest as water plunged down upon him. He floated up again, choking and spitting.

Jesse, hyper-focused on saving the boat, neither heard nor saw Arturo. Perilously close to being swamped, the stern of the Bongo sat low in the water, risking drowning out the engine. If he lost power, he would be at the mercy of the sea, and their chances of surviving this would be gone. If he did not clear water from the deck, the vessel would swamp and capsize. There was only one choice: he had to clear the water. Turning the bow downwind, he ran in the direction of the wave trains, surfing down the wave face and then staying, as best he could, in the calmer water between crests. His gut tightened when his trusty outboard coughed once and then again, but continued running. As he continued running, the excess water flooded over the transom. Regaining some stability, he hoped the bilge pump would take care of the rest.

"Mayday, Mayday, Mayday! RV Bongo, RV Bongo, RV Bongo!" Jesse held the microphone in one hand as he frantically tried to navigate with the other. "Vessel in distress! Vessel in distress!"

"RV Bongo, this is the Coast Guard Dauphin Island. What is the nature of your distress and location?"

"Taking on water. There are two people overboard. Our location is near the ship channel, south of Middle Bay Light." Jesse returned the microphone to its hook and tried to maintain course.

The radio crackled to life. "RV Bongo, a rescue chopper is already in flight."

Through the gathering darkness, Jesse fought the raging sea with one hand on the wheel and the other on the throttle. *They're never gonna find us!*

Throughout the ordeal, Jesse's thoughts and prayers were with Cherie. As the minutes passed, a feeling of guilt began to creep into his thoughts. Had he done the right thing? Still running downwind, he would have to execute a tricky maneuver to change course and find Cherie. To complete the turn, he would have to steer upwind, back into the face of these mountains of water. Momentarily broadside to the waves meant he would risk capsizing. Gripping the wheel, he turned into the oncoming sea and throttled up. Jesse's heart pounded as he leaned into the wall of water that rose to meet him. Like a stone across a farm pond, the boat slipped sideways down the face of the wave, slammed into the wave trough, and nearly capsized. Jesse screamed as he was violently thrown to the deck. Ignoring the pain, he quickly stood and managed to regain control. *If a slow turn won't work, then I'll try speed.*

Jesse buried the throttle, raced up the wave face, and made the turn. A torrent of water rushed toward the stern and flooded over the transom. Jesse held on like grim death and shouted as the boat reached the wave crest, took flight, and landed hard on the back side of the wave. Jesse was, for the moment, in control.

He powered the vessel up yet another mountain of water, and when he crested, a large object loomed just off his starboard side. "What the…!" Through the mist, Jesse could barely make out a large vessel; no running lights, pitching and rolling, with decks awash. Moving fast, carried along by the gale-force winds, the ghostly vessel was bearing down on him, and he had only seconds to react. Jesse buried the throttle and cut the wheel hard to port as the foundering ship narrowly missed his bow. Jesse breathed a sigh of relief, having narrowly avoided being run down. Strangely familiar to him, the abandoned shrimp boat drifted south and disappeared into the gathering gloom. As it passed, Jesse could just make out the name across the stern: *The Crimson Tide*. A chill went through his already cold body. However, he had no time to consider the coincidence or meaning of encountering the doomed vessel. Jesse course corrected and powered down the back side of a roller.

In the failing light, he topped another wave crest and spotted a barely visible flash of orange off to his left. He knew it was either Arturo, an empty life vest, or Cherie. If it were Arturo, he wondered if he would rescue him or run him over. Deciding he would cross that bridge when he came to it, he cautiously steered in that direction and prayed that it was Cherie.

CHAPTER 65

Ignoring the sharp pain in her right shoulder, a result of her struggle with Arturo, Cherie dove down and away. Holding her breath as long as possible, she swam as far as she could and surfaced to the sharp crack of several pistol shots. In the fading light, she could see Arturo, his bright orange life vest around his neck, firing at the R/V Bongo as it topped a wave crest. The boat was under full power and racing away from her. Arturo shouted something she could not make out, and Cherie realized she was too close to this monster. Pausing for just a moment to regain her breath, she began to breaststroke away. *I need to put as much distance away from him as possible!* Like swimming laps at the university pool, she thought. Although chilled to the bone while on the boat, the bay water felt much warmer, and she fell into an easy rhythm. Making good progress when swimming down the face of the waves, she struggled at each crest and was blasted by water as the now gale-force winds blew the tops out of each wave. She stopped swimming for a moment and checked her position. As she rode up and over a wave, she could see Arturo a safe distance away. Thankfully, Jesse had switched on his running lights, and when carried to the top of a wave crest, she could see the boat pitching violently in the distance.

Treading water and extremely fatigued, she scanned the ever-darkening horizon, such as it was. She thought she saw a patch of orange bob into view for a split second before disappearing between waves. *Was that the other life vest?* She waited and watched. Again, a patch of orange came into view and disappeared. *It has to be!* However, the wind was driving the object south quickly, and there was no guarantee she could reach it. With renewed vigor, she began stroking hard toward the vest.

Jesse kept the bow of the Bongo pointed toward the orange life vest bobbing along the surface of Mobile Bay. *Please, Lord, let it be Cherie! Please, Lord, let it be Cherie!* He kept up his prayerful mantra. Nearing exhaustion and fighting the wheel to maintain a heading, he finally drew close, and an empty life vest came into view. His hopes were dashed. Jesse throttled back on the engine and wallowed in the oily seas as the empty life vest floated past. The engine barely perceptible while idling, Jesse could now hear the sound of wind and water as the edge of Hurricane Allison assaulted Dauphin Island. *I'm not giving up damn it! I'll run a search pattern.*

Thanks to his Coast Guard training skills, he knew the most effective way to conduct a search, but he never dreamed he would be searching in a hurricane. Moving quickly, he removed a life ring from a compartment and attached a long length of rope to it and the other end to the boat. He removed his Q-Beam spotlight from the overhead compartment and switched it on. The million candle-power light came to life and then suddenly went dark.

"Are you kidding me?!" Jesse repeatedly struck the light with the palm of his hand, hoping he might jar it back to life. "AAAAAAHHHHHHH!!" In a rage, Jesse screamed and threw the light as hard as he could into the boiling sea. His fists balled, he shook from both hypothermia and anger. He sat on the boat railing, taking deep, calming breaths. Jesse had to hold tight as the Bongo rose to the crest of a wave and almost capsized. The urgency of the situation pulled him from the precipice of fury that he was about to fall into. Calmer now, he took the wheel and was about to throttle up when he heard the call of a lone seabird. *That's strange! Animals are too smart to be out in this mess.* He listened again and realized that it did not sound like a bird. *Could it be Cherie!*

Jesse shut the engine down completely and listened intently. In these seas, he could not sit for long with no power. He pushed the horn button, sending two blasts into the night. He listened again. A sweeter sound he had never heard. Two distant screams!

"Oh my God, that's her! But which direction? CHERIE, CHERIE!" Jesse sounded the horn twice and was answered again. "If only that damn spotlight was working!"

As a wave approached, Jesse was forced to restart the engine or risk foundering. He knew it would drown out any shouts from Cherie, but he had no choice. He pointed the Bongo in the direction from which he thought the sound came. Although his eyes were forward, there was nothing for him to see. Suddenly, lightning cracked, and for a moment, his surroundings were bathed in harsh, electric illumination.

A miracle! In the brilliance, Jesse saw an object on a wave crest, just off the starboard bow. He quickly looked down at his compass, noted the direction, and adjusted his course. He held the course for several minutes, topped a crest, and as he fell into calmer water, shut the engine down again. He sounded the horn twice and was answered by two screams closer now.

"Please, Lord! Please, Lord!" Jesse motored forward, shut the engine, and sounded the horn. Cherie replied very close by now. He knew now precisely the direction to take, but he had to be careful now or risk running down Cherie. He started the engine, throttled up, and slowly began in that direction. Another flash of lightning, and there was Cherie on the face of a monster wave, perhaps fifty feet from the Bongo. She was exhausted and was going down. Jesse threw the life ring with all his might. The wind caught it, and it fell far short.

Without hesitation, Jesse dove into the dark water and swam with all his might. He reached Cherie as she went down, pulling her to the surface. Taking her under the arms with one hand and with the other, he began stroking toward the Bongo, which was now drifting quickly away from them. *If I can just make it to the life ring!* The distance between the couple and the Bongo was increasing rapidly, and momentarily, the life ring would be out of reach.

Frustration finally took hold as Jesse screamed, and his inner demon surfaced. Like a man possessed, he stroked and kicked with strength that he never knew he possessed. Jesse reached out repeatedly, finding nothing but empty water. He reached again and, finally, his hand fell upon the life ring.

Jesse pulled Cherie to the ring. "Can you hold onto this? I need both hands to get us to the boat."

"Yes," said Cherie weakly.

Jesse pulled with all the strength he had left, and they arrived at the boat just as a wave crest approached. The Bongo, now broadside to the wave, pitched wildly as Jesse thrust Cherie over the railing and into the boat using the boat's momentum and brute force. He followed quickly behind, started the engine, and took control of the vessel.

Cherie lay on the deck, gasping and shivering. With no time to spare, Jesse removed a rain jacket from the center console and tossed it to her. "Can you put this on?" shouted Jesse over the roar. Jesse could assist Cherie no further as he fought to keep the boat afloat. The Bongo pitched again as the sea conditions further worsened.

"Yes. Give me a minute." Cherie sat up and put on the jacket. She rose using the center console for balance to stand beside Jesse.

Jesse had to speak directly in Cherie's ear. "There are two life jackets in this compartment." Without looking down, Jesse used his foot to kick the door of the compartment below the center console. "Get two out." Cherie carefully retrieved the two life jackets. She put one on and then helped Jesse put on the other.

"If you know a good prayer, now would be the time to use it."

Cherie read Jesse's face accurately. "We're not going to make it, are we?"

Jesse did not reply as he feathered the throttle with one hand and tried to steer with the other.

Over the roar, the VHF radio suddenly crackled to life. "RV Bongo, RV Bongo, RV Bongo. This is Coast Guard rescue helicopter 103. We are en route. What is your situation? Over."

"It's the Coast Guard!" said Cherie. "Look!" In the distance, the lights of a rescue chopper appeared low over the water while a bright search light could be seen passing over the ocean surface.

The radio message repeated before Jesse could reach the microphone. "Coast Guard, Coast Guard, Coast Guard. This is RV Bongo. Our situation is dire. Taking on water. We see you south of us. Over." Jesse glanced down at the compass to determine their position. "You are about 195 degrees south of us. Make course correction to 15 degrees north. Repeat. Course correct to 15 degrees north."

"RV Bongo, RV Bongo, RV Bongo. We are making course correction to 15 degrees north."

The distant chopper could be seen slowly turning to head in exactly their direction.

"Oh, thank God. They're coming our way." said Cherie hopefully.

At that moment, the Bongo's engine sputtered and fell silent. "We're out of gas!" said Jesse desperately. "Hang on as tight as you can." Jesse reached for the microphone. "Coast Guard,

Coast Guard. We have lost power! Assistance needed immediately!"

Jesse and Cherie crouched low, holding the center console and each other. The Bongo was adrift in a hurricane, and they would soon capsize. Riding over one wave crest, they were slammed against the gunwale and drenched with water. The Bongo slid over the crest and then righted itself as it surfed down the wave face.

"I don't know how long we can stay upright," shouted Jesse as he hugged Cherie. "If we go over, get away from the boat, or it could crush us."

"RV Bongo, RV Bongo, RV Bongo. We have you in sight."

Reaching the wave trough, an intense light shone down on the Bongo as the chopper hovered directly overhead. The chopper's downwash created a mini tornado amid this hurricane.

"RV Bongo, RV Bongo, RV Bongo. We have a rescue swimmer ready to enter the water. Secure your personal flotation device, abandon ship, and move away from the vessel."

Hesitating for only a moment, Jesse said farewell to the Bongo, and he and Cherie jumped from the boat. Jesse held Cherie, and he pulled away from the vessel. Under an intense spotlight, an individual from the chopper splashed into the sea a short distance away. The diver swam quickly to them.

"Good evening to you, Sir, Ma'am. I'm Lieutenant Mason, a Coast Guard rescue swimmer. I'm here to assist."

CHAPTER 66

Two weeks later.

The RV Bongo sat at anchor just offshore of Dauphin Island's west end as Jesse and Cherie watched the last rays of a late summer sunset. The cool air, with just a hint of the approaching fall, drifted on the breeze. The whisper of waves softly falling along the shoreline could be heard in the distance. Pastel pink, blue, and green painted the western horizon, while rays of golden sun shone through small puffy clouds. An almost full moon rose over the Mobile skyline. A group of shorebirds, silhouetted against Mother Nature's light show, skimmed across the glassy sea's surface. With fishing rods in their holders and lines trailing behind the boat, the two were settled in for a few hours of fishing and enjoying each other's company.

A rare respite from the worries of her investigation, Cherie's emergency call to the CDC led to a diazepam distribution program on the island. The effect was immediate and profound as new reports of deaths almost disappeared. Although still under quarantine while the virus lay dormant in many of the island residents, the drug provided precious time for labs across the nation to develop treatment. Shortly thereafter, the disease-causing agent was identified as the smallest virus ever discovered. The unusually small size of the virus explained the ease with which it was transmitted via aerosols and its rapid dispersion through the body.

Cherie sighed contentedly. "Incredibly beautiful, and just what I needed. Thank you for suggesting this."

Jesse turned his gaze toward Cherie as the sunset sparkled in her eyes. "Yes, beautiful is the word." Enjoying the scenery, the two sat together in the bow of the boat. "Maybe we'll see the green flash".

"OK, I'll bite. What's the green flash?"

"As the sun sinks below the horizon, just as the edge of the sun dips out of sight below the water, an intense burst of green light can be seen. You've never heard of it?"

"Is this one of your tall tales?"

"I'm serious. I've only seen it once when I was on a research cruise anchored offshore of the Florida Keys."

"Interesting."

"I doubt we will see it tonight. There are too many clouds, although that does create a much more beautiful sunset."

"It does indeed," replied Cherie with a yawn. "Sorry, it's been a long week."

"It's been a long month."

"That black eye and those bruises are all but healed," said Cherie as she drew closer to examine Jesse's face. "We've been very lucky recently. You need to be careful on that bike. By the way, what kind of bike do you have? I've never noticed it at your cottage."

Feeling the need to explain, Jesse decided it was time to come clean. "Uh… Cherie, I have a confession to make. I didn't crash on my bike."

"I knew you weren't being forthright with me," said Cherie accusingly. "What really happened?"

"Arturo broke into my house and tried to rob me."

"What?"

Jesse gave Cherie the abbreviated version of the event as she listened in shock.

A look of disbelief, she was almost speechless. "I am struggling trying to process all of this!" Her eyes filled with tears. "In the future, promise that you will not keep something like that from me."

"I promise."

"Why didn't you tell me?"

"I'm very sorry. I know I should have, but I did not want to burden you with it." Jesse got up and checked the bait on the fishing reels, found them intact, and tossed them back out again.

"Joe knocked him out?"

"He did."

"That's why Arturo said that he wasn't going to let you hurt him again," said Cherie as she now realized what he was referring to.

"On the bright side, it was fortunate that Gino found the Bongo ran aground."

"That was lucky. I assumed it would have capsized and sunk."

"I doubt it would have sunk, even after capsizing. The hull of the Bongo is loaded with flotation. Gino said the life ring that trailed behind the boat probably acted like a sea anchor, which helped keep the boat upright. It took a lot of work, but he got it fixed up and going again.”

“It was really thoughtful that Gino and the folks on Dauphin Island donated funds to pay for getting it repaired,” said Cherie.

“There are lots of fine people on Dauphin Island. Gino’s rough around the edges, but he’s a really good guy.”

“Have I thanked you for saving my life?”

“You have. Several times. But Chief East is the person to whom thanks are owed. He’s the one who put the pieces together. He figured out that Arturo kidnapped you and was trying to leave the island. He alerted the Coast Guard, and they began an immediate search. They were in the air searching before I ever made the “Mayday” call. That quick response is really why we are here today.”

“You don’t like taking credit, do you?”

“I don’t like taking credit when it’s not merited. You don’t know how much guilt I felt after you went overboard. I still have… nightmares… where I relive that moment.” Jesse looked away, embarrassed when he thought he was going to cry as well.

“You did what you had to do.”

“I guess.”

“I wonder what happened to Arturo?” asked Cherie. “Do you think he survived?”

“I doubt it. I was hoping the Coast Guard could have found him dead or alive. It’s not very Christian of me, but I wanted him to pay. I’ve never asked you this, but did he harm you?”

“Just a few bruises. I struggled when he kidnapped me, but I realized quickly that I could do nothing. Even injured, he was a very powerful man. The worst was having to listen to his rant about the utopia he was going to create. He saw me only as an asset to get to you.”

“Another reason you should not associate with me,” said Jesse dejectedly.

“Jesse Gates! That’s ridiculous,” scolded Cherie.

“I don’t know. A lot of crap happens to me, and I worry that I will draw you into it.”

"I won't put up with any more talk like that," scolded Cherie.

"OK."

"I have to admit, it has been exciting! Much more so than my life in Atlanta. Have you seen CC and Ross lately?"

"Yeah. They're doing OK. Although they're about to go stir crazy, like the rest of us. If that National Guard dude at the boat ramp will allow it, I'm gonna try to get them out on the boat later this week for some fishing."

"I'm sure they will enjoy that. I may not be able to go with you, but I can make arrangements with the Guard to let you launch your boat."

"Thank goodness you had your CDC credentials on you. Without that, he was not going to let us launch."

"Have you ever thought about the fact that the vessel that brought this disease to the island is called the "Crimson Tide," asked Cherie.

"Huh…I never made that connection. Weird! Did I tell you that I saw it adrift during that storm. It almost ran me down."

"The boat drifted by you? Weird."

"I guess it broke loose from wherever it was moored," added Jesse.

"Are you making any progress on your dissertation project?"

Jesse's normally upbeat demeanor suddenly changed, his brow furrowed, his shoulders slumped, and he sighed deeply."

"Well, that answers my question. Sorry, I brought it up."

"That's OK."

"Oh, I've got some exciting news," said Cherie. "They're going to name the virus after you. Since you were the person who discovered it."

"A deadly virus with my name on it. That seems fitting somehow. But shouldn't they name it after you?" said Jesse. "You worked hard on this."

"In actuality, it's named after both of us. The name given to it is *Carus gatesi*. *Carus* is my name in Latin. It's a completely new kind of virus."

"It has both our names? Well, that's cool! You know, it seems strange that Arturo, the person responsible for this mess, somehow avoided infection," added Jesse.

"I don't know if he avoided it or if he is a carrier. Just thinking out loud… he was devoid of human feelings. I wonder if a sociopath like Arturo would ever have the kind of emotional response that would lead to virus eruption."

"Wow! That's very insightful," said Jesse. "You know, the thought of being saddled with a mind that cannot feel emotion is very sad to me. I know that I am not good at expressing my emotions, even though I feel them intensely. But to feel nothing when you watch an emotional movie, hear a moving song, or see the beauty in a sunset." As if directing the developing sunset, Jesse waved his hand in an arc across the colored horizon. "That would be very depressing."

"It wouldn't be sad for the sociopath since they can't feel emotion."

"That's true," said Jesse, feeling a bit down.

"Someone like that could spread the virus all over. One more very endearing characteristic of this disease. There is so much we don't understand about this thing," said Cherie.

"And it has our name on it," added Jesse, chuckling. "Unfortunately, I seem to have little insight where it counts, particularly regarding my PhD project. I'm at a dead end."

"Jesse, a thought occurred to me the other day. This may be far-fetched, but is it possible that the changes you've been observing in sharks around the island could be related to this virus in some way?"

Jesse paused. A faraway look came over him. It was as if he were no longer in the present. And indeed, he was back in the laboratory. In his mind's eye, the numbers paraded across the monochrome computer monitor: the diminished stress response in sharks, the heightened response in infected humans, and the date when the first aberrant sharks appeared around the island.

"Earth to Jesse," said Cherie jokingly.

"Holy smokes! That's it. Cherie, you're a genius!" An animated Jesse rose and paced across the boat's deck, such as it was, as he pulled the puzzle pieces together in his mind. "It all makes sense now. The date when the Crimson Tide ran aground coincides, almost to the day, with the appearance of the first aberrant sharks. The altered stress response. That's the piece of the puzzle I've been looking for. Those sharks had to have been exposed to the virus; it somehow changed their physiology, and it has spread throughout the entire population." Overcome with excitement, Jesse suddenly embraced Cherie and kissed her fully on the mouth. "God, I love you so much!" Jesse stopped and pulled away as his expression turned from excitement to embarrassment. "Oh…oh…Cherie, I am so sorry. I was overwhelmed and…and…"

Cherie took his hand and pulled him toward her. Before Jesse could say another word, her hands were on his face, and their lips met again. The kiss was soft at first, but urgent, filled with raw emotion. The sexual tension that had been building for weeks was finally broken as both realized how much they'd longed for this moment. The world around them no longer existed. The boat, the sunset, the rhythmic sound of the water, all faded to distant echoes. All that mattered was the warmth of her lips on his, the feeling of her heart beating against his chest. The moment stretched, delicate and fragile, suspended in the golden light of the evening. She was breathless, her eyes closed, her hands warm against his face, her thoughts filled with something deep and unspoken. They both stood there, caught in the aftermath, unsure of what to say next, but both knew that everything had changed in that one, spontaneous kiss.

"I love you, too!"

CHAPTER 67

The driver of the old Ford pickup crept along a Dauphin Island backroad, trying to avoid detection. With the lights off and pulling a weathered fishing boat, the vehicle meandered along the gravel road. Its driver chewed on a *Slim Jim* beef stick and held a beer between his fat thighs. Empty cans strewn across the floor jostled at each curve and pothole. A 30-06 rifle with a scope lay across the passenger seat. Normally, the sight of a fishing boat on its way toward the boat launch after dark would create no suspicion. But these were not normal times. Instead of fishing gear, the boat was loaded down with an odd assortment of items: a duffel bag of mostly dirty clothes, bottles of whiskey, boxes of rifle cartridges, and cases of beer and canned goods. Two large gas cans were stowed in the rear of the boat.

Charlie Peron was angry, and his anger was held in check only by the alcohol that coursed through his body. His brother gone, his job in jeopardy, and the island on lockdown, it felt like his world was crashing down around him. He was leaving the island, whatever it took, and God help the man who tried to stop him!

"Damn, sons-of-bitches can't make me stay on this shit-hole island!" Charlie had recently developed a nervous twitch in his right eye and an unsettling habit of talking to himself and sometimes answering. "Robert East, the National Guard, the Coast Guard, they can all kiss my pasty ass. What gives those idiots the right to tell me what to do? No right at all, that's what."

"Oh shit!" Charlie panicked as a pair of headlights appeared in the distance. Making a quick turn onto a side road, he drove several blocks and shut the engine down. He watched for a few moments, his right eye twitching annoyingly, as a National Guard truck passed through the intersection and continued driving west. "Whew, that was close. Bastards are patrolling everywhere!" Restarting the truck, he headed toward the launch again. The road he drove bordered the water for a few miles, providing a view across the Mississippi Sound. The lights of Mobile blazed across the distant northern sky.

"Look at that water, slicker than owl crap!" Seeing the boat launch in the distance excited him. "I'll be in Fowl River in less than an hour and then… Mobile here I come!" He pulled the truck off the road, out of sight but still in sight of the launch. "Damn it!" In the glow of the street light, he could see a single National Guardsman stationed at the deserted ramp. "Shit!" Charlie thought for a moment. "What are you gonna do now?" asked Charlie. "Shut up!" answered Charlie.

He guzzled the last of his lukewarm beer and tossed the empty out the window. The can clattered noisily down a rip-rap embankment. The Guardsman suddenly turned and looked in the direction of the sound. "Shit!" whispered Charlie, ducking down in his seat. "That was a dumbass thing to do. I'm not a dumbass, you're a dumbass!" Charlie grabbed another beer and waited. "Why not use the gun?... I'm not going to do that!... You're a whimp! Shut up! You could just look at him with the rifle scope. That won't hurt anything." He pondered the idea for a moment. "OK, I could do that."

Charlie took the rifle from the front seat and quietly got out. In shadow, he crouched next to the truck and laid the gun across the hood to steady his aim. With an unobstructed view and a powerful scope, he sighted in the soldier, making out his every movement, every feature of his young face. The soldier took a package of cigarettes from his shirt pocket, removed the last one, and lit up.

"Don't forget to take the safety off," whispered Charlie.

*****

Cherie held fast to Jesse's arm as the RV Bongo gently rose and fell, easily slicing through the long, low swell. The silvery moonlight cast a shimmering path across the ocean's surface as the couple motored toward shore. Pushing ahead in utter darkness with the cool night air rushing past was exhilarating for Cherie. But it paled in comparison to what she felt in her heart. She took Jesse's hand and entwined her fingers in his, feeling the warmth against the coolness of the night. Jesse looked down at Cherie, her face soft in the moonlight, and smiled. For Jesse, the stars that pierced the velvet sky seemed brighter, the air sweeter. The quiet between them spoke volumes—a shared understanding, a quiet joy that needed no words. They were both caught in the afterglow of something new, something raw and electric, a feeling that colored their every thought.

The street light of the boat launch appeared in the distance, and Jesse throttled back on the RV Bongo as they entered the *No Wake Zone* around the launch. For a long moment, they simply sat there, watching the land approach, both of them savoring the sweetness of the moment, the feeling of the ocean beneath them, and the knowledge that despite the world around them, something had shifted.

Jesse shut off the engine and allowed the boat's momentum to carry it into the slip. The National Guardsman strolled along the dock, and Cherie tossed a bow line to him. The young man tied the boat to a piling while Jesse prepared it to be trailered.

"Thank you, sir," said Cherie.

"No problem. You're the folks from the CDC?"

"Yes," said Jesse. "This is Dr. Belon from the CDC, and I'm her trusty sidekick, Jesse Gates." Jesse and Cherie extended their hands as they stood in the boat. "Nice to meet you."

"Same here," replied the guardsman. "I'm Tracy, Tracy Cooper."

"Where did the other fellow go?"

"His watch was over. I have the late watch."

"Lucky you, huh?" asked Jesse sarcastically.

"Oh yeah. A real trip to the moon on gossamer wings."

"Ha! Ha," chuckled Jesse. "I thought I was the only one who used that expression."

"Well, I'm a literature major at the University. The National Guard gig is, of course, part-time. Did y'all have any luck?" The guardsman sat atop a pier piling as the two tidied up the boat.

Jesse caught Cherie's eye, and they smiled at each other. "The best fishing trip of my entire life!"

"What'd you catch, trout, flounder, redfish?"

"Didn't catch a single fish," said Cherie.

"Nothing?" said the Guardsman, obviously confused. "That would be a bad fishing night in my book." He paused for a moment and then noticed their furtive glances…"Ohhh…Ok. Yeah, I guess you did have a good trip."

Cherie blushed.

"Could you guys do me a favor? Would you mind watching the boat ramp for a few minutes? I need to find a restroom like right now, and I'm out of cigarettes too."

"No problem," said Jesse. "The Pak-N-Sak, just a few blocks from here, is generally open late."

"Thanks! You're the only folks I've seen here since the quarantine. Everyone knows that the launch is closed, so you won't have to do a thing."

"We'll wait until you get back. As long as my boat is in the ramp, nobody can launch. Take off," said Jesse.

"Thanks, man!" He ran to his vehicle and left in a cloud of dust.

"Did you see the look on his face?" asked Cherie.

"What look?"

"He thought we were *faire l'amour*." Cherie smiled coyly.

"You'll have to help me out?" said Jesse, shaking his head.

"He thought we were making love."

"Seriously? On this boat? Like I said, I don't easily pick up on stuff like that."

At that moment, a vehicle, its headlights flooding the dock, turned into the boat ramp.

"Is he back already? That was fast," said Cherie. They both squinted as they looked directly into the lights, attempting to discern who was behind the wheel.

"That's not him," said Jesse. There's a boat behind that truck."

The truck door swung open, and a large man approached them.

"Crap! That's Charlie Peron," said Jesse.

"Who is that?"

"Let's just say he's not a nice person and there's bad blood between the two of us. In fact, there's bad blood between him and practically everyone on the island. I haven't seen him in a while, but they say he hasn't been right in the head since his brother died from the virus. Cherie, stay in the boat. I'll talk to him."

The words were barely out of his mouth when Charlie shouted, "Get that damn boat out of the ramp. I got me a 'pointment in Mobile." Charlie staggered down the ramp and onto the pier, still clutching the 30-06 rifle in one hand and a fresh beer in the other.

Jesse met him halfway but stopped short, hoping to avoid physical contact.

"Well, well, if it isn't the pussy surfer boy!" said Charlie, noisily slurping his beer.

"Charlie, get back in your truck and drive away! You know you can't leave the island!"

"Just watch me!" Charlie stepped closer, and Jesse stepped back.

"Charlie, you're in no condition to be running a boat in broad daylight, much less after dark," said Jesse, trying to reason with him. "You're gonna kill yourself or you're going to be arrested. The Coast Guard has boats everywhere, and their radar sweeps the entire island."

"Ha! That's what you think," slurred Charlie. "I'm gonna run under the bridge all the way to the mainland. That radar will never see me."

"You idiot, you just told them what you are going to do," said Charlie scolding himself, his eye twitching wildly now. "Now, they're going to tell the Coast Guard after you leave." "Shut up!" shouted Charlie.

Jesse was confused and very concerned as Charlie argued with himself. "Charlie, listen to me, you're gonna hurt yourself. That boat is too small and old, and it's overloaded. You'll never make it."

Realizing the seriousness of the situation, Cherie stepped onto the dock behind Jesse. "I'm Dr. Cherie Belon from the CDC. You don't have to do this. We have a treatment for the disease now, and the quarantine will be lifted soon." A half-truth, but Cherie was having a very bad feeling about how the situation was developing.

"My, my aren't you a pretty little thing," said a leering Charlie. "Maybe I will just take you along with me for fun. Would you like that?"

"Charlie, put the gun down and leave NOW!" demanded Jesse.

"Huh?" Charlie looked down and realized he was holding his rifle. "You're too big of a wimp to shoot them, aren't you,

Charlie?" He dropped his beer, brought the gun up, and leveled it at Jesse. "Shut up! said Charlie to hmself."

"Jesse! Please get back in the boat," pleaded Cherie. "Mister, we'll move the boat."

Jesse moved forward to stand only a few feet in front of Charlie, the rifle now pointed directly at his chest. "Charlie, that's a Remington Woodsman 742. It's a classic deer rifle."

"Move your damn boat!" demanded Charlie. "You got to kill them both now. But you're a pussy just like surfer-boy." "STOP TALKING TO ME!" shouted Charlie, barely able to hold the gun steady.

"Charlie, you're not going to hurt anyone with that gun. Look at the gun just ahead of the trigger guard. See that hole, that's where the magazine goes. Your gun is unloaded," explained Jesse as he directed Charlie's attention to the missing magazine.

"What are you talking about?" Charlie turned the gun over to examine it. "You ain't got walking-around sense. Dumb as a sack of diapers, that's what you are. Stop it, stop it, STOP IT! AHHHHHHHHH," Charlie screamed. With the gun now pointed elsewhere, Jesse charged Charlie and knocked the weapon into the water. Charlie's demeanor suddenly changed. His face contorted in pain, his body wracked by convulsions, Charlie grabbed Jesse. Blood poured out of his contorted face as he projectile vomited.

"Oh God!" screamed Cherie as she watched the virus tear through Charlie, knowing that Jesse would be next.

"STAY BACK!" shouted Jesse as he pushed him away. Charlie stumbled off the dock and disappeared below the blood-stained water.

Jesse stood alone, covered in blood, knowing what was going to happen.

"I am not going to let you watch this. Goodbye, Cherie. I love you!" And with that, he dove into the Mississippi Sound and disappeared.

"JESSE!" screamed Cherie as she fell to her knees and fainted.

EPILOGUE

No one on Dauphin Island could remember a service as beautiful as the one held that fall evening on the beach at the island's west end. Many believed it was providential when, against a crimson sunset, a cloud formed, roughly in the shape of a shark, and then was whisked away by unseen winds. The crowd that attended was so large that many had to park their cars blocks away and walk. Some were unable to attend at all and stood at the roadside to witness the procession. Before rows of folding chairs, Pastor Cummings stood behind a flower-adorned pulpit, atop a snow-white dune overlooking the sparkling waters of the Gulf of Mexico. With a well-worn Bible in his weathered hand and draped in an indigo preaching robe, his sermon resonated with all in attendance.

"I want to thank everyone for coming this evening." The Pastor looked out over the sea of faces and over the flowers that covered the dunes, to the placid waters of the Gulf of Mexico. "There are four major transformative moments in the lives of the faithful. Some of you have heard me speak of these before. I call them the four B's. The first is Birth. There is nothing that speaks more powerfully of the existence of God than the creation of new life. A new being, formed in the womb, in the image of the Almighty. I see the affirmation of that power in the eyes of every newborn I have ever held in my arms. The second B is Baptism. For Christians, the symbolic rebirth heralds the acceptance of Jesus Christ as their personal savior. A dedication to walk, as closely as mortals can, in the footsteps of Jesus, to turn away from sin. The third transformative moment is Betrothal. When two people take the vow of holy matrimony. A sacred vow between Man and Woman to begin their lives together in faith. Faith in each other and in their beliefs. A vow that should never be taken lightly. And finally, Bereavement. Christians should not fear death, and the faithful should take comfort in knowing that our loved ones have moved on to a better place. However, we nevertheless long for the warm smile, the tender touch, and the comforting words of a departed loved one. Death visited our close-knit community and touched the lives of every person here. I know many of you are still in mourning over the loss of loved ones, and that makes your presence here even more meaningful. We continue to keep those who have departed in our most heartfelt prayers."

Pastor Cummings drew a handkerchief from a robe pocket and wiped the tears that welled in his eyes before continuing. "Although our little slice of paradise was tested, was knocked down, was dealt a terrible blow, it did not break. That speaks volumes regarding the strength of this community. We've all emerged from this nightmare stronger than ever. We all know the names of the two individuals who are largely responsible for saving Dauphin Island. Those individuals are Jesse Gates and Cherie Belon. Thanks to their selfless acts, insight, dedication, tireless work, and the guidance of the Almighty, many lives were spared on our island, and countless lives were saved worldwide. However, we are gathered here, not in mourning but to celebrate the union of two young people in holy matrimony."

On cue, someone pushed "play" on a recording of the wedding march as those attendees not already standing rose and turned their attention toward the rear of the gathering, where a covered gazebo stood. A curtain parted as two of Gino and Betty Patronas' children, followed by CC, looking beautiful, walked slowly along the length of carpet between rows of folding chairs, spreading flower petals. Behind them came the *Best Dog*, Bongo, on a leash held by the *Best Man*, Ross. An utterly radiant Cherie emerged from the gazebo on the arm of her father, as the march reached a crescendo. In a simple white wedding dress, a garland of gardenia blossoms in her hair, she made her way to the pulpit to meet Jesse who was dazzled by her beauty…

"I now pronounce you man and wife. You may kiss the bride!"

And the crowd erupted!

Through a hailstorm of rice and heartfelt well-wishes, the newlyweds rushed from the service and into the El Camino that was now adorned with nuptial slogans, shaving cream, and tin cans tied to the bumper. Jesse held the door for Cherie, ran to get behind the wheel to make their escape, and plopped into his seat without looking. "Ouch!" He cringed and raised himself off his seat to find a crudely wrapped package. "What the heck?" He slid it across the seat. "Whoa, that thing is heavy! Must be a late wedding gift." Jesse started the El Camino and slowly pulled away amid continued cheers and applause from the wedding guests. Well-wishers lining Bienville Boulevard waved and cheered as their vehicle slowly passed.

"Good grief, I think the entire island is here," commented Jesse. "I wish they wouldn't make such a big deal out of this."

"Jesse. No matter how you look at it, this was a big deal. The discovery that you were immune to the virus led to the therapy that is right now protecting everyone on the island and will be used around the world to prevent virus infection."

"Well, then Ross should get the credit. He was responsible for injecting me with shark blood. It was just a chance occurrence. It could have been anyone," argued Jesse.

"Yeah, but you're the one who had a huge storage of frozen shark plasma. Analyzing that plasma at the CDC jump-started the development of the therapy," said Cherie.

"Scientists would have discovered it eventually."

"Perhaps. But how many people would have died before they discovered it? It's really interesting, from a scientific point of view, that sharks responded so differently to the virus. You know, I read an article that took an interesting angle on this whole thing."

"What was that?"

"It floated the idea that sharks may have a completely different kind of immune system, which explains why their blood can be used for this therapy."

"I do like the idea that sharks, not the most popular group of animals, are saving the lives of lots of people."

"That is cool. That should go a long way toward changing some opinions on sharks and conserving them."

"One thing that I will agree with. Your suggestion that the change in shark physiology may be from their exposure to the virus was spot on. That piece of information is why I now have a PhD."

"Dr. Jesse Gates. I love the sound of that," said Cherie, smiling broadly and clutching Jesse's arm.

"I love you," said Jesse and gave Cherie a quick kiss as he turned north onto Dauphin Island Parkway and headed off the island.

"Love you, too. What's in that package?" asked Cherie.

"I don't know. Take a look."

"Gosh, it is heavy!" Cherie pulled the wrinkled brown paper away to find an intricately carved box. "Wow! Beautiful." She held it in her lap, marveling at the creatures carved into the dark, burnished cypress. "I know who this is from. Look at all the animals on the cover. This has to be from Joe. Nobody can do work like this except him. And look at this tiny handle, it's a dolphin!" Cherie was practically giddy as she raised the box lid. "Oh, my Goodness!"

"What is it?"

Wide-eyed, a speechless Cherie turned the box toward Jesse to reveal its contents.

"Whoa!" Jesse pulled the El Camino off the road and stopped."

"There must be 100 gold coins in this box!" said Cherie.

"Son of a gun! I can't believe it! Joe found Lafitte's treasure! I wonder where he is now?"

*****

The cheers and applause that went up when Jesse and Cherie kissed were so loud that folks claimed it could be heard from both ends of Dauphin Island. The noise startled a flock of gulls that headed squawking toward the mainland. From that dizzying height, looking down, the small boat below would've appeared as a speck. A dark-skinned, wizened old man, paddling a brand-new pirogue, paused for a moment to watch the passing birds, cocked his head slightly, and listened. Joe smiled knowingly and continued across the wide expanse of the Mississippi Sound toward parts unknown.

ACKNOWLEDGMENTS

I am most grateful for the kind assistance provided by my wife, Cheryl, my son T.J., and my daughter Erin. In addition, I would like to thank Betty Burroughs, Cindy Vines-Butler, Christy Chambers, Matt Gaylord, Dr. Jan Hoover, Meredith Hunter, Dr. Paul Lago, Barbara Lago, and Dr. Eddie Vines. I would also like to thank three of my South Florida shark fishing buddies: Randy Hochberg, Kristi Killam, and "Nittany". Finally, I thank all those who read Chapter 1 on Write Your First Novel and the Dauphin Island, Alabama, West End Beach Fan page.